# ASH
# FALLS

## A NOVEL

### WARREN READ

PUBLISHING

**NEW YORK, NY**

Printed in the United States
First Edition
10 9 8 7 6 5 4 3 2 1

Ig Publishing
Box 2547
New York, NY 10163
www.igpub.com

ISBN: 978-1-63246-047-9

*For Margaret, and the journey down from the mountain.*

# Ernie

He came out of the cage just before dawn and moved quickly down the corridor lined with dozens still asleep, their deep, gouging breaths and heavy snores pushing him on his way. He was dressed in state-issued jeans and a t-shirt under a thin, denim jacket. He wore running shoes, and the men shadowed him as if he were a child, one stationed on either side of him, so close their arms brushed against his as they walked past all the others, down the concrete steps and through three separate rooms, out the metal doors and into the morning chill.

It hadn't occurred to Ernie that the sky on the outside of the wall could look so different from the one that spooned out over his cell window. This was the kind of sky that went on forever, reaching in all directions, billowing black and gray cotton, pinhole stars pushing through where they could. He'd had weeks to consider what a move like this could mean for a guy like him, a guy who had done what he'd done. But Christ almighty, the breaking day was surely something to behold from the outside. Before the men ducked him into the back seat, he took in one more breath of the brand new air.

The men sank into their seats and slammed their doors, almost in unison. In the fading dome light, Ernie listened to the sound of keys tumbling and tapping against the ignition. The one in the passenger seat had turned to his left shoulder. The silhouette was something out of a comic book, a Dick Tracy cutout, all angles and hard edges.

"The fact that you're going from maximum to medium doesn't mean a damned thing," he said. It was a voice pushed down, forced to a place unnatural for its speaker. Ernie knew a thing or two about that. "Don't think you'll be sitting back there with your arm out the window, shooting the shit with us up here. This ain't no Burt Reynolds movie. You keep your mouth shut and do what we tell you, when we tell you."

The words bounced around the inside of the car and knocked him upside the head and rang his ears.

"You hear me?" The profile ticced. "This transfer today means you're on the downhill side of your sentence. So don't fuck it up by doing something stupid."

"I know."

He had imagined he would take notice and find some satisfaction in watching the valley disappear in his wake, but by the time they came out of Walla Walla he was already beginning to drift. It was an old sedan with real good shocks, and it cruised over the roadway as if it were floating him downriver. The heat was set on high. He settled himself against the door and touched his hair to the cool window and closed his eyes, listening to the humming on the pavement like it was a hundred thousand mosquitoes. They hovered just outside the screen like they always did, sometimes lighting, usually knocking against the mesh, and then he felt the warmth of his young son at his side as they laughed over dumb ghost stories and named all the fish they'd caught that day.

Ernie had been a good father and a decent husband most of the time, but he was also a man who liked to drive into the mountains at night by himself, in secret, when the rest of the house was sound asleep. He would drive until he found the perfect spot, and then he'd park and carry his folding chair close to the creek and listen to the distant yodel of coyotes as they cried. And sometimes they sounded so close the noise would raise the hairs on his neck and cause his skin to shrink to his bones. And then just as daylight began to edge behind the mountain, he would make the long drive home, where he shut off the engine at the corner and coasted into the driveway and slipped inside noiselessly to wait for his son to wake up for school.

In the front seat the men talked to each other in tones too low for him to piece together. Here and there a streetlight gave a momentary fade in and out and, when he opened his eyes, the whitewash of sagebrush or a lone, green exit sign appeared. Once, just as he dipped into sleep, the red bloom of fireworks burst into his mind, smashing neon against the back of his skull. A flash of heat spread over his chest, and his foot kicked at the seat in front of him. He pressed his teeth together and cleared his head of the smoke and forced himself to follow the drone of the road still beneath him.

"Convict."

His eyes jerked open, and his forehead knocked against the window. The one with the freckled neck and the red hair snapped the dome light and stared at him through the visor mirror, blue eyes shot and narrowed.

"Shut the fuck up."

"I didn't say anything."

"You calling me a liar?" The man had turned now and was looking over his shoulder, his arm stretched along the seat ridge. A flat, gold wedding band corseted his finger.

Ernie swept his palms over his eyes and sat up straight, a chastised little boy again, a bottom dweller, a peon. The road ahead came at him through the headrests, and the pavement hummed beneath them, crawling through his boots, along his legs, and into teeth ground together like the legs of a cricket. The fat driver fidgeted and checked the mirrors and gauges, his bald head shining from the approaching headlights, the flesh spilling over his collar as he bobbed right and left. It was he who had gripped Ernie's arm and pinched the flesh over his elbow as soon as they moved out of the deep acoustics of the final processing room. It was the fat driver who hollered through the open window to the gatehouse guard, as if they were the best of friends. It had been a short exchange between the two men, but Ernie was smart enough to know that the whole thing was a ricochet conversation meant for his ears, the convict on his way to his new home.

"Two and a half hours to the summit," the fat driver had said. The whole east cellblock could likely have heard him.

The guard asked then, "With how many stops?"

"No stops," the driver said. "Be no stops on this run."

A few more miles down the road, and the redhead seemed to have forgotten Ernie altogether. The man gazed out through his own window, the dim light carving a clenched jaw and thick brow driven to the bridge of his nose. They passed under a streetlight and the face held like a sculpture, chiseled and cold. Through the mirrors, the white ball of an October sun was just beginning to emerge.

In the dashboard lights, the clock glowed emerald green, and Ernie's thoughts fell to Patrick again. He could be at school already. He would be in the eleventh grade now, he thought. A year from graduation. And Bobbie, she would be there too, of course, in and out of her nurse's office, the hovering mother hen that his actions—the hair trigger temper, his great failure as a husband and father, as a man—had forced her to become. But he would be two hundred miles closer now, and this was a good thing for all of them. He was a better man, better than he had been before, and besides, there was so much unfinished business. Bobbie and Patrick could make the trip to see him once in awhile, now that he would be in Monroe, hardly a mountain to separate them. His letter to Bobbie had gone out weeks earlier—four pages of apologies and promises. She hadn't answered yet.

The vista shifted quickly from wheat fields to a wide spread of stunted trees, perfect geometrical grids of them that stretched on forever, naked branches reaching up, shocked, as if crying out to be released from the roots that anchored them into the cold earth.

They came through the orchards as the sun finally shone white over the rugged scablands. The driver suddenly wiped a thick hand over his head.

"I'm gonna get off here," he said. "Get something for my stomach."

"What are you, sick?" his partner asked. He pressed against the door and looked over at him as if he could be contagious.

"No I ain't sick. Goddamned acid reflux."

He steered them from the highway onto a breakaway road, taking them some distance along a crusted route that rose and dipped through sage-covered mounds. About four miles out they came upon a cinderblock gas station dropped smack in the middle of nothingness. They stopped alongside the building and flung open the doors, his included.

"Half a cigarette and a stop in the toilet if you need it," the redhead said. "But make it quick."

The man walked behind Ernie, nearly on his ass, but Ernie kept his pace slow lest the guy think he was making a break for it, as if he would try something like that, out there in the center of Mars like they were. He could outrun the driver, but the redhead looked like he could move. And anyway, either one might have a gun. Ernie wasn't much of a runner, not anymore, even though he had the right shoes for it. Running was for people with plans, and destinations. He was on the downhill side of his sentence; where the hell could a guy like him land out in the middle of this hellhole anyway?

The john was no bigger than his cell, and it was coated in a mossy green paint and bordered with a train of cloudy glass blocks along the ceiling. The redhead stood at the sink and took a comb from his back pocket, then crouched under the static of the fluorescent bulb as he leaned into the mirror. Ernie glanced briefly at his own image as it passed against the wall. His shoulders slacked under the loose-fitting shirt. His beard was long overdue for a trim. It looked like a costume hooked over his ears, cupping a face that had been scooped into shadows and feathered by the harsh light. He'd take care of it all before Bobbie came with Patrick.

"Five minutes," the man said without looking up.

Ernie crowded into the stall, latched the door behind him, and sat with his elbows on his knees as he began fill the stall with the stench of Walla Walla. He bunched his jeans in his hands and considered the vast diorama that surrounded him. These were people with pens and knives and too much disposable time, men who could leave their marks and then hit the road, to drive or hitchhike to Spokane or Reno or wherever the hell they wanted to end up. There were cartoon faces with crackled, golf ball eyes and horsey teeth, and crude drawings of tits and cocks, disembodied torpedo-like things, each of them in violent eruption. There were phone numbers with the names of queers who wanted it and girls who needed it, and a few rhyming poems. There was even a haiku, not half bad:

*I just saw Elvis*
*Filling up with premium*
*He liked my Pacer*

It was the first time in years that he had sat on the john without another man in plain view, thumbing through a magazine or carrying on a conversation with him between muscle flexes and the spin of the toilet paper roll. He wanted to make the moment last, as if the mere act of shitting in privacy was a prize earned in annual celebration. The walls were near his elbows and his thighs, but the square above the stall went straight to the sky, a perimeter of white trembling with the turn of the fan. This place wasn't the worst he'd been in, not by a long shot. There were johns and then there were latrines, jungle latrines that had better ventilation and the added task of checking for spiders or tripwires. He was thinking of light coming through the boards and of the dank heat and the sounds of helicopter blades cutting the sky, and then he pulled the image of Patrick into his mind again, as he always did when his mind started to slide like that. Patrick as he was when Ernie last saw him, pimpled forehead and too skinny for his height, sitting with Bobbie on the other side of the glass, his eyes fixed on his own chewed fingernails. It wasn't right that a father should depend on his son so much, but goddamn it. He needed that referee in his head. To quell the noise and separate what really mattered from what had been over and done with a long time ago. The outside door suddenly banged open, and the morning poured in, brilliant and crisp with the light lacing of sage.

"Get that bastard out of there," he heard the fat driver say. "We gotta hit the road."

Ernie walked past the clock in the station window and caught that it was half past nine. Normal people were at work now, at their desks answering phones or filling out papers. It would be another hour and a half until he reached the midpoint, where the guys from Monroe would be waiting to take him the rest of the way to the reformatory. His legs crawled with a kind of electricity, like the crackling veins that ran over the owlish cartoon eyeballs scrawled over the stall walls. From the station, the ragged terrain stretched low and wide in all directions as far as the eye could see.

The men directed him into the backseat and shut the door behind him, then held an abbreviated conference from opposite sides of the car. They talked back and forth over the hood, the driver's round face flush as he leaned elbows on the fender and worked his mouth like a sock puppet. The redhead nodded and closed his eyes, then after a couple false starts he held his hands up in surrender. There were a few more words exchanged, and then they climbed in and slammed the doors in unison.

The driver threw a pill back into his throat and pulled out from the lot, hooking hard to the left onto the road as he held a Styrofoam cup of coffee like a torch. The redhead said, "Buckle up, cowboy," and Ernie drew the seatbelt from beneath his leg, and cinched it tightly over his lap.

He sank into his shoes and watched the passing wires as they flatlined through the view of rolling scablands, trailed over the mounds of tawny grass and chunk rocks that tumbled to a distant, marbled sky. He yawned, and the glass bloomed to a silver fog. This is where it is, he thought to himself. A never-ending reach of openness. A guy could get past that first snag of barbed wire and just walk on forever, never meet another living soul.

They had dipped over the second ridge when the driver suddenly squeezed out a cry, mottled and phlegmy, as though it was being forced from deep within the gut. His thick body lunged to the right, cutting the car from the highway to the graveled shoulder. A spray of rocks hurled against the undercarriage as he grunted and growled, pulling at his shirt with one hand, while the redhead lunged at the wheel and yelled for him to hit the goddamned brakes. Tires plowed the gravel, and the fat driver spit and bobbed his head like it was on a coiled spring. A thin train of barbed wire raked over side window. They were a good distance from the gas station now, and the highway was nowhere.

Ernie took hold of the seat edge, his damp hands sliding freely over the fabric. For an instant the car rediscovered the pavement, skipping and seeming to take hold. The craggy plain stretched gloriously from the rear window, barren fields spotted with brambles and boulders, just like the old westerns he once stared up at from the front row seats. He gripped the armrest and tightened his stomach against the straining seatbelt. Over the fence, the dappled dips and swells rolled into distance as the car began to nose back from the highway to the shoulder. His mind went again to his boy Patrick and the last things he'd said to him, the details of which he could not bring to the surface. And then he felt his legs lift from the seat and the ground falling beneath them. Fence posts slammed against metal, and barbed wire clawed the glass. He pressed his chin to his chest, closed his eyes, and succumbed to the roll.

The crash itself was finished in the time it took him to lose a single breath. One moment his body was being jerked in all directions and the next he was hanging like a fish, still hooked tightly to the belt. He looked up into a swirl of dust and grit. A hard pang stabbed his side, and his legs felt as if they were just coming out of a coma. From the front seat, one of the men mumbled in low tones; Ernie could see through the turning cloud the tangle of arms and legs, bare skin feathered with crimson. The right rear door looked straight up into the sky. He undid his buckle and leaned to the front headrest to see the redhead crumpled over the driver, thick neck glaring through settling dirt. His body shifted and his arm moved from his side, ever slightly.

"Oh Jesus!" He wailed like a stung child. "Jesus oh Jesus!"

Ernie reached forward and put his hand on the guy's side.

"Don't you fucking go anywhere," he said to Ernie.

Red dust churned the interior, the taste of iron and grass settling in Ernie's mouth. His movements seemed to come without thought, his belly over the seat back, hands snatching wallets from pockets, swatting the redhead's feeble hand away. A .45 pistol sat in the glove compartment, the safety still engaged.

"Don't you do it," the passenger said, a voice flooded, washed in spit or blood, Ernie made no effort to check which. He took the gun and sat back on his haunches and pulled the cash from the billfolds.

"I never hurt you," he said, tossing the wallets back to the front. He tucked the pistol into his waistband. "No matter what, you make sure they know I never hurt either one of you."

Wire spilled in through the broken window, and he separated the strands with care and intention, as if it might explode in his hands. He slid through the shattered window, the scratch of glass against his jeans and the metal teeth of the barbs biting at his skin. And when he hit the ground he scurried the slope to the road that was ice against his palms, and a breeze crept its fingers down the front of his shirt.

It was wide open; in all directions there was nothing but sage and boulders and sky. In the distance behind him, where the blue and red chevron glowed over the little cinderblock station, a big rig was just pulling out from the pumps. It swung a wide left and took to the road, stuttering into gear as it climbed the hill toward them.

The shouting from the car faded as he ran on, every step over rocks and the sandy soil a drumbeat into the bottoms of his sneakers. There came a flash vision of An Khe again, of endless rice fields and the crying of insects, and his throat burned as he fought to pull air into his lungs. He thought of the place west of the mountains, the weeping green cedars and clouds of moss, of the whisper of Patrick's voice at the other end of the phone and the feel of Bobbie's hair as he wound it loosely through his fingers.

Taking the pistol from his hip, he held it, feeling the smooth steel against his palm. He was no stranger to guns, but it had been a long time, and he sure didn't remember the weight being so noticeable. He reached back as far as he could, as far as Walla Walla maybe, and launched it through the air. It sailed in a grand arc, almost disappearing against the ashen sky before finally dropping behind a swale of rock. Behind him, the noise of a big rig swelled as it came closer, and he picked up his pace, stumbling over the raw terrain as he trained his eyes on the tiny farmhouses freckling the far horizon.

# Marcelle Foster (Otherwise Known as Marcelle Henry)

The girl who had waited almost a full year to take the name Mrs. Eugene Henry pushed her husband's leg from her own and slipped carefully from beneath the sheets. She dropped the cotton robe over herself and took the staircase from the basement to the kitchen in a complete darkness, her hand sliding along the wood paneling all the way until she felt the light switch near the top. She moved through the doorway like she was air, and then she tiptoed through the dimly lit space to the sink. Turning the cold halfway around, she let the water run freely down the drain so that the swirl and the lapping would echo throughout the small kitchen and hopefully mask the noise she would soon be making.

Outside it was full night. The cone of light from the streetlamp did nothing more than illuminate a gray-blue spot beneath it, but the neat line of houses across the street, the strip of contorted, half naked Japanese cherries, and the serration of low mountains that stood behind them all gave but thin hints of their presence. Marcelle pulled back the drapes, and a vaporous light seeped in.

Her stomach rolled. She was wearing the threadbare cotton robe over drugstore-bought underpants and an old t-shirt that belonged to Eugene. Her hand lay over her ample belly, and she peered back at the closed basement door. She glanced to the pantry then stared back into the silver shimmer of the moving sink pan. Marcelle considered how the kitchen felt cleaner in the fog of night when she was up and around and everyone else was in bed, dead to the world. The business of stained, daisy-riddled wallpaper and mismatched hand towels hanging from cabinet and oven handles and mugs dangling from knobby racks all blended into a muted background of random shapes and shadows of the kitchen that was not her own. The whole world was sound asleep. The people in this house, and outside, all down Shale Street probably clear into town and as far as anyone could go. Nobody was up. Only her, like she was the last human standing alive in the world.

She was so damned hungry.

"What if I went into the pantry," she asked herself. "Just opened the damn door and took whatever I wanted, ate every last thing in there and to hell with them all. They could kiss my big round ass," she said with only the curling of a smile, and she leaned back against the counter and bounced herself from its edge a few times thinking about what she should do next. She wanted to eat. She wanted to eat something, anything, and then go back to bed not with Eugene but next to him. Then she wanted to sleep in a little, and she didn't know what should come next. "It'd be nice," she thought, "if I could get dressed up and go to school today." Of all the stupid ideas she had been violated with repeatedly over the years, the last thing she ever imagined would come back to get her would be that she would actually miss school. But it was true. To be back in Mr. Walner's biology class with all her friends, or any friend, whatever friend might be left there, to just sit there and listen would be wonderful. And she would write the important things down and eat her lunch on a tray in the cafeteria and talk to her teachers. Real conversations this time, though. No arguing.

But the thing was, married girls didn't still go to high school. She had said these very words to as many people as would listen, and a few who told her to just shut the hell up and go already. She'd left school for the pure reason of proving to everyone just how much she was ready to settle down like a grown woman and be married to Eugene Calvin Henry from over on Shale Street in the cedar-shingled house with the Japanese Cherries across the street. Did they know Eugene Henry, she would ask, and they'd roll their eyes and say, "Oh yeah, we know him. Everyone knows Eugene." But at the time Marcelle had only been in Ash Falls just over a year. She had no way of knowing the trail of dirt her boyfriend had left behind him in that town.

"But we're in love." She caught herself saying this aloud, as she searched the dimly lit pantry for what she wanted right then. They were in love, she had insisted to others. And people in love should get married, no matter if they're sixteen or twenty-three or whatever.

And even though her own mother said, "Marcelle, you're too young to be even thinking about moving out, much less getting married," Marcelle would not cave. Her mother began to cry then, and in turn, Marcelle cried louder, and when her mother repeated, "You're not old enough to get married," Marcelle coughed out, "I am too old enough!" Her mother whimpered some more before she got up from the sofa and walked to the kitchen.

When she took her keys from the counter she swung them by the ring and sighed. "Well, Marcelle's going to do what Marcelle's going to do, so I suppose there isn't a whole hell of a lot I can say about it. Just don't expect me to keep your room made up for you."

And she didn't. Even more, Marcelle's mother cleaned the whole apartment out within a month after the wedding, leaving Ash Falls altogether, gone over the mountains to Spokane where her sister and her husband ran a biker bar that needed a waitress to work the swing shift.

There was a hard clanging, and the furnace kicked, and a rush of warm air spilled out from the grate in the wall across the floor and over Marcelle's socked feet. It then rose in a pleasant updraft, tickling the thin hem of her bathrobe and rising to warm her naked skin.

The plastic on the cookie bag was so loud, like snapping kindling in a fire, louder even than the running faucet. Her stomach rumbled again, and her mouth was watered, and when she moved from the pantry to the sink her socks skated easily over the linoleum. Still, everything she did now made far too much noise for someone standing in the kitchen in the middle of the night. She considered going all out, all at once, just ripping open the package like it was a bandage over a scab. Fast as a blink and then it would all be done.

She managed to tear it enough to slip out a half-dozen cookies from the tray, and then she quickly returned the package to its shelf. He would ask about it, probably, the next day as he packed his lunch for work. He would blame her, but she would play dumb when he held the package into the air and accused her of eating them. "Maybe it was your mom or dad that got into them," she would say then add, "How am I supposed to know what they do during the day, I don't watch their every move." They would deny it if he asked, but he would have no compulsion to trust one over the other, so Marcelle would at least be in a three-way possibility, and she could live with that until the weekend when he'd finally let it go.

If Marcelle's mother had raised the roof over the marriage, Eugene's own parents barely issued a word. Mr. Henry asked Eugene what his plans were after the wedding, how he thought he would support a wife and children. "Because kids," he said, "have a way of showing up whether you want them to or not."

"I'll figure it out," Eugene said, and then Mr. Henry just laughed and repeated what Eugene had said.

"You'll figure it out, huh?" he said. He looked at Marcelle then, shook his head as if she had just been swindled of everything she owned, and walked out the door to his job in Lake Stevens, where he worked the drive-through window at a bank.

When they told Mrs. Henry not a half hour later, Oh Dear was all she seemed to have the capacity to say. She'd been making lace at the round table in the dining room, the wood bobbins fanned out in front of her like the rays of the sun. And she just stopped short, gone from a live movie to a snapshot on a page. Her dry lips pushed themselves out, and her brow caved like a skinny old screech owl, and she stared hard at her hands that still held tightly to the bobbins. She blinked a few times, and then just as quickly she broke loose from her trance, continued lacing and spinning out that tangle of a doily that might as well have been her own private web.

"I suppose that means you'll both be staying in the basement then," she said.

Eugene answered, "Where the hell else would we stay?"

"Well all right then."

There was a sudden creaking behind Marcelle. "What's the matter, you can't sleep?" The voice was dry and sickly, and Marcelle knocked her knee against the cabinet when she heard it. She tried to shove whatever cookies she hadn't eaten into the clutter of canisters and small appliances that sat at the far reaches of the countertop. Mrs. Henry stood in the kitchen alcove, thick terry-cloth robe nearly smothering her tiny body as it seemed to wrap itself twice around her and then some.

"You get hungry all of a sudden?"

"No."

"There's oranges in the wood bowl, probably some chicken in the fridge still from dinner unless Mr. Henry ate it all before bed."

She came into the kitchen, and the blue light from the window washed over her and made her a ghost. She always reminded Marcelle of a giant bird, always pinched tight and nervous, her movements clumsy and random, and little comma-like eyes that darted from one place to another when she talked. Sometimes Marcelle would make sudden noises on purpose, drop a book or slam a drawer, just so she could see Mrs. Henry jump and fan herself with her bony hands. She reached behind Marcelle and found a cookie that had been too slow to escape.

"Marcelle," she whispered.

"What?"

"You know what. I know Eugene's been on you about your weight."

"Not so much."

"Oh come on, now. Eugene doesn't do anything not so much." She tucked the cookie into her robe pocket and shut off the running water. "You know, it's normal for a wife to put on a little weight after getting married, but you don't want to let it get out of hand. You should have an orange." She glanced nervously around the kitchen. "Is everything on schedule?"

"On schedule?"

"You know." She jutted her chin out and peered at Marcelle's stomach. "With your monthly."

"Yes ma'am." Marcelle hoped it was. Things had been normal so far, but her next period wasn't due to come for another couple weeks or so, so anything was possible. They were being careful. Most of the time.

"Well, you're going to drive yourself crazy sneaking around like this," Mrs. Henry said. "But I guess you're still learning."

Marcelle wrapped her arms around the fullness of her waist and fiddled with the elastic band of her underpants. Her cheeks felt hot and her heart pounded below her dropped chin. Mrs. Henry had taken the sponge and was wiping the crumbs from the tile.

Finally Marcelle asked, "Learning what?"

"Learning what," Mrs. Henry mimicked her. She shook her head and tossed the sponge back into the sink. Her beady eyes gleamed black in the dull light and her head moved in little tics as she talked. "Learning how to be a wife. You kids think married life is like playing house, nothing more than dating with no curfew. But it's not, young lady. Boys will put up with things in the back seat of their car that they won't tolerate in their own house."

Marcelle didn't know what Mrs. Henry was saying, but she thought it sounded like she was talking about sex, even though sex was something Mrs. Henry would never talk about, not to anyone much less her son's wife. Marcelle looked to the robe pocket and wondered what the plans for that cookie might be.

"Eugene doesn't have to put up with that much from me," she said.

"Well," Mrs. Henry said with a tilt of her head, "It's best to keep it that way." She walked past Marcelle and stopped at the doorway to the hall. "I won't say anything to him about the cookies. But, honey, it would be a good idea if you'd try harder. Pay attention to what he says more and stop sneaking around like this. It would make things easier all the way around."

Marcelle listened to the bedroom door close, and then she retrieved the two cookies that had made it into the shelter of the dry goods canisters. As she rolled the chocolate and cream with her tongue she added up the numbers again, and she figured that it had been almost five months since the wedding.

It had been held here, in this house, on a spring day that was overcast and sickly gray. The vows were read from a book riddled with paper note cards, on the other side of the wall, in the living room, among a small collective of family members and just a few friends.

It was quiet, more a funeral than a wedding really. The minister was someone they didn't even know, from East Monroe, as no minister in Ash Falls would marry them. They'd considered the justice of the peace, but the one thing that Mr. and Mrs. Henry had wanted out of the wedding was that the two kids be joined by a man of God. The bouquet of carnations and baby's breath had come from Marcelle's mother, and the white veil was the only genuine wedding touch that Marcelle had been allowed to wear. Eugene's mother gave it to her to borrow, but only because Eugene had insisted.

The kitchen had been something else altogether, though. The food—green sherbet and soda punch, Jello salad with pears and whipped cream, twice-baked potatoes, tuna casserole, and chicken fingers. And then there was the spinach dip in the giant dugout bread loaf—it had all been positioned over the expanse of the white hexagon counter tiles like a promise of the bounty that would surely come to such a beautiful young couple. And the cake. Marcelle had drawn it out herself on paper, wrote the poem, and made up the intricacies of the curled border, and brought it to Stan Halvorson at the Red Apple on her own. She asked him to bake it just as she had drawn it, and while he hadn't been exact, it was close enough. She was able to brag to everyone that it had all been her. It was the best part of the whole wedding.

It was cold in the basement where the furnace lived its loud life yet refused to share its heat. Eugene had splayed himself over the entire width of the mattress, and when she prodded his thigh he snorted and raised his head from the pillow.

"What's going on," he mumbled. "Why are you up?"

"I had to pee."

She crawled under the layers of quilt and afghans and he leaned into her not to kiss her, but to smell her. "You been eating chocolate." His voice was clear now, and hard.

"No," she lied.

"You must think I'm stupid." And then he took his index finger that still had the odor and grit of engine grease, and he dug into her mouth, ran his callused skin over her gums until she snapped her head to the side. She heard the click of his lips kissing away his finger, and he said, "I can taste it Marcelle. Bad enough you've got to sneak out of bed in the middle of the night so you can stuff your fat face with my cookies, but then you got to lie to me like I'm some retard, like I don't know Oreos when I smell them."

He went on, only quieter or maybe it was because Marcelle began to close her ears to his voice. It was just the same, and she was used to it, and it was probably what married people did anyway. Fight, curse, cry, and then go to sleep, and wake up in the morning like nothing ever happened, like the whole sad thing had been only a dream.

# Bobbie Luntz

Bobbie Luntz finished what she had to say and leaned against the door with arms folded across her chest. She glanced up at the clock that hung over Jerry's head and scratched at her elbow through her sleeve.

It was out now, and she could stop sweating about it. The late night rehearsal in front of the mirror hadn't resulted in much since the news dumped out of her in a completely different way, in pieces, one half of it tangled into the other half. Just the same, it was done, and that was all that mattered.

Jerry sighed and thumbed through a stack of papers on his desk, eyes fixed on his clumsy hands. The desktop was a collage of invoices and student folders, pink detention slips and half-sheet memos. A mug of sharpened pencils sat adjacent his brass nameplate, which Jerry always kept turned toward himself. As if he might forget who he was.

"Okay," he said slapping the paper and looking up at her. "What am I supposed do about it?"

"You're the principal. I figured you should be in the loop." She shrugged her shoulders. "Just in case, I guess."

"Just in case?" Jerry Brewster labored a heavy sigh and worked his fingers over his temples. "So, you're saying he could just show up here?"

Bobbie sucked in her breath and tightened her fingers over her arms. The door began to warm against her back. His voice was getting louder, which meant that the conversation was probably spilling over to the secretary's desk on the other side.

"I don't know," she said. It occurred to her then that maybe she should have kept her mouth shut about it. Just gone straight to her office like usual, doling out Midols and Ritalin all day without saying a word. She stared down at her Keds. They had been white when she started the year, but now they were gray at best, with black smudges edging the toes. "I don't know what the hell I'm saying, Jerry. Never mind."

Bobbie Luntz turned and walked back to the door in a nauseous fog. Jerry stayed in his seat, filling the space in his office with the noise of rusty springs, as he shifted his fat self from one cheek to the other. The whole thing, this conversation, should have lifted the weight in her stomach —that's what unloading heavy news was supposed to do. If anything, it was worse. It all still sat there like a sack of rocks.

Connie stood behind her desk and tipped her cocoon of hair to her shoulder, and raised a penciled eyebrow at Bobbie. It was a look that suggested sympathy, but Bobbie knew better. Secretaries were cut from the same cloth everywhere. Bobbie faked a smile and moved past without a word.

She went quickly to her own office, where she began the busy task of Friday inventory. She pulled down the prescription bottles and drugstore counter painkillers that crowded the labeled, plastic crates like pharmaceutical Easter baskets. In the ledger, the names of various students fronted long rows of her own handwriting, and she ran down the midday column, scratching her initials into a half dozen boxes. She fought to keep herself focused, but the whole thing blurred to a blue haze as her fingers drummed over the page. Someone had come that morning for a Benadryl, she knew, and there were a couple aspirins that had gone out. But she'd forgotten to write them down, and now she couldn't even remember which kids got what pills.

"Jesus God," she said. "Your mind is all over the damned place."

Bobbie closed her eyes and sucked in her breath. She held it behind her teeth. Get it together, she told herself. There's not a damned thing you can do but wait and see how it plays out. Her fingers massaged her eyelids, and she tried to force her head into the present day, to remember who had been in to see her that morning. There was a girl in glasses and a red hair clip, but it wasn't someone she knew.

He could show up at her door tomorrow, and then what? What's the worst that could happen? He'd show up is all. It wouldn't be like him to hurt her. The letter had been a long one, but it wasn't angry. Emotional, of course. Accusatory, here and there. *Maybe now you can take time out of your weekend to bring him to see me*, he'd said. *He's my son just as much as yours.* But he hadn't made any threats. If he showed up, she'd just tell him to go on back, that she was calling the cops, no two ways about it. There had been an accident. Maybe he hit his head and he hadn't been thinking clearly. The best thing to do was to turn right around and see the rest of his sentence through. The whole interaction, whether it happened on her porch or outside the school, or even at all, could be done and over with in ten minutes.

"Oh, screw it," she said. She grabbed the pen and simply wrote out the names of three girls she knew who played on the softball team.

She checked her supply of gauze, bandages, and Ace wraps, and tampons and pads and then she looked up at the analog clock that was inset into the wall above the door. It was two minutes until second lunch. She refilled the cotton ball jar and took a couple Tylenol for herself, then re-tucked her blouse into her blue jeans. She pulled back her red hair and re-clipped her barrettes before locking the whole cabinet down and going to the door that opened from her second floor office out into the long hallway.

The bell was original to the building, and it was mounted to the wall directly over her head. And even when she was ready for it, she was never really ready for it, the moment the thing screamed at everyone to get into their classrooms or get out of their classrooms or go to lunch or go home or get to whatever lousy after school job might be waiting for them. Then at last there was the nerve-jarring alarm and piles of students poured out from flung doors.

They swirled all about in a river of flannel, and denim and moussed hair framing acne-specked faces and flashes of metal on bricklike smiles. Bobbie stood on the banks against the wall with her leg now beginning to ache. Maybe it was the phone call the night before that was making it worse than usual. More likely, though, it was the constant mist or rain or thick fog that had held such a tight embrace on the mountain for the past two weeks, because God knew her leg was in a constant throb. This time of year, everything was wet. Always. Even the air in the hallway lent a distinct clamminess to her bare arms. She stood waiting, the toes of her tennis shoes mere inches from the tumultuous flow.

From behind a wall of fluttering lockers he appeared, tossing a glance in Bobbie's direction. The rocks in her stomach tumbled, and her hands began to needle, and then everything washed to a kind of numbness, like they often did when she saw her son in the hallway, in his element.

Patrick was uncanny handsome. But with his noodle arms and legs and the goofy puppet-like way he moved from one place to the next, it was clear that he just hadn't grown into himself yet. He was a late bloomer, she told him. Some people took longer than others to reach where they would eventually be. It was all just a frustrating requirement of the teenager phase. He seldom mentioned girls to her anymore, and she'd stopped going there long ago. But she still found herself wishing that he would find some-one—anyone—that he could share himself with. So he wouldn't feel like he had to shoulder everything all by himself. But she had to believe things would turn out the way they were supposed to and her task was to be patient with him. He was a stunner, with his shock black hair, and that custard-yellow bleached stripe he had down the bangs, and hard, steel-cut cheekbones. Like his father, those chiseled cheekbones, and that one fact ripped Bobbie Luntz clean down her middle, straight from top to bottom.

Today of all days, she wanted to go to him, just bear straight through the thickness right there in the middle of the school hallway and take him into her arms until he disappeared from the world. It took every bit of herself to stay by that door and keep her hands to her sides. He was so helpless, so alone among the crowd of jocks and braniacs, and rockers with ratted hair and torn black t-shirts who passed by him as if he were nothing. She could turn away, she thought, but in the next second he might be gone forever. It was her pathological fear to lose her son again, and on this day it was worse than ever, as if a coming storm could suddenly appear and sweep him from her at any moment. She waved to him, and he turned away quick and shouted down the hall to someone Bobbie couldn't get a bead on. A round-faced girl with big, moon glasses and a stack of books mashed protectively against massive boobs stood next to him. She elbowed his arm and leaned into his ear.

Patrick nodded, rolled his head to one side and stepped off from the edge, falling into the current, crossing over to where Bobbie stood.

"What's up?" She tried to be casual. She shoved her hands into her jeans pockets.

"I was gonna go up to the quarry this weekend."

"Are you asking or telling?"

He tossed his bangs aside and rolled his eyes to the ceiling. "Asking. Can I go to the quarry this weekend."

Bobbie knew well that the chances of Patrick actually going to the quarry were questionable at best. He could be headed there or he could be off to Seattle again, to that Mama Whats-her-name's place and those castoff kids that she gave shelter to. Bobbie didn't care for either possibility. Still, she knew the kinds of things that went on up at the quarry, and the idea of him spending a night or two at an old woman's house, rather than drinking beer and burning campfires and leftover fireworks, didn't seem so bad. If that's what was going to happen.

"Seems like you just went up there. Two weeks ago?"

"Three."

"Who else is going?" She played along.

He glanced over at his friend by the locker. She was talking to someone else now, and it looked as though they were both about to leave. "Just some guys. Greg Hardeman, and I don't know. Vince Stewart, maybe. You know 'em."

She didn't know them, but she let it slide. It was sometimes easier to avoid asking too many questions, to dodge the holes that too often showed up in his answers than to press too hard. "Pick your battles, babe," Ernie used to say to her, back when the battles were little ones.

"You'll be home before noon Sunday this time? I don't want you dragging it out into evening."

"I'll try."

"You'll do more than try, sir, or you can forget about asking me next time. And don't forget you have Tin's, before you take off."

"I won't forget."

"It's a job. It's important to be on time, every time."

Patrick's voiced hardened off, and he said, "God, Mom. I'm not going to forget about Tin or the stupid minks. I've been there every day already, why would I forget now?"

Bobbie said, "Alright, alright. Have fun, and be smart."

He gave her a smile that Bobbie knew was charitable at best. Then he broke from her, to fall back into the current with the rest of the fish.

She watched the churning of bodies and sifted through the mental Rolodex of the various injuries, stomach and skin conditions, the heavy periods and the missed periods, and all the generally nonexistent sicknesses that made up the menagerie of teenagers that moved past her. After six years, she was still only a four-day-a-week nurse, and even then, most days amounted to little more than taking temperatures and writing gym passes for girls with cramps and boys who likely just didn't want to shower in front of the other boys. There was the occasional parent meeting, carefully spoken phrases such "first term," "next steps," and "several options left," shared across the small, kidney-shaped table. Now and then there might be a phone call to police or a jaded social worker, the divulging of telltale bruises or tearful stories involving uncles or new stepfathers. But for the most part, as far as Ash Falls High School was concerned, there were some days that Bobbie Luntz felt like nothing more than a glorified Band-Aid dispenser. And on most days, this was just fine by her.

She locked the door to the health room and walked down the hallway, between students who darted past her or simply moved to the side, or didn't move to the side, until she reached the staff lounge at the end of the hall. Already she could smell the menthol, and her teeth took on that veneer of chalkiness that came with sitting in a smoke-filled room. She never understood how people could eat their boxed lunches of warmed-over spaghetti and flaccid iceberg lettuce salads while bundled in blue, smoky filth. But there was a part of her that still ached for it, a need to belong on some level. So she found herself putting up with the nastiness without so much as a whimper. Christ, she thought. You're just as much a lemming as any one of those kids.

A swale of laughter rushed out from the lounge, and then someone said, "I'd have loved to be a fly on the wall for that one." Then Bobbie swung open the door, and there was a hard freeze in conversation, and a half dozen faces bucked at her as she stood in the doorway. Fisheyed, all of them. Mike Walner, Tom Cowen, and Tina Reiter and all the rest of the math and science team stared at her as if she might turn right around and run back down the hall to find the principal and rat them all out. Then just as quickly faces set to neutral, and everyone seemed interested only in eating again. It was a scene she had gotten used to long ago. The dropped conversations. Averted glances.

"Don't everyone shut up on my account," Bobbie said. She

glanced at Tina who kept her back to her.

"So yeah. I'm guessing we'll get to the finals this season, but there ain't no way in hell we're going to state." Tom Cowan was red-faced, jowly, and gin-blossomed as he sputtered through gobs of egg salad. "Don't tell Jerry I said so, though."

Bobbie took a seat at a small round table by herself. Tina got up from the men's table and carried the last of her lunch over to where she was.

"Do you remember that night? Mike Walner said. "When they actually took state?"

"Hell yes, I remember that night," Tom choked. "Like it was yesterday, and let me tell you that son of a bitch Jerry owes more to Troy Bonneville than any chalkboard diagrams he ever scratched out."

Bobbie tuned it out as best she could. It had nothing to do with her, or with Patrick. Tina reached to the clamshell ashtray and stamped out her cigarette.

"You going to The Flume later?" she asked Bobbie. "TGIF, you know."

"I'm not feeling up to it."

"You sure? If you're not there I'll be the only woman in the pack. You know how they can get."

"Then don't go."

"Come on." There was an edge of desperation in her voice now, and it was getting under Bobbie's nerves. Tina was probably the closest thing to a friend that Bobbie had anymore at the high school, but she could also be an emotional drag, especially when she got a few drinks in her. Like Bobbie, Tina had arrived in Ash Falls by way of Seattle, in a limping station wagon overloaded with cheap furniture and a shitload of personal baggage. And like Bobbie, she was learning fast that baggage loves a small town.

"So. Is it true?" Tina leaned in close to her, her lips barely moving as she spoke. "About Ernie?"

Bobbie glanced over Tina's shoulder to the men, who still

mumbled to one another in the midst of all the blue haze. She tilted her head, looked back to Tina and took a spoonful from the small yogurt cup.

"Oh God." Tina froze in her seat. "So Connie wasn't shitting. He really is out."

"Who's out?" Tom Cowan piped up. "Not Ernie."

"Yeah, Ernie," Bobbie said. "So what of it?"

"You gotta be fucking kidding me," Tom said.

"Jesus, Tom," Tina said. "Nobody was even talking to you." She straightened herself, sat tall in her chair, and pushed her chest out, and the other men followed her posture as if she were dancing. Her rouged face cocked to one side, the neck craning to look out the window, toward the cars whose chromed grills jammed up against the curb in a gleaming line.

Bobbie accepted that there was no sense in fighting it. From where they all sat, from the boxed in, smoke-sickened corner room on the second floor, they were equal prisoners—all of them. They were prisoners of the neglected two-story brick behemoth that contained them all, a building aged and grandly pillared and choked with a suffocating layer of untamed ivy and dying wisteria and steadfast tradition and, too often (if you asked the right people), a small town's general inability to see the horizon beyond its own cracked and rutted streets. Did Ernie really want to come back to this?

Tina asked, "So what happened? They didn't let him out just like that?"

"No they didn't let him out. There was an accident, and I guess he ran off."

"Goddamn, Bobbie," Tom said, looking over his shoulder at the door. "When did this happen?"

It was out of the bag now, there was no use parsing words. "I got a call from the sheriff out in Monroe yesterday," she said. "They were moving him out there from Walla Walla. The driver had a heart attack and drove off the road." She rubbed at her eyes with her fingers, imagining again Ernie tumbling through a rolling car, jaw clenched beneath a shrubby beard, guards in the front seat, out cold. In some of her visions, he tries to help them, radio in somehow. Other times he just kicks the door open without a moment's hesitation and crawls out. And just like that, he's gone.

Tina leaned in to her. "So you told Jerry."

"Yes I told Jerry. And it sounds like Connie started in on the phone tree as quick as she could get her fingers on the buttons." Bobbie stood up from the table now and cut the blue air around them with her hands. "But who gives a shit, right? People are going to find out soon enough as it is."

Bobbie could see now that Tom was full-on sweating, tiny beads forming all down the slope of his neck.

"Jesus Tom," she said. "You look like you're about to have a coronary."

"Yeah, well he made his presence known to more than a few lives here, Bobbie, mine included. I'm sorry to put it like that, but goddamn. That son of a bitch better not show his ass back here."

"You don't have to worry, Tom. If anyone's got a reason to sweat it's me, okay?"

"Not just you." It was Mike Walner. Bobbie looked over to him, but he kept his eyes on his half eaten sandwich. He picked at a rippled edge of lettuce. "There's a few others in this town that might have reason to worry."

She got up and walked to the window and looked out over the parking lot. The morning drizzle was supposed to have burned off by now, but yet here it still was, a stubborn, lingering annoyance that refused to loosen its grip on the mountain. Pelting the glass in tiny specks like Tom Cowen's neck. Still, just across the street, old Mrs. Gilman knelt on a yellow pad in her garden digging up bulbs and laying them in a tidy pile in the middle of her fractured walkway.

"The sheriff said they got everyone out looking for him," Bobbie said. "It's just a matter of time. She looked down past

Mrs. Gilman's house, down the long stretch of Main Street. "He won't set foot in this town," she added. "So you can quit worrying about it."

Tina came and stood beside her at the window. "I know you're not trying to minimize this Bobbie. But he killed someone, and half the town was there. Some of them still teach right here in this school."

"I know that, Tina. I was there too. Right there."

"Yeah, then I know I don't need to remind you of why he did it, either. Honest to God, I'm not trying to lay guilt on you for that. You say he won't be coming around here, but you don't know that for sure. I know men, and I know men who have been away for awhile, if you catch my drift." She put her hand on Bobbie's arm. "I don't want to scare you, Bobbie, but you can't be sure of anything."

Bobbie nodded. Her hair had broken loose from her barrette and was falling down over forehead into her eyes. She worked her knuckles into her palm. "I just don't want to make a big deal out of it."

Tina moved in closer. "Have you talked to Hank?"

Bobbie shook her head and felt the pressure of blood against the back of her eyes. She glanced over at the men. They were eating again now, and Tom seemed to be on his way back to his natural color. The last thing she wanted—besides involving Patrick—was to drag Hank Kelleher into this hornet's nest all over again. But she guessed it was unavoidable.

Tina took hold of Bobbie's hand now and pressed her thumb to her wrist.

"Why don't you just come out for some drinks later? We can talk more about it there, if you want. You don't want to be alone tonight."

The bell signaling the close of lunch drilled on the other side of the wall, and the roar of disappointed voices washed through the door. Bobbie glanced at the men who were now sweeping their trash into their hands, eyes glued to their fingers and feet. They pushed past her, out the door into the rush of teenagers streaming past.

# Patrick Luntz

He crowded into the phone booth and the overhead light hummed and flickered through a ceiling mosaic of dead flies and fat, downy moths. Names and phone numbers layered the box and beckoned all along the glass and not a single one of them was somebody he knew or had even heard of. It was hard to believe that, in a town as small and dead end as Ash Falls, there was anyone within reach of a local phone number that he didn't know. He dialed the operator.

"I'd like to make a collect call." He recited the nine digits, burned into his memory. "Collect from Spooky."

"From who?" The operator had a crisp, short way of speaking, as if she were judging him for even asking. As if this person with the weird name would have to explain himself first, convince her to place the call for him.

"From Spooky. It's just a nickname, but they'll know who it is."

The line at the other end rang and rang, and Patrick prayed that the operator would give it time before cutting in, because it always took forever for anyone to pick up there. When at last the receiver clicked and the soft, deep voice on the other side said, "Sure, I'll accept," Patrick Luntz leaned against the cold glass of the booth and began to cry.

He was a mile and a half outside of town before he rebalanced the Supersonics gym bag over his handlebars and veered the Schwinn from the highway onto River Road. He downshifted and drove hard up the swaybacked hill, past the old water tower to the tall, chain link gate that did a decent job keeping wanderers from venturing uninvited onto what was officially the Dorsay property, but what most people in Ash Falls still called The Old Dahlstrom Ranch. He fished the key from his pocket and undid the lock and swung the tall chain link gate, then pushed his bike past the aluminum post, through the salmonberry brambles with their seedy orange nubs, most of them dried up or already picked clean by birds. After closing the gate behind him, he took his gym bag and tossed it into the undergrowth. Then he repositioned himself on his seat and pushed off, lifted his feet from the pedals and let loose, coasting balls-out crazy down the rutted grassy drive to the bottom of the hill.

This was his favorite part of the trip, the ride down the long drive to the minkyard where the wind could blow his hair back from his face and he could feel the fingers of the forest teasing his arms and legs as he made his descent. Here he flew beneath the low hanging hemlocks with their soft, feathery needles, and a gauntlet of bracken and sword fern and the occasional mammoth fan of a devil's club with its needled stalks leaning ominously out into the drive. Near the bottom he came out into the bogs at last, where the understory was open and cathedral-like, and giant nurse logs lay rotting beneath blankets of moss and deer fern and pale yellow lichens, and tags of thick, rippled shelf fungus. Here the skunk cabbage grew in occasional stalks, their bright yellow flowers rising like erect dicks poking from behind leafy capes. Here, the sweetness of the long ride began to fade and the heaviness of a dank musk reminded him of the whole purpose of this long journey.

At the north border of the yard the Stillaguamish River rolled by, icy and sluggish, with occasional pinwheels on the surface that liked to hold up the fallen leaves and errant branches on their journeys to Port Gardner Bay some sixty miles downstream. The waters of the Stilly have the kind of unnatural slate-green that exists only in the deep veins of a glacier fed river, and from this river Tin Dorsay hauled in rainbow and cutthroat, and steelhead, which he usually kept for himself, but sometimes sent home with Patrick, each wrapped in aluminum foil like a heavy bar of silver.

Old man Tin stood at the tongue of the first mink barn, a pair of chunky saw horses on either side of him and several sun bleached two-by-four planks stretched between. At his feet lay a corded Skilsaw, and a light fall of sawdust scattered down his back and around his boots. Patched denim trousers hung loose from his twig body like paint-splotched drapery while taut, bright blue suspenders looped necessary over his shoulders. The flannel shirt-tails billowed from his beltline, and he paused between jerks on the tape measurer and hard pencil marks to tip his baseball cap and wipe down his shiny cue-ball head. He kept at this business as if he was a machine, his toothless grimace forming something of a duckbill and when he caught sight of Patrick out of his periphery he laid down the tape and waved him over.

"Well if it isn't old skunk head," he called out. "Get on over here, boy, and let's get started. Christsakes, where you been the day's almost over." He tottered to the door of the barn, legs in a wide gambrel. Patrick laid down the bike and hustled over to him. "What'd you get lost on your way over here?"

"I'm only a few minutes behind."

"Yeah, well, I got things to do." Tin yanked open the door and the eye-burning odor rolled out with it. "I been wanting to talk to you, kid. We lost a couple at the end. You know anything about it?"

"They got out, or they're dead?"

"If they was dead, I'd of said they was dead," the old man snapped. "They got out. Gone. Run for the hills. Capeesh? You must have been monkeying with the cage when you was here yesterday."

Patrick looked at Tin's face and he was biting down on his lip, the flesh wrapped down tight over his gummed jaw like it was a dinner plate. The old man looked over the long rows of teeming cages.

"I don't mess with the doors. And I always double check them," Patrick said. "Like you told me."

"Yeah, well, you must of no-checked that one cause it was wide open this morning when I come through with the feed cart. Them sonsofbitches are long gone."

He wide-stepped down the aisle between the cages, and all around him the weasely critters twittered and paced, and some snapped at the mesh as he passed them by. Patrick followed him. The boy kept his hands in his pockets the whole way and took pains to avoid eye contact with the minks. Too often they worked their ways into his head at night while he tried to get to sleep, all marbley eyes and razor teeth. The more he could do to keep them at bay, he thought, the better off he was. Just as Tin was turning around one of the minks to his left, a good-sized silver blue male, made a hard lunge at the screen. Tin took a jolt back and gave a raspy report.

"Yeah, yeah. All piss and vinegar now but we'll see where you stand in a few weeks."

Patrick stole a glance at his watch.

"You got somewhere you'd rather be?"

"No. I got a bus to catch is all."

"A bus? Where the hell you got to go?"

"The city." It just came out, and it seemed okay to Patrick that it did. There wasn't a reason to lie to Tin. After all, who did he have to tell?

"Goin all the way into Seattle? Well, with that stripe in that hair of yours I suppose you'll fit right in." They got to the last rows and Tin waved a bony hand at the empty cage, its door laid open against the frame. "So what of it? This empty goddamned cage cost me pert near forty dollars. You got forty dollars to pay for it? I ought to make you work the week for free to pay it off." He slammed the lid closed and latched it rough, like he was showing the cage a lesson more than he was showing the boy.

The door creaked opened from the far end of the shed. It was

Gus the Indian and he froze, staring with his mouth drooped, as if he had walked in on a murder.

"What do you want?" Tin called.

"The feeder won't start."

"You check the gas?"

"Yeah." He bounced against the open door, casting a strip of outside light that breathed into the shed.

Tin looked at Patrick again, and at the empty cage. "Goddamn it," he said.

Patrick didn't say a thing. He had better sense than to implicate himself in something that was, more likely, the old man's fault than his own. Tin Dorsay finally skulked off and Patrick reached into his pocket to switch on his Walkman, dialing up the volume so The Clash filled his head and drowned out the sounds of the squalling mink.

He took himself from cage to cage, sometimes talking to the creatures, usually to himself, the driving guitar blasting from the headphones and drawing him closer to the memory of the music and the people he wanted so desperately to be with, the people like him, that packed the old church and pressed sweaty against each other as they danced, and climbed on the speakers where they swayed in shorts and no shirts. The musk that wafted up brought him back to bodies and machine smoke, and vortex of spinning lights and the boy Shadow who held his pose against the back wall, one foot propped behind him, two cigarettes hanging from a crooked grin.

Patrick scooped out the soiled bedding, always tolerating the rips to his gloved fingers, grateful for the protection of leather. On a typical day he might take in a dozen mink bites to his hands and wrists, and at least as many sprays if he let himself face the ass end of any one of them. The first day at work his mother barred him from even coming into the house before stripping down in the mudroom and sealing his clothes in a plastic garbage bag. From then on a knee-length terrycloth robe always waited for him to the right of the kitchen door.

Tin had brought in a truckload of alder shavings earlier in the week for Patrick to work into the straw for the mink nests. He moved from cage to cage on autopilot, each step and process mindless in its execution. Twist the latch open, sweep the mink out of the way, clean out the soiled bedding, refill with clean. Nasty animals pacing to the rear of their cages, or huddling against the sides, or sometimes hooking teeth into his leathered hands. Do it again. Twist the latch open, fill the bed, latching it closed, tight. One after the other, there wasn't the slightest amount of thinking even required in a job like this, a monkey could do the same job and still get it right. Goddamned Tin, he thought. Who the hell is he to accuse me? Forty dollars my ass. Only an idiot would have left that cage open and I'm not a fucking idiot.

In an hour, the minks were pawing through fresh chips, or were curled in the corners of cages, sleeping off the trauma of Patrick's intrusion. He came back through the rows and double-checked the latches he had already checked once before. Tin walked through with him and did the same, painfully slow, before finally handing over the cash and setting Patrick free.

The drive was now almost completely dark under the dense canopy, and Patrick barreled up the hill, standing straight up on the pedals and kicking until he thought his chest would rip open. At the gate he fished his bag from the bushes and flung it over his shoulder, then he pushed hard through the chilly drizzle to the open highway. He came into town, zigged through parked cars and alleyways to Junction Service Station, where he ducked into the bathroom and stripped himself naked by the sink. He filled the basin with cold water and hand soap and gave himself what he had once heard called A Whore's Bath—which if he were to be honest, seemed fitting. As he stood there in the harsh light of the gas station john, toilet paper strewn on the floor and swabbing at his pits and ball sack with soap-soaked paper towels he wondered if the rancid air in his head was the room or his own mink-soaked body. He stuffed the farm clothes into his bag and slid on the bleach-splotched jeans and the Joy Division tee-shirt, which he covered with his heavy winter parka. He put on his red Converse shoes, splashed himself with a coat of cologne and then he was out, was back on the road, right on schedule, racing to the bus stop on Main Street where he shoved his bike deep into the bowels of the giant holly tree that hulked against the post office wall.

Even though it was already close enough to dark, and the streets were quiet enough, and even though he only had a few minutes to kill he sat in the shadows of the awning behind the columns just in case. In case his mother should happen by or any other person on their way to The Flume who might say I saw your kid waiting for the bus to Everett and I hate to say it, Bobbie, but he looked a little queer to me.

At six twenty-five, the wheezing transit rounded the corner. Three people stood with hands on dropped ceiling loops, hunched down and peering out the rain-soaked windows. They seemed to be looking right at him, staring at the lone young man with a skunk stripe down his head, a boy desperately waiting to leave the godforsaken mountain behind.

# Hank Kelleher

Hank Kelleher stood in the center of a circle of gleaming white alder quarter trunks, remnants of a listing tree that he had felled by himself that morning with only a 16-inch Stihl and a tightly stretched cable. The cable he had cinched to a come-along, which then was attached a spar tree of sorts, a big cedar some distance from the cabin. He had winched the thing as far has he could, enough to draw the tree from the cabin toward the cedar spar. He braced his body against the saw, sinking the bar the rest of the way in to the gnarly trunk. There was a sharp crack and the trunk broke loose, kicking back from the stump and almost taking his legs along with it.

Hank was thrown a few yards, into a clump of sword fern, the whole thing giving him more of a start than anything else. Close calls had happened before. With trees and such. This was his forest and he knew it well. He had for himself a tidy collection of second and third growth Doug Firs and red cedars, and Western Hemlocks and moss-covered stumps of the same with springboard notches that looked out from beneath the underbrush like the toothless grins of old men. The ghosts of men who had lost limbs of their own or whole lives, even, taken down by the errant descent of a widow maker or the man's own careless action. Or both. He brought down four or five trees on average each year, so to him this situation with the bucking alder was a minor one.

He took out his pocket watch and flipped back the nickel cover. It was almost noon. He'd split the entire length of the alder already, and by two he had planned to stack it all in the shelter of the cedar grove and cover the whole thing with the new tarp he'd bought at the Coast to Coast that week, to let the wood season for burning the following year. This would give him plenty of time to get cleaned up and changed before she arrived.

The air was cool and wet, still holding onto what felt like the last bit of the morning's rain. There were low clouds covering the west face of the mountain and the high peaks poked above like jagged, floating white islands. It was coming down, all of it, the whole sky. In two hours' time it would be pouring again, and Hank still had probably half a cord of wood to get under cover.

His dog Toby was a wiry-haired mutt, more hound than terrier, and he scrambled on the west side of the creek bed, pacing the edges of the giant fern-pocked nurse log and scouring its perimeter. He pawed at the bed of oxalis and bleeding hearts and bunchberries with an almost giddy energy. A screwy pinch grabbed Hank's lower back and he gave out a loud call. The dog stopped what he was doing and cocked his head in Hank's direction, wagging his tail as if the call had been for him. When Hank took off the canvas work jacket and broke loose the suede gloves and sat down onto an upturned chunk of wood, Toby bounded through the low creek and came to him, and nuzzled his palms and cleaned the callused skin. Hank scrubbed at his ears.

"Ain't you the nursemaid," he sang. "Checking up on the old man."

Hank arched his back and worked his fingers into the muscle above his belt loops and Toby climbed onto his lap. Hank felt it everywhere: his back, across his shoulders, even in his damned knees. There was a time when he could buck and split timber all day like this and not feel the least pinch the next morning. Still, he could point to a half-dozen men his age that wouldn't last an hour with him at the woodpile. He was barely on the north side of sixty. There was still plenty of mileage left in him.

The crunching of gravel drew Hank's attention to the long driveway, and he gave the dog a firm pat on the ribs, pushing himself up from the ground. He ambled to the porch where he reached inside the door for his rifle, a Remington with bolt action, standard for the casual hunter, not that Hank would ever put himself in the category of either Casual or Hunter. The squirrely man in Coke-bottle glasses who lorded over the gun counter at Jerry's Surplus had declared it a good rifle, for taking out deer and whatnot. "Pick that sonofabitch off from a hundred yards," the man promised, and the latter fact was one that appealed to Hank. He never liked the idea of shooting at anyone but if he had to, he hoped it would at least be from a good distance away.

He leaned back in to steal a glance at the clock. It was just past twelve. He gave a whistle to the dog, which jogged from the alder cuts to the porch where he took his place dutifully at Hank's side. Hank rubbed at the dog's ears and told him he was a good, good boy, but he held his eyes straight down the drive to the dip in the roadway.

The toothy grill of one ugly Ford wagon rose up over the ridge, a mousy tap coming from its horn. A slender arm unfolded from the window and waved to Hank. At once, his blood seemed to warm and his lips drew back in a smile, and he set the rifle behind him. He raised a hand in mutual greeting, careful to show surprise over happiness. The car came to a rattled stop then knocked a couple of times before giving a final cough.

The door swung open and Bobbie Luntz stepped out, wearing waffle-soled boots too big for her body, and a red flannel shirt filled well in the chest and tucked into her jeans. The shirtsleeves were cuffed neatly to the elbows. A knit handbag swung heavy over her shoulder, and as she rounded the front of the car there was that lack of symmetry in her walk. The long car ride out of Ash Falls, he imagined. Probably aggravated her leg for her. She gave a squeeze to her hip and leaned against the fender, and his heart fell again.

"Well I'll be damned," she called out. "The Professor lives and speaks."

"What are you doing here?"

"You forgot about our date? Figures."

"I didn't forget, but you're a few hours early. You should have called first," he said. "I could've shot you."

"I did call. Twice. Better check your phone line to see if you haven't cut it again with all your digging." She pushed off from the fender and walked toward him. "I haven't seen that famous blue Chevy of yours in town lately. Is there a reason that you're keeping yourself holed up?"

"I've always got some reason to keep holed up," he said. He came down from the porch. "Besides, the truck. It's slipping gears some and I haven't had a chance to take it in to have it looked at. But I guess I'm gonna have to do it soon. I gotta run down the back side to Darrington at the end of next week. The last thing I need is to get stuck halfway between here and there."

"Well, all right. I suppose Benny could use the work." She dropped the subject of the truck and quickly turned her attention to the scattering of firewood. "I see you've been busy."

"I'm always busy, you know that, too. That thing nearabout came down on my roof." He fumbled with his hands, first in his pockets then picking his shirt buttons. He rambled on, filling the air with details about the tree-felling that he knew were neither interesting nor important to her. The cable winch, the reach of the lowest branches. It filled the space more than anything else, since it was the only way he knew to talk to her anymore.

"It was a tricky thing," he said, nodding to the pile of wood. "But there she is."

"Well, you know. You could have called me, Hank. I'd have come out early and lent a hand."

"You're already early. Just not early enough."

This was the Bobbie he'd always known, unfailingly willing to offer herself up for help around the property, wood cutting, brush clearing, whatnot. Ever since the snowy night at the Flume shortly after she'd started at the school, when she slipped his keys from his coat pocket and announced that she was driving him home, whether he liked it or not. That night had been the spar tree. Stripped clean, solitary, and cabled to every other event that had touched his life since.

"You know, you shouldn't worry yourself so much about the old man in the woods."

She reached up and grabbed hold of his whiskered chin. "You're not so old. But you could do with a shave. There's no reason to grow into the mountain like moss, Hank."

There was something about her on this day that was different, maybe her hair, not that he knew a thing about that sort of business. It could be the light coming down from the thickness of the canopy. Perhaps everything was just extra bright today. Something. The orange washed from her temples and fell down to the shoulders like the sunrise.

She reached down and grabbed a few chunks of firewood and tossed them into a nearby wheelbarrow. Hank said, "Come on now," but she just smiled and shook her head at him.

"Come on yourself," she said. "Let me do this one load. Fun first, then business."

She commenced to filling the barrow, one piece at a time, while he stood there gawking at her like a waiter.

"I was flipping through the channels last night," he said. "Couldn't sleep. Came across that old horror movie with Steve McQueen. 'The Blob'."

"Oh yeah. That's a good drive-in picture."

"Dumbest thing I ever saw. Big pile of strawberry jam, eats up the whole town."

"I forget how it ended."

Hank said, "They killed it with a bunch of fire extinguishers."

"Oh yeah." She bit down on her lip. "It was a stupid movie, but you didn't turn it off."

"Well, I was already too far into it to give up. I had to see how it all ended."

Hank trucked the barrow into the cedar grove, and Bobbie added each piece neatly to the growing stack, and only when she clapped her hands together did Hank take the wheelbarrow from her and push it back to the alder field next to the house.

"Okay, now," he said. "Time for business."

Bobbie nodded with conviction and said, "Time for business." She kicked at a curl of bark and followed him into the house without further discussion.

There was still the smell of wood smoke in the room, remnants of the morning fire that Hank had built to cut the waking chill. There were a few mismatched plates on the counter, a couple of errant glasses and a red-checked hand towel left draped over the edge of the sink. But for the most part, the place was clean. Hank took pride in being the kind of man who was cognizant of the space around him, a person who appreciated a semblance of order and predictability but who did not demand it.

The details, as they should be, were in the construction of the house and it showed. Hank had built it over a period of years with his own hands, when he still lived and worked in Ash Falls. It was a mix of Doug Fir, alder and Western Red Cedar, all lumber that he had milled onsite. He was especially proud of the dovetailed cabinetry and hand-routed moldings, the tongue in groove paneling and even the woodstove that he had welded together from a salvaged oil drum, set into a hearth of river rock that he carried in from the nearby riverbed. There was no hint now of what had once been on site, not even a faint scar of the ramshackle cabins and canvas-draped tents that cluttered the land decades earlier, when the entire valley was owned and inhabited first by Hank's grandfather Malcolm and then, Hank's father Henry Senior.

"Damn that thing puts out the heat," Bobbie said. She undid the button at her neck and pulled her shirt back and forth from her chest. She glanced to the sofa, where the finer clothing that Hank had lain out still waited for the change that would no longer be taking place. "Just like your dad, I suspect. It could be the middle of July and you'd have a fire in the stove."

"It gets cold up here in the mornings. You forget that, living down there in the big city. It might only be twelve miles but it's almost six hundred feet up. These bones freeze easily."

"Those bones are just fine, Hank." Bobbie stood in the doorway to the kitchen, her shoulder leaning against the jamb and her hands in her jeans pockets. She looked at Hank in the way she always did when she was poking fun. Deadpan, one eyebrow raised.

"Business."

In the pine-paneled pantry, behind the canisters of black beans and chickpeas and dried cornmeal, and wheat flour, and a false cedar panel, were the tiny gasket jars filled with the Medicine, and that was exactly what he preferred it to be called. Medicine. Anyone who happened to come by his cabin and refer to it as anything else would be given a single correction and then it would be, "Off my land for good and don't come back." It was one of several reasons Hank saw so few people at the cabin anymore. It was just too much to ask some people to be respectful of what he did and how he did it. Bobbie got it. She was smart and she kept her priorities in line with Hank's. She hadn't needed a reminder at all, not even once.

"Any of these your own?" Bobbie stood back from the shelves. She peered studiously at the jars, then glanced back over her shoulder, out the front window. "Are you growing yet?"

"Hell no." The last thing he needed was the headache of a grow operation. "I don't need but a little bit here and there, you know that. These down here I got from my guy in Darrington, and the rest are from a grower up in Sedro-Wooley. It's all good stuff, but this right here is something new." He pulled two jars from the shelf and handed them to Bobbie, then took two more. They walked to a small table in the kitchen and set them down. "Open that lid there and take a whiff of it." He motioned to one of the jars closest to Bobbie.

"This one?"

"Yeah."

She bent down the bracket and popped the glass lid back, and put it to her freckled nose. She closed her eyes and inhaled deeply.

She smiled, the first full, genuine smile he'd seen all afternoon.

"Grape Kool-Aid."

Hank took the jar from her hand and reached in, pulling out a thumbnail-sized nugget and holding it up. It was a tangle of thick, meaty fibers with sparse wisps of purple hairs woven in.

"They call it Grape Krush. My fella in Sedro-Wooley, he brought in about twenty plants. Gave me first dibs on it."

"That's generous."

"He's that kind of guy."

Bobbie took it from him and rolled the nugget between her fingers, and lifted it to her nose to give it another smell.

"What's the strain?"

"Sixty indica, forty sativa. All grown inside, believe it or not. He's got these new sodium vapor lights. Like something out of NASA. He tells me it cuts grow time almost in half if you can believe it." The two of them, talking business, science. Like she was any other customer.

Bobbie picked up the jar and tipped it to one side, and brought it to her nose where she took in a deep breath. She leaned back and exhaled, and ran her hand through her hair, scratching at the back of her neck with her fingers. "What about couch lock?" she said.

Hank rolled his eyes and whispered, "Couch lock? Come on."

But Bobbie held up her hand in defense. "Hank I have to ask. I can't be giving up my whole day."

With the amount of medicine that Bobbie had been buying from him lately, Hank found it hard to believe that she wasn't already giving up her day. They never talked about how much she used, or whether or not she was sharing with someone else. It was better for Hank to stay in the dark about what his buyers did once the product left his hands, and that went double for Bobbie.

"No couch lock," he said. "Christ Almighty. If I have something that's going to shut you down I'll tell you up front, you know that. Enough of this couch lock bullshit, you know me better than that." The sound of his own voice—the rising tone, the slight tremor, the self-righteous indignation—needled him, and he felt the flush of embarrassment rise in his face. Jesus Christ, Hank, he thought. Get it together.

He took the jar. "This strain right here, this'll be real nice for you. It's got a slow build up and a warm blanket for the rest of the night."

Bobbie nodded. "Fine Hank. It's all right."

After the metric scale and the plastic baggies, and the cash transaction and the coded notations there came the coffee and the scratching at the door. Bobbie let the dog inside, and Toby knocked against her legs and then Hank's legs before he found the softness of his bed near the stove. Hank said, "Dumb dog," and his tail thumped against the floorboards.

Bobbie leaned back in her chair and took a drink from her mug, and set it down on the table with a smirk and undid another notch on her shirt, and fanned herself. "Damn Hank," she said. "Every time I forget what pond muck tastes like I just think about that stovetop percolator waiting for me up here on Silver Mountain." She laughed.

"Yeah, well," he said. "It can't be much worse than that shit they cook up in the staff room. If memory serves, that stuff could melt the spoon before you finished stirring in the sugar."

Bobbie laughed again and said, "Oh, it's still bad but it'd be a far stretch to say that this is much better."

Bobbie slid down in her chair, and Hank felt her knee come to rest against his. She was looking at his eyes, and he looked away, to stare at the jars in front of him, not really looking at them at all. Then she took another drink of the wretched black coffee. Their knees stayed as they were, unmoved, neither of them speaking a word.

In those few moments, a hundred thoughts ran through Hank's mind, and not all of them pleasant. Hank circled her face with his eyes, studying the tiny crescents hanging over the edges of her mouth, and the glistening sheen of her eyes. There was a pleading there, he thought, a hunger that he both understood and shared. It seemed to rise up from the floor and overtake them both, like that ridiculous thing from the late movie. It had taken three years from the night that Ernie killed Ricky Cordero to be able to face Bobbie in even the most pedestrian of circumstances without feeling as though he should die at her feet. The last thing in the world he thought he could ever do was walk through that door again, to even hope that he'd come out the other side alive.

"What's happening here, Bobbie?" he said. "Something's on your mind. It's been there ever since you got here."

She broke into a pained, forced smile.

His insides blinked but he held back, stayed put. "You can tell me."

Bobbie put her fists over her eyes and shook her head. Her whole body tensed, and she released a heavy sigh.

"Shit, Hank," she cried. "I don't even know where to start."

There was a tension in her voice, a rubber band wound up ready to snap. Hank drew his leg back.

"Is it Patrick?" he asked. "He's not running off again, is he?" In those months after Erie had gone to jail, Bobbie's boy would disappear for days at a time, once as long as two weeks. The news came through others, so the details had likely been all mixed up. He'd wanted to call her then, to try and be there for her. But the crevasse between them had grown too wide. Uncrossable.

"Patrick's a good boy," Bobbie said. "He's fine. He got a job, you know. Some mink farm outside of town." She nodded quickly. "After school mostly. Sometimes on weekends, if the old guy needs him."

"He's working at Tin Dorsay's? Damn. Well that's just great. You know, Tin's my uncle. That place goes way back."

"Is that right?"

"Sure. Uncle Tin, he's been running the minkyard on his own since...I don't know...maybe fifty-five? Used to be a commune back in the old days. A religious group—"

Bobbie looked past him and it was clear that whatever he might say about this place would fly right over her. She didn't want to know about the ranch, not now. And it was all just as good, anyway, because he didn't really want to get into it.

"Shit, there isn't enough time left in the day to get started on that story." Hank leaned onto his elbow. "At any rate, you tell Patrick to keep his fingers away from the cages."

"He knows that already."

"Bastards will take 'em right off without so much as a warning. I've seen it."

"He knows, Hank." Bobbie scratched at the table with her thumbnail.

Hank watched her eyes, waited for her to look up at him. But she wouldn't. She kept staring at those fingers of hers and working the nail into the varnish, not making progress on anything in particular. Her hair had fallen over her face now. He wanted to reach across and smooth it away, to see what might be happening with her eyes but his own hands felt like lead weights, anchored to the table in front of him.

"So it's not Patrick," he said. "That's good. But hell sweetie I wish you'd—"

"It's Ernie," she interrupted. She looked up at him finally, eyes welling, nodding slowly as if he had already guessed the answer.

"Ernie?"

"Yeah. He's out. Loose in the world as it would be."

Hank pushed himself back from the table, pressing his back against his chair. "You ain't shitting. When did this come about?"

"Couple days ago. Some sheriff called."

"Goddamn, honey, I'm awful sorry to hear it. I know you don't need that in your life."

"Nobody does."

"You tell Patrick yet?"

"God no." She got up from the table and went to the kitchen

and dumped the coffee down the drain, and rinsed the cup and filled the cup and took a long drink before putting it down again. "I know I have to tell him sometime, but I guess I'm hoping they'll catch Ernie first." She stopped and put her hand to her mouth. "He's been doing so good. Patrick. He just doesn't need any more to deal with right now."

"Well Bobbie, I think he has a right to know. I'm not saying Ernie will come this way but it'd be a hell of thing if he did decide to show up on your stoop one night. You can borrow my gun if you need to."

She stood up straight. "I don't want your gun. Jesus." Her voice was a tremor and he could tell that the tension struck even her as odd. She closed her eyes and drew in her breath, and held it before letting it out slowly. "I know Ernie's in a bad place right now. But he wouldn't hurt us. I know he wouldn't hurt Patrick, anyway."

"Honey you can't be sure," he said. He didn't want to argue with her. But this was something different. "He's been sitting in there with nothing on his mind but this place and the people who he thinks did him in. I don't want to lay any more on you than you've already got, but I suspect I'm not saying anything you haven't already thought about."

Bobbie went to the table and gathered her purse into her arms. "You know, it doesn't matter anyway because by now the whole damn town knows. If he so much as sets foot on the mountain Ray Hardy or any one of his deputies will be on him like flies on shit and it'll all be over."

Hank nodded in agreement, and forced his gaze toward his lap. He smiled, and recognized it was time to leave the subject. "Well I'm here if you or the boy needs anything," he said. And this offer came so naturally, without hesitation that Bobbie told him she would take him at his word that he was being sincere. He said, "I'm serious as a heart attack, honey," and then she smiled and patted him a good one on the chest.

Hank collected the jars and returned them to their places on the shelf, slid the panel back into place. Then he reached into a canister and pulled out a handful of small chocolate cookies.

"Here. I made these the other day." He brought the cookies to the table and set them down in front of her. "They're not the best, but they're pretty good. I'm messing around with a butter concoction. It seems to be decent. Go ahead and try it and let me know what you think of them. These are from the Ambrosia, so it's fine to have one in the middle of the day. Should help you on those rainy days. And slip a couple in your school lunch if you want."

"Yeah," Bobbie said, tearing a paper towel from a nearby roll and wrapping them up. "That'd go over like a lead balloon." She put all the baggies into her purse, and touched Hank on the arm, lightly. "I'll let you know when I know."

"Well, you know I'm no cook."

"I wasn't talking about the cookies. But if these are any good, it might be something to think about," she said. "Cookies and brownies and stuff. Sometimes I wish I had something that didn't require a flame."

"You're pretty good in the kitchen," he said. "Maybe I can talk you into doing some baking for me?"

"Hell Hank, I'd consider it but you know half of Ash Falls is downwind from me."

# Lyla Elizabeth (Kelleher) Henry

Lyla stood at the kitchen door, the drapes pulled back from the window as she watched Eugene and Marcelle out in the carport. The front end of Eugene's car was propped up on metal stands, and his legs spilled out from underneath as if he was being consumed by it. A perfectly good pair of blue jeans was now streaked with black grease, from his knee all the way to his shoe. Not more than two feet away from him, Marcelle sat in the old green lawn chair with her hands tucked between her thighs, her oversized parka bunched around her chin. A white glow of light pooled from where Eugene lay, spreading out to Marcelle's tennis shoes.

There didn't seem to be enough holding that car up. A couple of flimsy metal teepees were the only things propped under it and as Lyla watched, Marcelle kept leaning forward, putting the weight of her whole body against the fender to retrieve and swap out tools whenever Eugene slid them from under the car. She'd rest on it, and lean herself down to dig around in his toolbox, then toss whatever she pulled out into that pool of light. Twice she got out of the chair and knelt onto the floor so she could mess around with him, tickle his stomach and squeeze his knee. When she did this he'd kick at her, and she would laugh and put both hands on the car again as she stood up. Three times Lyla thought she saw the car tremble over her son.

When he was a boy Eugene sat in a chair, maybe the same chair Marcelle was taking up now, while Jonas monkeyed with the car, changing the oil or a pump or a filter, or whatever else he was able to fix himself. Eugene was so small his feet would not even touch the floor. They swung back and forth as he fidgeted and looked around at the walls or out into the street when a car or bicyclist passed by. Lyla thought the whole thing was ridiculous. A boy his age should be on his own bicycle or down at the school playground, burning his energy, not cooped up in a garage watching his father tinker with the family car. But Jonas was insistent. It was the kind of thing a father and son ought to do together, he said. The making of a man. But it was always too much to ask of Eugene, and he'd hop down from the chair and begin to wander about, and fish through the toolbox for things he could turn into swords or pistols. He'd hand off a pliers when he'd been asked for a crescent, or a flathead screwdriver instead of a Phillips. Like clockwork, Jonas would start to holler and swear, and Eugene would cry, and Lyla would finally come outside to put an end to it all. To this day divots marked the paint, lingering reminders of the wrong wrenches having been hurled against the walls.

She opened the kitchen door and leaned out into the cold. "I'm putting on soup," she called out, her breath clouding the porch like smoke. "Are you hungry?"

Marcelle said, "Yes ma'am," and stood up from the chair. Eugene said nothing, but slid his feet back and raised his knees into triangles.

Lyla came back inside and took the soup from the refrigerator, the chicken noodle she had made from scratch the night before, and put it on the stovetop to heat. Neither Jonas nor Eugene ever complimented or commented on her cooking, but they usually ate up everything on their plates, and that was enough for her to hold onto as any kind of approval. She wasn't someone who needed a big show of appreciation.

But Marcelle, now she could be thoughtful in that way. She often told Lyla that her food was much better than her own mother's had been, and even asked if Lyla would teach her to cook, since she could barely make a sandwich without getting it wrong. "It's important for a wife to make good food for her husband," she said. And even though the words echoed Lyla's own parents' constant haranguing, it pleased her to hear it anyway.

She'd certainly do that sometime, Lyla promised, and she meant it. There would come a day, she guessed, when neither she nor Jonas could pretend that Eugene's wife wouldn't always be there.

There was a rattle at the kitchen door when Marcelle came in, taking off her jacket and draping it over the back of one of the kitchen chairs. Her face was flushed and her hair was hanging down over her eyes. She went to the stove and lifted the lid off of the pot, and peered into the broth.

"This smells good," she said.

Lyla took the lid from her and put it back over the soup. "It's not ready yet," she told her. She edged her way in and Marcelle stepped aside, moving to the counter by the sink. There was a spot of black grease on her chin, a mark Eugene had probably left on her.

"Is he coming in?" Lyla asked, lifting the lid again and stirring the soup.

Marcelle shrugged. "He said he has to finish before Mr. Henry gets home. He said he'd be in big trouble if the car's still in there."

Lyla had moved to the table and was setting the bowls out when Eugene entered the kitchen. He dropped his coat on the floor and walked over to Marcelle, coming up behind her as she washed her hands in the sink, his shoes tracking dirt behind him. He pressed himself against her backside and leaned into her, whispering something in her ear; Lyla couldn't hear what it was. And then his hands found Marcelle's waist and slid around to her stomach, and when he pressed in harder Marcelle pushed back at him.

"Oh, you want to fight?" he said, pushing against her again.

Marcelle said, "Quit, Eugene. You're gonna get grease all over my clothes."

"You're already dirty," he said.

Lyla said, "Knock it off, Eugene. She said stop, so stop."

He glanced over at Lyla with the only briefest acknowledgement, the way a dog will look at its owner before bolting through the open gate, out into the street. Marcelle had turned to face him now and she held her hands out in front of her, still wet and dripping water onto her clothes. He pushed into her again, but she moved away, and gave him a slap along his shoulder. It wasn't a hard slap by any means, certainly not something that Lyla or Jonas or any reasonable person would make a deal out of. But as Marcelle left the sink, Eugene took hold of her sleeve and gave her a hard spin.

From Lyla's place by the dinette, she watched the way Marcelle suddenly tangled over her own two feet, her awkward body stumbling in the open space in front of the stove. Her eyes grew wide with panic and fear, and her hands grasped at the air as if something might magically drop from the ceiling to help her. Lyla made a move toward her, but it was too late. The girl's body knocked into the stove, her arm catching the edge of the pot and dragging it into herself, a cascade of steaming chicken soup dumping down the front of her clothes and all over the floor.

Marcelle let out a wail and fell to her knees, and the pot rattled back in place on the stovetop, steam spitting from the spiral burner beneath it. Lyla rushed to her and took her arms to look at them. They were red, but they would be all right with some cold water. Half of the soup was on the floor.

Lyla shoved Eugene aside and grabbed a hand towel from the oven handle, giving it to Marcelle. She was furious; a rush of heat swelled, as if the soup had poured over her instead. "Damn it, Eugene!" she snapped. "Why does it always have to be like this?"

"Like what?" he shouted back at her. "She hit me first."

"I barely touched you," Marcelle said, holding the towel in her hand like it was a dead animal.

"I barely touched you," Eugene mocked, his voice high and scratchy. "It's not my fault you're such a stupid klutz."

"Just grow up already," Lyla said. "Both of you need to grow up and act like adults for a change."

She told Eugene to get the mop and clean up the mess, but he said, "The hell I will. I didn't want any fucking soup, anyway." Then he stomped out the back door, slamming it behind him.

After what seemed like an eternity, Marcelle finally stopped crying and picked herself up from the floor, then went to the basement to clean up, leaving Lyla to fill the basin with soapy water and retrieve the mop herself. She attacked the spill with intention, pushing the sponge in tight rows, soaking it up, rinsing, mopping, continuing the pattern from where the soup had landed. And then she moved farther out, stepping back slowly, all the while studying the clutter of papers that covered the refrigerator.

That door had once been a mosaic of crayon drawings and scrawled notes and shopping lists, and Lyla would sit at the table drinking tea and staring at it all, praying that there would someday be more than what was already on it. Other people had glowing report cards to display, accolades from their child's teacher, a gushing comment in the corner of an essay. When the crayons went away for good, Lyla was left with citations and juvenile court dates to post, and appointment times for counseling and doctor visits, things that sucked money from their bank account but never really resulted in anything worthwhile. The refrigerator door became nothing but a collection of mementos proving Lyla and Jonas' great failings as parents.

There was a hollow grind outside and then Eugene's car suddenly roared to life, the rhythmic pumping of the accelerator washing through the walls in great waves. By the time Lyla got to the window, he was at the end of the driveway, the brake lights burning red. She opened the door and he stomped on the gas, tearing out into the street, leaving twin stripes of tire tread on the pavement as he disappeared. In the carport, his toolbox sat with its lid wide open, wrenches and sockets scattered all around.

In the beginning of it all, when Eugene was still small enough to take by the hand, she had come to Hank for help, hoping he could offer something more than what she already knew. "You need to beat his ass for him," he said, and her heart sank. He reminded her, "That's what Dad did for us."

"Yes he did, didn't he?" Lyla said. "But we're not like that, Hank. Jonas and I don't want to be like that."

"Your boy's out of control," he said. "You've got to do something before there there's nothing left that you can do."

Hank stood there staring at her, in his tidy living room with all of its contents neatly in place, the unwrinkled pillows tucked against the arms of his couch, and the books stacked perfectly on the side table, books that he had all the time in the world to read. He lived in his quiet house with his quiet dog that lay curled up and motionless on the rug, and he had the audacity to tell her what, in all honesty, she already knew.

"We just can't hit him," she said, going to the sofa and sinking down into it, the pillow pressing against the small of her back. It was firm, as if it had not been leaned on once since its creation. Hank looked down at her. His eyes were ringed with red, and glazed in wonder and confusion and frustration.

"You just don't understand," she said.

"Help me, then."

She leaned forward, her elbows pressing onto her knees. "You can't tell Jonas I told you this," she said. "Promise."

"All right, I promise."

"It'd humiliate him," she said. "He wouldn't ever be able to be around you again."

"What is it, Lyla?"

She slid to the edge of the sofa. "I love him, you know. Eugene. I do love him."

"I know that."

"But that boy has a way of pressing my buttons like nothing I've ever experienced in my life. And you know I've got buttons. There are moments when I get so mad at him, I'm afraid that if I take a switch to him like I want to, with his little body, I could hurt him real bad."

"Oh Honey, you wouldn't ever," he said. "You have better control than that."

She took the pillow from behind her and laid it on her lap, and leaned her body over it. It had a sweet smell to it, like cedar. Like fresh cedar boughs. "You think I'm exaggerating, but I'm not." She looked up at him. "I've done it, Hank. When Eugene was really little, so little I could pick him up from the floor and drop him again, just like that."

"Okay, Lyla," he said.

"I can't hit him."

"I know."

"I can't hit him and Jonas can't hit him. Neither of us can."

"All right, Lyla," he said. "All right."

# Marcelle Foster

Eugene's mother Lyla had talked to Melvin White already and told him that Marcelle would be there by 8:15 this time, no later.

"I put my neck on the line to get you that job," she told Marcelle, while she scrubbed her son's breakfast from the griddle. When she spoke her eyelids fluttered and she stole looks at Marcelle in sideways glances. "So I'd appreciate it if you didn't mess it up. I'd really appreciate it."

Marcelle tore a sheet of plastic from the roll and bunched it around the peanut butter sandwich that she had made on wheat bread. On the counter was a big red apple, waiting for her. It wasn't even 7:30 yet, and Mrs. Henry was already agitated with her.

Lyla took a paper sack from the cupboard above the sink and handed it to Marcelle. "I don't mean to pounce on you like that," she said, her wet hands soaking water into the brown paper edge. "You're a young woman now, Marcelle. You're expected to work. Contribute to your husband's income."

Mrs. Henry didn't work. She stayed home during the day, when Mr. Henry and Eugene and now Marcelle were gone to their jobs. The house was always clean anyway, so there wasn't a lot for her to be doing all day except cook dinner, which didn't seem to be a big deal to Marcelle. Turn on the stove, put the meat in. Boil some vegetables. Maybe Mrs. Henry had worked once, and Eugene being born changed everything. Having a baby, Marcelle decided, was what it took to be able to stay home from work.

She left the house at 8:00, right after Eugene pulled out of the driveway for the garage. It was seven blocks to where the Sleep Inn Motel sat on the corner just down a bit from the Red

Apple, on the way out of downtown. It was raining some but that was to be expected in September, or any month between September and July, really, and while Eugene could have dropped her off on his way to the garage he told her he decided it was a good thing for Marcelle to walk, seeing as how none of her clothes seemed to be fitting her anymore.

She put on her raincoat and her tennis shoes, and her glasses, and did the walk down Shale Street all the way to Main, then she turned right toward town. Cars passed by with their headlights still on, splashing spray up over the weedy planting strip onto her tennis shoes. She hugged the edged lawns of the Main Street bungalows until she got to Maple Street. Here she made an unanticipated turn, then walked a short distance to where the Luntz home stood.

She stopped to squat down and tighten her shoelaces. She took her time, tugging at the laces so that her feet felt completely embraced. And though it was a school day and she had every reason to know that there was nobody at home, she still found herself looking up, staring for a few minutes at the white paned windows, with their blue curtains drawn tight. If there was a movement there, she thought, a little pull at the edge and the face of a boy appeared, she decided she would give a smile this time, and a little wave. And maybe—just maybe—he might do the same for her.

She stood and fixed the drawstring on her hood and left the house behind her, quickening her pace until she got to the parking lot of the Red Apple. She cut through the black sheen and wove through the trucks with wheelbarrows and cut wood and tarped loads, and then down the graveled alley behind the post office where the potholes were already full and getting fuller. Here the small houses that had once been millworker cabins still stood, tarpaper poking through shingles and backing up to the alley so tightly that sheet-draped bedroom windows looked out over dented and overturned garbage cans. At the end of the block there was a row of stubby, dried out juniper shrubs sticking up from a bed of rust-colored beauty bark. This was the rear entrance to the Sleep Inn.

The back of the building was still unpainted, crusty and dropping sooty flakes on the dandelion-pocked ground like dead, molted skin. Some years earlier, Marcelle didn't know when, Melvin White had simply run out of paint when he'd only gotten through the street-facing half of the place. And then for one reason or another he never drove himself back to the Coast to Coast to get another couple gallons. So there it sat, half-dressed but cleaned up on the only side that really counted anyway.

Marcelle settled herself into the wicker chair against the office wall, listening to guitar and static on the small dial radio, and the clatter of dishes and cupboards coming from the room behind the front desk. She swiped a Kleenex and cleaned the fog from her glasses. She kept her hands on her stomach and studied the paintings of men on horses, cattle drivers climbing sloped trails that hugged wildflower-covered mountainsides. There were snowy peaks beyond them, and snaking rivers below, and Marcelle wondered if such scenes really existed anymore, or if ever.

The dribble of brewing coffee falling into its glass globe gave an idea of warmth, even though her pink hands were still ice. She heard his footsteps at last and then Melvin came through the door into the office. He gave Marcelle a dismissive look and a heavy sigh before swiping a cup of coffee from the still running stream. He flipped open his ledger and began scratching pencil to paper. His hair was combed over his head in a limp white ducktail and the soft blue legs of a voluptuous tattoo woman poked out from the cuff of his shirtsleeve, ankles crossed like she had simply drawn blankets over the wrong half of her body. He wrote and wrote, and thumped a chunky stamp onto the paper three times before closing it and taking hold of another booklet where he started the whole thing again. After carrying on like this for another a minute or two, he finally spoke to her.

"Are you going to just sit there all day, Marcella?"

"It's Marcelle, Mister White."

"Marcella. Marcelle. Are you going to sit there all day?"

"Well, no."

He continued on with the business, shuffling papers and punching numbers into a desk calculator. He wasn't doing anything really. Marcelle knew. She'd stood behind the counter once before, when Melvin had to run to the Red Apple for smokes and there was never anything to do but stare out the window or sometimes answer the phone. He clicked his tongue at her.

"There's rooms need cleaning," he said.

"That's what I needed to know."

"Marcelle, you been here two weeks now and every time you come in here it's the same thing. You gotta take initiative. Don't sit there waiting for me or Roxanne to tell you what to do." He pointed a knuckly finger at the wall to his right. "If there's no key on the hook then the room's either occupied or it was till this morning. Go get your cart and start knocking. Jesus Christ girl, it ain't rocket science we're talking about here."

Roxanne's cart was parked outside room number three, and she was stripping the bed and singing to herself. Marcelle didn't know the song or even recognize the tune but she was going at it like she was on a stage, loud and full-throated. She moved like a machine, with much more energy and intention than Marcelle ever felt in her life. Roxanne was old enough to be somebody's mother but there was nothing the least bit motherly about her. She was snippy as could be and showed an impatient streak if Marcelle didn't move fast enough or if she cut corners with the wipe downs or got the cleaners mixed up. And when they worked together, Roxanne didn't split the tips fair.

"Number five is all yours," she said. She talked through her teeth with her jaw clenched tight. Her lips barely moved. "It sure would be good if you could get here on time for once."

"I had to walk."

"From where? It's not more than eight blocks to anywhere in this town, honey. It's not like you came all the way from Everett."

"Well I wasn't planning to walk."

"You live with Eugene Henry. You should plan for anything."

Marcelle knew full well about plans, she had been making plans around Eugene since the first overnight up at the quarry. When he laid her down on the sleeping bag and slid his hands beneath her shirt, put his tongue against her neck and that first wash of electricity rushed through her—from that moment on she was his, completely. The quarry became the place where things could happen at their own pace, without fear of slamming car doors or footsteps on the ceiling, and it got so that she hungered for it, if not the words, then the touching, his fingers moving over a body that she could not bring herself to even look at in the mirror.

"We should get married," he'd said one night, simple as that.

It was within a conversation about something she couldn't recall, inside a two-person tent in the shadow of the sheer granite cliff, surrounded by empty beer cans and the smoke from a dying campfire. It just came out of him, from nowhere. He said it and she pictured it, clear as daylight. A little house somewhere that she kept tidy for him, a wife there for her husband, there for him like nobody else would or could be. She would fix everything in him that was broken, like he said that only she could do. She answered then, "If you want to, sure," and then the chain kicked in and just like that, the roller coaster was on its way, no stopping it even if she had wanted to.

Roxanne stood up at the foot of the bed with her hands on her bony hips. She arched her back and gave a low grunt. Her ponytail dropped down to her shoulder blades and moved in circles as she rolled her head from side to side and said, "Criminy I'm sick of this."

She dressed herself in shapeless jeans and a plain blue smock every day, and she was skinny in a way that Marcelle never wanted for herself. Boobs like tangerines, and nothing at all in the way of ass, just an empty sack of denim back there. Marcelle wasn't a beauty, and she never claimed to be. But at least she had some meat for a man to grab hold of. Roxanne was a scarecrow, grizzled and spindly, and lonely in her place at the foot of the stripped-down king-sized bed.

Marcelle creaked her cart two units down, to the lacquered blue door. She rapped the paint and called out, "Housekeeping," but there was no answer. She keyed it open and called again, and stuck her head inside. It was dark and moldering, and stank of underarms and cigarettes, and of spilled beer on old carpet. The cheap linty bedspread tumbled down over the foot of the bed and both pillows lay on the floor side by side as mates. On the nightstand were three dented cans of Rainier and an opened yellow bag of potato chips. There was no suitcase.

"Housekeeping."

A thin line of yellow crept through the base of the bathroom door but again there was no sound, and she had called out twice and both times had gotten no answer. And she was already running late. So she swung the room door full open and loaded her arms with cleanser and spray bottles and rags and made her way to the bathroom where she pushed her way in.

The man was in the bath, with the yellow plastic curtain drawn wide open and the water crystal clear, no cloud of soap or bubbles or even so much as a washcloth to cover his business that stood straight up through the surface like it was the periscope of a submarine. He held it as such, too, so that there would be no mistaking his intentions when whichever housekeeper happened to stumble into the unlocked bathroom. Marcelle froze on the tile with her hand still on the door and the bottle of Fantastik pointed like she might shoot him dead right there in his bath.

"I'm sorry sir," she managed to cough out. "I said housekeeping. Twice."

"Hey, no harm no foul," he said. "Don't let me stop you from your work."

He was old enough to be her father and as he talked his furry round stomach rolled, and the water sloshed around him as his tool bobbed one way and then another. Marcelle hadn't seen many in her life and this one looked pretty much like the others, though there was a little crick to it that she wasn't sure was supposed to be there. He pushed himself to the back of the tub and sat up.

"I can close the curtain if you want and you can just clean around me."

Marcelle stumbled back from the doorway and slammed it closed, and then she rushed out from the room into the walkway under the eaves. Roxanne was standing at her cart pushing dirty bed sheets into her hamper. She looked up at Marcelle.

"What the hell's the matter now?" she said. "You find a rat in the toilet?"

Marcelle rested her hand on her cart and took deep breaths while the stacks of towels and baby soaps and shampoos rattled. She was surprised at how keyed up she was, it didn't seem like such a big deal at the moment but of course it was very much a big deal, anyone would say as much. She had walked in on a stranger in the bath, a man who was in the middle of working himself over, or maybe just at the beginning, and besides she wasn't so stupid that she didn't know full well what that whole scene was all about. She imagined what Eugene would do if he found out, if he would come and give the guy a piece of his mind or knock him clear off the mountain, or if in the end it would all be her fault for being dumb enough to put herself in a situation like that. "You must not have heard him," he would say. "Jesus Christ, Marcelle, sometimes you are so fucking ignorant."

"Oh don't tell me that's Trucker Otis' room," Roxanne bellowed. And then she leaned back on her scarecrow legs and laughed with her clench-jawed face to the sky. "Holy Jesus, you got to meet Trucker Otis."

She wound her arm in a giant sweeping motion and Marcelle looked back at the door and then she ran over to Roxanne. The older woman took the younger's arm and dragged her into the empty room behind her. It smelled of lemon and bleach and even in the midst of all of what was happening, Marcelle wondered how she could possibly manage to get these rooms smelling so clean in the time it took Marcelle to probably lose her job.

"What did he do?" Roxanne crowded her, hissing into her face. "Was he on the bed or was he hiding in the bathroom? Oh I'm sorry hon, I should have warned you but this isn't even his usual day."

Marcelle's whole body was shaking now and her mind swirled, thoughts bouncing around in her head just like Trucker Otis' business in the bathwater and all the while Roxanne laughed and held her ribbed body and said "Oh my God I gotta pee so bad," and she broke loose and ran back into the bathroom. "Don't say anything to Melvin by the way," she called out. "He don't want to hear it."

"But the guy's a pervert," Marcelle hollered back. "He's just sitting there waiting for us to come up on him."

"He's harmless," Roxanne said. "Really, girl, you need to grow up. All he wants to do is lay there while you clean the room around him. Just pretend he's not there, he won't touch you or even talk to you. And he'll leave a huge tip."

"That's being a prostitute, Roxanne."

At this the woman laughed, full-throated. She leaned forward on the toilet, her contoured face tilting into view in the open door of the bathroom. "Oh give me a break, Marcelle. It's nothing at all like that. Don't think you can stand there at all of seventeen years old and try and explain life to me, kid, you haven't experienced enough of it to even have a learner's permit." The toilet flushed and Roxanne stood in the doorway doing up her jeans. "Fine then. If you don't want to do his room, I'll do it."

Marcelle leaned out the door and looked down the walkway

at the blue door two units down. It was still closed and her cart still stood blocking it. A baby bar of soap was on the ground and one of the towels had somehow come unfolded and was hanging down over the edge.

"I'm doing number 8," she said, and then she closed the door behind her and walked the long stretch to the far end of the building.

# Bobbie

Bobbie liked to think it would surprise people to know that she sometimes sat alone on her back porch singing quietly to herself, far away from the glare of the streetlamps and rattle of cars filled with people returning home from the swing shift. She preferred the old country-western songs, the ones that had played on her father's old radio with an echo and crackling like they could have spilled through the open window of a roadside tavern.

She also collected salt and pepper shakers, one of the few silly hobbies she allowed herself to waste time on. At first it had been a kind of investment; she only wanted ones that she thought might go up in value one day. But the oddities gifted to her over the years from Patrick and Ernie, and well-meaning friends, eventually widened her collection to include tiny twin mushrooms, windmills, outhouses, telephones and other objects that any decent person would never place on his or her kitchen table, but were fine to be displayed in a smoke-glass curio as complete kitsch. They were ridiculous and a little embarrassing, but now and then she'd go through them anyway, just to make herself laugh.

Bobbie was still smiling as she climbed out of her car and took the shopping cart closest to her, one that had been left right out in the open so anyone could have run into it. She walked it up to the front doors and passed the bag boy with the earring, who stared at her as if it was the first time she had ever walked into the place. Just the same, she had the sense that every single eye was on her, watching her as she strolled through the fruit section, then over to the cereal aisle. It wasn't so much that they were all looking at her, but they were watching her just the same. If such a thing was possible.

At the far end of the aisle a man stood looking over the granola. He was familiar, with his receding brown hairline and lumpy shoulders, but it was only when he took out his glasses to read the label that Bobbie pinned him as the therapist who worked out of the offices of the old Hargrave Mansion. Patrick had seen him for a few sessions some years earlier, around the time that she was bringing him to the prison to see Ernie. She couldn't remember his name to save her life.

"Hi," she said.

He looked up, searched her face for some semblance of recognition. Finally he broke into a grin and said, "Oh, hello there. It's been some time." He stood up straight and beamed in that way people do when they are trying not to appear completely lost.

"You used to see my son Patrick," she said low, leaning in. "You'd remember him if you saw him."

"I'm sure I would," he nodded. "And how is he doing? Well, I hope."

"He's up and down," she said. "But he is seventeen."

"That's great," he said. "Just great." He smiled broadly but with his lips together, still holding the granola in front of his chest, and Bobbie could tell he was fighting the urge to look down at it, to continue what he'd been doing before she interrupted him.

"Well anyway," she said. "It's good to see you."

"Nice to see you, too," he said. "And please tell your son—I'm sorry, what was his name again?"

"Patrick," she said. "He's working now."

"Working? That's great." He put the granola back on the shelf and nodded as he moved his cart from the aisle. "That's just super."

Bobbie was also fond of driving her station wagon out of town up the highway, into the mountains with the windows rolled down and her flannel shirt unbuttoned halfway to her waist where she could feel the evening air rush over her skin and tug at her clothing, and maybe—just maybe—she would catch the eye of a logger on his way down from the clear cut to the mill. It was something she let herself do now and then but she told no one, not even Ernie. She liked to think that it wouldn't have bothered him; it might have even given him some kind of thrill. Ernie was a guy who was full of surprises, that much was true.

Like most young couples, she and Ernie had started off sexy. They could find it just about anywhere, at any time, drunk or sober. In the pool hall men's room, behind Zeke's Bait Shop at Lake Cassidy, in the middle of trout season. In the back of the station wagon, halfway through "Bonnie and Clyde." But the leaves on that tree curled pretty quickly. Ernie went over and did his year in Vietnam, and came back different, like they all did. By then he was drinking an awful lot, and there were the nightmares. Ernie was better off than a lot of them, though. Bobbie knew one gal whose husband beat her up one night and didn't even remember doing it. They liked to say that part of them was still lost in that jungle somewhere. Ernie had his demons, but Bobbie had always felt like she could handle them. Then Patrick came along, and everything more or less settled into a world of routines, of pot roasts and babysitters and the occasional night of pool and darts at the local tavern. Somewhere in midst of all of it, she couldn't remember when, she and Ernie came to an agreement. A kind of understanding.

Bobbie nearly ran into Lyla's cart before she realized it was her standing in the middle of the aisle, peering at a list in her hand, her head inches from the paper, lips moving as she went through it. There was no way to turn around without creating a situation more awkward than it already was. Bobbie looked down into her own cart. A bunch of bananas, a gallon of milk, Noxema and a bottle of red wine. Lyla's cart was already half filled with several packages of toilet paper, a dozen or so boxes of pasta and a scattering of canned vegetables.

She used to check her son Patrick's things regularly, going through his room, never privately but publicly as he stood passively to the side. She did this in the guise of putting his clothes away, or "helping" him thin out his closet, or clearing pockets in preparation for the hamper. She always asked him what he was thinking and what he was doing when he wasn't at home, but she seldom asked him what she could do in order to make him happy.

That first winter, Ernie's first in the state penitentiary, Bobbie drove Patrick down to Seattle where she splurged for a single weekend at the Westin. They took in the giant gingerbread house display, and watched The Nutcracker ballet, and stood back as the men threw giant fish from one person to another as if it was the most acrobatic thing in the world. She took him to the restaurant of his choice, a big place on the water with cloth napkins and lobster on the menu and when they were done, she had Patrick sit with the Nordstrom Santa for a portrait. On the way home, he told her he'd had the best time of his life.

"Excuse me." Bobbie edged her cart alongside Lyla's.

Lyla looked up from her list, hand on her hip, her green eyes expanded behind owlish glasses. She said, "Oh." It was almost a whisper, a quick breath of recognition and a sour lemon pucker as she glanced down at Bobbie's cart.

There was a dance of sorts next, a do-si-do of shopping carts as they both tried to clear the aisle enough to allow passage. Bobbie said, "These stupid things. They never work the way they're supposed to."

Lyla said, "It's the wheels."

"They need to replace them altogether," Bobbie said.

"They won't."

Lyla moved past, her arm brushing Bobbie's as she did so. She bristled at her own error, keeping her gaze straight ahead and Bobbie could see some of Hank in that profile, in the even slope of the nose, and the skirt of the jaw line. Even the hard stare was almost identical, but where Hank's showed a kind of strength and quick determination, Lyla's was just cold.

Bobbie pushed her cart to the end of the aisle, to the vinyl-covered chairs opposite the pharmacy counter. She took a number and then a seat, and listened to the old woman at the window ask question after question about her blood pressure, and the gout in her hand, and why her Medicare did not cover everything.

All along the back of the grocery, people politely stepped around one another, or lingered at the ends of aisles with carts abandoned in the middle of the floor. A few stood with hands on cart handles, making small talk. Smiling. It was like they had all come to this place not just to shop, but to see one another, or just be in the presence of other humans.

"I can't sleep though to the morning!" The old woman at the pharmacy leaned into the open window. She stretched to her full height, chunky heels lifting off the floor.

"The medication is keeping you up at night?"

"No," she said. "They're giving me bad dreams. Like someone's chasing me in the woods."

Bobbie often had nightmares, never about being chased, though. In her dreams, she'd be driving her car up the mountain with the windows down and the air hot against her face. She'd drive until the incline bent to vertical and the roadway disappeared behind her and the car would begin to slide backward. Sometimes she made it up over the top of the ridge, but more often than not, she would lose her grip and fall, plummeting down the face of the mountain. Always, she would wake up then, her tee-shirt stuck to her chest, and she would lie still, feeling her heart beat in her temples and stare out of the window as she breathed deeply, watching the fingers of tree branch shadows ripple against her drapes.

# Hank (Henry) Kelleher

Their mother's wake had been crowded into her own home, in the very house that Lyla and Jonas now shared with that son of theirs. Overall, the whole thing had been a disaster and Hank wanted nothing less than to be able to completely wipe the entire day from both his and Lyla's memories.

When she'd called him to talk about the wake, she had been standing on the line between control and collapse, a precarious balance that Hank didn't come to appreciate until much later. Her voice hummed like a violin. She was rambling on about photographs and keepsakes, and a guest list that swelled so large that Hank could feel the claustrophobia from weeks away. He pressed the phone to his ear, the earpiece sweating against his head.

"I don't have any need for something like that," he'd said to her. "I don't understand why this has to be laid at my feet."

"Everything's not about you, Hank," she said. "She was our mother."

The entire gathering had been a collection of ascending incidents, one smeared over another, the finer, important details misplaced in his memory over the years. He remembered that the house had been so goddamned hot, that someone had built a fire in the stove. It was November. Hank recalled the feeling of near suffocation, the heat and the grief, and the weight of guilt, guilt over his inability to bring himself across the room to his own sister, who seemed sentenced to spend the whole afternoon standing at the window, just staring out at the street. And Jonas in and out of the kitchen, always eating, and people touching Hank on the arm, or the shoulder, or the small of his back, all the while kids ran in and around the legs of adults. Eugene, the worst of the lot, as always. Spoiled, squat and demanding, Eugene the undisciplined animal, constantly clamoring for attention.

Hank should have gone over and talked to Lyla, but it seemed like there had been no clear path to her. Looking back, there had perhaps been a moment when it was possible, but then suddenly there was Eugene in the kitchen. Jonas said something in hard tone and Eugene gave a belligerent shout, and then came the overturned table. And just like that, a tear of anger flashed within Hank that had been too quick to rein in. He was there, and his hand jerked from his side, an impulsive, backhanded swat, landing someplace on the boy that had been unintended. It was a spot that was hard against his knuckles and, God help him, it felt so good.

The people scattered like pigeons then, cars flew from the curb in droves. He had gone to the kitchen to begin cleaning, but Jonas had taken the dishtowel from his hand and suggested he leave. When he said it, his eyes met Hank's with a curious look of understanding, and his hand pressed the back of Hank's arm like a gentle escort.

And so when the snapshot of him and Lyla appeared in his school mailbox some days later, the photo of him leaning close to her ear, her turned away, smiling gently and staring into the empty air, the weight of that afternoon fell right back upon him, along with an added blanket of confusion. So many times he had slipped the photo into a drawer or a cabinet, when the reminder had begun to crawl beneath his skin. But then the details would dig at him, and the photo would find itself on the shelf again. When? he'd wonder. When were we standing like that?

Hank leaned back in his chair so that the cedar shingles scratched the nape of his neck. He tipped the mug against his lips and watched the last drips of coffee run in black rivulets, down the pearlescent walls to his tongue. At the far side of the drive his old pickup truck sat waiting. A lame mule.

"It's like it's having fits half the time." He pulled the phone cord and it scratched along the door frame. "I'm worried it'll leave me at the side of the road somewhere in the middle of nowhere."

"Well," Benny said. "If you can get her down here we'll take a look at her."

"You don't think you'll need it all day, do you?"

"Now Hank, you know I can't answer that till you get her in here," Benny said. He didn't sound as optimistic as Hank had hoped. "But you know, it ain't likely it'll be a twenty minute turn-around."

Hank hung up and lifted the receiver again to make the second phone call. This number he dialed more slowly, and he brought the phone inside where he could sit while he talked to her.

"I'm not sure how long, Lyla," he told her. "Maybe an hour. Maybe longer. I don't know." He fingered the cord and studied the tiny brass-framed photo on his shelf, the pale, faded snapshot from the wake.

"You could probably go down to Reid's for a haircut," she said. "You must be due."

"I don't need a haircut."

There came a heavy sigh at the other end of the line. "Well I guess that'll be fine," she said. "I can't commit to the whole day though. I have things."

Hank filled Toby's bowl and gave him one last scratch between the ears, then locked the house down tight before climbing into the pickup. It was the time of mud and muck and creeping molds, the kind of season that sent a good many Ash Falls folks into a spiral of gloom and regret, the mobile ones to Arizona or Baja. But for Hank, the dankness of autumn could hold a certain thunderous romance, if only for those winding drives into town, where he would find himself stealing glances in the rearview mirror to watch the glorious rooster tail of yellow and red billowing wildly behind him. Not enough people appreciated that. The turning maples and dogwoods that hovered cathedral-like over the roadway, racing down the snaking mountain highway, flanked by the breathtaking gauntlet of granite and basalt cliffs and the intermittent rush of late summer melt forcing its way down the slope toward the chugging Stillaguamish. Most times, it was the only thing that made that coming down the mountain worthwhile.

Gravel sprayed from the tires, and the Chevy bucked hard as he steered from his drive out onto the highway. Just as quickly it stopped, and a few errant chunks of firewood launched themselves against the cab as he wrestled with the gearshift. He peered up the roadway, eyeing the point at which it disappeared past the culvert, and he tried to force the rod to first, but it kicked back, knocking into his bony knee. His heartbeat rolled up into his head, and his whiskered neck began to dampen under his collar.

"You sonofabitch." He cursed at the rod, but even more he cursed at the stony old hands that seemed never to do what he wanted anymore. He knocked the stick in and out of the pathways of the big H, and his palm was sweating, and his knuckles were rusty, and he imagined that he might be able to push the truck back off the roadway if it wasn't for his back, the dull aching that seemed to a constant companion now. He gave it one more shove and there was a connection of sorts that rolled through his arm. The pickup shook violently, and Hank's left foot numbed from the grinding beneath the pedal. An acrid odor crawled in from the floor and the truck rolled slowly forward. It strained against the gentle slope of the roadway until it reached the crest, then it finally settled itself on the downhill grade into town.

Hank trembled his hand across the dashboard, leaving a black swipe through the layer of dust. "All right then," he said. "Let's just get into town and all will be forgiven."

As the truck choked into the garage parking lot, Benny West

lumbered through the office door and waved Hank into an empty bay. Benny was a man who led with his giant belly, and a toothy grin that stayed put whether he was actually smiling, listening intently for a rattle in the engine compartment, or just thumbing through the sports page at his desk.

Hank rolled into the bay and cut the engine. Benny walked around the front end of the truck, and Hank wound down the window, halfway. There was a worker at the far side of the garage hunched over a screaming grinder, a spray of yellow sparks shooting outward from his hip.

"Damn, Hank," Benny shouted over the noise. "You burning toast under that hood or what?" He wiped his hands off on a scabby rag he'd pulled from his coverall pocket. His lips stretched tighter, and the edges of his gums appeared in thin, pink stripes. Benny's version of a genuine grin.

"It's been awhile since we've seen this old girl."

"It's been fine till now," Hank said.

"Yeah well, we'll see about that." He winked at Hank. "You got someone to take you back home? Just in case?"

Hank drummed his fingers on the steering wheel and gazed at the dashboard gauges and lights. The clock read 9:47. His mind spun the hands forward, passing over a list of walking errands that was way too short.

"You really think you're going to have to keep it beyond today?"

"Well Hank, I have to get under there so I can see what we're looking at first." Benny's fingers rested on the edge of the open window. He pressed his lips together but the teeth still strained against them from behind, and for the first time Hank thought how strange it was that Benny must work to do that, to cover up those big, grinning teeth.

Benny extended his hand through the open window and Hank gave up, laying the keys into his open palm. Benny opened the door like a valet then, and led Hank into the tiny office carved into the side of the tin building.

"I'll be as quick as I can with her, Hank," he said. "Where do you want me to call you?"

"I should be at my sister's," Hank said.

Benny stopped and turned around, slack-jawed, eyes wide. He dangled the keys out from his round stomach as if they were something offensive, a used tissue left on his desk, a remnant of some anonymous customer.

"You're going to Lyla's?" he said.

"I believe so. Yeah."

"All day?" He shifted his eyes from Hank's, to focus on a spot beyond the office, someplace in the garage, maybe. "It's been awhile since you've done that."

Hank considered the collage of papers thumb-tacked to the walls of Benny's office. There were framed certificates, lily white behind grease-smudged glass, and cartoons of men fishing, and men hunting, and men crowded around a muscled hot rod with a big-breasted woman perched behind the wheel, the captions all too small to read. Behind Benny's desk hung a window-sized framed photograph. It was a picture of Mt. St. Helens, before she'd blown her top. A turquoise lake, clear as glass, fronted the regal mountain like a jeweled necklace. It was a place he'd always intended to see in person. It was too late, now.

"You really think you'll need to keep it that long?" he asked.

Benny walked around his desk and sank into the chair, leaning forward and reshuffling the mess of papers spread out before him.

"If it's the clutch," he said, "I could probably have a new one in her by this afternoon. If not, and I have to keep her overnight, I'll drive you home myself. And I'll come on out in the morning to bring you back."

"No." Hank dug his hands in his pockets and shook his head. "I don't want you to do that."

"Hell, it's no problem. I don't mind the drive."

"No. I'll ask my sister if I have to."

"Yeah," Benny grinned. "You'll ask Lyla all right." He slid a bowl of pistachios across the desk to Hank. "Here, take a handful of nuts with you. I can't stand 'em."

"Why don't you throw them outside for the squirrels?"

"Cause I hate the squirrels more."

Hank left the garage and walked up the street until he hit Main, then cut right and took the sidewalk under the blistered awning of Henning Jewelers, and the crusty ferns that hung in front of the fabric store, past storefronts plastered with starburst advertisements until he reached the rows of clapboard bungalows where the townies lived. At Shale Street, he hooked left and walked to the cedar-shingled house with the Japanese Cherries across the street.

The sedan was parked in the carport, jug-eared with its doors wide open, a water bucket crowded against the fender. Lyla Henry's slippered foot stretched from the passenger side, her rear end rocking back and forth as she worked feverishly at something inside.

He stopped at the curb and took his billfold from his pocket. He thumbed through his cash, then looked up again. Lyla stretched her body over the bench seat, her leg extended past her cuff and kicked behind her. There was still time. She hadn't yet seen him. He'd call her later and apologize, tell her that it turned out he didn't need to stick around in town after all. She shifted her weight and brought a bucket of water from the floor to the pavement. He put his wallet away and walked up the driveway toward her.

"Hello Lyla."

She bolted upright, sending a scrub brush sailing from her hand to the fissured concrete. Her legs wound beneath her body as she tried to turn and face him. To Hank she was a landlocked mermaid, dark water stain pooled around her feet, her body twisting on the bench seat like a trout.

"Darn it, Hank," she said. "You about scared me out of my skin." She climbed out of the car and stood up, and pressed a hand into the small of her arching back.

"Jesus Lyla," Hank said, looking past her at the sudsy carpet on the passenger floor. "Something die in there?"

"No, something didn't die," she said. "Jonas dumped a whole thermos of cocoa. And then like always he left it for me to clean up." She craned her neck to scan the street. Her head moved in fits and jerks. "What's the deal with your truck?"

"It's with Benny for a while. Said he'd call." Hank reached down and picked up the scrub brush. "I can finish that up."

"No you won't."

"I got nothing else to do."

She decompressed, sifting her breath through her teeth and shaking out her fingers. "It's clean enough." She walked away from him. She took the porch steps hard and without turning back said, "You might as well come in. I'll put on a pot of coffee if you'll drink it."

Hank's own home was tidy, and he preferred to keep it that way. But his sister's reeked of the kind of order and almost un-real, unshakable consistency that a person would see on display behind a glass case. Potted plants and fanned magazine displays, and fringed throw pillows were exactly as they had been on his previous visit. Their mother's old crystal hanging lamp, the one that had cost two year's pin money to have shipped from Chi-cago, hovered alone over an end table. It stretched its dim light over the chevron-patterned afghan quilt that Lyla had crocheted in those months after her surgery.

He'd asked her for details on the procedure. She said it was a private matter. But there were comments between the layers, words about waning motherhood, and of choices made late in life. So Hank made assumptions. The whole afghan was draped over the sofa back like a saddle, its tassels combed neatly against the upholstery.

They sat across from one another at the living room coffee table, he at the sofa and she in the recliner. It had been like this so many times over the years in this house, the two of them on opposite sides, their mother positioned between them, the weary referee. Lyla gave a rattled sigh and pressed her knees to one another, and kneaded them softly with her twiglike fingers. Her smile was pinch-lipped.

Hank started. "So how are things?"

"Fine. Just fine."

"And Jonas?"

"He's good, too." Her eyes darted cooly around the room.

"The place smells like vanilla. Something in the oven?"

"No," she said. She rubbed at her eyes and crossed one leg over her knee. "It's one of those popup things. They were two for a dollar at the Red Apple. I thought I'd try them."

"Oh. Well, it's nice." Hank leaned back against the afghan. He laid his hands over his knees and looked around the room, at the portraits with spotless glass and gilded frames, glossy photos of Lyla and Jonas perched behind a plastic fence rail, or crowded into a swanlike wicker chair, their arms entwined like a prom couple.

He swallowed and formed the word. "Eugene?" he said, his throat tightening. "How are he and that girl doing? What's her name again?"

Lyla tilted her head and rolled her eyes. "Why do you always do that?"

"Do what?"

"You know good and well what. Like I don't spend enough time thinking about those kids when they're here underfoot," she said. "For crying out loud. This is my time. My time to lend my thoughts to other things. I don't want to talk about them."

Hank knew the sequence that came with a flare up like this. Lyla held her hands out in front of her, fingers extended and spread out, like the preening tail feathers of a peacock. She pinched her eyes closed for entire sentences. And then, just as quick, she leaned back in her chair and ran her finger over the pleat of her pants.

"I went to lunch with some ladies from church," she said. "They all asked about you." She went over their names like roll call—Ruby, Mary, Diana One, and Diana Two—and then she proceeded to fill him in on what she deemed the most important items in their lives. She listed various maladies, the gout and glaucoma, and joint replacements, and updated him on the many places the grandchildren had flown off to, parts beyond the mountain.

"It's nice to know that there are those who do eventually leave the nest," she said. "We're making a quilt for the First Baptist Church of Haysville, outside Wichita." She looked up from her hands. "The tornado."

Hank stared at her, unblinking.

"Hank. You must have read about it," she said. "It was all over the news." When Hank shrugged his shoulders she said, "I can't believe you haven't heard about it."

"I don't get the paper anymore, Lyla. If it doesn't come in over the radio, I don't know it."

"I don't see how you even manage," she said, shaking her head. "Anyway, the whole thing was absolutely horrible. Cut through half the state, apparently. Janet said it came into Haysville and just…crushed the whole town. Oh, there was a house here and there all by itself, because you know that's how those tornadoes work. Drop down to destroy things and then all of a sudden pick right up again, just like that."

She was leaning in toward him now, her hands cupping her knees. "But here's the amazing thing," she said, almost in a whisper. "When it finally went, there was nothing left. Nothing except, get this: the elementary school, a couple of stores and the Baptist church." She sat back in her chair and folded her arms over her chest.

"Can you believe it?" she said.

"Believe what?"

"God. Was. Looking out for them."

Hank lowered his head and gave a gentle laugh. If there was the chance of finding the smallest shred of divinity, even in the most unlikely of places, Lyla would find it. She did it when they were children, when two classmates had been taken by the river. She did it when their father's heart suddenly stopped and before dying, he somehow managed to steer clean through traffic, putting the truck in a deep ravine. And it was what brought her solace when Ernie Luntz killed the boy, Ricky Cordero, who had been seated under a leafy chestnut tree alongside her son Eugene that muggy evening. God took some, and spared others.

"Well," he said. "A quilt is a nice gesture. The church folks will appreciate it."

Lyla stared at him for a moment, and Hank could see the dissatisfaction pulling at the edges of her mouth. But she pushed through it and rubbed her hands on her knees.

"How is that dog of yours," she asked. "What's his name?"

"Toby," said Hank. He sat up straight on the sofa.

"They got a spaniel across the street," she said. "One of those nasty things with matted ears and no tail. I've chased that thing off of my lawn no less than a dozen times this week. Jonas told me the perfect birthday present for him would have been seeing the dog pound truck parked at our curb."

"Jonas had a birthday this week," Hank said.

"Oh, don't worry about missing it," she said. "We didn't do anything. You know how he is. He says that each passing birthday is like the passing of a kidney stone. A necessary pain along the path to the final exit." She curled her lip in a wry grin.

The familiar sensation began to rise in him, the monster again, hot and suffocating, rolling up and over his entire body. He was trapped with her, two children pressed against clammy windows of their clapboard house, this same house, both of them waiting for their mother to come home from the grocery store, cigarette in her lips yet not a single bag of groceries in sight. Conversation flowed from Lyla in a torrent, as if she had been locked away from human interaction for so long that she was afraid of never having the chance to talk to another person again. She moved from one story to another like a prisoner set free in a buffet, with only her need to take a breath allowing for interruption.

"Are you feeling okay, Lyla?" Hank jumped in.

She sat up straight and her eyes narrowed at him. "Something wrong with how I look?"

"Just wondering—with the rain and all."

Lyla looked down at her hands resting on her knees. She bent her knuckles upward, stretched out her fingers and laid them flat again. "It's not so bad right now," she said. "But it's autumn. I know what's in store for me."

"It doesn't have to be like that." He looked up at her with his chin to his chest, pensive and wary.

At first Lyla said nothing, and the air hung between them like stagnant coal smoke. Her eyes were tiny glistening marbles and her jaw clenched and ground against itself.

"Henry Kelleher you know I won't ever touch that stuff," she said. "I wish you'd quit trying to push it on me. Mama would roll in her grave if she knew you were back messing with that. And haranguing me."

"Hell, I don't think Mama would've given one minute's thought to it."

Lyla stood up from her chair and went to the window. The drapes had been pulled closed and she drew them to the side and peered out into the daylight. She kept her back to him and said nothing, but Hank could sense what was in the back of her mind. It was the stench, the strain of the damned wake, all over again.

He leaned over the coffee table and thumbed the corner of one of the magazines. Lyla glanced over her shoulder at the noise.

"You know what I think?" he said.

"What do you think?"

"She was just lonely, that's all."

"Who was lonely?"

"Our mother. With Dad up at the camps half the time. The two of us, always fighting each other. She just got lonely."

"We didn't always fight," she said. "We didn't always do anything." Lyla kept her back to him, and her body began to sway on skinny, precarious legs.

"You can't tell me you never thought of that, Lyla. That Mama wasn't grocery shopping. Not every time, she wasn't."

She turned sharply, a deer catching the snap of a twig. "I don't know if you heard," she said, "but Ernie Luntz broke out the other day." She stared at him, her head tilted back in self-satisfaction.

Hank leaned his elbows onto his knees. "I did. But from what I hear, it was more a walk-off. Not that it matters much."

"It matters that he's probably on his way here right now," she said. "I don't know how you feel about that, but it gives me cause for concern. And I have a lot less reason for it than you do."

Hank shook his head slowly and smiled. He said, "I'll be fine, Lyla."

Just then the telephone rang. She let go of the drape and walked quickly to the kitchen. He heard her answer sharply, then soften. "No," she said. "I can do it. No, it's not a problem, why would it be a problem?" Hank walked into the kitchen, and Lyla stepped into the hallway, the coiled cord straining around the corner and out of sight.

He stood at the counter stirring honey into his coffee, letting his eyes roam the cluster of canisters that lined the tiled countertops like rotund soldiers and specked fruit that tumbled from the same wooden bowl their own mother had used for bananas and apples and plums when they were in season. He gazed at the fading floral wallpaper that still clung to the kitchen walls, remembering the long weekend of helping his father and his Uncle Tin lay that paper. He could smell the sweet, wheaty scent of the paste that dripped and clotted over his forearms as the men laughed at his efforts and crackled emptied cans of Rainier beer in their callused hands. There was not one ounce of appreciation that existed within those walls now, not for any of it. Not from his sister Lyla, or anyone else in that family of hers.

"That was Benny," Lyla said, returning the phone to the receiver on the wall. "He's keeping your truck till tomorrow. I'll drive you home."

"You don't need to do that, Lyla. Benny'll take me. He said he would."

"He can't get away till four." She sighed and put a hand to her forehead. "Let me think a minute."

This was something he hadn't prepared himself for. A car ride to the cabin. With Lyla. "You want to just go now, then?" he asked.

She looked at him and said nothing. She seemed to be studying him, looking for a solution somewhere in his face. "Why don't you go and get a haircut," she said finally. "You're starting to look like a hitchhiker."

He put a hand through his hair. She might be right about his needing a trim. "Lyla," he said. "Let's just—"

"Eugene's going to be home for lunch any time now." She reached for her purse sitting on the kitchen table and pulled out a ten from her billfold. "I'm not in the mood for the two of you in the same room," she said. "Now go get a haircut."

# Patrick and Mama T

His mother used to try and hide it from him, when he was younger. When she worked harder at keeping things from him. She probably thought she was being clever, slipping into the bathroom and flipping on the exhaust so she could smoke her bowl freely, the fan rumbling through the walls and the window left wide open whether it was June or January. He knew the smell then and the habits, even as young as twelve or so. As much as she and all the others seemed to think so, he was not so stupid.

Now she lit up whenever she felt the need—which seemed to be practically all the time lately—although she usually kept it to the bedroom or the back porch. It would start with her massaging her fingers over her hip and then he'd hear her talking in a low voice, as if she were explaining it all to herself, justifying what she was about to do. Then she would walk out the kitchen door and sit on the steps, and the skunky smoke would rise in a hazy cloud on the other side of the window.

Patrick was a month past his 15th birthday and standing in the alley behind The Sanctuary when he had his first hit of MDA. With fingers warm and salty Shadow placed it on his tongue, then gave him a bottle of root beer to wash it down with. They sat on the curb against the chain-link fence, huddled close to one another until the purple lights finally blasted from the steeple into the darkening sky. Then Shadow took him by the hand and stood him up, right there in front of everyone, and led him through front doors into the smoke and the pressing crowd. He took him to the place where the music was the loudest and the crowd was so dense he could barely move his arms from his sides. And the balloons overhead lifted and fell and held Patrick's eyes as if they were calling him, and bodies pushed against his own while the pounding bass pushed at him and penetrated his insides, bodies shirtless and soaked in sweat and blistering hot. He raised his head to find the air above and for a moment his mind flipped from one side to the other, and then his mother was on him, her body holding him down while the fireworks exploded over them, and the sweep of police cruiser lights washed over the grass like a blue tide, her body convulsing in sobs and speaking words he could not understand.

"You feeling it?" Shadow shouted into his ear, his arm encircling his waist, the smell of rawness in his breath as he mashed his face into Patrick's. "Fucking amazing."

"I love this!" Patrick yelled it to the ceiling, and Shadow moved in and pressed his lips to his, and sqeezed him so tightly Patrick thought he might melt into him.

He leaned back, and the music was infinite, blade lasers and archways, boomerangs that carried him from one end of the club to the other and back again. And hands on him, sliding along his stomach and down his back and finding the curve of his ass and working around his thighs, hands that must be Shadow's but too many to know for sure, hands slipping under his shirt and over his chest and working the buttons of his fly, the sultry breath against his neck and the music lifting him from the floor and holding him in its arms like a mother, cradling him and rocking him gently with the kind of love that he had never felt in his life.

"Patrick. I said how long you been out here?"

He hadn't heard the door open, or Mama T's voice, not until she nudged him with the toe of her slippered foot. It was four months past his 15th birthday when he returned to her. To Shadow. His backpack was wedged beneath the small of his back, and his head was in a fog.

"Why didn't you ring the bell?" she asked.

The truth was, he didn't know. He remembered sitting down on the steps and thinking about ringing it, but then he must have fallen asleep.

"What time is it?"

"Eleven thirty-five. You was snornin." She stood in the doorway of the stoop a cutout of brown paper with the faint glow of dreadlocks falling snakelike from her head. "Get inside before somebody calls the cops."

In the living room a broken conversation was happening, and it wasn't until Patrick was in the doorway that he realized it was the television. Something in black and white, and the kids were all flat on their stomachs in a neat line of three. They were infantry soldiers, prostrate with hands cupped under chins, each of them staring at the flickering screen with glassy and unblinking eyes.

"Hey," he said. "What're you guys watching?"

"Outer Limits," said Freddie, his voice seemingly deeper than the last time Patrick had seen him. Freddie was the oldest of the three who lay there and therefore the one closest to the television. He could reach the channel if he'd wanted. It was the rule, that the oldest have dominion over the channel. It was an honor Shadow had given over months earlier, when his time at Mama T's started to be more static.

"Hey Danny. Nicco." Two little faces turned slightly to look at him, both giving a quick chorus of *Hey* before recalibrating themselves back to the show.

"You hungry?" Mama T was at the fridge now, harvesting Tupperware containers into her full, lovely brown arms. She wore her flannel robe and the same faded pink headband up under her dreads. "I can heat up some leftover spaghetti. There's some bread in the pantry if you want."

"Thank you, Mama T." There was gunfire on the T.V. then and the boys' toes were curling. Patrick said, "A little bit of spaghetti sounds real good."

He was halfway through his second plate when Mama T talked to him again. She had been sitting next to him the whole time, watching him with her olivine eyes steady on him, not saying anything. Once she pushed up his sleeve to look at his arm and rub her soft fingers over the bolt of veins that ran up to his elbow. "You sure you doing okay?" she asked.

Patrick shrugged his shoulders and took a drink of milk. Looking down the hall from the kitchen to the bedroom door he could see the clutter of papers and colorful lettering still claiming territory. Mama T caught him looking and she patted his arm. "We need to talk about things."

"I know."

She got up from the table then and started putting the food containers back into the refrigerator. She hummed to herself as she cleaned up, but the knocking of glass on glass was deliberate.

"What are your plans this time?" she asked. She looked over her shoulder at Patrick. Not knowing what to say, he shrugged his shoulders again.

"Well honey, you gotta have a plan of some kind." She turned around and leaned against the fridge, her lovely arms folded across her full bosom. "Least of which you know we got to talk about things. You know you can't be just comin and goin like this."

"I know." Patrick's voice was becoming strained now. He turned back to the hallway and looked at the bedroom door. Mama T said nothing, but kept her eyes trained on him. He looked back to the living room and Nicco had dropped off to sleep, his caramel-colored arm folded under his little face, mouth agape and drooling over his bare skin.

Patrick asked, "Is Shadow around?"

"Not at the moment, hon," she said, "You know I always like to see you, but if it's Shadow you're coming for, you best call first."

Every noodle Patrick had eaten seemed to come to life then and begin to coil around the walls of his stomach and weave themselves into tight little complicated knots. He glanced at

Mama T, and he could see that her green eyes were glassy now too, and staring off into the room where the boys still lay beholden to the strangeness of the unreal people who carried on, on the other side of the glowing screen.

"Can I sleep in there anyway?" Patrick asked. "Just for tonight?"

"Honey, you can stay as long as you need to," she said, the slightest edge of hardness in what was usually her molasses voice. Now she swept the plate and glass from the place in front of the boy and brought them to the sink, where she began scrubbing it hard, as if she intended to remove any hint of his having ever touched it. "I got to tell you, though. Your mama, she called me some time back."

Patrick pulled away from the table. He looked up at her. Her shoulders shrugged as she worked, the ropes of black hair brushing against down as her head rocked back and forth.

"Must of got my number offa the phone bill." She turned and looked over her shoulder. "She sure does love you, Spooky."

His throat closed in on him, and he felt his eyes welling up. The crecent moons in his fingernails seemed to come alive, brighten so white that they felt like they might lift from his fingers and drift away.

"You hear me?"

"Yes ma'am."

Mama T turned to face him, leaning with her back against the sink. "Kids come past this place time and again who'd give anything to feel that kind of love." She folded her arms over her chest and then she gave Patrick the smile that was one of the things that brought him back in the first place. "She told me about what happened."

What happened could have been any number of things, but most likely it was the fight he and his mother had had about going to Walla Walla again. The last time he had gone to visit his father Patrick had told his mother on the ride home that he wouldn't do it again. He was sick of it, he said. All of it. The pat downs, the stale vending machine food, the loud, buzzing gates and crashing iron doors. That godawful, long drive over the mountain pass and the dry Eastern Washington flatlands, all so he could sit on the other side of a window and stare at his dad, who never had anything to say, everyone pretending that life was just great, ingorning the reason they were all sitting there in the first place.

"I don't fault you for it, if you thinkin otherwise," she said. "A boy and his dad ought not be separated by bars. But it is what it is. I reckon they're just doing what they can to try and keep you all together in some way."

Patrick heard what she was saying, heard the words, and they made sense to him. But even coming from Mama T it was all more an idea than a reality, not something he could really to take to heart. He looked down the hall at the door with a patchwork of drawings and scrawled signs taped onto the wood.

"Yeah that's Shadow's room still," she said. "Might be, anyway. Might not."

"It depends on Shadow?"

"Yes sir, it depends on Shadow." Mama T went to the living room. She stood in the alcove with her hand gripping the molding and called to the boys still staring at the television. "How long till that show's over?" she asked.

"About ten minutes," said Freddie.

"Well, I'm going to bed," she said. "You put the little ones in when it's over."

"Sure," Patrick said.

"I wasn't talking to you." She stopped at the entrance to the hall. Without turning around to face Patrick she said, "You welcome to stay tonight, in Shadow's bed. If you're still here when I get up I'll fix you some breakfast, and then I expect you'll tell me then what your plan is."

"Plan?"

"How long you plan to be here this time. Before you go on back to your own Mama's arms." She kept her back to him, talked as if there were someone else down the hall from her. "You know you always welcome here any time. But it sounds to me like you got a nice home, with a loving mama just busting to get her baby on back to her. A mama who's been through a lot, for sure. Maybe she's done things she wishes she could change, but it sounds like she's ready to do what she can to make things right." She turned and looked back at him. "That's something these boys here would kill to have."

Patrick swallowed back the knot in his throat. "I'll try."

"That's all I'm askin," she said. She walked into the deeper curtain of the long hallway, past the door that had always been Shadow's, but perhaps was not any longer.

Patrick sat on the sofa and watched the rest of the black and white show over the tops of the boys' heads, not really paying attention to the woman in the headscarf who ran from room to room crying, calling out somebody's name. He thought of his own mother, in their living room with too many pillows on the sofa and knickknacks on the shelves and photos of people who had died before he was born. She was waiting for him to come home, and maybe she was crying too. Who could be sure what she was doing really? He put his pack on the floor with the zipper still closed, and while there wasn't a lot he knew about his "plan" he did know he would be heading home first thing in the morning.

And when the credits began to roll up the screen, Freddie crawled to the television and pushed the button and blackened the screen then pushed on the two boys and they all collected their blankets, and they said *good night, Spooky* as they went past, bleary-eyed and silent to the large back bedroom where they fell into their twin beds that were probably still arranged in little rows, like cots in a barracks.

# Hank

If he had to point to the moment when things changed between him and Bobbie, when things really started to go sideways, it would not be the killing. It wouldn't even be the trial afterward, or Hank's decision to put his house up for sale and move to the mountain. No, the moment when the whole thing really began to unravel was the day that Eugene busted up her leg.

It had come to be that on most days, Hank would ford the divide from his classroom to her office, to sit on the papered cot near her desk. They would talk about the upcoming pool tournaments and a town that would soon be packed with motorcycles. They'd laugh over all the on-the-job retired teachers still lingering and debate over who would be the next to fall. And Hank would note how funny it was that beer could taste so much different when you drank it with the right person. They'd talk about the day, about the coming weekend, and all the weekends beyond, and some of the times Hank could see himself in those, with her, ridiculous as it all seemed now. Every once in awhile the conversation would turn to Patrick, and Bobbie's forehead would wrinkle, and her eyes would well up. Then Hank would make another crack about himself, on getting old, and she'd smile with her lips apart, and sweep the bangs from her eyes. In the end, no matter what aches he'd brought with him, he always left her office feeling cured.

They had made plans to meet up at The Flume for beers. It was Friday. "There might be other people there," she'd said. As if it would make a difference in anything they might do. There had been others plenty of times before, when she tipped the mug back to drink the last of her beer and stepped out through the back door to get some air. When he'd followed her out and walked farther back into the parking lot with her, and they stood against one another, the sweat of his shirt soaking into hers, her back against somebody's pickup trunk, arms locked around his waist.

He'd kissed her more than once, in places other than The Flume, though the parking lot would forever be associated with Bobbie's hands tucked into his back pockets. There might have been more, had there been more time, if he'd been more daring. And it shamed Hank that there were moments he found himself thinking, *If it hadn't been for that goddamned Eugene, she could have gone home with me that night.*

He had seen his nephew through the door window, across the hall, slouching against the lockers. Classes were in session again, and Eugene had no business being out there, but he was a senior and it was three weeks to graduation, so there wasn't a whole hell of a lot Hank could or would do about it now. The best thing for a situation like that was to simply move to the side so he couldn't see out the door.

The students had finally settled down and their books were all open on the same page, and Hank had just asked Monica Toomey to read the sidebar on Piaget. She'd only gotten halfway through the first sentence when the scream came.

Bobbie lay on her back near the top of the stairwell, her left leg out to one side, the knee bent at an unsettling angle. A blue line of liquid dish soap scribbled up and down the hallway, stretching from his door to hers. A single racing track began outside Bobbie's office and ended with her shaking body.

Hank yelled for a student to call the main office, then he went to her, moving over the floor as though he were crossing thin ice. Bobbie looked up at him, her face twisted in agony. "Jesus," he said. "Tell me it wasn't the fucking kid."

"He was going for the fire alarm," she said. "I went after him and he took off down the stairs."

Bobbie was on sick leave the rest of the school year, Eugene's diploma instantly became contingent, and things got especially ugly between Hank and Lyla. One night, she and Jonas showed up at Hank's house well after ten o'clock. They stood in the entry-way and kept their coats on, Lyla rocking on her heels while Jonas danced around the issue, finally zeroing in on the suggestion that Hank should pick sides—Eugene's side, preferably—and plead a case to go easy on the kid.

"He didn't mean it to happen," Jonas had said. "I know he can be a pain in the ass, Hank. He did a dumb thing, but he shouldn't have to have his life ruined over it."

"He put her in the hospital, Jonas," Hank said. "She might never use that leg in the same way again. The next dumb thing he does might end up with someone dead."

Lyla had laughed then, a single, throaty cough. "I'll be in the car," she said, walking out the door and leaving Jonas to finish pleading his dying case.

After that, Friday nights at The Flume became that thing that used to happen in a past life, to a completely different person. Bobbie still called Hank on the phone every so often, usually late at night when Ernie was asleep and her leg was keeping her awake. They'd talk about the things she wanted to talk about. Some black and white movie she was watching on television, an old girlfriend of hers from the city who'd stopped by the house. A fight she'd had with old man Corley, the old guy next door with the Pekingese that never stopped barking. One night she had phoned especially late, waking him up from a heavy sleep. It was just before midnight.

"You could call me sometime, you know," she said. He sat up in bed, in the near dark with the streetlamp coming in through the thin curtains.

"What about Ernie?" he said.

"What about him? Ernie doesn't believe in keeping people hidden away," she said. "I can have friends."

*Friends.* It was a word she had used often with him, in her office, against the fender of his pickup truck, her fingers circling over his ear. And every time she said it, the word both cut and secured him.

Reid Hanlon stood over the old codger, slapping the brush over his shoulders and scattering hair clippings to the floor. It was Oscar Schultz, from over at Frontier Bank. Reid looked up at Hank when he came in, but Oscar sat still with his eyes closed. A fellow that Hank recognized as the husband of one of the school lunch ladies sat in the seat closest the window, his nose in a magazine.

"Hank Kelleher," Reid called out. "Take a seat. Be with you in two shakes."

Hank fanned out the stack of magazines, settling on a Field and Stream. The little black and white television on the shelf showed the snowy image of a golf game, the audio low and crackling. Nobody seemed to be watching it.

"If you'd told me ten years ago we'd be having a goddamned Hollywood has-been running this country," Reid said, "I'd have packed my shit up and moved to Saskatchewan."

"You still could," the lunch lady's husband said from behind a *Playboy*. "I got a nephew lives up in Vancouver. They got a Prime Minister there, I guess. Different from a president."

Old Oscar creaked up from the chair and took his billfold from his back pocket, while Reid took the broom from behind him and swept what little hair there was on the floor into a tiny white cloud. Hank noticed then that all the men had begun to look over at him with quick, intermittent glances. The door opened and Charlie Gumm came in, his bulky mailbag sagged over his shoulder, a clutch of envelopes in his fat hand.

"Morning." He laid the stack on the counter then looked over at Hank. He smiled and shifted his weight, and put his hand inside the bag. "Professor Hank."

"Charlie."

"Or should I say, 'Medicine Man'." He flashed a toothy grin

at Hank. "That's what I hear folks calling you these days."

"Ain't nobody calling me that," Hank snapped.

"Maybe not to your face."

The old man walked to the coat tree, took down a wool blazer and snaked his arms into the sleeves. "How's that mother of yours, Charlie?" he said.

"She's alright. We got her moved into a home last spring, out in Arlington."

"Yeah, I heard you went and did something like that."

His grin fell, and Charlie moved his bag from his shoulder to the floor. "So Reid," he said, his voice dropping, as if there was anyone in the barbershop who might not hear. "That thing we were talking about earlier." He looked over at Hank again. "No news come through on my end, yet."

Reid sighed. He looked up at Hank, then over to Charlie. "That mail ain't gonna deliver itself, Charlie."

There was a soft chuckle, and then Charlie said, "Well okay then. Hope you're good, Hank. It's been a long time since we've seen you down here."

"I'm here for the haircut," he said, pointing to his head. "That's all."

"Well, that's what they do here," he said. He wrestled the bag back to his shoulder and stumbled out the door, followed by the stooped figure of Oscar. The door swung shut, the chain of bells knocking against the window as the two men disappeared down the sidewalk.

Reid tucked the draping around Hank's neck and sprayed a mist of water over his hair. The comb moved quickly up the back of his head, scissors snapping away, and the clippings whispered against the vinyl sheeting as Reid hummed a song Hank couldn't pin down.

"Sorry about that," he finally said. "About Charlie."

The lunch lady's husband had found a new magazine, folded it so he could hold it with one hand. He sat with one leg crossed over the other, clean posture, and was alternating his gaze from the page to the television.

"It's just that—people are talking, Hank." Reid pinched the top of Hank's hair between his fingers and sheared the excess in a single cut. "That's nothing new."

"Yeah well, just because that's the way it is, it doesn't mean I have to participate."

"It's been a long time since that night, you know. Four years and then some. This news of Ernie getting out, it's all brand new. You can't blame folks for getting riled up over it." He talked through quick combs against the grain of the hair. "Don't tell me it hasn't kicked loose a few things in your mind."

Hank clenched his teeth.

He had seen her the night that Ricky was killed. She was on those crutches of hers, and as she hobbled through the gates, Ernie on one side and Patrick on the other, she looked in his direction. And it seemed to Hank that she had seen him, too. The air was gray with smoke and it reeked of sulfur from all the cheap fireworks. He had been standing with bald Dave and his wife Tawny, holding the neck of his Rainier bottle and pretending not to notice as Bobbie made her way over the grass slowly. Dave had been talking about a retaining wall, and Tawny was pulling on his sleeve, saying, *Let's go sit down, the fireworks are gonna start soon.*

Reid filled his palm with foam and rubbed it along the back of Hank's neck, warm against his skin, menthol clouding the space. From the side mirror, he could see Reid stretch the leather strop from the wall and slap the razor along its length, back and forth.

"Do you even remember much of anything?" he said to Hank. "About that night?"

"No."

"It was sure a lot of crazy," he said.

"You almost done?"

Hank had finished his beer, and Bald Dave and Tawny had just turned to leave when there was a sudden explosion of shouting back in the direction of the big chestnut tree, followed by a gut-ripping scream. The crowd of people around him shifted at once and began to move en masse toward the commotion, and Hank instinctively turned to join the stream. It hadn't occurred to him that it could be Bobbie, but maybe some part of him had to have known it, and that was why he threw himself into the crowd without thought. Somewhere along the way, though, he was swept aside and knocked to the ground, where the weight of several piled on top of him and held him down, giving throaty warnings into his ear to stay put, to not go anywhere near it. He lay beneath their knees for what seemed like forever, breathing in cut grass and dirt, as the screams of others rose and fell, and the flash of sirens ribboned among fireworks that continued to thunder and bloom overhead in spite of it all.

"That Ernie," Reid said. "Something sure made him snap. Something that Cordero kid said. I don't know if it was about him, about the wife, or that kid of theirs." He shook some tonic into his hands and rubbed it through Hank's hair. "But it was something."

Hank stood and brushed the hair from his pants legs, and the clippings fell like snow. "You know, Reid," he said, taking a five from his billfold and laying it down on the counter. "You got that striped pole that lets you call this a barbershop. Truth is, you ain't running anything different than Louella's next door."

"What are you talking about?"

Hank walked to the door and rested his fingers on the knob. He wanted to wrench it from the frame, let the glass shatter as he swung it to the wall, but he held onto that knob like it was keeping him from lifting off the ground and being sucked into the edge of a tornado.

"Bunch of old farts sitting around all day telling stories they don't know a thing about," he said. "You oughta just knock that wall down, so you and Louella can share both the shampoo and the bullshit."

He left and crossed over Main and walked down to the end of the block, beyond the vacant lot with its cluster of bare plum trees, then he hooked around up Douglas Avenue to where the high school stood, bound by miles of creeping ivy and choking vines.

For years he had watched teenagers spill from those doors, packing into cars that cost more than his own, Bic lighters flaring amid the roar of engines. They usually raced south, hightailing it out of town to go raise hell in the city. Sometimes, though, they turned north, cruising up the mountain highway to cut onto graveled service roads, where they raised bonfires and littered the creek beds with mashed beer cans and busted bottles and empty shotgun casings, and the milky, slug-like sheen of discarded condoms. Whenever Hank found himself waxing nostalgic about his days in the classroom, all he had to do was take a short drive off of his property to be reminded of what being free of those kids really meant.

He stood at the edge of old Mrs. Gilman's yard and scraped his boots at the loose dirt that had spread from her flowerbed onto the sidewalk. Looking up at the school, he imagined Bobbie Luntz near the back of the building, just down the hall from the main office. She'd be sitting in her rolling chair, her eyes glazing over a thermometer that jutted from some pockmarked kid's trembling mouth, probably holding his clammy hand, the boy green in the gills, her telling him, "Now then, you'll be all right." And all the while she'd be praying he wouldn't throw up on her floor, if he hadn't already.

Hank turned in his resignation three days after the murder. The trial kept Bobbie tied up for the next month or so, going back and forth to Everett, probably spending most of her days sitting in court listening to testimony, or couching in the waiting room of the county jail, maybe going in to visit Ernie, sometimes not. Hank had wanted to call her, but every time he imagined the conversation that might unfold between them, the whole thing fell apart. He wanted to tell her how sorry he was, for everything. Maybe he was wrong but it pounded at him over and over again like the unrelenting litany of fireworks that night. If he had stepped back, his head told him, just left her the hell alone—none of it would have happened.

A few weeks into the new school year, Hank sat at his kitchen table tying trout flies and working on his second pot of coffee when Bobbie phoned. It had been three months since Ricky's murder and more than a month since Ernie had been shipped off to Walla Walla.

"I miss seeing you around here," she said. Every bit of distance between them hung in those words.

Her voice washed over him like a bore tide, and he walked the telephone across the kitchen to hang by the window, where he could see the top floor of the high school rising over the Main Street rooftops. Under the gray clouds the bricks were cut layers of rust.

"Do you think there'll ever be a time when we can sit down together?" she said. "Just talk?"

"I don't know," he said. He chose his words one at a time. "We could shoot for it. I suppose."

There was a heavy sigh at the other end of the line, then silence. The flag that stood at the school's corner lolled in and out from the pole.

"You there?" he asked.

"Yeah."

"What are you thinking?"

"I was going to ask you the same thing," she said.

He went back to the table and sat heavy in the chair. He swept the thread and beads and hooks from the center of the surface back to the edge of the tackle box. The phone was warm against his ear.

"The thing is," he said, "I'm just sitting here on my ass, staring out the window doing nothing, day after day. And I can't stop thinking about that boy and his family. Lyla's not talking to me and might never again, which I guess has its own sliver lining. But Christ, something's gotta give. Cause I think this whole thing's trying to eat me from the inside out."

"God damn it, Hank," she said. "It's my baggage, not yours. I brought it here with me."

"It's killing you, too," he said. "And I just feel so goddamned bad about it all."

His throat felt as if it were being strangled. He wanted to be there with her, to hold her and tell her that he didn't give a damn that she'd brought it with her. Wouldn't it be easier if they shared the burden together?

"I just don't know what happens from here on out," he said. "It's like I'm caught underwater and I can't make my way up. I'm pushing sixty. I ought to know better."

She said, "Stop it, Hank." Then there was a beat before she spoke again.

"You can't have it," she said.

"Can't have what?"

"I said it's mine. I won't give you my blame."

There was a silence then, and he felt his legs ice over, as if something had come loose and drained everything from his lower half.

"Are you there?" she asked.

"Yeah."

"Okay. Well, Hank. I'm gonna hang up now." There was a long pause before he finally heard a click.

# Hank and Lyla

Hank was ready to be home now, away from Ash Falls and the plum and cherry trees, and the open sidewalks where anyone could see the rusty walk of this man who wore his self-loathing down to his boots. He cinched his coat to his neck and stepped up his pace. Tipping his head back, he took a look at the sky, and the cool air whispered over his eyes. It was barely two o'clock, but it sure felt like dusk was already coming down.

Lyla's house smelled like frying butter. She stood at the stove with her arms folded, a greasy spatula jutting from her hand. Eugene sat at the dinette with his back to Hank, hunched over like a Neanderthal in tarry coveralls, with cropped, grimy hair. Lyla looked up at Hank.

"Let me finish this up and then we can go." She flipped the cheese sandwich from the pan to a plate and laid it on the table.

"I'll wait outside." Hank turned back toward the door.

"Hold up." Eugene picked up the sandwich with a blackened hand and bit off a good-sized portion in one take.

Hank took hold of the doorknob as Eugene chewed slowly, and he felt himself shrink in the waiting. He turned the knob, and Eugene held up his hand.

Hank asked, "What do you want?"

"You should know your gear assembly's fucked."

Hank watched as Lyla tore a square from a roll of paper towels and draped it next to Eugene. She brushed her hands over the front of her pants, looking at the partially eaten sandwich on his plate.

"What do you know about it?" Hank asked.

"What do I know about it? That's what Benny said. He said

it looked like that tranny ain't seen a drop of clean fluid since the day it rolled off the line."

"That's a bunch of bullshit."

"Hey, I'm just saying what he told me." He took another bite of the sandwich. "Anyway, I'll see you tomorrow."

Lyla looked at Hank and shook her head. Christ how he wanted to reach over and take him by the hair. That filthy, greasy hair of his that always hung in his eyes, that he tossed to the side constantly as if he couldn't just take a pair of scissors and cut it out of the way.

Hank walked out to the driveway and began circling Lyla's car, sweating through his shirt, his heart working its way up into his throat. His head told him he was being weak, that in letting the boy push his buttons again, he was giving up the battle. Benny could hire whoever the hell he wanted to suck oil from cars, who was he to question it? But Christ. He'd sooner run his truck into a tree before he'd let that shitpile put his hands on it.

At some point he leaned against the side of the car and allowed the coolness of the window against his back to bring him down. Lyla was at the door, keys in hand, her blue windbreaker open to her waist. She stared at him through her giant owlish lenses.

"I wish you wouldn't do that," she said. She came to him and put her hand on driver's side door handle. "You know how he is. You act like you're the only person in the world who's ever had to put up with him." She opened the door. "Now get in, so I can take you home."

She climbed in and swept her seatbelt over herself like a sash. "I have a few errands to run first," she said, leaning into the ignition with the whole right side of her body. "It won't take long."

There were always *a few errands*. A stop at the grocery, the bank, a friend who needed something that Lyla was more than willing to loan out. These were the tracings of the next hour, periods of time when Hank sat in the passenger seat with his feet growing cold, studying the veins on his hands and running a budget in his head as he waited. It was getting late and he needed to get home. By the time they were on the open highway, heading to his house on the mountain, it was already past four.

"What's the matter with you?" She stole glances at him as she drove exactly the speed limit, her hands glued at ten and two. "It's a truck, for goodness sake."

"I don't like being stranded. I need a working vehicle."

"You're the one who put yourself out there in the middle of nowhere. Living on that land like a hermit. Not to mention the little side job you've decided to keep."

"What's that got to do with anything?"

"People talk, Hank."

"Oh Christ almighty, I'm getting tired of being reminded of how this town can't keep its mouth shut."

"Well, you don't have to hear it like I do."

They came to the three corners, where the Tollefson farm stretched over both sides of the highway and Jeffries Road wove down to the old lumber mill. Lyla came to a complete stop, even though there was not a single car in sight. A tractor sat abandoned in the middle of the field opposite the house. Two Australian cattle dogs jumped down from the porch and started running down the long drive toward them.

"What you need," she said, "is a woman to occupy your time."

"Yeah well I tried that," he said. "And it didn't work out so good."

She looked at him. "Well, one would hope that you'd be smarter about the next one."

She punched the accelerator and plunged them into the cover of the forest. Hank stared out the window into the stands of Doug Fir and spindle alders that raced past them. The trees stood like bristles on a brush, evenly spaced with a floor almost entirely of salal. Half the mountain at this point was third growth, planted by hand like lettuce starts, regimented according to someone's master plan. These trees were living and breathing and providing homes and food for many. But they were waiting. Waiting to be felled again, to be run through the saw and cobbled into somebody's cheap furniture, or toilet paper, or the guts of the sort of matchbox houses that had begun to sprout along the lower highway like fungus.

Lyla pulled the headlights.

"There goes the day," Hank said.

"It's November," she said, not looking at him. "It's worse up here, though. Always under shadows."

"You'd get used to it."

Lyla laughed. "Never," she said.

She slowed at the bend and turned into his drive, and by now the headlights washed along the trees and over the mottled road like paint. It always set his nerves on edge, the sight of his empty house, unguarded, just waiting for him. There were times that his mind got the better of him, and he saw things. Flashes of movement in the trees. Probably an owl, he'd tell himself. Or a squirrel, up late. Now and then he caught a glint of something against the window glass and he imagined that there must be someone in his home. And in those moments, he was glad for the rifle in the back window of his pickup.

"Wish you had a gun in here," he said to Lyla, knocking on the dashboard.

"Well, keep wishing," she said.

He thanked her for the ride and she reminded him that Benny would be out the next day to get him but when Hank asked her what time, she couldn't remember if Benny had given a time.

"It's fine," he said. "I'll be here."

He leaned over and gave her a kiss on the forehead and let himself out. She stayed where she was until he was up on the porch, and the door was open, and the dog had bounded out and slapped his paws upon Hank's stomach. And only when he turned to wave her off did she put the car in reverse and hook around. She rolled back almost to the big maple stump, then she straightened out her wheels, gave a tap on the horn, and drove off down the drive, out of sight.

# Lyla and Jonas

It had been uncharacteristically warm that spring day, when Jonas Henry showed up at Lyla's church in his slick blue suit, his hair clipped short and stiff like a parched lawn. He had come to town by way of Tacoma, an Army buddy of somebody's brother, Lyla couldn't remember whose. But there were the whispers from the pew behind her, one of the Snyder sisters telling the other what she knew about this new face who just sauntered past everyone, showing his teeth and smelling like English Leather. He had fought in Korea, she said. And he was single.

The sermon had been a long one, about keeping faith in the moment of despair. The Soviet Union was already in outer space, and they were testing missiles. There was a man running for president who was unlike anyone who had run before, and for the first time in memory Lyla was excited to be able to vote. But he was so young and unproven, Lyla's parents liked to say, and on top of it all he was a Catholic, so what could be expected in the way of foresight and temperance? It seemed like every day they were predicting the end of everything, one minute begging her to hurry and find a man already (she was thirty, after all), the next minute shrugging their shoulders and lamenting, "What's the use?"

When the minister finally finished, Lyla followed the congregation as it spilled out into the yard, where the idle gossip always rose up, people chattering about everything but the sermon. Jonas was down the slope near the old drain pond—a handsome fellow standing beneath the big willow with a group of people Lyla knew from her high school years, though she hadn't spoken with them in some time. She took her purse from her shoulder and clutched it in her hand, and walked on down to the tree like it was the most natural thing in the world for her to do. She was almost upon the group when he looked up at her.

"Who are you?" he asked. He spoke loudly, and Lyla shrank in the anticipation of turning every head in the yard.

"I'm Lyla," she said.

"Lyla," he echoed. "Lyla." He repeated it twice more back to her, as if it was a brand new word, a sound he'd never heard before in his life. And now the eyes of those gathered around the tree were upon her. These old schoolmates who'd been talking among themselves and not paying her the slightest of notice were suddenly interested in what might happen next, and Lyla drank in the attention as if she'd been famished her entire life.

The next months were something of a heady time for her, a blur of spaghetti dinners and live music in the basement of The Elks Club, and of church women leaning into one another, nodding in twitches as they peered at the two of them from across the room. Jonas got a job at the Coast to Coast hardware store in Lake Stevens, and right away moved into an apartment over the Gamble furniture store on Main. Sometime later, a few months maybe, he asked Lyla to marry him. She had a clear memory of his proposal shouted over the noise of a brash number the swing band was playing downstairs at The Elks. He'd recall it differently when asked, saying it had been in the parking lot afterward, the two of them nuzzled together while the car radio played in the background. What they both agreed upon, the memory that each recalled to perfection, was that Lyla's parents were in near ecstasy over the engagement, practically packing her bags for her the moment she and Jonas broke the news to them.

"I wonder what Hank will have to say about this," she said aloud later that evening, as they left the club and walked arm in arm between the cars in the parking lot. She had said "yes" and had already begun to think about the wedding, if not the marriage.

"What does Hank have to do with anything?" he asked. The way he stared at her then—that half-cocked smile and single raised eyebrow—it was as if she had suggested the family dog should first give permission. She had approached some line that was not to be crossed, she realized. If she wanted the proposal to stand, she had better leave her brother out of it.

Today, as any other day, they sat on opposite sides of the table, each with a different section of the newspaper folded neatly in front of them. Lyla worked her crossword puzzle more out of routine than desire, writing out the easy ones, stealing glances at the wall clock every few minutes. Jonas thumbed through the sports pages. Now and then he'd tap the page and remark on something Lyla knew nothing about, like which team was headed for the playoffs and who was not earning his salary, or which coach was probably on his way out at the end of the season. These things didn't interest her, but she'd stop what she was doing when he spoke anyway, nod or raise her eyebrows for him in feigned surprise. Between them, coffee steamed from matching cups.

"She was up again last night," he said. He held his eyes on the paper. Lyla lifted her pen and looked up at her husband. There was a yellow smear of egg yolk along the edge of his lip. He said, "I could hear her walking around."

Lyla shrugged her shoulders. "She sneaks food," she said. "I thought you knew that."

"I didn't know that." He took long drink from his coffee, peering over the rim at her. He seemed to be studying her, searching her eyes for some indication that she was feeding him a story. "I thought maybe he was keeping her up," he said finally.

"Keeping her up with what?" Now she sat up straight in her chair, her back rigid.

"The noise. The talking."

"You mean, in his sleep?" She pushed air through her teeth. "He hasn't done that since he was a boy."

"Oh come on, Lyla." Jonas turned the page. He went on, reminding Lyla of the middle-of-the-night shouting, the phantom conversations through the wall that woke both of them, right up until he finally moved his bedroom to the basement. "It hasn't been that long," he laughed.

It was hard to believe that there was ever a time before Eugene, when he didn't dominate every part of her life: her pocketbook, her emotional bank, even the very air she breathed each day. From the moment he was born, Eugene fastened himself to her, a kind of emotional parasite that seemed to need her constant presence in order to survive.

"I saw a 'For Rent' sign up at the Gamble building," he said. "It might be a good idea to talk to the two of them again."

Lyla felt herself tense. "Good lord," she said. "Anywhere but there."

"You forget I lived there when we were starting out," he said. "It's fine for a young couple."

"A lot's changed in twenty years, Jonas," she said. "It's squalor now. Nothing but alcoholics and welfare recipients. Something with turn up eventually."

They used to talk so much about what "eventually" meant, she and Jonas, of the kind of world that waited for them after Eugene finally grew up and left home. There were a hundred little things they would do just as soon as it was the two of them again, with no child to chase or clean up after. On the morning after their wedding, Jonas asked her to name all the places she wanted to see in her life, and she told him the Redwoods in northern California were first on her list, and then Monument National Park. Death Valley, too. Lyla dreamed of being in the desert, of scanning the endless stretch of sand and tumbleweeds, and stands of spiny cacti spotting the horizon.

"You got it, Pumpkin," he promised her. They lay in his double bed, looking out the window at the tar-splotched rooftops of the Main Street shops.

They made it to Eureka once, about six months after the wedding. But that was it. Lately, it was getting harder and harder to imagine that any of those places even existed anymore, much less that she would ever get to see them.

"You know why she sneaks, don't you?" she said.

"I suppose it's because he's always bugging her about her eating," Jonas said. "Well, he won't change unless she toughens up."

Lyla set down her coffee and gazed over at him, at the stony bridge of his nose, at the gentle, white hairs that lay like spider webs on his fingers as he ran them over the newspaper. Jonas was a man who had always been generous with her, with the money he earned, and the time he had. Even if her life didn't turn out the way she'd imagined and if there were moments when she dreaded the thought of thirty more years of awkward conversation over the morning newspaper and fried eggs, he was always there for her. If nothing else, she could count on him to listen to her when she talked and come home from work every night when he was supposed to do. That kind of thoughtfulness was more than a lot of women got.

He tried to show that same generosity to his son, but it was clear he could never figure out Eugene. "I don't understand you," he'd say from behind the steering wheel, eyes locked on the rear-view mirror, fiery. Even though the school was less than a half-mile away, those drives home were eternal. "Why can't you be a good kid and just do what you're told?" The Army would never put up with it, he'd say. "Why do you always have to be Johnny Smart Ass?" The whole time Eugene would sit in near silence, sobbing quietly into his coat or—as he got older—brooding, glaring stoically out the window at the passing houses.

Lyla pushed her chair back and stood up from the table. When she touched the edge of his cup and tipped it to one side Jonas shook his head, so she removed it from the table and added it to the breakfast plates that were already soaking in the sink. As she ran the water, she looked out the window, down the block at the streetlights that still shone down onto Main Street. Now and then a car would drift past. People were already beginning their days.

"I saw her at the Red Apple the other day," she said.

"Who's that?"

"That Bobbie woman. The nurse." She reached into the water with the washcloth and found a plate to scrub.

"Hank's gal?" Jonas said. "Well hon, she doesn't live but six blocks from here. You're bound to run into her sometimes."

"I know that."

"It doesn't make it news."

"I never said it did." She dropped the plate into the rack. "I'm just making conversation, Jonas." She glanced over her shoulder at him. He looked at her with a curious expression, as if he had no idea why she should be irritated. The newspaper draped over his hand like a wilted flower. "I wish you wouldn't let her get under your skin like you do," he said, going back to his paper. "It was the husband who did it, not her."

"I know that," Lyla countered, running both cups under the faucet at once. "But she had a hand in it."

"There were quite a few hands involved in that whole mess, Lyla."

She pulled the stopper from the sink and watched the soapy water melt down the drain. She knew he was right. In her heart, she knew what he said made sense, but it was like he was standing on the other side of a locked door, telling her to just walk through already. She couldn't do it. That woman didn't deserve to be let go so easily.

There was the sound of voices downstairs and the ache of water through old pipes. Lyla turned around from the sink in time to see Jonas fold his paper and get up from the table.

"I guess I'm off," he said.

She said, "You wouldn't want to be late."

"No," he said. "I wouldn't."

She went to the refrigerator and took out his lunch, a Tupper-ware bin of leftover meatloaf and roasted potatoes, something she had put together for him the night before. She had no way of knowing if he actually ate the lunches she packed for him. He said he did, and the bins he brought home with him were always empty. But there had to be plenty of decent restaurants in the shopping center where the bank was. She supposed it didn't re-ally matter.

He was at the kitchen door now, his arms fighting the sleeves of his sport coat. His tie was knotted too loosely and she could see his top button, even from the other side of the room. The egg yolk was still there as well. For a moment she felt a sense of satis-faction, that he might see the mess himself in the rearview mirror of his Buick, or in the restroom at the bank sometime later that day. He would think of her then and wonder how she could have missed something so obvious.

She brought his food to him, and he took it and gave her arm a squeeze, and kissed her on her cheek before turning to leave. Outside, daylight was just beginning to break, and the cold rushed in as he swung open the door. The air was crisp, carrying in the smell of early morning, before the logging trucks started thundering through on their way to the mountain.

"Just a minute," she said, turning him to face her. She slid the Windsor knot to his throat and tucked down his collar, then she licked her finger and used it to wipe the food from his face. He smiled at her, kissed her again, and told her he'd see her that evening. He'd pick up a bucket of chicken on his drive home if she wanted. She just had to call and let him know.

She went to the window and watched as he backed out of the driveway and drove off down the street, a cotton-white cloud billowing from the back of his car as he rounded the corner to the highway. There was more noise below her. Eugene and Marcelle were up now, opening and closing drawers and speaking to each in hard tones. What could they possibly have to talk about, she wondered, the two of them, with what little they knew about the world outside of that basement. Maybe they didn't say a single word that had anything to do with life beyond the next two hours of their lives. Where had Marcelle put his socks? Could he pick up his own towel? Would Eugene drop her off at work on his way out so she didn't have to walk?

She went to the sink and pulled the frying pan from the dish rack. There would come a day eventually when the two of them would no longer be living in that basement with their queen-sized bed and thrift-store vanity, and their shelves made of cinderblocks and boards, playing at marriage. There would someday be a time when Lyla didn't have to watch them pretend they were something more than two kids trapped by circumstances and a stupid piece of paper that called them "husband and wife." And as Lyla imagined a basement devoid of Eugene's decrepit furniture, replaced by her mother's sewing machine and boxes of linens or anything else she chose to put down there, it suddenly hit her: What then? What waited for her and Jonas when there was no longer Eugene and that girl to clutter up her conversations and thoughts and efforts?

She went to the corner desk and took a sheet of paper and a pen from the drawer. In block letters she wrote GAMBLE APARTMENTS, then walked to the refrigerator and clipped it to the freezer door.

# Bobbie and Tin

Friday afternoon came sooner than expected. Bobbie did her final inventory, locked up the office and went to the hallway to wait for the bell that would bring in the weekend. She twirled her keys in her hand, watching two women teachers talk on the lower landing of the stairwell. They leaned in so close their hair touched, and they occasionally glanced up at Bobbie. They were young, new to the school just last year, and Bobbie wasn't even sure what they taught.

She looked at the floor outside her office door, a habit now, always checking for hazards before stepping out. Patrick took his sixth period—American Lit—at the opposite end, from Peggy Chapman. Bobbie had heard that Peg was merciless in her grading, and spoke to the kids as if they were graduate students. But Patrick seemed to be holding his own, even though he seldom had a book in his hand.

The bell rang and bodies poured from doors. Patrick appeared amid a swirl of classmates and they cut in and around him, shoulders knocking shoulders. He came toward her as if he was crossing a river on stones, his chin dipped, yellow bangs tumbling over his eyes. She wanted to go right to him, smooth that hair back from his face and kiss him at the temples, like she did when he was a boy.

He came to her and she touched his elbow.

"Hey," he said.

"How was the day?"

He thumbed his hair from his eyes. "We had a test."

"And?"

He shrugged his shoulders. People flooded all around them

and Patrick shifted his weight from one foot to the other. "I gotta stop by my locker," he said. "And I gotta go to work."

A girl in a blond ponytail and plaid skirt brushed past them. Patrick reached out and tugged at her sleeve. She spun around and smiled, toothy, the fleshy gums showing pink. "Hey hey," she said. "Hi, Mrs. Luntz."

Bobbie smiled, though she had no idea who the girl was. It was typical. Kids she knew ignored her, and those she felt like she'd never seen before bellowed her name from the parking lot of the grocery store. Bobbie turned back to Patrick.

"I thought I'd drive you."

"I got my bike."

"We can put it in the back." She leaned to one side to catch his eye. "Hey," she said. "I'd like to meet the old guy."

His face screwed up at her.

She said, "Don't give me that." This was an argument she didn't want to have, not now, not here in the hallway at school. Why couldn't he just say Okay and be done with it? "Buck up," she said. "It'll be a good thing."

Patrick laughed. "It'll be a frigging mess." He reached up and put his notebook on his head. His eyes closed, the jaw pulsating as he ground his teeth together. This was a thing of his, when he found himself backed in a corner. When he didn't want to lose it and wind up in trouble on top of everything else that might be happening to him. It was one of a few things he'd picked up from watching Ernie, early on. After a good thirty seconds, he gave a heavy sigh, and brought his notebook back to his side.

"Whatever. Okay."

Out in the parking lot, Tina Reiter and Sam Gish, the history teacher, were already climbing into her Datsun. It was too early for TGIF. There was an unwritten rule that teachers wait for the lot to clear of students before locking up and heading out for the weekend. It could be that Tina and Sam were abandoning the mountain for the night, getting an early start. Whatever the case, this coupling was news to her. She glanced over at Patrick, but he paid no attention to them.

While he fiddled with the radio, Bobbie asked about his plans for the weekend, if he was getting with friends, if he had any homework. What did he like about Tin's, if anything. Small talk. He gave a word here and there. Being civil. Bobbie was fishing, feeling for any indication that the beans had been spilled about Ernie. Patrick seemed like Patrick. Concise. Evasive. If anyone had said something to him, he wasn't giving it up.

By the time she came upon the turnoff to the mink farm, he had a tight hold on the passenger door handle. "Just drop me at the gate," he said. "Up here." He nodded his chin at the windshield and snatched his gym bag from the floor to his lap. "You'll just get stuck at the bottom."

"I'll be fine," Bobbie said.

*I've been in tight spots before, she thought to herself. You try navigating your way out of the Blue Moon Lounge parking lot, six-drink-drunk at two a.m. in a Buick Skylark.* Giving the wheel a spin, she coasted through the open gate and took the decline to Tin's slowly, rocking over ruts and divots the whole way down.

Patrick sank against his seat and let his head bounce against the window while he stared out through the glass. All around them, the forest stood dense and black with shadow, still holding onto the day's rain. He was not so different than the little apple-cheeked boy who had once called out street signs from the backseat as Bobbie cruised the taverns looking for Ernie's Firebird.

She wasn't bending. She was determined to take Patrick all the way to the river's edge, whether he liked it or not. The fact was, he had money to spend. She was his mother. She had the right to know exactly where, and how, he was earning it.

The car came to a stop in a clearing of patchy sod, the rolling Stillaguamish a starry, green-blue ribbon filling her view. At the far side, thick cedar boughs hung like curtains over the water, rippling loosely in the breeze. Through the closed window she could hear the whisper of the water's flow, and the tinny chatter of chickadees. "Sweet Jesus," she said aloud. "I might even be willing to deal with all those mink if it meant I could wake up to this every morning. Just me and you, way out here with nobody else."

The old man was already coming up from the riverbank, whip fishing rod in one hand, a clutch of slimy trout dangled from the other, mouths sucking air, bodies slapping at his leg. He was a giant tortoise, hunched forward, craggy head bobbing from the loose opening of a mossy wool sweater. His legs angled over the uneven ground. He was old, even older than Bobbie had imagined.

When he saw them he hollered, "Well if it isn't Skunk in a car!"

Patrick climbed out and went around to the back of the wagon, pulling his bicycle out and walking off without so much as a goodbye. When he got to Tin, he paused and said something. The old man responded with a few words and a wave of his arm, and Patrick pushed his bike toward a cluster of buildings in the distance. Tin broke into an eager march to Bobbie's car.

"So you must be the famous Mister Tin," she said, getting out of the car and taking support from the closed door behind her.

"Just Tin," he said. He laid the fishing pole against the fender and took her hand in a cold grip. "Dorsay's my last. Most people think it's Irish, but it's French." When he spoke his tongue ran over the entire topography of his toothless mouth.

"So that's your boy?" he said.

"That's my boy." Bobbie nodded her chin at him. "All seventeen years of him."

Patrick stood near the mink houses, hands deep in his pockets as he gaped back at them. The jeans weighed loose on him and his jersey hung too far over his beltline. He could stand to gain some weight, Bobbie thought, or have a mother who would take him shopping more than once a year.

"Clock's running, fella," Tin hollered. "No pay for staring!" He looked at Bobbie and gave her a wink. Patrick walked away, disappearing into a small silver Quonset adjacent to the mink houses.

The land was a clutter of hovels and dwellings and rusted out vehicles, windowless and resting on oil-splotched cinderblocks. Pitch-roofed barns huddled against the edge of the forest opposite the creek, ringed with sprays of thick, yellowed crabgrass and brushy sorrel. Plywood shutters, propped outward like sleepy eyelids, extended from each hut. These were low-rise barracks, regimented in close rows.

An algae-stained travel trailer pressed snugly against a cloud of naked blackberry brambles, connected to a meaty maple by a lone, sagging clothesline. Further back, far from all the clutter, stood what Bobbie assumed to be the old man's place, nestled at the deep edge of the cleared land. It was a two-story farmhouse with lattice-paned picture windows and a wide, swaybacked porch.

"So can I get a look at them?" She nodded at the barns.

"The minks? God. Them nasty goddamned things."

They walked to the barns, each lopsided in their gaits as they stepped over the lumpy sod. She had caught a whiff of the creatures as soon as she had come into the river bottom, but now that she was out, the closer she got to the buildings, the more pungent the air became. Not unlike skunk, she thought. Heady, musky, and miles thick.

"I think if I lived here I would spend half my day hoping for a strong breeze," she quipped.

"Hell," he said. "Thirty odd years. You get used to it."

Tin swung the door open and the full scene rolled over Bobbie like an unexpected, breaking wave. The stench was more than she had imagined. She remembered vividly how she had made Patrick strip in the mudroom on that first day back, and the memory gave her heart a pinch. Twin lines of crowded boxes lined the walls of the barn, wire mesh cubes with spots of blue-gray, scurrying, scratching, some gnawing at the wire. Others lay still, curled into furry balls in the farthest corners of their pens, oblivious to the racket. She had imagined a lot worse, given Patrick's complaints. But Jesus, those things did stink.

She kept her hands tucked into her jean pockets, walking squarely in the middle of the aisle. As she kicked at the sawdust flooring, she traced the rough-hewn beams that propped up the tin roofing, and she thought about just how much Ash Falls was made from the grain of its own forest. Hank had rambled on for over an hour about this once, as they sat on his cabin porch, passing a roach back and forth between them in the dark.

"There isn't one person in this town," he'd said, "who appreciates the history that lives in the walls of their house." He patted the shingles over her head. "This piece of wood," he said, "was in the ground when the Declaration of Independence was signed. How can that not just blow your mind?"

Bobbie squatted down in front of a cage. "I wasn't expecting them to be so cute," she said. "Hank told me they were mean sons of bitches."

"They are mean," Tin said. "Get too close to em, they'll show you just how mean they can be."

*Probably being kept like this*, she thought to herself. *Walled off from the world. Fed and watered, just kept alive so they can wind up stitched to the collar of some rich bitch's ski jacket.*

"How come they have to be so small?" She asked, nodding at the row of boxes. "The cages, I mean."

"A den in the wild ain't no bigger than these. Food and shelter on top of it all. They ain't got it so bad."

"I heard you had a couple get free."

"Free?" He gave a phlegmy laugh, kicked up a real cough and spit a quarter-sized wad into the sawdust. "These things won't last two, three days out in the world. They got no skills for these woods. Spend their whole their life in this barn. If a coyote don't get 'em the first night, a logging truck will the second."

The door creaked open and Patrick came in, dragging a plastic garbage can behind him. He went to the cages at the far side of the barn and began sliding out trays and dumping the soiled wood chips into the bin. He kept his back to them. A thin cord ran from his jacket pocket to a pair of headphones that cupped his ears.

Tin gave a nod toward the door and began walking. Bobbie followed. When they got outside he continued walking from the barn, across the open space toward the river, where he stood at the high bank and stared off into the current.

Bobbie said, "I'd like to thank you."

"Thank me? What for?" he said.

Bobbie's breath seemed to dodge her, each word a labor. Her brain, working a tangle inside her head. "I guess I'd say that there ain't a whole hell of a lot of people in this town who would give that kid a chance. Either of us, really. But especially him."

"'Cause of you being Ernie's gal?"

The sound of that name, so sudden, nearly buckled Bobbie's knees. She looked over at Tin, at his searching eyes. Big, white eyeballs that hovered atop sagging folds of thick, ruddy skin. And then he gave her a smile. Gums pink and as shiny as the gaping trout.

"I'm not Ernie's gal anymore," she said. "Haven't been for a long time."

"Didn't mean it like that. Word is he got out, though."

"You heard that all the way down here?"

"This ain't the middle of the earth. And I do go up that hill sometimes."

Bobbie caught herself smiling at that. This was a man who didn't mince words.

"That was something else, that thing at the fairgrounds," he said. "Stirred up a lot of coals in the fire."

"I know."

"Do ya?" He cocked his head at her.

She held him in her gaze for a good five or so seconds, an ungodly amount of time to stare and say nothing. He kept himself fixed on her as well, big eyes misted, his lips framed the edges like hard parenthesis.

"Well anyway," she said finally. "I hope that doesn't create a problem for you. Him working here, I mean."

"Long as he works, I don't give a goddamn what his old man did. It ain't his cross to bear."

Bobbie glanced back toward the mink barn, then squinted at Tin. The sun had come from behind the clouds, just breaking off the edge of the old man's crown.

"Patrick doesn't know yet. About his dad." Tin dipped his chin and peered at her, and Bobbie said, "I know it's bad. And I will tell him. I just can't seem to find the right moment. Every time I think it's there"—she sucked in her breath—"I just freeze up."

He moved back from the bank and began to walk back toward the barns. "Well," he said. "Christ knows I ain't raised nothing, not unless you count them minks, which I sure as hell wouldn't. But like I said, people around here can't keep their mouth shut to save their lives. The boy ought to hear it from his ma."

"I know that."

As she steered to the top of Tin's drive she thought of Patrick still down there, burlap sack in hand, walking up and down those endless rows of sharp teeth. From her window just before she'd left, she looked over and saw him standing in the doorway, and he glanced back her and gave her a quick wave. And for a moment, in spite of the squalling and the stench and the low, filtered light she could see the boyish face that she missed so much. That face that she remembered from before. Before she or Ernie—she wasn't even sure who to blame anymore—had ripped their lives apart.

# Bobbie

She hadn't imagined that Ernie would want to go to the fairgrounds. Everything that he hated, standing shoulder to shoulder with other people, all in the middle of smoke bombs and bottle rockets going off everywhere, would be there. It was why he wanted to move to the mountain in the first place, to get far away from the crowds and the chaos.

"Everyone in town's going to be there," she said. "It'll be a sea of blankets and Styrofoam coolers." But Patrick had asked, and Ernie was feeling good.

"Sure, buddy," Ernie had said, pouring another bowl of cereal for himself. "We can go watch the fireworks."

Bobbie didn't remember thinking about Hank then, though it was hard to imagine that she wouldn't have. Her mind was on Eugene. "He'll probably be there," she warned Ernie. "If you see him, you have to promise you won't say anything."

"I didn't last time."

"Yeah well, he was by himself then," she said. "He'll probably be with friends this time. And they'll be drinking, I'm sure. He'll get cocky like he does."

Ernie looked over Bobbie's leg, plastered and scrawled with smudged messages of sympathy. *Ouch. Hang in there. Cast-Away.*

"Yeah, well he's just a dumb ass kid, right?" he said. "And he already got smacked over it. You said 'Let it go.' I'm letting it go."

Bobbie kept quiet then. She had said a lot of things in the days after the break, unsure how Ernie would take it, not sure what she wanted done about it, or what could even be done. Anyway, she was healing now, it was summer, and Eugene would not be at school when the term started again in September.

Under the hazy apron of lamplight, Bobbie skirted the edge of the huge chestnut canopy, Ernie and Patrick on either side of her. Her head throbbed and her armpits were killing her. She was convinced that by the time she got the hang of those fucking crutches, the cast would be off. It weighed her whole left side down, and it felt like an army of ants had found its way inside and were devouring her leg. She was already sweating down her back.

So the last thing she either wanted or needed at that moment was to hear Eugene Henry's donkey laugh. A commotion of sorts arose at the chestnut, some jostling and hushed laughter. She could make out a small crowd of teenagers crouched together on an outspread quilt. Heads bobbed in and out of the huddle, hands slapping backs.

Ernie looked at her and smiled, and gave her a quick wink. "It's gonna be a great show, Peanut," he said. And the way he said it, crisp and singsongy, Bobbie imagined that it actually could have been.

Then somebody said, "That's him right there."

"Say it, Eugene." A different voice.

"Shut up, Allen." This one was Eugene, shaky though, not like him.

Ernie slowed his pace. Bobbie told Patrick to walk next to her. "Ernie," she said. "Let's just keep going."

There was another punch of laughter, and Ricky Cordero's nasal croak floated above all the noise. It was a voice Bobbie could pull from a crowd as well, the kind of voice that could strip paint from walls. She'd once heard another teacher describe it as something like an old woman's who'd lived her whole life on whiskey and Camel non-filters.

"Hey dude," he called out. And then he said something that Bobbie didn't hear, something that resulted in a momentary hush in the group. A girl said, "Damn, Ricky."

Ernie faltered. "*Ernie, you promised*," Bobbie reminded. But he wouldn't look at her. He just stared back over his shoulder, to the crowded spot under the tree.

"Who said that?" Ernie called.

There was a pause, and the burst of air escaping from a popped can.

Patrick reached out and took Ernie's sleeve. "Dad, let's just go."

Ernie snatched his hand back and repeated, "Who said that?"

"Nobody, man." Eugene said. "It's nothing."

"Nothing, my ass." This time it was Ricky again. "She needs to find her boyfriend, wrap a little blanket around the two of them and cuddle under the fireworks. Love, American Style!"

Bobbie stopped and pivoted on her good leg so she was facing the chestnut tree full on. Ernie still hung back, his jaw pulsing, his fingers moving at his sides. She reached out with the tip of the crutch and tapped his leg, and he glanced almost nonchalantly down at it. When he looked up at her again, his eyes were almost transparent, as if she could see through him, right out the other side at the clot of boys that ringed the trunk of the massive tree. He blinked his lids, so slowly. As if he wanted to feel the soothing wash over his eyeballs, one last time before he looked back.

Ricky laughed again and said something Bobbie couldn't make out. An empty beer can rattled against something. "Dude," he said. There was some jostling in the group and then Ricky said, "He ain't gonna do a goddamned thing about it."

"Ricky, you're drunk," someone said. "Be cool."

"Everybody knows about it. Big fucking deal," Ricky said. "I guess some people are into that kind of thing."

There was a sharp explosion. The fireworks had begun, blooming overhead in giant red and green globes. Bobbie could see the dappled light falling through the branches, passing colors, the boys crouched against the huge trunk of the chestnut. There were beer cans tucked against legs, and orange cherry tracers from cigarettes on the move. Ricky clutched a beer in his hand, sporting a grin so big his face was a skull.

Patrick took shelter behind Bobbie. He was crying now, his sniffles bucking against her body as he held to her waist. Bobbie reached out a hand. "Ernie," she said. "Let's go."

"Don't." He jerked his arm away from her. His eyelids collapsed, his teeth clenching so that his beard seemed to retract into his face. "Don't tell me what to do."

Another cut of laughter burst from under the tree. Ernie's fingers knuckled against his sides. Ricky spoke again. Something. Bobbie couldn't tell what. Then there was jolt at her arm, and she was spun like a top, arms flailing for balance until the weight of her cast dropped her to the ground. She lay on her side, stunned and out of breath, one crutch wedged beneath her ribs. Patrick knelt beside her, still crying, his fingernails digging into her arm. By the time her eyes found Ernie, he was almost to the tree, the second crutch jutting from his hands, its handle swinging in broad, preemptive loops.

She screamed, a desperate push from her lungs that seemed enough to turn her entire body inside out. But it was all too much, the chaos raging from all around and the screams and shouting, and the rockets still blasting overhead, as if not a single terrible thing were happening beneath it all. The wash of red and green fell over the bodies scrambling from under the tree, lights flashing against aluminum as Ernie swung the crutch from so far behind him, over and over, like he was splitting knotted logs into kindling.

She grabbed Patrick by the hand and pulled him to the ground with her. His body collapsed onto hers, his face buried against her neck, and she took in the scent of his hair, the smell of apricot and grass, and it mixed in with the choking smoke and the flash of colors against her eyelids, and the incessant racket of fireworks that seemed as if they would go on forever.

"I'm sorry, honey," she whispered. She locked her hand to her wrist and pulled him in even tighter. "Oh Jesus God."

# Patrick and Ernie

There was a stretch of time when Patrick would wake in the middle of the night to the tinkling of glass against glass, or the static of bunched cellophane, and chair legs scooting over linoleum. If the room were cold, Patrick would bring his knees to his chest and burrow deeper under the covers, cradling his pillow, safe knowing his father was in the next room making a snack, or fixing a drink of whiskey and Sanka. When they had lived in the city, in the shady half of the flat-roofed duplex, this routine happened at least once a month.

On the Saturday before their last Christmas in the duplex, Patrick climbed from under his quilt and walked on rough wood floors from his bedroom to the living room. The red lights tacked to the neighbor's eaves glowed through the windows into their home. It gave Patrick a feeling of warmth, though he had heard his mother once whisper to his father that it made the bedroom look like a whorehouse.

His father was on the sofa in the darkened room, hunched over the coffee table, smoking down a blunt cigarette and humming. A fat mug and a soupy bowl of Corn Flakes sat in the middle of the table, the spoon sticking out like the handle of a shovel. His father's beard was just coming in then. By the light of the outside porch lamp, Patrick could see the sandy outline of his jaw.

"Hey kiddo," he said to Patrick. "I thought I was being quiet."

"It's okay."

"Well, I was at it again." His father nodded, and wiped a shaky hand over his mouth. "I hope to Christ it never happens to you," he said, looking up at Patrick. "Wake up in some strange place, no idea how you got there."

Patrick never knew what he was supposed to say when his father talked to him about these. Sleepwalking. It gave him the creeps, like his dad was the walking dead, knocking around in the middle of the night with no idea he was even doing it.

"I fell out of bed once."

"Hey," his father said. "I guess that's far enough."

Broad shadows filled the room, swiping over the glossy family portraits and street market art, and the cracked glass curio that stored his mother's chintzy salt-and-pepper-shaker collection. Near the window, the unlit Christmas tree stood in the corner, a shadowy Sasquatch. In the dark of the room his father looked years older than he was, cheeks hollowed as he sucked on his cigarette, face glowing orange, his eyes glassy, strained, and starving.

"Twenty minutes ago I was all the way down on Fourth Avenue," he said. "Woke up standing right there on someone's lawn. Lucky I didn't get shot." He took another hit from his cigarette, held it in, then let it out slowly, controlled.

"This one time, I came to right in the middle of the loading dock, way the hell over at the shipyard on Twenty-Fourth. I was standing in the pouring down rain in my long johns and slippers and no shirt. Can you believe that?" He laughed. "I couldn't even find a way out that didn't mean climbing the fence. Don't ask me how the hell I got in there."

Patrick said nothing, and his father tapped the edge of his bowl. "You want some Corn Flakes?"

"What time is it?"

"Too late for a ten year-old to be up."

"I'm eleven."

Patrick padded in bare feet to the other side of the room, brushing against the tinseled branches to stand at the sweaty picture window that looked out over the street. Up and down the sidewalks the lawns were layered with frost, hard squares glowing blue under the high street lamp. The air was a thin mist, so close to snowing. Their driveway sat empty, a blanket of glitter.

"Where's Mom?"

His father cleared his throat and got up from the sofa, stepping long over the coffee table. He dropped to his hands and knees and began crawling over the carpet toward the tree, humming a tune deep in his throat as he went. At the tree's skirt he shoved packages aside, then moved further into the branches, fumbling with something in the far corner. Suddenly the tree was ablaze in lights, and the room was saturated with colors, winking a staccato of red and green and blue in the branches, along the walls, and across the sparkled popcorn ceiling.

"Come on down here," Patrick's father said, patting a space beside him. There was a sharp crackling of paper as his father made room for Patrick. Lying on his back, he dragged his body beneath the lowest ornaments. "Make like you're a present from Santa. One of them Misfit Toys."

Patrick looked out again to the empty driveway then turned back to the tree. His father still lay under it, unmoving. He lay there with his hands folded behind his head, and Patrick knew he would probably stay till daylight, whether there was the sound of a car driving up or not. He stared up into the lights, a sleepy grin drawn across his face. Patrick thought he looked like a toy himself, a life-sized puppet with his eyes blinking red and green, waiting for someone to push the button behind his ear to make him talk.

Patrick crouched to the floor, then slid on his stomach into the branches, the needles of the fir crawling over the bare skin on his neck. The ornaments tapped together as he brushed them, and he finally reached his father's side, curling against the flannel shirt. It smelled of cigarettes and sweet cologne.

Then his father said, "See the lights?"

Patrick rocked his head to the side and stared up through the branches. The colors went on forever, layered and hidden, some almost touching his face, others so far away they were almost invisible, entire strings disappearing and then suddenly appearing again. He relaxed his eyelids and let his vision blur, and he was drifting through a multicolored universe, farther than anyone had ever been before.

"Maybe we'll just drag our sleeping bags out here and camp under this tree, huh?" His father's chest rose and fell against Patrick's arm, a gentle rocking, and Patrick thought he could do that, just go to sleep right there, curled against this dad's musky old shirt.

Patrick said, "Where's mom at?"

His father sucked in a deep breath, then said, "She's out. She had her office party tonight."

"What time is it?"

His father's hand reached up and touched a glass ball just above Patrick's face. It was a white ball, with glitter stenciling stretched around it, of reindeer pulling a sleigh. It rotated slowly, catching red and green in its reflection as it went.

"This time next year, we're gonna have a tree twice as big," he said. "You, me and your mom, we'll go out in the woods and cut it down with our own hands."

"I never cut down a tree before."

"You're gonna do a lot of things you've never done before. Fish every weekend if you want. There's rivers and lakes everywhere, all of 'em full of trout or bass, or steelhead. You know, your grandpa took me up there when I was your age. This one summer, we spent a whole week camped out on the edge of the river, just pulling in fish one after the other, and hanging them up over the fire like they were laundry. Just reach over, pick em off the chain, pop 'em in your mouth."

Above his head, just out of reach, a teardrop ornament turned on its own. It was a small turn, so small that Patrick imagined his father didn't even see it. Some of the glitter and silver paint had been scratched clean, and he could make out a single white bulb hiding out on the other side.

"Over in An Khe," he said, "we'd all be deep in the bushes, with the bugs and God-knows-what all buzzing in my eyes and in my ears. You know what I'd do? Just put my head a thousand miles away. My M16, well that was a fishing rod. In my mind, I was sitting on the banks of the river, just waiting to drop my line in the fishing hole." He laughed softly. "I know it probably sounds stupid as hell, but it made a difference to me."

"It doesn't sound stupid," Patrick said.

"Everyone needs at least one good memory to go back to," he said. "Something to pull you through later on, when things get bad."

Patrick said, "I saw a cartoon once where a guy sleepwalked into a place where they were building a tower. Every time he almost walked off the building, this big beam would go in front of him, and catch him." Patrick reached up and brushed his hand against a fall of tinsel. "I don't remember how it ended."

"That's only a cartoon."

"Still. You could wake up way out in the middle of the woods. You might get ate by a bear. We'll have to build a fence around the house."

His father laughed. "No way. Do that, and all I'll be thinking when I go to sleep is how much I want to get out. Just get me the hell out of this city. Open up that sky and bring out the stars, man. Even your mom agrees with that. And you know she's always the smartest one in the room."

A wave of white light came through the window and washed over the wall, followed by the slam of a car door. Patrick lay still under the tree, his father beside him, both of them staring up through the branches toward the front door. There was the sound of feet pounding the steps and the jingling of keys.

His father said, "Speak of the devil."

The door rattled and creaked open, and his mother slipped inside.

"Well, look at this." Her voice was dry and smoky. "This is

almost the weirdest thing I've seen tonight."

"We were just enjoying the lights," Ernie said.

"You should come down here, Mom." Patrick rolled to his side and stared at the cuffs of his mother's white pants. They were frayed and spotted with mud, and they brushed the laces of her blue-striped sneakers.

"Scoot on out from under there and get yourself back to bed."

She walked over to the coffee table and took his father's coffee mug in her hand and brought it to her nose.

Patrick slid from under the tree and stood up. His mother put a hand to his forehead, and smoothed his hair from his eyes.

"Everything okay, honey?"

"Yeah," he said. "I woke up and Dad was here. We were just talking."

"Well you go on to bed. It's my turn to talk to Dad."

Patrick walked the long hallway to his room and closed the door behind him. He quickly slid under the blankets, which now were ice cold through his pajamas. His parents' voices hummed on the other side of the door, words coming in and out. *Tired. Gone all night. Like an idiot. That boy.*

Outside his window, over the peak of their neighbor's gabled roof and the bead of red lights, the sky had begun to bruise.

At the end of the day, Patrick stood at the mouth of the Quonset with his bicycle leaning against his body, the frame bleeding cold into his legs. He watched Tin climb the paint-splashed stepladder to the low shed roof, a can of tar patch swinging in his hand. It was all of about eight steps to the edge. It was an easy pitch and even a person as old as Tin Dorsay could heave himself up and over the top rung, and crawl onto the roof without much trouble.

Patrick pushed his bike across the patchy ground to a spot under the eaves, where Tin knelt above, slapping black glue over a buckled seam. The light was going, but there was enough white sun still hovering over the west mountain to send long pencil tree shadows running up the barn sides. Now and then, Tin scraped at the composite with his putty knife, lobbing clods of moss over the edge onto the ground.

"I'm all done." Patrick kicked at the green puffs.

"You put the buckets away?"

"Yeah."

"The right way this time?"

"Yeah." Now would begin the twenty thousand questions before Patrick would be allowed to go.

"Cause last time you stuck 'em inside the door, and I tripped and near about broke my neck." Another chunk of moss tumbled from above. "You check the cages good?"

"Three times." There was the sound of the brush licking the roof again. He wanted his pay for the week. But Tin would not be fishing cash from his pocket now, not when he was stuck on the roof, wrist deep in tar.

"So anyway," he said. "I can come back out tomorrow, if you want. For pay and all."

"Hang on and I'll get it for you." There was the sound of dragging, and Tin brought himself to the edge of the roof where Patrick could see him clearly. He had black streaks to his forearm. He wiped his hands down the front of his overalls.

"There's a bunch of change in the console of the truck. Count yourself out some quarters and let me know what you got."

"It's okay."

"No. You did good work. You're due your pay."

Good work. Those were two words Patrick hadn't heard in a long, long time. Through all the sickening feed and the shit, and the scatter of tiny scabs over his arms from frayed mesh, all he ever heard from Tin was bellyaching. But all that was gone, if only for the moment. Patrick turned his handlebars and started toward the pickup.

"Hold up a minute," Tin said. "I wanna talk to you about something."

Patrick pressed down on the seat of his bicycle. The tires sprung under his weight, squeezing mud from underneath. The old man reached up and scratched at his nose, leaving a black smudge.

"The thing is," he said, "pelting time is in a couple weeks. If you're up to it, I could use your help. I'd pay you good. If you're up to it."

"To kill the minks?"

"Kill 'em. Jesus Christ, kid, you make it sound like I'm Jack the goddamned Ripper." His eyes swung under a folded brow. "I ain't asking you to kill em. I got a guy with a truck for that. All you gotta do is bring the cages to the guy. When it's done, if you help out with the processing and whatnot, well, that'd be good."

"All of them?"

"No, not all of em. Just the ones that are good enough for fur. The rest I hold onto, wait till spring. Let 'em shack up for awhile and how-dee-do, pretty soon we got us some babies." He winked at Patrick. "Naw, I just need you to help bring 'em to the guy, and that's it. It don't take long. There's a system. I got plenty of other things for you to do." He looked over Patrick's face, then turned back to his work. "If you don't wanna do it," he said, "I can get someone else."

Patrick bit down on his lip. A light tickle rattled his throat, the realization that the time had finally come, that moment when—for some of them, anyway—the feedings and the pacing and the box scraping would be done. He hadn't thought Tin would ask him to take part in the killing, even though there was no reason that he shouldn't ask. The old man needed his help. He *needed* him.

"Can I think about it?"

"Of course you can think about it. Just don't think about it too long."

He swung a leg over his bike and settled himself on the pear seat. The old man's face shrunk together as he grinned, his lower jaw reaching all the way up to his ears. A balloon grew in Patrick's chest with a lightness that wanted to lift him from the ground.

He made it to the base of the hill then stopped himself with his feet in the gravel. He cranked the handlebars, turned around, and pointed himself back toward the shed.

"Hey Tin!" he called out.

"Hey what?" He craned his neck in a labored attempt to see over his shoulder.

"How come you never got married?"

"Who the hell says I didn't?"

Patrick gave a single pump on the pedal, coasting to the shed. "So you did."

Tin turned back and continued slapping tar. "Jesus no."

"Ever get close?"

"Depends on what you mean by close." He held both hands over his head, palms facing one another. Slowly, he brought them together, bringing them to a stop about three inches apart. "I had a pretty little gal," he said, dropping his hands, "used to cook up at my brother-in-law's logging camp. She stayed on with me for a couple years."

"What happened?"

"Oh, it got so she hated the rain. I told her she was in the wrong place for that. Last I heard she went off to Texas."

"Texas?"

"Can you believe it? You gotta hate something pretty bad to end up in Texas."

Patrick rode the hill to the River Road standing up all the way, legs pumping like pistons. And the balloon swelled so that it might bust open. He would do it. He'd show up and be a man, get right in there with all the other guys and do whatever he had to do. Skin them, haul the bodies away, he didn't know. However hard it might be, he would stand up and do it. His mind stormed like this all the way up the drive. He reached the roadway, slipped through the gate and around the posts, brushing against the stripped salmonberry bushes. He had once seen a deer, skinned, hanging from the garage rafters of a friend's house. It had been upside down, its body pink and shiny in the naked glare of the nearby trouble light. A swarm of flies had moshed all over its eyes and mouth. It would probably be the same with the minks, only smaller. Everything would be smaller. It wasn't a big deal, to kill an animal. As long as it was quick and it was for something important. Tin needed the money. He'd raised them up. Fed them and watered them. They were his, and he could do whatever he wanted with them.

The lights from town rose into the darkening sky, a white haze reaching above the jagged ridgeline of the forest. Patrick pedaled hard, his knees bucking all the way to his chest, the quarters weighing down his pocket, five dollars and fifty cents' worth, tugging at the beltline of his jeans as he rode. He zipped along the middle of the empty road, zigzagging among the yellow dashes, working the looped handlebars back and forth like a pro. A rooster tail of water lashed a stripe up his back as he raced into town. It was Friday night, and he owned the street.

The payphone outside Rexall Drugs was at the far edge of the building, as far from the front door as you could get without being in the parking lot. He leaned his bike against the shingled wall and searched with numb fingers for the coin slot. The fluorescent rod hummed and flickered above the phone, erratic and hardly useful as he carefully punched out the eleven digit number.

It rang in his ear. Once, twice…five times before it was picked up.

"Who this?"

"Mama T? It's me, Spooky."

"Spooky? Well hey there little man. It sure is good to hear your voice." Mama T's voice was soft and warm as velvet, rolling out from way down in her throat, just like always. "How're things up there in Ash Falls? Got snow yet?"

"No. I wanted to surprise you by calling with my own money

for once."

"Well, it sure is a surprise."

Patrick held onto his words, the cold earpiece pressing against his skin. The parking lot was a patchwork of tiny lakes, each reflecting the blooming night sky back at itself. His breath came like puffs of smoke, fogging over the metal telephone receiver. A hundred miles away, Mama T's own breathing was a warm wind through trees.

"I'm doing good," Patrick said. "I have to help kill the minks in a few weeks."

"Well. That's a ugly thought."

"It's okay, it's part of the job." He ran his fingers up and down the ribbed metal cord. "Is Shadow there?"

There was a pause, then Mama T said, "No honey. Shadow ain't been here for a couple weeks, now."

The words pulled at his insides. He wanted to slide down into his haunches, but the phone wouldn't reach that far down.

"Do you know where he is?"

"No, honey." She clicked her tongue. "You know don't nobody stick around Mama T's for too long. But I reckon he'll be on my stoop any day now. Shadow's just like his name. Here one minute, gone the next."

A bank of lights panned over the wall, and the sound of rusty springs and thumping bass stirred up Mama T's words. Behind him, the rumble of an engine cut short and a door groaned open.

"Don't tell me what to buy with my own money, bitch."

The door slammed. Patrick turned around. Eugene Henry leaned against the primer-splotched fender of his sedan, baseball cap tilted over his eyes, one thick leg crossed over the other. He held his wallet at his belt buckle and worked the open flap with his meaty fingers, tight 501s worn pale in certain places, cuffs bunched over the laces of mud-caked boots. Behind him, in a near silhouette, sat Marcelle, in the passenger seat. She stared straight ahead.

"What the fuck are you looking at?"

Patrick brought his eyes back to the car. Eugene slipped his wallet into his back pocket, cupped a hand over the full pouch of his crotch and squeezed.

"You see something you want, boy?"

Patrick turned his back to the car. "I better go Mama T," he said. "Love you."

"Yeah," Eugene called out. "You better turn away. You wouldn't know what to do with this monster anyway." He laughed, deep and gravelly.

"Love you too, baby." Mama T. kissed him through the phone. "You know my door's open anytime. All you got to do is be clear-headed when you here, okay? Them's the rules."

"Yes, ma'am."

He said goodbye, and placed the phone back on the receiver. From the corner of his eye, he watched Eugene pass through the front door. He turned around and saw that Marcelle had turned on the dome light. She was leaning forward, close to the rearview, smoothing her fingers over the skin beneath her eye. Her hair was longer since the last time he'd seen her. It was swept back from her head in big curls and fell down her neck onto her shoulders. And she was chubby in the face, her cheeks like soft, fleshy apples under those busy fingers.

He pulled his bicycle from the wall and mounted it, taking his time as he fussed with his bag and the handlebars, turning the pedals so they were just right under his sneakers. He moved the bike from the payphone out into the glare of the big Rexall sign, keeping his eyes on the front seat of Eugene's car. He worked the gears as he rocked back and forth on the seat, rolling forward a few feet to watch the chain shift over. Finally, Marcelle looked from the mirror and out the window at Patrick. She froze in position for a moment, then reached up snapped off the light.

Patrick gave the pedal a single pump and coasted around the trunk to the passenger window where he waited. The glass reflected a ghostly image of himself, a goofy kid whose hair was dirty and too long, strung back in ropes from his zit-pocked forehead, staring stupidly into the cab.

The window slid down a few inches. Marcelle was leaned back in the seat, her face turned only slightly, looking at him through the sliver of space.

"Hey," he said.

"What are you doing?" she asked.

"Just using the phone."

"Why don't you use the one at your house?"

Patrick said with a stumbled laugh, "You know why."

"Oh," she said. "So you're still sneaking off to see that Shade guy."

"Shadow." He rubbed his thumb over the reflective tape on the handlebars. It was already layered with moisture from the dropping clouds. "But no. He took off."

"Took off?"

"Yeah."

He wouldn't say it, not in a million years. But more than anything he wished they could be somewhere alone, just the two of them, him and Marcelle. Marcelle Foster, not Marcelle Henry. He wished she would put her arm around his shoulder, hold onto him and tell him it would all be okay, like she used to do. He wanted to say to her that it was like someone was pinching his throat with their fingers, squeezing so tight that it felt like he might never talk again. He wanted to lay his head down on her warm lap and feel her polished nails comb through his hair, and hear her say that she would always be his friend, forever, that it would always be the two of them no matter what. And maybe then the claws grabbing at his neck would finally go away.

"It's probably good, you know." She was looking at him straight on through the window now. He could see, even in the dim light of the cab, the dark smudge under her eye.

"There's people getting sick all the time, Patrick," she said. "I see on the news, they look like skeletons. It's awful. That church is closing down, too. But you probably already know that."

"It's not a church."

"A club. Whatever. Used to be a church. You know what I mean. You have to be careful, Patrick. You don't know if Shadow has it or not." She looked to the front of the drugstore. "Just don't be stupid, okay?"

"So how's married life treating you?" he said.

She shifted in her seat and looked at the rearview again. "He's gonna come out any minute," she said. "You oughta go. He's been in a nasty temper since he heard about your dad getting out. Waking up in the middle of the night, yelling out Ricky This, Ricky That. Cussing and snapping at everyone for no reason."

It was an explosion in the pit of his stomach. It raced like fire up through his chest and down his arms, burning hot in the tips of his fingers. He looked up at the Rexall sign, then over his shoulder, down the street. There were two cars idling at the traffic light, farting clouds of white smoke into the intersection. A station wagon with wood sides and a little convertible with a black ragtop. Convertibles didn't belong in Ash Falls, not in November.

"What do you mean my dad got out?"

Marcelle's face froze, a sickly white, her mouth held in a perfect O. The glass door to the store swung open and Eugene stomped out, a purse-sized paper bag at his side. He walked to the other side of the pickup, rattled his keys, and peered around the windshield at Patrick.

"Getting beauty tips, Luntz?" he said. "Wasting your time there." He wrenched open the door and climbed inside, tossing the bag onto Marcelle's lap. The engine cranked and immediately the air was sliced with the jagged assault of an electric guitar and the raw, high-pitched wail of some metal singer. The car shot back from the curb, its rear end swinging outward as Eugene spun the wheel. In the passenger seat, Marcelle's body rocked from side to side like a doll as the car swerved, stopped hard, then kicked forward again, roaring out of the parking lot out onto the highway toward town.

His bike was half a ton as he slogged along the sidewalk, and the storefront windows were dark as he watched his own reflection pass over them, a pathetic and wrung-out mink not even good enough to skin and throw into the pile. He lived in a town where not only did things remain the same, people were dead set on things staying firmly and forever in place. The Fotomat still showed the same portraits, pigtailed girls hugging ribboned dogs, men propping limp deer carcasses, dusty, faded remnants of some era prior to his moving there. Louella's Shear Genius Salon advertised women with hairstyles he'd seen on black-and-white sitcoms, piled high over pearl earrings. The half mannequins in Hinkle's loomed likes ghosts behind the darkened window, still dressed in last spring's polo shirts, washed out from two seasons crowding the storefront. The half-hearted effort that Mr. Hinkle had made by tossing in a few paper leaves and cardboard cornucopia barely forced the whole thing into Thanksgiving,

Patrick wanted out so badly it kept him up nights. His father was out, whatever "out" meant. A cage left open, somebody having failed to double check. Patrick knew his dad would need to be careful of trucks passing too close to the shoulder. He'd need a place to be sleep at night, someplace warm, and he'd have to take food from the garbage, or wait for unfinished pizzas to be put out behind the parlor. He would be coming back to Ash Falls. Somehow. And when he did, Patrick would be ready to say what he had to say.

He climbed back on his bike and turned hard from the sidewalk to the street, shifting up, working the gears with all his weight and picking up speed before hitting the open road leading out of town. And he cried out as loud as he could, a cry that cleaned him out, pushing until his throat hurt and the blood pulsed behind his eyes. The wind rushed his face as he rode, pulling the tears from his eyes and drawing icy lines to his temples, and wetting his hair before finally making warm pools in the pockets of his ears.

# Hank and Susanna
## (and Nels)

The sun had dropped behind the alder grove, and its hard light cut through the naked stands in stinging, white stripes. Hank peered from beneath the visor as he drove along the long, rutted drive. The countless potholes spotting the ground had already begun to frame themselves with thin, papery edges of ice. He passed right over them, sending arcs of mud over the flanks of bracken and sword fern, and then just as he reached the rotted stump with the lichen-choked springboard notches, he turned into her driveway. The gauntlet of overgrown Rhodies raked the sides of his truck as he went, their leaves curled under like cupped hands. Susanna's place was the last stop of the day.

In the clearing beside the Elcona singlewide, an old car was propped on stubbed posts of cinder block, its wheels stripped and stacked against the trailer. It was a '65 or '66 Rambler, or Valiant. Hank wasn't sure. At any rate, both the car, and the broad-backed, coveralled man bent over its open engine compartment, were not supposed to be there. The glow of a trouble lamp shook against the underside of the hood as the man's thick arms bucked back and forth.

Hank stopped and cut the engine, and the man pulled himself from the car's mouth. He turned to Hank and pulled a blue bandanna from his pocket, and rolled it casually around his bare hands.

Hank stepped from the pickup and stretched himself to his full height. He slid his Stihl cap onto his head and tucked his bag under his arm, pressing it tight against his body. The man took a few steps toward him and stuffed the rag into his pocket. Hank's toes curled inside his boots.

"You lost?" the man asked.

"I'm here for Susanna. She's expecting me."

"You the caseworker?"

Hank slipped his hand into his denim jacket and took hold of his car keys and ran his callused finger over the notches. The man's lower lip hung heavy, showing a cobbled assortment of horsey teeth.

"Oh I know," he said. "You're that guy from up on the mountain. The old teacher."

A sudden heat bloomed from Hank's chest to his shoulders, then raced down his back. He felt his face flush, and his mouth turn to chalk. He glanced over to his pickup truck, then back to the guy. Susanna hadn't said a goddamned thing about a boyfriend or anyone else being here.

"I'll just go on in." Hank intended to add kick to his words. But the sound was weak, a tremorous ribbon that fluttered limply to the ground.

"Fine by me." The man thumbed at the trailer. "She oughta be up."

Hank stepped from his truck, keeping the man in his sights. The bulky figure stood guard, hands kneading the blue rag, monitoring Hank as he climbed the mud-slicked steps. Hank slipped his hand from his pocket and pounded at the cold aluminum door. Immediately there was a shout for him to come in. He held the doorknob and breathed in the crisp, clean evening air, letting it fill his lungs and soak into his head. He closed his eyes and drew his concentration to the surrounding forest and its understory, the hanging mosses and composting leaves and dried out cedar springs that blanketed the floor. And only when he felt like he could carry those things with him, did he turn the knob and step through the door.

Inside, the place was misery, a miasma of mildew and sweat and breath and cat shit, and overripe fruit, all forced into a tepid swirl by the blast of a growling furnace. What had been stacks of clutter on his previous visit were now towers, precarious columns of boxes and magazines, and wadded clothing. Reams of loose, useless papers and unopened mail blanketed every desktop and shelf and window ledge in drifts of specked white. At the same time there was the nauseating sensation of airborne algae clinging to Hank's skin, as if he was swimming into the depths of an untended fishbowl.

Susanna was poured into an orange recliner against the far wall, her body a rolling landscape wrapped in paisley. She sat beneath the umbrella of a floor lamp, working a jigsaw puzzle off the surface of a TV tray that straddled her full lap. She studied the scene like a giant owl, eyes darting about, chin swollen and taut, her thin, graying hair swept back clean over her head.

He slid a chair from the kitchen table. A tabby hissed and launched itself from the seat before scurrying behind a column of trussed newspaper bundles. Hank came to Susanna and set his bag next to the chair. He could feel a beating in his temples. He sat down and took a full breath of the thick, murky air, and found his fingers falling together in knots as he tried to work the zippers on the bag.

It was moments like these—when things came unexpected, when the money didn't match the promise, when caterwauling kids wandered from back bedrooms to paw at his things and ask nosy questions, or strangers suddenly showed up from nowhere—moments like these Hank found himself wondering what the hell turn he had taken in life to end up where he was. In a moist tin box dense with the smell of cat piss, choked with water-spotted furniture, shoeboxes coughing out forests of paper, and flaccid houseplants that looked the way he felt.

"How are things?" he asked.

"Okay, I guess." She picked up a small puzzle piece and pressed it to the tray then retrieved it, returning it to its original spot. The orange tabby reappeared from the kitchen and sauntered over to lie at her spongy ankles.

"Tough time for some folks," he said. "All this rain, and now the frost. Hard on the bones."

"Well I don't like to complain." The woman lifted the tray and set it aside. "I hate this puzzle. Just a bunch of jelly beans. It's too hard."

Hank unpacked his bag and laid an array of jars at his feet. He had a system, very specific and regimented. It was a bit of irony he hated admitting. Lyla had been made almost crazy with her own systems when they were children. Her chest of drawers and crayons and paints, and their shared toys and board games. She could be obsessive, demanding that they be organized by hues, or by name, alphabetically, to the point of little blue veins rising from her neck. Hank had loved that he could drive her to tears simply by refusing to follow her dictate, or by sneaking in after the fact to move things around. And now, here he was.

He took Susanna through the various selections he'd brought, casting recommendations for her complex, ever-shifting needs.

"This right here is a good one for the morning," he said, resting a Mason jar on his knee. He turned it over in his hand as if it was a laboratory specimen. "For getting out of bed. Stiff joints. Sore muscles."

She leaned over her lap and snatched a jar from the floor, then sprang back up, holding it to her face. Her eyes narrowed, her lips drawn to a rosebud.

"What's a Cinderella?"

Hank took it from her and returned it to his feet. "That one's candy," he said. "Goofy. Not an everyday thing."

"What do you like?" She continued to reach for the jars herself, to tip the lids and shake the medicine, and put them all back in the wrong places. Hank reshuffled them and slid the bag closer to his feet.

"What I like has no bearing on what's best for you."

They moved pinches of medicine from jars to the scale, from the scale to bags. Money was transferred from purse to hand to envelope. Hank took out a pad and wrote down a few numbers and nothing more, and when the transaction was complete, and Hank had the medicine stowed neatly away in his bag, he breathed in the thick air, cupped his hands over his knees and leaned into her.

"Susanna," he said. "I don't want to make a big deal about this. But I need to be frank."

She looked up at him with her eyes that were always weepy and yellowed. A heavy mask of worry fell over her face. Hank had set her feelings on edge, as he had intended.

"That fellow outside," he said. "Who is he?"

"Nels. He's my brother."

"Well, your brother Nels threw me for a real loop when I pulled up here. Asked me all kinds of questions. He even called me *the old teacher*. I just about turned around and drove on out of here."

The woman dipped her balloon chin to her chest and pushed out her lower lip.

"I'm sorry," she said. "He's only here a couple weeks, till he gets on his feet. He don't know why you're here. Probably he was curious is all. He ain't seen no regular people here."

"Regular people?"

She looked up at Hank, her eyes wide. Glassy droplets sagged from the lower folds. "You know," she said. "Nice-looking. Hardly no one ever comes around here. Just church people bringing food and puzzles and stuff. Them or my caseworker."

"He said *teacher*, Susanna. You didn't have to tell him that."

The woman rested her chin to her chest and wiped at her eyes. "I'm sorry, Hank. It's okay if you don't want to come back, but can I get a little bit more? To hold me over till I find someone else? I'll give you a check but you gotta hold it—"

Hank put up his hand. "Susanna just calm down. I never said I wouldn't come back. But I don't want Nels or anyone else here when I come. Don't talk about me, don't talk about the medicine, not to anyone. Those are the rules."

"But Nels—"

"I don't care. If he asks, you tell him it's none of his business. This is your place and you can do that. Okay?"

"Okay, Hank." Susanna heaved herself from her chair and took hold of a four-pronged cane that lay propped against the wall. With tiny steps, each one seeming like it was planned out days before, she moved slowly past Hank to the refrigerator. She swung the door wide and began to knock through the shelves.

"Want something to eat?" she asked. "I got some leftover casserole, or I can cook some eggs if you want. I was gonna make supper for me and Nels anyway."

"The roads are icing over," Hank said. He slid the chair back into the kitchen and traversed the wide path through piles of plastic bags and wadded clothing to the front door.

Nels leaned against the front bumper of the car, holding a carburetor in his hand, digging at it with a screwdriver. He looked up as Hank closed the door behind him without saying a word. The sound of metal picking metal cut the air.

Hank climbed in the cab and fired up his engine. Nels came sauntering over. Hank pretended not to notice, but the dull rap on the glass gave him no choice but to roll down the window.

"All good?" Nels' lip hung like a cut of raw liver.

"Fine," Hank said. He squeezed the steering wheel, cold under his knuckles. "What can I do for you?"

When the man leaned into the cab, Hank pressed himself against the seat and reached over to take hold of the stick shift. If he were to punch the gas, there might be enough time for Nels to pull back. He might be able to pull back in time to keep from leaving his head behind in Hank's truck.

"You hear that?" Nels said.

"Hear what?"

Nels cupped his hand to his ear and tilted his head. He waited a few seconds, staring intently at the dashboard. All of a sudden he snapped his thumb and forefinger into a pistol. "There," he said. "Hear it? Like a little mouse squeak."

Hank listened and sure enough, about thirty seconds later, he heard a squeal, high-pitched, barely perceptible. If it hadn't been pointed out to him, he'd likely have never noticed it.

"Well how about that."

"Better have your belts checked," he said, pulling his head back out into the evening. "Be a bitch if one of 'em snapped between here and your house. Be stranded up there. That's how bears and cougars get fed." He winked.

Hank forced a smile then watched Nels amble back to the Rambler or Valiant, his lumpy hand slapping against his thigh in some nonsensical rhythm. The heat began to spill from the vents over Hank's hands, and the blood slowly returned to his fingers.

It was well past supper by the time he came into town. The parking lot of the AM/PM was already swarming with high school kids, their cars polished, trunks raised with stands of teenagers passing cigarettes and bags of chips back and forth. Hank recognized Tom Cowan at the pump island, lurking behind the rear fender of his car. He was holding the pump nozzle at his crotch as if he was pissing in his tank, watching the kids, probably deciding whether or not he wanted them to notice he was there. Teachers did that all the time—skated between being cool when encountering students outside of the classroom, and staying completely invisible until Monday forced itself upon them again.

This had once been Potter's Bog, and longtime locals still referred to it as such. Potter's Bog had been his and Lyla's playground, the site of post-Sunday-school searches for the fat frogs that dwelled among tall, downy cattails and sedge grass. Always, they were searching for the evasive. Lyla at his side, ever hopeful, confident that Hank knew best, even when he didn't.

At the base of the lit sign, a teenaged girl sat with her head in her hands. Another knelt at her side, hair ratted out like a halo, staring dreamily at the sky while she rubbed a hand over her friend's back. None of these people—Tom Cowan included—had the foggiest idea what lay beneath them. Thousands of tadpoles listening for spring, for the moment when that beam of sunlight would finally break through the asphalt and set them free from their slumber.

He turned off past the minimart, taking the side streets beyond the charred remnants of Mick's Laundromat, and the Tanner Mill cottages, where all the old timers, the lumberjacks and blacksmiths sat alone in their kitchen nooks, drinking whiskey and Metamucil, waiting for the last shift whistle to blow. He backtracked from Main Street so that he could wind through the cul-de-sacs littered with hockey sticks and basketballs and toys that, once upon a time, might have been made not of cheap Japanese plastic, but of American-forged metal and hewn wood. This is where the Henderson's buffalo farms once stood, where young boys separated barbed wire with bare hands, slipping through to run wild among the bison, whooping war cries and racing for the safety of giant, craggy maple trunks. He cut east, over to the power transfer station, with its humming castle-like glass spires, the subject of routine city council meeting diatribes, doomsday prophesies of twenty different kinds of cancer, certain to come. He rolled down his window, pushed out a whole afternoon's worth of pent up gas, then drove on back to where he'd begun, finally spilling back out onto the highway just at the center of town.

The vacancy sign out front of the Sleep Inn Motel flickered red, the reader board advertising free HBO and coffee for $29.99. Beneath it, a woman bounced on tennis shoes, pinching her ballooned parka to her chin with one hand. The other hand was stretched out from her like a fishing pole, thumb wiggling away at the end. Even in the pink glow of the motel signs, Hank could see she was no teenager, in spite of the bounce and the too-tight blue jeans, and the little Kewpie doll ponytail that sprouted from the top of her head. It was already nighttime, and it was cold.

He pulled to the shoulder and reached across, unlatching the door.

"Where you headed?"

"Home. Up the highway a ways, but I'll ride as far as you can take me." She leaned into the open cab. Her face was gaunt and pockmarked in the hollows of her cheeks. She reached her hands up to her mouth and blew on them.

"Just got off work." She nodded back to the motel.

"You work for Melvin?" Hank waved her in. "Hell. You deserve a ride home."

She climbed in and drew the seatbelt over her lap, then stretched her hands over the defroster vent to catch the warm air. "I sure appreciate this," she said. "It's so damn cold out there I thought my fingers were gonna fall off." She kept her teeth together when she talked, and Hank thought it was an odd thing, but perhaps it was because of the chill.

He said, "My place is just past the big clear cut."

She said, "Just a little bit on this side of me. I'm up at North Fork Road."

More than a little bit, Hank thought to himself. The North Fork was a good eight miles past his gate. He hesitated, and she said, "I can give you a couple bucks for gas."

Hank settled back in his seat and worked the pedals. "That's not called for," he said. He let out the clutch too fast, and the pickup leapt from the shoulder out onto the roadway. She grabbed hold of the dashboard, her fingernails scraping the metal.

"Sorry about that," he said. "This new clutch still has me a little whipped."

He tapped his boot to the highbeams and opened up the throttle. In minutes, they were climbing the mountain, heading into thick clouds of feathery hemlock and red cedar boughs. His lights panned the blacktop, reflecting the oncoming road delineators. Every hundred yards or so a mouse or a vole would appear from the shoulder and dart into his path. Sometimes it would make it to the other side, sometimes not.

She laughed. "That is some crazy shit."

"What's that?"

"These little guys. The mice. They got all night to cross over. But the second a car comes and the headlights hit the road— Bam. Off they go."

Another one darted from the shrubs, scurrying over the roadway. It halted for a second, backtracked, then took off for the opposite side again. Hank drove straight over it, a faint tick under his tires.

"See?" she said. "I just don't get it."

"Well," Hank said. "They're in a panic. They're in the bushes; they can't see a damned thing. They think something's coming. They sense the light. It terrifies them. Since they don't know which way is up, they run out in the open, where it looks the safest."

"Well, looks can be deceiving."

Hank smiled and said, "Yes, they can be." He turned the heater down a notch and adjusted the rearview mirror. From the edge of his sight, he could see her staring at him. He looked over, and she raised her eyebrows.

"You don't remember me, do you?" she said. She leaned her back against the window and grinned at him through sugar cube teeth. "Roxanne Dugard. Ash Falls, class of '64."

Hank slid closer to his door. This kind of thing happened too often, an out of the blue recognition, some student's mother or father, and him never knowing if there was a statement of appreciation coming or an ass-chewing for a failing grade.

"Give me a minute," he said. "How were you so sure it was me?"

"I wouldn't have gotten in your truck if I wasn't. Well, probably not, anyway." She took out a pack of Winstons and tapped them against the palm of her hand. "Care if I smoke? I'll crack the window."

She punched in the cigarette lighter and slid one from the pack. "It's okay if you don't remember me. It was a long time ago." She rubbed at the crease between her eyes, seemingly deep in thought. "Be twenty years," she said. "Jesus. You gave me and Doreen Finkbeiner after-school detention for calling that Chinese girl a gook." The lighter popped out, and she retrieved it, and pressed it to the tip of her cigarette. Her cheeks collapsed, and her skeletal face disappeared behind a veil of smoke.

"It's probably good you don't remember," she said. "Otherwise you'd have never stopped." She leaned her hand to the window and held the cherry near the opening. "You probably would've run my ass over instead. I was kind of a bitch back then."

"Well, it looks like you turned out fine. Whatever the outcome of the detention was."

"Yeah," she laughed. Her teeth pressed together when she did this. "We never showed up." She nodded and took another drag from her smoke. "But I am doing okay, all things considered. Got a boyfriend. He's in treatment right now, but he's supposed to be done in a couple weeks. We got a decent place by the river. I'm working steady there at the Sleep Inn. It's a shit job, but it's work, and these days that counts for something."

"Yes it does."

It figures, Hank thought. Bounce this girl from the classroom twenty years ago and she winds up right back in his stead, mouth running all over his cab like a busted faucet. He turned up the radio, and when the slow tide of slide guitar rolled from the speakers he asked her if she liked country or if she wanted to hear something else.

"You know," she said. "I always wondered about something. I wanna ask you, but you gotta promise you won't get all mad and throw me out."

"I promise not to throw you out, but that's it. What do you want to ask me?"

She took a deep drag and blew it from the side of her mouth, out the window. "I just always wondered what the deal was with you and that nurse."

Hank lifted his arm to take a look at the speedometer. He gave the gas a little more weight.

She said, "I got a little cousin, well, he ain't so little anymore. His name's Cal. Anyway, Cal used to run with Eugene Henry back in the day, who I know is your nephew. It was always the story from Eugene that you and that nurse were having this heavy thing. And he said that when this gal's husband found out about it, he went crazy. And that's why all that shit went down at the fairgrounds."

"Eugene told you all this?"

"Not personally, no. I said my little cousin used to run with him. But then I asked Eugene's wife Marcelle, who works with me at the motel, and she said that wasn't it at all. She told me that Eugene said it was about that kid of theirs, that Ricky said something to him, or about him. And the dad, he just snapped like a rubber band."

Hank turned down the radio. "She said it was about Patrick?"

"Well, she said that, but I wouldn't take it as gospel. Marcelle, she's her own piece or work, but that's a conversation for another time. Anyway, it just always had me wondering is all."

"Yeah, well there's a lot of things in this world that don't make sense," Hank said. His voice began to tremor and he held it in place before speaking again. "Like the fact that the people in this damned town have to pick apart every goddamned detail until it looks like someone threw a hand grenade into it. Just leave things the hell alone, I say."

Roxanne shook her head and sucked another drag from her cigarette, then flicked the remaining stub out the window. She blew out, the silver train sucked through the gap.

"Don't have an aneurism over it," she said, cranking the window closed. "That was a big deal, and don't pretend that it wasn't.

Lots of people knew you, and they knew that lady, too. And Ricky. And hell, everybody and their mother knows that fucking Eugene Henry, and he was right there in the middle of it all. No, it was a huge deal. Still is, like it or not."

The highway opened up, where the asphalt runway reached uphill to Colby Ridge, the southern edge of the Weyerhaeuser seed boundary. This was the halfway point between Ash Falls and Hank's property. A pair of lights drifted down the slope toward him, the only other vehicle Hank had seen so far on the mountain. At the base of the ridge, the lights suddenly turned off the road, disappearing from view.

The base of Colby Ridge was where the old Granite Quarry service road switched back from the highway. In a few months, when spring arrived, this would be the spot to watch as cars braked without notice and turned in, never a signal to warn of the last minute decision. Convoys of pickups would snake in and out, kids stacked in the beds, howling like wolves and flashing ridiculous signs with their fingers, likely obscene. But now, here in November, with the pond frozen but too thin for skating, nobody went up there.

Roxanne drew the zipper down from her parka, and Hank looked over at the sound. She had turned in her seat to face him. She was wearing a loose smock beneath the jacket, and he could see the lacy pattern of her bra breaking through the fabric.

"You heard he's out, right?" Even as he heard his own voice it didn't make sense to Hank, that he should throw Bobbie out of the conversation only to replace her with Ernie. But it was the track his mind took, and he was stuck with it now. He looked back to the road and drummed his fingers on the steering wheel.

"Who? Not the crutch guy."

"Yeah, the crutch guy."

"No shit. When?"

"About a month ago."

"A whole month? That fucking Marcelle. She never said one

word to me about it." Roxanne shook her head and glared out the window. "See if I tell her another goddamned thing."

Hank said, "Well, everyone's on edge. Thinking he might come back."

She spit a puff of air from her lips. "Shit, he ain't coming back." She furrowed her brow and jerked her bony chin back. "You think not?"

"I know not. Come on. If the guy's got half a brain, he'll leave this whole corner of the country behind. Get his ass to L.A., or Mexico, or someplace like that."

When Hank's drive came into view, he knew something was wrong. The gleam of the metal gate that always peeked from the dogwood reach wasn't there. And there was a sense in his core, nothing he could explain if he were asked. A kind of pressure working from the center outward, holding heavy just behind his skin. As he got closer to his drive, he let off the gas pedal.

"That don't look good," he said. He pulled off the road and came to a stop at the entrance.

The gate was open, swung to the trees, its rusty chain hanging loose like entrails, tangled among the ferns. On the ground near the post lay a two-inch padlock, the bolt snapped clean in half.

He heaved a deep sigh and ran his hand over his face. He popped the gearshift to neutral and let off the clutch, then looked over to Roxanne.

"I ought to run you home first." He said this, but made no move to do so.

She was turned toward him, with her back against the door. Something about the way she looked weakened him, compressed his body, and drew his skin from his clothes. Perhaps she thought he was a coward, too afraid to face what lay at the end of the drive. Maybe she just wanted him to take a stand and make a decision.

He said, "You want me to take you home now?"

"I guess," she said. "I can stick around if you want, though. Make sure everything's okay."

"I don't want to put you at risk."

She shook her hair from her face and reached up, patting the stock of the rifle that was bolted to the rack over their heads. "Isn't that what this is for?" she said.

Hank considered that she smiled as she hooked her hand over the butt, not like it was something dangerous and unpredictable, but a tool she would and could use if she had to. That she had shot a gun before was a likely assumption, since she held onto that thing with a confidence unlike any he'd ever had. But what kind of a man was he to even suggest dragging a woman into his mess?

"To be honest," he said, "I'm reluctant to go down this drive. Guess that makes me something of a coward."

"No, it makes you normal. You want to turn back? We could go back into town. Or we could drive up to my place. You could call the sheriff from there."

"I'd just as soon not." He snapped on the dome light and took the rifle from behind her head. "Can you go in there and grab the cartridges?" he asked, nodding at the glove compartment.

She reached in without a word and took out a small box of Remingtons. It had been there for a year, unopened, and he took it from her, and the cardboard fought against his jittery fingers as he pulled one, then another shell from the tidy array, and he was painfully aware of his clumsiness in front of her. As he fumbled with them something caught his eye. He looked down the drive, at a small bit of movement caught in the beam of his headlights.

"That dog yours?" Roxanne said.

It was Toby. He paced frantically from shrub to shrub, ears flattened against his head, his tail tucked stiffly between his haunches. Toby had always been a porch greeter. Hank pushed the cartridge into the chamber and slid the bolt back. He swung open the door and gave a whistle. The dog's ears perked up, and he came running to the truck, leapt over Hank's legs onto the passenger side, and coiled himself on the floor at Roxanne's feet.

They rolled forward at a snail's pace, rifle lain across Hank's lap, the barrel nosed through the open window. Even in normal circumstances Hank felt a certain unease when coming upon his house at night. Headlights on a forested drive always brought out creatures that did and did not exist in his world. Naked salmonberry branches reached out from either side like giant blooms of electricity, while the fissured trunks of young hemlocks lurked ominously in the deep shadows of the understory. He pulled back from the trigger and worked the cramp out of his finger.

They came to a stop some yards from his house and took in the scene, bathed in yellow spotlight. Yard tools had been left on the porch, leaning against the shingles—his hard rake, the digging shovel, and the transfer shovel. A rotting pumpkin sat under the front window. His rattan chair faced the east. At the center of it all, his front door hung by a single hinge, blocking the doorway at a crippled angle. The frame was split, white alder shards poking out like splintered bones.

"Oh you got broke into all right," Roxanne said. "That's the shits. Rudy and I had two break-ins in the last year alone. But I guess that's the risk you take living in paradise."

They sat there, just the two of them, and the dog panting on the floor. Hank's window was down and the air was taut and cold and had that crystalline scent that comes only from water that spills from the mountain. Hank listened, straining to hear the noises beneath Toby's breathing, but there was nothing except the flow of the river and the occasional tumbling of a rock in the current.

"Doesn't look like anyone's here," he said.

"Probably not." She pulled on the door handle and the dome light blazed the cab. Dropping a foot to the running board she said, "Let's leave the headlights on till we get inside."

The walk from his pickup to his porch was a mile. Every rock dug through the soles of his boots, every whisper of wind through the understory raked over his nerves. He held the butt of the rifle against his hip and reached around through the open doorway to flip the lights.

The first thing to hit him was the mottled pool of agates, olivine, and quartz that were fanned across the floor. It was a kind of collection, these minerals that he'd collected along the riverbed, the only bit of silliness with which he indulged himself. The pickle jar that had housed them lay broken on the hardwood, shards reaching up like claws. Through to the kitchen he could see canisters, boxes, cupboard doors. Anything that could hold something was inverted or opened or emptied. Countertops were painted with a mixture of flour and sugar and cornmeal, washed over the edge onto the linoleum floor.

Hank kicked a path through sofa pillows and books and reams and reams of paper, and as he marched through the room, to the rear of the house, he couldn't make sense of the incredible amount of shit that had found its way from bookcases and desktops and side tables onto his floor. Open books, sharpened pencils and unopened envelopes covered the floor, while dozens of small twigs, cloaked in puffs of pale green moss, and shelf fungus, and crusted pine cones—things that had seemed just right on the shelves now looked as if they had been swept in by a heavy storm.

In the cramped space of the pantry, sauce jars and soup cans and cereal boxes littered the floor, a few broken but most lying peacefully against the cedar backboard that had been successfully jimmied from its place behind the dry foods.

His entire stock was gone, every last jar. It was a good three thousand dollars worth of medicine, maybe more, plus a couple grand in cash—several weeks worth of road trips and coffee table dealings. He tipped his forehead to the door, and his mind spun through a dozen possibilities, none of which had a chance of fixing this mess. It wasn't so much the money and the waiting clients, though they were immediate problems that definitely needed solving. It was the violation, the savage rape of his home. The only thing that kept him from putting his fist through the wall was the sheer weight of shame and disgust that glued his arms to his sides. He had been warned. They'd all been hit before, every single grower and dealer, city or county. But he had been above it all, pretending that his spot carved in the side of the mountain would keep him immune. But the truth was there was no way to do it, no way to build a fence strong enough, and he knew that. He kicked at the cedar panel, driving it into a pile of boxes.

"Everything okay back there?"

"It's fine," he said. "What are you doing?"

"Just cleaning up some."

"You don't have to do that," he called out.

"Busman's holiday," she said. "It's fine. Unless you want to keep it for the cops to look over."

Hank pulled the backboard from the rubble and reengaged it into the wall. He took the jars and cans and stacked them along the shelves, conveying a sense of normalcy. He kicked crescents of glass through mounds of rice.

"Maybe I'll call him later," Hank lied. "I just want to pull my head together first."

"You think it was the crutch guy?" She was picking the glass from the floor and stacking it in her hand. "Maybe I was wrong about him not coming back."

Hank put the last of the boxes on the shelves and pulled the chain for the bare bulb. He went to the kitchen, closing the pantry door behind him.

"No," he said. "It wasn't Ernie."

"How can you be so sure? Looks like whoever it was just wanted to tear shit up. Stereo's still here. Anything gone from back there?"

"No." Hank took the broom from behind the refrigerator. Roxanne came into the kitchen balancing a tower of broken glass in her hands. He slid the bin from the lower cabinet and held it as she dumped them the shards the trash.

"Nothing's missing? Not a single thing?"

"Everything's fine," he said.

She took the broom from him and began to sweep the dry ingredients from the floor. She snapped the dustpan from the handle and passed it off to Hank.

"I'm not trying to be a bitch," she said, "but it feels an awful lot like you're bullshitting me."

He squatted to the floor and held the pan against the mound of powder. She stared down at him, her lower teeth glistening down at him, her eyes narrowed accusingly. She pressed the broomstick to her shoulder. One edge of her mouth drew up in a fishhook.

Hank slid the pan to the powder, and she swept it in. He dumped it into the bin, went to the living room, and took up some books from the floor.

"You know," he said, "it wasn't as salacious as it sounds."

"What's that?"

"The word?"

"I know what Salacious means," she said. "What are you saying wasn't salacious?"

"The deal with Bobbie. The nurse. I mean, there was a thing, if you have to know." He handed her a few paperbacks. "I wouldn't say it was a big thing, but I guess we were careless, and it turned into a lot bigger thing than it should have. She's a good woman. She didn't deserve all the crap that came down afterward. Nobody did. Hell, not even that shithead nephew of mine deserved to have that happen to him."

Roxanne gathered the cushions from the floor, laying them in place on the sofa. She didn't say anything. She kept her back to him, positioning the seat cushions, fluffing the pillows and placing them gently at the edges. She picked up the woolen blanket from behind the sofa and spread it evenly over the back.

"I guess I just keep waiting for things to just move on," Hank said. "But maybe that's not even possible. Maybe there'll always be a big, goddamned black cloud over this mountain. It doesn't matter whether Ernie Luntz is loose or not."

"There's no gate keeping you or anyone else up here. All you got to do is get in your truck and drive. People walk around this town like a bunch of trapped animals, but the only ones trapping them are themselves."

"That's a mighty deep statement."

"Seems pretty obvious to me."

She stayed with him for a while longer before she let him take her home, until his house was put together well enough that the edges seemed smooth again. Hank kept up the conversation, steered the talk toward Roxanne's high school days, who her teachers were, what things she remembered from his class, until he could finally see the young girl in the third row, with the acne and braided hair and the sharp tongue that made him consider retirement twenty years before it was even possible. This once seventeen year-old girl, all grown up now and smarter than he'd expected, but still awkward and perhaps a little self-conscious, and certainly still too young to be standing in the kitchen of a dealer of marijuana, smoking cigarettes and playing at psychology.

## Lyla and Tin

In Lyla's memory, Henry Kelleher Sr. was a man who wore a frown more often than not, his mouth curled down hard at the edges, the brow constantly gouged with worry ruts. He was protective of his solitude, and Lyla liked to hide in the shadows to watch him in the pre-dawn lamp-lit kitchen as he simmered his pot of coffee over the wood stove, whispering the old Irish folk songs, *The Cliffs of Doneen* and *Lark in the Morn*. In those moments, she could often catch the faint lift of a smile.

He told Lyla and Hank stories of his own childhood in St. Paul, tales of schoolyard scuffles and ice fishing and of litters of kittens that seemed to appear in different corners of the house each time he told it. One night, when he had drunk too much whiskey, he told them of the frigid winter morning when he found his grandmother dead, slumped over in her own porch rocker. She was dressed only in a flannel nightgown and wool socks, and dusted from top to bottom with the thinnest layer of snow.

"You need to have plans," he said to them. "You don't want to end up alone, no one around to be there when you most need help."

"I got plans," Lyla told him, since she did. She had a clear idea to run away from Ash Falls the first chance she got. The world, she decided, was waiting for her.

He turned to Lyla. "I don't mean plans to go up and cook in the logging camps, either. So help me, if I ever catch you so much as breathing the same air as one of those lumbermen, it'll be the last breath you take."

"I'm not cooking for anyone," she said. "I'm gonna go to

France and make dresses, and eat in restaurants."

Hank laughed at her, and their father furrowed his brow at her and shook his head. "Don't mistake dreams for plans, Lyla," he said. "Dreams are what happen when your eyes are closed. You'd be smart to keep yours open."

It was almost 9:00 a.m. when Lyla pulled into The Sleep Inn parking lot with Marcelle seated beside her. There had been a hard rain the night before, some fir branches thrown down onto lawns and such. But the sun was out now, and the pavement had enough of a gleam in it that Lyla swatted down her visor.

"I might not be there when you get home," she said. "It'd be a good time for you to run a load of laundry."

Marcelle nodded and tugged at her dirty coat sleeves.

Lyla said, "I noticed Eugene's been wearing the same jeans the last three days."

"I know," Marcelle said, "He does that even when he's got clean ones." She didn't look at Lyla when she said this, but she thanked her for the ride then got out and walked quickstep to the motel office. The girl was getting bigger in the behind, Lyla observed. And everywhere else. There were men out there who liked that kind of thing. Maybe Marcelle would be better off with one of them.

The wet roadway hissed beneath her as she gunned the engine, gliding over River Road like she was floating downstream. As she approached Tin's gate she caught sight of movement on the inside of the fence, a streak of blue-gray that flashed along the chain link then disappeared into the underbrush. Another escapee, Lyla told herself. Tin was usually careful with the cages, but every now and then one didn't get latched right, and a pair of minks would break free and run for the hills. Most times he reclaimed them eventually; he had traps for situations like that. Still, it wasn't unusual to see a stray pop up in the surrounding woods, or worse, a stripe of fur on the pavement along River

Road, the remnants of one that had managed to dig out and run straight under the wheels of a passing car.

She descended the hill slowly, easing through the potholes and instinctively ducking as the low cedar boughs feathered over the car roof. Coming out into the familiar clearing, she brought the car to a stop just outside the first mink shed. Tin poked his head out and showed his gums in a broad grin. The grading cart was parked just outside the door.

"There you are," he called out. He held a thermos up in greeting, as if he might offer to share. "How's life this morning?"

"Oh, you know." She did up the front of her jacket. Actually, it was Jonas' jacket, a canvas thing that weighed heavy on her but it kept the warm in. "Just life." There was never a story to tell Tin that was any different than the one she'd told him before, and the thought of repeating any of it for him exhausted her. "Just life."

She took hold of the cart handle and pulled it into the shed behind her. Tin asked how Jonas was, and she said he was fine, and then he brought up the fur auction that was in a couple months' time. It'd be in Seattle again, as always, but he talked about it like it was brand new.

"There's gonna be folks there from all over the state, some from Idaho and Oregon, too," he said. "Last year a group of Chinese came with a shitload of black pelts. Drove the price way down for those poor sonsabitches that brought the same. I been talking to Bill Gallagher up in Deming and the guys at Coolie Farms down in Chehalis. Figure we'll get together and sell as one block, just in case them yellow bastards show up this year with what we got."

Lyla did her best to look like she was following him with interest, nodding at the right moments. But there was work to do, and more than anything she really just wanted to get going and be done with it.

They started at the northernmost cage. Tin took his handling gloves from his coat pocket and slid them on, like gauntlets.

Snapping open the cage door, he reached in and took hold of a fat mink. It squalled and squirmed in his hands, kicking its legs until he laid it down on the curved tabletop and pressed his palm onto the back of its head.

Mink grading, deciding which creatures would live to breed another season and which were destined to be skinned, was a process Lyla was plenty used to, but not one she ever cared for. She harbored no particular feelings toward the minks. How could she? They were nasty things, angry and vicious. And when it came to their smell, they were far worse than skunks. As far as she was concerned the only purpose for their existence was to line the collar of a coat, or lie draped over the shoulders of the type of woman Lyla would never know. Minks were no different than cows or chickens, things bred and fed by humans in order to fulfill their desires.

"I saw one up by the gate," she said as she slid her fingers along the mink's back.

"Yeah, I lost a pair a while ago," he said. "I got the male, but the female, she's a stubborn one."

"Sounds more smart than stubborn," she said.

"So smart she don't know what's best for her. Either way, it don't make no difference. If I don't catch her, something will."

The inevitability was certain, one way or the other. Still, there were times when Lyla would look directly into the face of one of them, and it would stare back at her with its stony eyes, and the sensation would grab her in the gut. The connection and the feeling that came with it were always unexpected. And in those moments Lyla found that she wished she could just disappear from the spot. Like in one of those science fiction movies, where one could just vanish into vapor and then—just like that—rematerialize somewhere else.

The fact was Tin needed her, pure and simple. She had always been good at mink grading, skilled at finding the subtle colors in the fur, the density of the undercoat, and spotting the smallest of imperfections—scars, a kidney spot, the tiniest cuts. She'd always lent her eyes when she was called upon, and now her uncle's own eyes were failing him, and he couldn't do this part at all without her. That kind of need was a glove over a cold hand, a wool blanket, different from the way Eugene or Jonas or even Marcelle needed her. Most of the time they were like children banging spoons on empty dinner plates.

"You seen your brother lately?" Tin asked her.

Lyla ran her fingers along the sides of the mink. "He was down getting his truck fixed. He got a haircut. I drove him home."

"I'm gonna give him a call here soon, to come lend a hand with the pelting. I suspect he's doing all right."

"He seems fine." Lyla wouldn't bring up the fight with Eugene. It wasn't important and besides, it wasn't really a fight. Tin always took Hank's side of things, anyway. "I think that nurse still has her hooks in him, though," she said. "Maybe not intentionally, but his head's still wrapped around her. I can tell."

Tin released the male back into the cage and latched it closed, then went right to the next one and pulled out a female. She tried to turn back on him, but he had a good hold of her, and he pressed her down over the curve of the table, holding her head with his palm. "She's a nice enough gal, from what I can tell. Nice looking."

Lyla stopped. "When did you ever meet her?"

"I seen her around plenty," he said. "Before. I only just met her the other day, though. Her boy cleans cages for me after school."

Bobbie Luntz's son was working every day for Tin, yet when Eugene was that boy's age, Tin wouldn't give more than piecemeal work. Lyla raked her fingers over the mink's back. The undercoat was thick and lush and completely unblemished, just as the male's had been. She'd been with a good mate; they'd been easy with each other. She pinched around the sides and nodded approval, and Tin slipped it back into the cage, and tied a tag onto the mesh.

"Is that Patrick?" she asked. "Stripe of bleach down his head?" She twirled her finger over her bangs.

"That's him." He reached into the next cage and pulled out the female, and laid her on the cart.

Lyla combed through the fur. This one was pretty small. "Marcelle told me they used to be close." She laughed, quietly. "I guess they had a falling out the minute she set her sights on Eugene." She stopped at a spot behind the mink's ear. "There's a cut here," she said, rubbing her finger in a circle. A scab the size of a water drop showed through. "Can you see it?"

Tin leaned in close, to where Lyla held her finger. "Goddamn it," he said. He put the mink back in her cage, took his pen and marked the tag and tied it to the mesh. He stopped and looked over to Lyla. His mouth was drawn into itself, the lower lip hugging his gums, his eyes almost glowering at her.

"What's the matter?" she asked.

He turned and crossed to the other side of the shed, taking the cart with him. "The kid's been through a lot, Lyla," he said. "Don't come down on him."

Lyla held her tongue. Because of Ernie Luntz, everyone in that town had been through a lot, some more than others. Hank. Eugene. And what about Ricky Cordero's family? She couldn't begin to imagine what it must have felt like when that phone call came for them, the voice on the other end telling them their son had been beaten to death. Half the town right there, and not a single person had stepped up to do a thing to stop it.

They pushed through the remaining cages amid small talk. Tin made mention of a coyote he'd shot on the property and the many dogs he and her father had as a boy. Dogs that stole chickens and dogs that chased cars, and dogs that crawled under the house to die. By the time they got through the last of the minks it was past one. The sun was breaking through the clouds overhead, and the honking of southbound geese echoed in the far distance.

"You hungry?" Tin offered. "I got a pot of stew on the stove."

"You know I'm never hungry after grading."

She followed him back to his office, an old travel trailer that had been in one place or another on that property for as long as Lyla could remember. When he swung open the door, the smell of beef and onions wafted out, a welcome change in spite of her lack of appetite.

The place was mostly tidy; Tin wasn't one to just leave things lying around whenever he was finished with them. Lyla stepped up to the sink and washed her hands in the tap, and took the sponge from the basin and wiped down the counter of the crumbs and spots of coffee and gravy and who knows what else. Tin sat down at the small table, pulled the calendar down from the wall and took a pair of Coke bottle glasses from his pocket.

"Busy week ahead of me, that's for sure," he said.

Lyla sat down across from him, took the stack of papers and envelopes from the edge of the table and thumbed through them. There were notices and junk mail, and bills both recent and over-due. She set the pink ones aside.

"You need to get on these, Uncle Tin," she said.

"I will."

"I mean it," she said. "Before you know it, you'll have no pow-er and no phone."

He kept his eyes to the calendar, running his fingers from one side of the page to the other. His jaw moved back and forth as if he was chewing gum, as if she hadn't said a thing to him.

"Never mind," she sighed, "I'll do it." She tucked the stack into her coat pocket and reached up into the overhead cabinet for his check ledger.

The river tumbled blue green, beyond the lichen-spotted sheds, continuing south to where it bent around the old maple whose muscled branch still reached out over the swimming hole. Tin's land stretched on fifty yards or so past the tree, and it was another quarter mile before the rapids would get too rough for a person to wade safely along the shore. Lyla remembered watching

Tin and her father and mother in that trailer, playing cards and laughing over beers late into the summer evenings while she and Hank dropped from the maple branch into the cold, blue water and ran up and down the riverbed, heaving rocks into the current.

Tin signed the blank check for Lyla and thanked her for taking the trouble, and she said it was no trouble, since she had to sit down and write out her own bills anyway.

"You need to stay on this though," she said, waving the check at him. One by one, the men in this family seemed to be bound and determined to avoid responsibility, and since there were no women beside them to manage these details, she was stuck doing it. "If you want me to take this over for you, I will. But you need to tell me."

Tin nodded and pinned the calendar back up on the wall, then got up and turned the propane burner on beneath the stew pot. Standing with his back to her, leaning into the stove, he was so much smaller than she remembered, his seat invisible in the sagging trousers, cuffs bunched over his shoes like he was a child dressed in his daddy's clothes.

"Are you coming for Thanksgiving this year?" she asked.

"Naw," he said, stirring the pot. "They're doing a thing at The Elks Club."

They were always doing a thing at The Elks Club. Lyla was fairly sure Tin never went to any of them. She had extended the invitation to him again, and she would do the same for Hank, just like she had every other year. And like every other year, neither of them would show. Always, with other plans.

She gave him a pat on his back, his spine like carved wood under his shirt. "I'll tell Jonas and Eugene you said hi," she said. She smiled and Tin looked back at her, grinned, and tapped his finger to his head. It was a thing the two of them shared, the gentle reminder that he hadn't asked about them at all, but that the intention was somewhere inside there, tangled up in a hundred other things more important at the moment. Lyla opened the door and took the steps down to the dirt. Tin held back at the door.

"They're both fine," she said, on impulse. "Jonas is working a lot. Holidays and all."

"How is it the bank gets busier at Thanksgiving?"

"I don't know. He says they just are. Maybe people need money to get out of town." It didn't make sense to her, either.

"And the boy?"

"Eugene? He's..." She stopped, paused to shape the words that seemed to be tumbling in her head like a Laundromat washing machine. "Him and Marcelle," she said. She looked down at her shoes. There was hardly any mud on them, even after walking through four sheds and an acre of waterlogged sod.

"Kids, huh?" he said. He stepped down and patted Lyla on the arm. "Thank Christ I never had any. But they'll grow up sooner or later. We all do."

"Yeah well, let's just pray for sooner over later."

"I don't want to stir up trouble," he said, "but can't that husband of yours have words with his boy?"

Lyla looked up at Tin. He filled the doorway to the trailer, his brow every bit as gouged as her father's ever was. She had tried to make plans long ago, plans that saw Eugene in college, or in the Army. He would be on his own and calling her and Jonas once a week to check in, sometimes coming by with his wife and babies just to watch television and even share in the Thanksgiving dinner she had worked all day on to get just right. But those plans just weren't working out as she'd hoped.

"Jonas?" she said. "He's spent hours talking to him; twenty-three years of talking. He's a good father, you know." She zipped up her jacket and slid her hands in the pockets. Jonas' pockets, lined with soft sheepskin that smothered her hands in warmth. "Eugene wasn't an easy boy to raise. Jonas was patient in ways that I could never even come close to being. He took him camping when he was little, tried to get him involved in scouts. They went deer hunting once."

She looked up at Tin, and he nodded, as if he remembered at least some of what Lyla was telling him. She said, "He could never really understand Eugene. They've always been so different from one another, the two of them. Anybody could see that."

Tin leaned against the doorjamb and ran a hand over his bald head. "I never said you was doing anything wrong," he said. "Hell, what do I know? Only thing I ever raised is them minks out there, and look how good things turn out for them in the end." He laughed and shook his head. "That boy was always tough on you and Jonas; we all knew that. Kind of like a wild animal. Stuck in a world with rules that just don't fit his nature."

"A wild animal? That's what you think?"

"You know what I mean. No matter how wide the boundary is around him, he's gonna try his damndest to push his way out. He knows it's there. Just the idea of a fence around him—no matter where it is—he won't abide it."

# Marcelle

Before she was Mrs. Eugene Henry, she was just plain Marcelle Ruth Foster, and she lay with her best friend Patrick on an open sleeping bag on the playfield behind the elementary school. It was way past midnight on a January school night, and they were almost sixteen, close enough to one another that she could feel the warmth of his body through her sleeves. They ate corn chips and stared at the stars, and talked about things that stood out in their minds at the given moment.

"Sandy Bates started crying in Home Ec today," Patrick said. "We had a test on hand stitching."

"When I did that, I sewed the scrap to my pant leg," Marcelle said. "Mrs. Kirkpatrick had to get on her knees so she could give me a grade."

She closed her eyes and ticked off numbers from one to ten, as he had instructed her to do. She meditated on the icy air freezing the insides of her nose, each breath sharp on the intake, forgiving with the slow exhale. But when she opened her eyes and looked from the moon to the Big Dipper, everything was the same as before.

"Are you sure it wasn't aspirin?" she asked.

"Just wait," he said.

The night on the playfield had been right at the beginning of Eugene, but nobody knew about the two of them just yet. She decided she would tell Patrick before the night was over. She would tell him, and then it would be out, and she would be legitimate.

"I'm gonna drop out of school," she said to Patrick. "This Friday is my last day."

"Don't be stupid," Patrick said. "Losers drop out."

"I'm not stupid," she said. "And I'm not a loser."

Patrick cleared his sinuses, rolled to one side and spit out into the grass. "How come Friday, anyway?"

"There's a pizza party in choir. And I already put in my five dollars."

She closed her eyes again and felt a tickle along the back of her neck, like tiny spiders crawling out of her hair. She didn't like it, but it didn't scare her. She shook her head and brushed her hand over her collar.

"Look at my breath." Patrick sat up, and a white cloud billowed from his lips. It shrunk together in a cottony cloud just over her head, tumbling and rolling, before finally breaking apart and dissipating in tiny silver pinwheels. Marcelle sat up and wrapped her arms around her knees. The security lamp stood over the school building, a sharp cone of light dropping from the bulb. It broke through the mist, settling in a milky pool over the graveled courtyard. There was a slight ripple of movement in the cone and then it bent at an angle. Slowly, the cone rippled and bent, until it began to dance from side to side, like the gown of a towering angel.

Patrick stood and turned a full circle, once, twice, his arms open wide. He moved away from the sleeping bag and lay down on his back, arm stretched out from his sides. He ran his hands over the grass, the blades white and stiff against his fingers as he moved slowly, back and forth, caressing the fur of a giant beast.

"Can you hear it?" Patrick smiled at the sky.

"Hear what?"

"The frost," he said. "It's whispering in poems."

Marcelle put her ear to the grass and strained to listen, but there was nothing. Nothing but the scratching of wind licking at her hair.

There had been only two left. This is what Patrick had told her that morning at school. They were the very last ones, and they would do them together. They would hold hands and listen to each other's breathing, and when they did this she would finally, finally understand him. She would be connected to him in the deepest way, inside his head, and she would see everything he had ever seen in his life. And then she would never have to ask again, and he wouldn't have to tell.

But things went sideways, and she never got to hold his hand. Patrick spent most of the night combing the expanse of frozen grass, and she went through the entire playground, piece by piece—the swing set, the merry-go-round, the climbing gym with its domed arches—all of them, speaking the names of Eugene and Marcelle into every single one. Because then no matter what happened, no matter how it all turned out, their names would be forever bonded to the atoms or molecules that made up the cold metal against her lips.

Marcelle was awakened by the scraping of chairs over linoleum, above her head. On weekdays, Jonas and Lyla Henry would get up early and eat breakfast together. Marcelle had seen them on occasion, having white toast, scrambled eggs, and black coffee. Every time. They'd be sitting on opposite sides of the small, gray Formica table in the old flower-wallpaper kitchen talking quietly, so quietly that Marcelle could only ever hear the clinking of forks on plates. When they finished Mrs. Henry would clear the plates and then they would leave together, Mr. Henry to his job at a bank in Lake Stevens and Mrs. Henry to volunteer in the church office, where she would stay until mid-morning most days. Once in awhile the slamming of the back door and the rattle of the window over his head woke Eugene an hour and a half before his alarm.

When this happened, he might give a jump then fall back to sleep. Sometimes he wrapped his arms around Marcelle and clung tightly to her as he dropped off. He'd squeeze and she'd squirm and struggle to put a little space in there. But he could be one of those constricting snakes, a python or a boa, holding on as if he was terrified of letting her loose. In the early days she liked this kind of thing. Him needing her. Almost a year later, she lay there counting the pocks on the wall and waiting for him to relax his grip and turn over, so she could slip from under the covers and go up to the kitchen for a bowl of cereal.

On this morning, Eugene coughed and jostled next to her, and then there was the tinny click of his lighter. Marcelle caught the sweet smell of butane and then came the thickness of smoke. She rolled over. He sat up, the blankets bunched at his waist, his cigarette pointing up from the hand he rested on his lap. His greasy blond hair stood up like he'd been smacked.

"I don't know why you do that," she said.

"Do what?"

"That." She nodded her chin at the smoke rising from his hand. "You're gonna make your mom mad."

"She's not here, is she?" He reached up and picked a flake of tobacco from his tongue. "You get paid yet?"

She ignored him and rolled onto her side. He kept talking, going on about the motel and how much she wasn't working, and she tried to focus on the sound of his voice, not the words themselves. Like chocolate. He was standing in the bank parking lot in a bright orange vest, stuffing paper and cans into a plastic bag like he was one of Santa's elves. Marcelle had been with her girlfriend Tia. They'd come from the AM/PM, where they had bought vanilla ice cream sandwiches. They had already eaten them halfway down.

"Damn," he said when he saw her. "Where'd you come from?"

Tia answered, "Over there." She pointed over her shoulder toward the minimart.

"Not you." He nodded to Marcelle. "You're brand new. I like new." He put his hands on his hips and arched his back, pushing the thick crotch of his jeans at her. Right then, Marcelle was hooked.

She brought her knees to her chest and pulled the covers

to her chin, while he blew streams of smoke over both of them. Marcelle wondered what had happened to Tia. The girl had phoned a couple times after that day, and Marcelle had promised to call her back. But it had slipped her mind.

Eugene groaned deep in his throat and stretched his body, and then he reached over to her and dug right into her panties. He took her in a hard grip. She said "No," but he rolled his heavy self on top of her anyway and kissed at her with his filmy tongue, all the while she tried to get whatever air she could through her mouth, to try and hide the stale rawness of his breath. She pressed her legs together and pushed at his hand with her own.

"Don't," she said.

"What do you mean, don't?" He put his hand back and dug at her with his fingers.

"I mean, don't." She pushed at him again.

He said, "Goddamn it, Marcelle. What the fuck is with you now?"

She scooted herself back from him, knocking her head against the headboard. "What do you think?" She pulled her hair back from her face and looked at him square in the eyes.

"Jesus Christ. I said I was sorry."

"So what? Sorry doesn't automatically make everything okay."

Eugene dropped his cigarette into a can of soda on his nightstand. "I don't know what you want me to do, Marcelle."

"You're always saying sorry, and it doesn't mean anything." She pushed at his arm and slid out of bed.

"Fine, Marcelle," he called after her. "I'm not sorry. That make you happy?"

She bunched her clothes from the bureau and locked herself into the small bathroom behind the stairs. She dressed with the lights off, cracking the shade a tiny wedge. In the mirror, she was all shapes and shadows.

There was a time when she really thought she could solve Eugene's puzzle, when she believed she could help him find all his missing pieces. But it was useless. The more she tried to figure him out, the more he confused her. He could be so sweet, and when he was, he was all honey. The drives up to the river with the radio playing loud, and his smile with a dimple so deep she could put her fingernail into it. And the notes, folded white squares with hearts in pencil, some of them with the word Sorry in big, block letters. She still had them all in a shoebox, kept closed under the bed.

She raked out her hair and leaned in close to the mirror. She stared at her own mouth and whispered, *Stupid, Stupid Marcelle.* And then just before she went out, before she opened the door to leave, she took Eugene's toothbrush and gave it a good swirl in the toilet bowl water.

The night before, Marcelle had watched the drift of light snow-flakes outside the window, and it had made her think of Christmas. Today, though, it was nothing but a cold drizzle coming through the tumble of clouds, washing out what little white had collected overnight. She cut over slushy lawns, feeling herself starting to sweat under her parka, the itching and acrid odor working its way up through her open collar. She walked past the crippled, black frame of the old Laundromat, the chalky odor of charcoal still heavy in the air. For some time she had wondered if the smell would ever go away. But three years later it was a fixture in town no more unusual than the chemical sweetness that always seemed to spill from Sunrise Drycleaners or the constant barbecue of the Burger Barn.

For a while Marcelle wondered if it had been Eugene who set the fire, only because whenever the subject came up, his name rose out of it somehow. But she told herself he was too cute to be that much trouble. He was football-player-square in the shoulders, and he had a smile that could have been in a John Hughes movie. He was better than any boy she had ever been with, not that she had really been with any other boy. Not in the same way, anyway.

"They'll be hauling my ass in any day," he told Marcelle. "You wait and see." His thick arm ran along the edge of the car seat, and he tickled the back of her neck with his fingers. "I swear to God. A person can't fart in this town without everyone blaming it on me."

Marcelle walked up the empty staircase of the high school like an adult would. She held onto the rail and took the steps slowly, and looked over the multicolored fliers taped over the walls. She hoped no one would see her, but if they did, she wanted it to be matter-of-fact, not an uncomfortable reunion with a riot of squeals, and a million annoying questions about her life with Eugene, and her job. But when she came to an open classroom door she rushed past, using those moments to scratch at her eyebrow or casually turn her head to look the opposite way. A couple of girls appeared from around the corner and walked toward her, hot pink squares of paper fluttering in their hands. They were skinny girls, with giant eyes and goose pimple boobs, and they slid past her like scared stray cats. Freshmen. They had no idea who Marcelle Henry was.

Bobbie Luntz was seated behind her desk talking on the telephone, but she looked up when Marcelle opened the door. *It's no fun, I know,* she said into the phone. Her hair was longer than Marcelle remembered it being. Before, it had been cut to the collar like a boy's, but now it was pulled back in a ponytail that fell all the way down around her shoulder. She said, *You can put the clothes in the dryer on a high heat and it will kill them.* Marcelle could see that she had no makeup on at all. *Both the live ones and the nits.* Her Creamsicle eyebrows and naked lashes were like powder, absorbing into her pale face. She smiled at Marcelle and winked an eye, a blue pond on a freckled, ashy field. All right, she said. *Let me know how it turns out.* And then she hung up the phone.

"Wow," she said. "Isn't this a surprise?"

"Yeah."

She came from around the desk and met Marcelle at the door, taking her hand with one hand. She squeezed Marcelle's shoulder with the other.

"How have you been?"

"I been fine."

Bobbie leaned back, and her eyes zeroed in on Marcelle's bruise. "Really?" she said.

Marcelle tilted her head and let her hair fall over her face. "I'm pretty good," she said. "Still getting used to being a married lady, I guess." Her hands began to tingle. She pushed them into her pockets.

Bobbie said, "Okay." She stepped back and folded her arms over her chest. "Are you working?"

"Yeah. At the Sleep Inn, cleaning rooms. It's just for now, though, till I get something better."

"Don't apologize for honest work," Bobbie said. She studied Marcelle some more, then she reached up and brushed a finger to her own cheek. "What's going on here?"

"Nothing."

"It looks like a bit of something."

"No." Marcelle felt her face flush. Her underarms itched, and she could smel'       er own sourness drifting up.

Bobbie cocked     er head to one side and raised her eyebrows in twin arches. "No?" she said. "There's no issue whatsoever?"

"Well," she said. "A little one." She unzipped her coat and walked from Bobbie, and sank onto the butcher-paper-covered mattress. Bobbie pulled her chair from behind the desk and sat opposite her. She leaned forward with her elbows on her knees and nodded at Marcelle's eye again.

"So?"

Marcelle swallowed. She could feel the growing lump there and her eyes stung, and that made her angry with herself. She hadn't been there five minutes, and she was already falling apart.

And besides, the black eye wasn't even why she had come. It had just come along with her.

"That son of a bitch." Bobbie clenched her jaw and leaned back in her chair. She looked Marcelle hard in the face. "At least tell me this is the first time, then."

Marcelle stared down at her swollen fingers. The cuticles were raw from not wearing gloves at work, like Roxanne had told her to do.

Bobbie sighed, weary and weighed down. "Marcelle. You don't have to put up with that. When I said you could come to us anytime, I meant it. I still mean it."

"Okay."

Outside, the rain was peppering the windows in tiny drops that grew fatter and fatter, until they finally streamed down the glass to collect at the chipped wood panes. She should have waited, she told herself. Until the eye was better. The eye was making it all so much worse.

Bobbie said, "What do Lyla and Jonas have to say about this? They must know."

Marcelle slid her coat off and laid it on the cot next to her. "Most of the time they tell us we need to grow up and act like adults. Then Mr. Henry goes out for a drive and Mrs. Henry goes and makes lace in her room. When she catches me by myself, when Eugene's not there, she tells me I shouldn't be so hard on him. Says I have to work harder, go along with him, so he doesn't get all worked up."

Bobbie shook her head. "That's bullshit, Marcelle, sorry for swearing. One hundred percent. It's not my business, but Jesus. You don't deserve that. Any of it." She took Marcelle's hands in her own and squeezed them until they were warm.

The door opened and a boy came in. Marcelle recognized the curly black hair and crook nose as someone from back when she had gone there. But she didn't really know him. Bobbie got up from her chair and said to Marcelle, *Just a minute.*

She went to the counter at the far side of the office and drew a plastic tray from the wall cabinet. She spoke in a low voice to the boy, while the boy stood against the counter with his arms to his sides and drummed his long fingers against his legs. Bobbie set a single pill onto the counter, took up a pen, and started scratching notes on her clipboard. The boy looked over at Marcelle. He chewed on his fingernail all the while he stared at her face, and down at her boobs, and the hands that she cupped tightly on her lap.

"Take your pill, William," Bobbie said. "Then straight back to class, no lollygagging."

"I don't lollygag."

"And you need to be in here before the bell rings. Mr. Cowan doesn't like students leaving class for any reason. Not for meds, not for anything."

"I know," he said. "I just forget."

"Well, don't forget."

"That's what I take pills for, Mrs. Luntz."

Bobbie grumbled in her throat. He looked over at Marcelle and smiled a toothy grin, and when Bobbie gave him a nudge in the small of his back he sauntered out the door into the hallway. Bobbie came around and walked to the front of her desk, and leaned against its edge.

"So Marcelle." She gestured toward her own cheek. "There are people I can call. We can, I mean. Get you somewhere safe."

"I don't care about the bruise."

"You should care."

"That's not why I came, anyways." Marcelle looked down at her shoes. They were wet from the slush, the canvas ringed dark all around. She was cold now. She brought her jacket to her lap and tucked the zippered edges under her thighs.

"Why I came is I'm late on my cycle. About a month and a half. And since you're a nurse and all…"

Bobbie sighed, and cleared her throat. For a long time, she

didn't say anything. She just shifted against the desk, the wood creaking under her weight. She brushed at a spot on her jeans and folded her hands on her knees. Finally she said, "Have you taken a test yet?"

"No."

"You need to take a test, Marcelle."

"I'm afraid someone will see me. And anyways I'm never late."

"You don't need to be ashamed to buy a pregnancy test. You're married. And even if you weren't, women go in all the time to buy them. This isn't 1960."

"I don't care. I don't want anyone to see me."

"Did you call your mom?"

Marcelle's throat began to tighten, and she felt the wave moving up through her chest again, and her eyes well up. Her nose suddenly started to drip and she wiped at it with her bare hand.

"She said I made my own bed."

Bobbie came and sat down on the cot beside her. She slid close and tucked a tissue into Marcelle's hand. She didn't say anything, and she didn't hold Marcelle's hand or hug her, or pat her knee or anything like that. She just sat there, with her hip against Marcelle's, waiting while she wiped all the mess that ran from her nose and her eyes.

Finally Bobbie said, "What do you want to do?"

"I don't know."

What she didn't know was exactly how to put the words together, the words that would say she just didn't want it. Not the baby, not the marriage. Not Eugene.

Bobbie got up and walked to her desk and pulled a flat drawer out from the front. She grabbed a scrap of paper and wrote something down, then brought it to Marcelle. "Take this phone number." She put it in her hand. "No matter what, you can't stay with someone who hits you."

"It's probably really small right now," Marcelle said, putting her hand over her stomach. "Probably not even like a real person yet."

Bobbie looked up at the clock. She was looking at the time, as if what Marcelle had just said hinged on the minutes left in the day.

"Would I be a bad person if I got rid of it?" she said. She began crying again, and this time she just let the tears roll on down her face and fall onto her chest.

"You mean abortion?"

Marcelle nodded.

Bobbie looked at the clock again and then out the window. Marcelle followed her gaze. The rain had stopped, and there was enough sunlight that the drops glowed on the glass like tiny stars.

"It doesn't matter what I think." She put her hands on Marcelle's. "It has to be your decision."

"I think I'm sure about it, Mrs. Luntz. One hundred percent." She pulled her hand from under Bobbie's. "Could you take me? I know it's a lot to ask, but I don't know anyone else."

"It depends. Are you eighteen yet?"

"No ma'am. Not till February."

"Well then I can't. I'm really sorry honey, but you're a minor." She closed her eyes and sighed. "It hurts to even suggest this, but have you thought about talking to Lyla?"

Marcelle felt the tears coming again. It did hurt, even thinking about it made her stomach ache. "Oh no," she said. "Do you think you could? I can't even think…"

"Oh, Marcelle, I don't think so. I can't picture her listening to anything I have to say. We're not exactly girlfriends."

Bobbie took the seat behind her desk and stayed there for some time, rubbing her thumb over her palm, just staring at her hands, working them back and forth. There was a bowl of candy next to her hands and a glass mug, half-filled with milky coffee. Other than those and a pink notepad with a single pen crossed over it, the desk looked like more of a prop than anything else.

She finally stood up. "Give me a little time to process this, Marcelle. How about you call me tonight at home. You still remember our number?"

Marcelle nodded as she stood and slid her coat back on. "If you talk to her, can you tell her not to say anything to Eugene?"

"Call me at six."

"Mrs. Henry's gonna be sad. I sometimes hear her talk to Mr. Henry about having grandchildren someday."

"Yeah, well it's not your job to make babies so Lyla Henry can get what she wants." She took her own jacket from the hook beside her door. "I'll walk you out."

They walked all the way through the hallway and down the stairs, and out to the parking lot. The bell marking the end of first period rang, and Marcelle quickened her pace, leaving Bobbie behind, cutting through the parked cars toward the street. Bobbie yelled something to her. Marcelle kept walking and zipped her parka to her chin, pushing her hands into the pockets. She wanted to turn around, to see if Bobbie was coming after her. She wondered if she did turn around and look up at the windows, would she see the frantic scurry of kids in the windows, of hands pushing shoulders, and teachers whistling and clapping, and flipping the light switches for attention.

She finally stopped and looked behind her. Mrs. Luntz was gone. The reflecting sky whitewashed the entire wall of windows.

*This thing inside me. Part me, part Eugene.*

She was completely exposed, naked to anyone who might be looking out at her now. Marcelle Foster with her ugly black eye and moon face, standing like a fat old cow in the muddy parking lot, just staring up at us.

*Pretty soon it'll have his nose and my eyes, and fingers that push hard against the insides of my body. And then it'll be too late.*

Marcelle Foster, the same stupid girl she always was.

# Bobbie and Lyla

The night that Ernie first mentioned Ash Falls, Bobbie had left the Owl Tavern on her own, a good hour before closing time. She and the other shift nurses had been up to their elbows in drinks and barflies, and Bobbie was halfway through her third dance with an electrician by the name of Rico.

"I keep a boat docked down at the marina," he said.

"That so?"

"Yep. You should come see it. I got it set up real nice."

Bobbie shook her head against his shoulder. "I gotta get home," she said. "My kid's got a thing in the morning, real early."

"You got a kid? How old?"

"Eleven."

"Eleven years old and home all by himself." He slid his hand around Bobbie's back and tucked his fingers inside the waist of her jeans.

Bobbie smiled. "No," she said. "He ain't by himself." She took his fingers from her waist and pressed a kiss to his sandpaper face, right next to his mouth. He turned his head, but she pulled herself back from him.

"You ought to go over and ask Laurie to dance," she said, nodding to the booth. "She's the cute one with short black hair."

"Does she like electricians?"

"I don't know. She might like boats."

Bobbie slipped through the back where the outside lighting was best and went straight to her car. Seatbelt cinched tight, she drove off with the tape deck dialed up, singing along with Blondie and feeling damned good, her hands at ten and two with the window all the way down, her shirt unbuttoned to the middle and billowing in and out from her skin. She kept to the side streets all the way, cutting from Aurora Avenue to Greenwood Park then circling around to the Episcopal Church on the corner of Dayton Street. As she hooked south onto to 92nd, she snapped the headlights off so she might pull into the driveway unnoticed.

She rolled up to the duplex, and there on the front steps sat Ernie in gray sweats and a t-shirt, eating peanuts, a fat plastic bag at his side and a fist-sized mound of empty shells between his bare feet. A cigarette was balanced on the lip of a beer can, the thin tree of blue smoke growing from its smoldering tip. It was almost one-thirty, and even though Bobbie had stopped drinking two hours earlier, there was still a good buzz behind her eyes. All the house windows were dark.

"You sharing any of that with the squirrels?" She did up her buttons and walked around the front of the car, opening the passenger door, locking it then closing it again. "That's a lot of nuts for one person."

"I wanted something with salt," he said. "The shelling gives my hands something to do."

"How come you're sitting out here? I told you I was going out after work."

He took a final drag from his cigarette, then flicked the butt in a high, orange arc over to the side yard. He blew a plume of smoke into the air.

"I can't fucking sleep."

Bobbie climbed the concrete steps and took a spot beside him, the cold seeping through her jeans. She reached down between his feet and scooped a handful of shells, then dumped them off the side of the porch into the azaleas.

"It's not getting any better," she said. "If anything, it's getting worse."

"I'm not mad at you, babe. If you need to blow off some steam with your friends, go ahead. I told you, I don't care."

"I'm not talking about that. I'm talking about your sleeping."

She ran a finger along his temple and pushed a rope of hair over the saddle of his ear. "I wish you'd get yourself in to talk to Dennis."

Ernie pulled away and corrected his hair. "Dennis costs money we don't have."

"We got insurance." Along the street opposite, boxy bungalows crouched side-by-side, specked with a collage of pumpkins that winked and grinned, gap-toothed, from dimly lit stoops. She cupped her hands to her face and breathed into them.

Then Ernie said, "What would you say about us getting out of here? You and me and Patrick." He leaned back, putting his elbows against the step. His eyes narrowed and he stared up into the night sky, and the goofiest smile she'd ever seen stretched over his face. He said, "We could move out of this city, away from the traffic and the streetlights. Goddamned sirens every ten minutes. Think of it. We could just look up and see nothing but stars."

Bobbie drove her hands into her coat pockets and leaned over, pressing her stomach to her knees. She turned her head to the side and looked out over the void that was the side yard. Ernie reeked of cigarettes, but only cigarettes this time. Still, even out in this scrubbed October air she could smell him. How many butts, she wondered, would she find dotting the lawn when she came out to get the morning paper?

"I've only been a year at the hospital," she said. "Things are just setting in. The thought of having to look for another job all over again—God, Ernie. Can't you call Dennis? I'll call him myself if you want."

Ernie stood up, sending flakes of peanut shells fluttering from his lap to the steps, some of it onto Bobbie. He let out the groan of a man beat, and pressed his hand to her hair. He rested against it, gently, and Bobbie reached up and took hold of him. She didn't push him away, but she held his hand in place, and moved her finger against his cold skin. She didn't want this. It was too sudden, too drastic. It was possible that he was right, though, maybe he needed it. Maybe she needed it.

"Let's go to bed," she said. "We can talk about this in the morning."

"It's morning right now," he said. He slid his hand from beneath hers and walked into the house, closing the door behind him.

Bobbie stood at the kitchen window, phone in hand, watching the neighbor's garbage can roll from his driveway to the street. It was dented on one side, and it limped as it went, finally coming to a stop in the gutter against the curb.

The phone had rung five times in her ear before Lyla finally picked up.

"Hello?"

"Lyla"?

"Who is this?"

"It's…Bobbie. Bobbie Luntz."

There was the sound of breathing then, for several seconds, nothing at all on the other end.

"Are you there?"

"What do you want? Something with Hank that I don't know about?"

"No," she said. "I mean, not that I know of."

Old man Hart came down from his porch and limped to the end of the driveway, looking as though every ounce of his strength was being used to drag that bucket back to his garage. Forty-five years, he'd been there. It's what he'd told her one day, over the top of his pruning shears. Forty-five years. An entire lifetime.

"So why are you calling here? I don't have time for games."

Bobbie took a deep breath. "Can we meet?"

Bobbie waited for Lyla, in a booth at the back wall of Cook's Grill, a place twenty miles outside of Ash Falls that she had driven past dozens of times without consideration. She nursed a cup of smoky coffee and stared out the window into the parking lot. It was 10:30 in the morning and there was a dull ache going on with her leg. Not more than a half-dozen cars populated the lot. Four old timers crowded the bar.

Twice, the waitress had come back to ask Bobbie if she wanted anything to eat. She was fiftyish, with gray-streaked hair folded up into a heavy bun, too much foundation and a loose floral blouse with a nametag that said *Howdy*. She wore her shirt untucked, letting the whole thing tumble over snug jeans that stopped just above her ankles.

"How about a piece of pie?" she asked.

"Just coffee."

"We got apple and sour cream cherry, fresh made." She tapped her pen on the order pad. "It's real tasty."

Bobbie forced a smile. "I'm waiting for someone."

Howdy shrugged her shoulders and walked away. She retreated to the space behind the counter where she resumed her waitress banter, winking at the whiskered old men who mashed their potbellies against the bar. She poured coffee from the glass bubble and pushed slices of cream-topped pie at them as they talked over one another about the wives who didn't talk to them, or ex-wives who wouldn't leave them alone, and joints that didn't bend like they used to but other parts that worked just fine. Her head tipped back as she laughed and doled out saccharine terms of endearment:

"Oh, Punkin."

"You old Slydog."

"Mister Man, I will run you outta here myself."

Bobbie watched it all happen and tried to imagine what it would be like to be A Good Regular, like these old codgers. Just walk into a place and have folks drop what they're doing and give you a shout, pick up the conversation from the exact place it had been left earlier. She never had that in her old haunts, though The

Flume had been a little like that. Sometimes. Even so, it hadn't always felt good. The banter could be casual and light-hearted, but in the time it took her to pull the darts from the cork everything could turn nasty and deeply personal. Shortcomings and airy rumors quickly floated to the surface. And as such, Bobbie often found herself walking out at closing time with a crippling headache, a kind of a verbal hangover of long night of serrated dialogue. But these people over there, spreading conversation like they were spreading butter. They were fucking loving it.

Lyla Henry's white sedan turned into the lot and settled in the stall right outside Bobbie's window, and Bobbie felt her skin flush, down her back and over her legs. Her feet crawled with electricity. What the hell was she doing calling Lyla all the way out here? The woman hated her; she wasn't going to be able to get a word in edgewise. She had to be out of her mind to be sticking her hand in this hornet's nest.

Lyla slid the column shifter into park and dropped the visor in front of her face. Her elbows bent outward and moved in small circles, and when she flipped the visor back to the ceiling, there was a blue scarf tied down over her hair, framing her giant drop temple glasses. She saw Bobbie and froze, her hands curled at her chest like a squirrel. Bobbie waved, but Lyla just turned and shoved the car door open with her shoulder.

She came through the glass doors and made her way straight toward Bobbie, a mustard yellow cardigan falling over pressed, cream slacks that snapped as she walked. She didn't say anything; she simply slid right into the seat opposite and hoisted a bulky white purse onto her own lap.

Howdy came from behind the counter to their table. She stood to one side, her rear end directed at Bobbie, the heel of her hand resting on the Formica.

She said, "Who's hungry?"

"Not me," Lyla said. "I'll have some tea. Earl Grey if you have it."

"So don't nobody want food."

Lyla began to rifle through her purse, crowding the booth with the jarring noise of shrinking cellophane. This was classic Lyla, the kind of passive-aggressive behavior that Hank used to complain about so much.

Bobbie said, "I don't think we'll be eating."

"Well if you change your mind." The waitress turned and left, fanning herself with her order pad as she went.

Lyla took out a tissue and dabbed at her nose. She blinked behind her glasses, the movement taking up the entire lens.

"Well," she said. "Here I am." She pulled two napkins from the chrome dispenser and scrubbed at the space in front of her. "I can't wait to hear what this is all about."

Bobbie took a drink of coffee and went over the script in her mind, the conversation she had rehearsed all the way out. "Thanks for coming out here," she said carefully. "I know it's a long drive."

Howdy appeared with a thick coffee mug and a small pewter kettle and left it without a single word on the table between the women. Lyla pinched the string from the rim and poured the hot water, and gave the bag four or five rough bounces.

"What's so top secret that you couldn't tell me over the phone?" She blew over the rim of her cup and sucked in a sip. Pink lipstick bled from her puckered lips into her skin. "If all this is about that husband of yours, don't bother. Hank told me everything."

Bobbie leaned back in the booth and put her hand on her forehead. She felt feverish, nauseous. The image of Hank and Lyla gossiping over Ernie flared in front of her. "Lyla, come on," she said. She looked out at the tumble of gray clouds. The tree shadows that had earlier lain over the parking lot were now vanished into the darkening ground. Her leg was really starting to throb.

"It's about Marcelle."

"Marcelle." Lyla stiffened. "What about her?"

Bobbie sighed. "Where to start?"

"Is this about the black eye? We're well aware of it."

"And it doesn't concern you?"

"Eugene's got a temper. She knew that going in."

"It doesn't concern you, then."

"Of course it concerns me! What kind of a person do you think I am?" Lyla put a hand to her mouth and looked over her shoulder, back at the bar. The waitress still leaned over the counter, resting on her elbows. One of the men was talking with some energy, his knuckly hands opening and closing in front of him.

"They're still kids," Lyla said in a hard whisper. "It'll work itself out with time; they need to grow up is all. If there was anything I could do to make that happen any faster, believe me I would."

"Have you even said anything to Eugene about it? You or Jonas?"

Lyla looked at Bobbie as if she had suggested she call the pope himself. "If you think either Jonas or I can fix Eugene just by talking to him, then you don't know anything about anything. Believe me. If that girl had half a brain in her head she wouldn't even be in this spot. Those two made the decision to get married, in spite of anything I or the girl's mother had to say about it. So I say, let them stand in their own mess."

Bobbie tipped her cup and swirled the shallow black pool around the edges. This was turning into way more work than she'd imagined, and she hadn't even gotten to the heart of the conversation. She had begun to see something of the world that existed inside that house, the denial and excuses, and placating. It seemed that Eugene was less of a child and more of a creation, though she had always suspected as much. She also had discovered a newfound sympathy for Hank. It was no wonder that he couldn't say Lyla's name without simultaneously rolling his eyes or shaking his head.

She looked up at Lyla, who was now picking change from her

coin purse and counting silently. Bobbie took hold of the coffee mug and ran her finger over the handle.

"She's pregnant." There. It was out.

Lyla snapped the coin purse shut and held it to her chest. Her teeth showed between taut lips, and her eyes seemed look not at Bobbie but through her, to somewhere else, maybe to her own basement where she envisioned what lay ahead. Hopefully she saw what Bobbie saw, a miserable Eugene and Marcelle, and a big, fat, squalling baby sandwiched between the two of them.

"So that's it," Lyla said. "Well, I guess it was only a matter of time, wasn't it?"

"And, she doesn't want it."

Lyla shook her head and laughed softly. "What then? She'll adopt it out. Give it up for some stranger to raise, I suppose."

Bobbie leaned forward in her seat. "She doesn't want the pregnancy."

Lyla brought the mug to her lips. Her chin quivered, and she finally set the tea in front of her without taking a drink. "She told you that? And what about Eugene? Does he get a say in any of this?"

Bobbie slid the coffee cup to the far edge of the table, next to the window. "All she wants, Lyla, is to start over." It wasn't until she said it aloud that she felt the avalanche of possibility that those words carried with them. *Start over.* How many times had she dreamed of climbing back in time, finding the decision that, if done over again, would fix it all? Things could have been so different for her. For everyone.

Lyla reached up and took hold of her necklace and pinched the gold strand between her fingertips. She wound the chain around her finger as she stared out the window.

"He doesn't even know, does he?"

"No, he doesn't."

She took off her glasses and drew a tissue from her purse, and set to work on the lenses. "I don't know why you had to drag me out here and humiliate me in the open," she said. "You could have done this over the phone."

"Marcelle's scared half to death, and she needs you."

"Right. So she can just, *start over*. Pull that handle and reset everything. And won't that be convenient for her?" She glared at Bobbie with a hatred so real, so visceral, that Bobbie thought she might reach out and take hold of her right there in the booth. "People don't always get to just do whatever comes into their pretty little heads," she said. "When you flout the boundaries that God puts before you, there are consequences. You and Hank ought to know a thing or two about that."

And there it was, finally. "This isn't about Hank and me, Lyla."

"Oh, it isn't?" Lyla snapped. "Do you think we'd be sitting here if it wasn't for your little *thing*? You had a husband. Lord knows what life Eugene would have had in front of him if it hadn't been for that night. Don't sit there and tell me it's not about you and Hank."

Bobbie watched as Lyla ran her thumb around the rim of the cup, wiping the pink smudge on her napkin.

"I know that game plenty well," Bobbie said. "What if. What if those kids hadn't been drinking beer right there in the open; what if someone had actually taken it away and made them leave? Or better yet, what if there had never been soap dumped all over that floor? I wouldn't be sitting here with my leg feeling like it was ready to fall off, and I sure as hell wouldn't have had crutches with me that night, now would I?"

"You could have never come to Ash Falls."

"The same goes for you, Lyla." Bobbie slid forward in her seat and folded her hands on the table. "We could do this all day, name every choice made from this moment all the way back to the Mayflower. It doesn't matter now. What's done is done. What we have is right now plus whatever comes after."

Lyla put her hands over her face and slumped in her seat.

"This is one of those choices that can set the path for the rest of their lives," Bobbie said. "There's no reason it has to trap them, and you know it. In your heart, you have to know that."

"Why are you telling me all of this?" Lyla dropped her hands to the table. "That girl can and will do whatever she wants. She can walk out that door tomorrow and do whatever she wants to that baby."

Bobbie leaned back in the booth. The conversation was sliding quickly, and she hadn't even gotten to the point at which Lyla would either agree with everything or clear the entire table with her arm and storm out.

"Marcelle's a minor. Her mother won't be bothered with her, so like it or not, you're all she's got."

"It seems like she's got you. Why don't you take her there and get it done?"

"Marcelle has your last name, now," she said. "If you go with her, you can say you're her mother. Nobody has to know any different."

Lyla sat bolt upright, as if she had discovered some grand secret. "You can't be serious."

"Try for a minute to forget that it's me sitting here," Bobbie said. "Pretend you never met me in your life and just consider what I'm asking you to do. I can think of a dozen different outcomes if you shut this out. And there aren't many good ones there."

They sat for awhile, Bobbie busying herself, thumbing through the sugar packets, counting the famous landmarks on the wrappers. Lyla refilled her cup with water and let the teabag seep, but didn't drink from it. Outside, the rain began to pelt the window. It grew more rapid and denser, fat drops running in rivulets down the glass and drumming on the hood of her car, round drops bouncing off the asphalt and filling up the low spots. Lyla gathered her purse onto her lap and slid to the edge of her seat.

"I'm going," she said.

Bobbie reached out a hand. "Will you at least think about it?"

Lyla pulled back. She scooped up her purse and her scarf. "Good lord," she said. "How in the world could I not think about it?"

## Marcelle and Lyla

"Richland, Washington. For Vic Foster. No ma'am. V-I-C."

Marcelle put the lid back on the boiling pot and leaned against the sink, the coiled telephone cord circling the expanse of her waist. She reached up and penciled a drawing of a star into the window sweat with her finger.

"It's my dad," she told the woman on the phone. She drew a long, arching tail from the star and a sharp crescent moon in the corner. "What about Victor? Is there a Victor?"

"There's no Vic or Victor Foster in Richland or anyplace in the vicinity."

Marcelle thanked the operator while turning a circle to free herself of the cord. She put the phone back on the wall receiver and returned to the window. She had added several more stars and traced the entire perimeter with a long, snaking curl when Lyla came in through the back door.

"I wish you wouldn't do that," she said. "To the window. It gums up the glass."

"I'll clean it." She grabbed the hand towel from the dish rack and swabbed the window. Lyla came over and took the rag from Marcelle.

"Just never mind," she said. She lifted the lid from the pasta, turned down the heat and set it back off the rim. Marcelle moved to the kitchen table and sat down in the chair against the wall. She took the weekly grocery flyer and began to thumb through it, looking at the cereals and produce ads, dog-earing the corners as if she might come back to it.

Lyla filled a glass from the faucet and drank the entire thing down without a breath; then she folded the dish towel over the edge of the counter. She smoothed her hand on the terrycloth and straightened the fringe.

"I talked to that nurse this morning," she said, not looking at Marcelle. "But I guess you know that."

Marcelle nodded.

"Did you hear me?"

"Yes."

"Did you ask her to call me?"

"No," she lied. "She said she wanted to talk to you."

"I'd have rather not spent my morning having tea with that woman. To have her be the one to tell me about this."

Marcelle felt a bubble roil somewhere under her stomach and she shifted in her seat to press herself against the chair. More than anything, she wanted to leave the kitchen, go to the bathroom or go outside. Anyplace that Mrs. Henry was not.

Lyla took her glasses off and set them on the counter. She looked up sharply, and when she did this the smallness of her eyes was jarring to Marcelle. She knew she had to have seen Mrs. Henry without glasses before this. But at that moment, it felt to her like a discovery of sorts. That Eugene's mother's eyes were akin to little blue thumbprints on her head.

"So you're dead set on this?" Lyla said. She pushed her lips out. She waited and tilted her head to one said. "You've thought this through carefully? This is the path you really want for yourself?"

Marcelle nodded. Her head felt like it weighed a hundred pounds on her shoulders.

Lyla came over and sat down across from her. Her eyes were red, as if she had been crying. "You silly girl. Think you know everything but you don't. You don't know a darned thing about what the Lord intends for you. None of us does."

The skin on Marcelle's hands was so white, with blue veins running like a road map to her knuckles. "I don't believe he intends that me and Eugene stay married," she said, not looking up at Mrs. Henry. "I don't believe that. I think he knows it's a mistake."

"So He made a mistake when He blessed your union?"

"I think me and Eugene made a mistake when we asked the preacher to bless it. Yeah."

Lyla groaned and worked her fingers into her temples. "Oh Marcelle. And what about Eugene? You know he ought to be a part of this decision."

"No," Marcelle said, shaking her head firmly. "If he finds out then he gets to choose, not me."

Lyla's eyelids fluttered. She got up from the table and hurried to the sink, and took the dishrag and put it to her eyes. She kept herself facing the window, staring into the glass that by now had fogged over again, bringing up Marcelle's galaxy once more.

Somewhere in the midst of Mrs. Henry's sniffles and trembling shoulders, Marcelle burst into tears. It had come surprisingly hard, from nowhere, and her own shoulders bucked and rolled as she sobbed. She scrubbed at her face with her shirtsleeve, gasping and sucking at the air, and snorting all the sudden looseness back up into her head.

Lyla dropped her head back and put a hand to her face. "Oh criminy," she said. She reached over and tore a sheet from the paper towel spool and rushed over. "Don't do this," she said, thrusting the square at her. Marcelle took it, and Lyla stood back from the table, her arms over her chest, inkblot eyes bearing down pitifully.

"Look at you," she said. "Good lord, you're nowhere near ready for any of this."

"I wish I was." She spoke between forced breaths. "I wish I could be like you. And Mister Henry. Me and Eugene. We wouldn't fight over anything. Ever again."

"Wishing is all fine and good, but it doesn't get the bills paid or keep the house clean. You need to learn, Marcelle, that life is hard. It's hard work, every minute of every day, no breaks." She walked over and turned off the stove. "Your noodles are done."

She wasn't hungry anymore. In fact, as she sat there wiping the tears and snot from her face, she had a hard time believing she'd ever been hungry.

Lyla made a noise in her throat, a kind of low growl, and she went to the lower cupboard where she took out a colander and brought it to the sink. She grabbed hold of the dishrag again and used it to take hold of the pot handles. When she tipped the contents into the sink, her entire face vanished in a plume of steam.

"How old were you when Eugene was born?" Marcelle asked, finding her breath again.

"I was older than you, that's for sure," Lyla said. She turned the cold faucet and let the water run over the pasta. "I'd been married longer than a few months, too."

"To Mister Henry?"

"Yes to Mister Henry." Lyla rolled her eyes and kneaded her fingers through the cooling macaroni.

"Was it an accident? Eugene, I mean."

Lyla swung her head to her shoulder, giving a wide-eyed look to Marcelle. "No, it wasn't an accident," she said. She turned her attention back to the sink. "It was unexpected. But not an *accident*."

"Still. You wanted him."

"I wanted a baby."

"Did Mister Henry?"

Lyla went to the cupboard and brought down a glass bowl with a red, plastic lid. She took the colander and dumped the noodles into the container, sealed the lid, then put the whole thing into the refrigerator. Snatching the dishtowel from the countertop, she walked to the window and scrubbed at the foggy glass.

"I told you that putting your fingers all over this would gum it up. I'll be looking at that picture of yours all week, now."

Marcelle reached to the center of the table and took the salt shaker and poured some crystals into her palm. She licked her finger and pressed it to the salt. When she put it to her tongue, she ran her eyes over the whole kitchen, over the faded flower-papered walls and the mismatched, out-of-style appliances. She studied the glossy painted cabinets that gleamed in icy blocks on the walls, and the ruffled yellow drapes that twitched as Lyla brushed against them with her towel.

"Sometimes I think I might want a baby. Someday," Marcelle said. "But then I think, how can I be a mother when I don't even know how be a wife?"

Lyla tossed the towel into the sink and leaned against the counter. "Oh Marcelle, stop being such a martyr," she said. She had put her glasses back on, and she looked at Marcelle with the stare of an old owl. "And let's both stop pretending that life with Eugene is anything but exhausting, all right?"

Marcelle coughed a weak laugh and wiped at her nose again. "I don't know what that means," she said. "Martyr." She looked up at the fat wood burl clock that was mounted on the wall over Lyla's head. It was almost 1:30.

"I suppose you're off to work soon," Lyla said. "It would be a good idea to start socking your money away, somewhere safe. If you haven't already been doing it, I mean." She walked over to Marcelle and patted her forearm, then touched her hair, just on the edge of her face, where it was still wet from crying.

Marcelle took in a breath to say something, though she wasn't sure what it might be. But Lyla just picked up the grocery flyer and walked away, flipping through the pages and talking softly to herself as she moved down the hallway to her and Mister Henry's bedroom.

# Patrick Luntz

Patrick sat in the passenger seat, not fully awake yet, buttoned into an oversized flannel shirt, the scent of his father's cologne and beard like a scarf over his face. Ernie squinted into the orange glow of the dashboard and punched the radio selector, finally settling on an old country station with a woman's bell-like voice warbling under the tinny sway of a slide guitar.

"Kitty Wells," Ernie said with a snap of his fingers. "Goddamn, that woman could sing. That's real country, son." He drummed on the steering wheel with his fingers and sang along with her.

*How far is heaven, when can I go. To see my daddy, he's there, I know.*

He sang in a deep tone, his chin pressed to his chest as they cruised down Main Street, well under the speed limit. The heater blew cold air up over the dash into Patrick's face, and his father reached up with his sleeve pulled over his hand to wipe the fog from the windshield.

Along the street, shop windows were dark, the doorways like the mouths of caves. A&M Electronics, the attorney and bookkeeping offices, Annie's Fabrics—all of them were hours away from opening. Even the Red Apple lot was only visible through a gauze of light, thanks to a single stuttering fluorescent. A dark sedan sat at its base, draped in a frosty layer of dew. Ernie thumbed the lighter into the dashboard. He pulled a pack of Winstons from his shirt pocket and gave it over to Patrick.

"Draw one of them babies out for me," he said. Patrick took the pack and picked at the opening with useless, chewed fingernails, and Ernie said, "No. Tip it over and smack it against your palm." He clapped the heel of his hand against the steering wheel. "Bam, like that."

Patrick thumped the pack against his hand and launched a few cigarettes from the pack to the floor. His father laughed softly and held two fingers out in a V. He said, "I didn't know you had a problem with cigarettes." The lighter popped, and by the time the cab was filled with a blue haze of swirling smoke, Patrick was wide awake and leaning over the back of his seat, fishing through the cooler for something to drink.

They drove up the mountain, the high beams illuminating a snapshot of trees in an unnatural glare. Mile markers were winking jewels. Patrick watched the dark spaces for coyote eyes.

"Talk to me," Ernie said.

"About what?"

"I don't know. Tell me about school."

Patrick shrugged his shoulders. "School's boring."

"How about girls? Any girls in your life?"

Patrick sighed and played with the dial on the radio, scanning waves of static. His feet were starting to cramp in his boots.

"What about that Marcella girl that came by the other day?"

"I don't like her that way."

"Really. Huh. What's her story?"

"I don't know. Her mom and her live over the furniture store."

"The Gamble Apartments? Damn. That's some major welfare."

"She's nice." The air was blowing hot now and making him sweat under his shirt. He turned down the thermostat.

"All right. I been there." He leaned back in the seat and held the steering wheel at arm's length.

"Back in the eighth grade," he said. "Just like you. This girl's name was Angela Jackson. A real beauty, and man she was all over me. I could have had her before I even knew what having was all about. But Angie was a black girl, and back then, that was not okay. Black and white. I could be her friend and all that. But if anyone ever got the idea that it was anything more than that? Shit. I'd have been a dead man."

Patrick said, "No one cares if we go together."

"So what is it?"

Patrick took a drink from the can of orange soda that had been pressed between his knees. He looked over at his father, whose beard quivered from all the grinning.

"I just don't like her that way," he said.

"Fair enough." They rounded a bend in the highway, and Ernie nodded to the road ahead. "This is it right up here."

He let off the gas and coasted the last distance into the graveled turnout. Through a small grove of trees sat the old Trout Creek Station House, a boarded up shack that had once been the entrance to the old Kelleher logging camp. Patrick had gone past the place before, with his mother, on the way to pick up a cord of firewood from Hank Kelleher's property. "That little shed," she had told him, "is more than eighty years old if you can believe it."

By the time they gathered the tackle box and the cooler and made their ways to the switch-backed trail that descended behind the shack, the sky was beginning to break with color. Through the stand of trees, Patrick could make out the soft palm of a lake at the base of the trail. The air was waking up with the pepper of chickadees and warblers, and the serrated call of an obnoxious crow. A thin cotton fog blanketed the water. At the edge of the shore, a ruddy old rowboat stood tipped against a tree.

"Pretty sweet, huh?" His father laid the boat into the water and waved Patrick in. "Buddy of mine took me up here a couple weeks ago." He tossed the oars into the boat, and set the cooler and tackle box down on the floor at Patrick's feet. Patrick held on to the sides, and his father pushed off, and the boat cut through the mist, a reversed panorama of the mountain rippling off the bow.

"Are you ready?" his father asked, settling into the seat.

"For what?"

"Let's liberate some fish from this pond."

Patrick stood in the dark at the kitchen counter, stirring a cup of warm instant cocoa he'd made from the tap. The streetlights outside were still on, and all the windows along the block were black. He didn't like waking up so early, but he did like being up. At times like this, when everything around him was quiet and still sleeping, he liked to imagine that he was the only person in the world left alive.

He heard his mother's door open, and the sound of her feet shuffling down the hallway toward him. She came into the doorway and turned on the overhead lamp, and he turned around, shielding his eyes from the light. She was wearing her blue bathrobe, and her hair was bunched on one side of her head like a sunburst.

She said, "Are you ready for today?"

"Yeah," he answered. It didn't really matter whether he was ready or not. Tin would be here in a half hour.

"Okay," she said. "I'm gonna go back to bed. Call me when you're ready for me to come pick you up."

He had dressed himself for the frost, canvas pants and a thermal shirt under his father's old flannel. His mother bought him wool socks when he'd complained of cold feet, but they itched. So he layered them over the top of a pair of cottons and laced his steel-toed boots over the whole thing. He waited in the dark living room on the sofa, peering out the window, not hungry but thinking of the food he'd packed for the day, and wondering if it would be enough. He pictured the minks waking up to the sudden light, blinking their black eyes and rattling their whiskers, looking up for food and stupid to the reality that this morning would be their last. A horn sounded in two, short pinches. Tin's pickup rolled up to the curb.

Patrick jogged down the driveway, sliding on the ice before coming to a stop against the passenger door. He took hold of the handle, but it gave way, and the door swung open on him.

Staring at him from the passenger seat, bleary-eyed and dopey, was Eugene Henry. Eugene Henry, with the lumpy red plaid hunter's cap, earflaps hanging down like a hound's. Eugene, bragging a bottom lip fat with chewing tobacco, clutching a dented beer can to his chest with his oil-stained hand.

"Make room," Tin snapped, knocking him on the shoulder. Eugene flinched and mumbled. He grabbed a large grocery sack at his feet and crowded over, next to the old man. Patrick climbed in and closed the door tight to his hip. Eugene was looking at him, his breath smelling of menthol, and his leg warm against Patrick's. Tin punched the gas and broke away from the curb, taking a hard corner at the end of the block. Eugene's body leaned into Patrick's, and objects that couldn't be seen slid from one end of the dashboard to the other.

"So what's up, Luntz?" Eugene took off his hat and tucked it between his legs.

"You two know each other?" Tin practically shouted.

Eugene said, "Yeah, I know him." He lifted the can to his mouth and spit into the opening again. His voice came from his sinuses, and it was dry so that it croaked like a frog's. He said, "Him and Marcelle used to run around together."

Tin leaned forward. "That right, Skunk? You got history with his lady?"

Eugene said, "No. They were just friends, unless she's been lying to me all this time." He jabbed his elbow into Patrick's ribs. "Is that it, Luntz? She been lying to me? You get a little piece of that meat after all?"

Patrick looked over to Tin then touched his forehead to the window. They were coming to Rexall Drugs, at the edge of town. The traffic light blinked red. Tin coasted through it.

"Oh Christ," Tin said. "Forget I even said anything."

They came through the gate and rolled down the drive, into the openness of the yard. The mink barns glowed white under the moon, with a single shed lit up through side windows like a passenger train car. In the open doorway, a figure stood, square-shouldered and holding something in his hand, one arm resting against the jamb. The pickup pulled to the side of the Quonset, and the man looked back at them. Tin cut the engine.

"Here we be," he said. "Skunk, you head on over to that fellow there. Eugene, you get going on the stretchers. The White-horse gals will be here in an hour to take over."

Eugene raked his fingers through his hair. "The stretchers? Come on."

"It's where I need you, so quit your bitching. Jesus. Ain't even light out yet and already you're a pain in the ass." Tin stepped out and slammed the door behind him.

Patrick collected his lunch from the floor and got the hell out of the cab. The ground crunched under his boots as he walked, and he kept his eyes forward, doing his best to ignore Eugene. A stream of black juice splashed onto the ground beside him.

"Yo, Luntz." Eugene jogged to catch up to Patrick. His breath came in white puffs and hung heavy with the smell of tobacco. He slapped a hand on Patrick's back and it reverberated through his whole body. Eugene said, "It is my duty to tell you that today you will leave this place a changed man."

Patrick quickened his pace. The shed and the man were a good fifty feet away. The air began to swell with the high-pitched complaining of the minks.

Eugene said, "The shit you've seen and done here, dumping slop, digging out wood chips. Scooping shit. That ain't nothing."

"I'm not doing any killing," Patrick said.

"It don't matter." He nodded to the illuminated shed. "Every single one of them in there, in two hours they're gonna be dead as fucking doornails."

"Eugene!" It was Tin, and he was standing at the far end of the yard with a flashlight in his hand, waving the beam along the ground. His free arm swung a loop through the air. "Them stretchers ain't gonna wrap themselves."

Eugene stomped off into the darkness, and Patrick cut to the barn where the figure stood alone inside the doorway, holding a clipboard in his hands. He was stooped over writing something, his clipped, gray hair poking out like metal shavings from under a baseball cap.

It had been some time since Patrick had seen Hank Kelleher. Sometime after his father had gone off to prison, Hank had come by the house. Patrick answered the door. He'd acted strange, not looking at Patrick in the eyes, hanging back from the door, his heels almost to the edge of the steps. He wore cowboy boots, the toes pointed and shined to a glassy finish. He mumbled something that Patrick couldn't make out and then asked if Bobbie was at home. Patrick yelled for her, and she came to the door, and then they talked outside while Patrick watched them through the picture window drape. They didn't stand close to each other. Hank kept his hands folded in front of him and nodded over and over as Patrick's mother did all the talking. Then Hank left, and she came back inside and gave Patrick a quick, hard glance before walking back to her bedroom, where she stayed for the rest of the afternoon.

Hank motioned Patrick into the shed. They came into the light and stood within the warm reach of a hissing, kerosene heater. A mass of gray-blue fur skittered all around Patrick, in boxes up and down the rows. Two men milled around near the end, fingering tabs of paper that had been fastened to the mesh.

This was it. Weeks earlier the full time guys had been doing nothing but moving cages, separating next season's breeders from those destined for the fur auction. Countless boxes had had to be lugged to the pelting barn, and Patrick had helped with some, weathering the frenzied lunges and gnashing at the elbow-high welding gloves he wore. And now here they were.

"You'll be helping to move these things out to the truck when he gets here." Hank hung back from the heater and thumbed at the pages on his clipboard.

"Okay."

"He told you that, right?" The arches of his brows pulled downward and he glanced only briefly at Patrick, then he looked over to the door. He wore jeans too loose for his body, bunched at the top of work boots that were caked in mud up to the laces. Overhead, the ceiling lights retreated in a shrinking row of white circles, all the way to the end where the men still flipped the paper tags and talked to each other out the sides of their mouths. Hank watched them, still not looking at Patrick, body stiff as a fencepost, his whiskers like coffee grounds around tight, drawn lips. He dropped his eyes to his clipboard again and looped a page back over his hand.

"Did Tin say anything to you about fleshing?"

"Fleshing?"

He flipped another page back. "Hell," he said. "I don't know."

He mumbled something more under his breath, and lifted his cap from his head, and scratched at the thick, silver hair. None of it made any sense. Patrick didn't know stretching from fleshing from anything. Tin hadn't given any details, other than the fact that Patrick would not be doing the actual killing of the minks. He wasn't expecting Eugene, that was for sure. Or Hank. Tin hadn't said who else would be there, and Patrick hadn't thought to draw out the family tree. All those days he'd trolled up and down the rows, warily brushing his glove up against the mesh and avoiding the black, glassy eyes of the frenzied mink as they hurled themselves at his hands, the only thing he thought he knew for sure was that he would not be there when the killings started.

Hank drummed his fingers on the clipboard. He growled a heavy sigh, then reached up and hung the board on a nail beside the door. Turning to Patrick, he looked at him for the first time. He folded his arms over his chest and studied him closely, his eyes looking over his whole face as if he was counting each freckle and every zit. Patrick's legs itched. The minks were getting louder. They would not be getting fed this morning.

"Okay kid," Hank finally said, walking a wide circle around Patrick. "Follow me."

The window light threw shadows over the frozen ground while the two of them walked, black forms that cut back and forth, finally fading into the dirt by the time they moved beyond the final building. Hank was probably taking him somewhere private, away from the eyes and ears of the other men. Maybe he wanted to tell him what he and Patrick's mother had talked about on that day. It could be that he wanted to know things about her and this was a chance to dissect Patrick's brain and find out things that his mother would no longer say to him herself. From somewhere up the hill, near the road, the quarrel of a truck engine sounded, rolling down at them through the trees.

"That'll be Jasper," Hank said. "We got about a half hour."

From the corner of his eye Patrick could see Hank doing up his jacket and folding the wings of his collar. "Tin says you're a good worker," he said.

Patrick became suddenly conscious of the ground beneath his feet, the uneven sod and loose gravel, all of it hidden by the dark. He faltered in his step. He knew he should have responsed to what Hank said, but nothing would come to him. If it was an attempt at conversation, Patrick wasn't interested.

"Anyway," Hank said, "I thought you ought to know that."

"Thanks."

They came to a pair of twin gable-roofed sheds set back near the trees, like single car garages with latched double doors at the front. Light spilled through the cracked door of the left hand shed, and Patrick could hear the echo of boots on wood floor coming from within.

"Those are the tumblers," Hank said. "That's where the pelts get cleaned. You don't need to worry about that, but you might carry the pelts from there to the stretchers."

As he listened, Patrick felt an overwhelming urge to tell Hank to shut the hell up already, that he didn't care about tumblers or what had gone on between Hank and Patrick's mother, not anymore. The only thing that had been more humiliating than listening to stories about the high school nurse and the history teacher kissing behind The Flume was that they imagined they could somehow keep it a secret. Had they even tried to hide it? It was old news, and besides he was fairly sure it was all over between them. Still, it didn't mean he needed to stand there and pretend that it had never happened. If he had to make a choice between spending the whole day with Hank or Eugene, suddenly killing the minks didn't seem so bad anymore.

They went next door into a space that was about half the size of the mink sheds, warm with the smell of pinewood. Dozens of wooden boards ran the perimeter in short stacks, like weathered fence pickets made of old skis. Eugene stood halfway down the length, shuffling through the stacks, a pile of newspapers strewn at his feet. He cast an annoyed glance over his shoulder, tipped a board from the wall and wrapped a layer of paper around the upper half. From his pocket, he took a swatch of masking tape and secured the paper, then moved to the next board.

Hank said, "These here are the stretchers. When the pelts get brought in here, the girls slide them over the tops."

"Like putting on a rubber," Eugene called out.

Hank shook his head. "The newspaper soaks up the fat." He went on casually, and Eugene wrapped the wood like he was dressing wounds, every tear of the tape a chore in and of itself. The air felt thick in the room, and the humiliation seemed to radiate from Eugene, humiliation that Patrick should be standing at the door watching him work, watching as he carefully layered paper over the ends of those boards.

Behind them, the door opened, and a rainfall of high-pitched laughing broke the soberness.

"About fucking time," Eugene hollered to the ceiling, his hair crushing against his collar. He pitched the roll of tape to the floor. "I am so done with this."

They were girls from the reservation, around Patrick's age. They had tucked their hair under knit hats and written on black eyeliner and rosy lip-gloss that was greasy under the overhead lamps. Likely they had shared the makeup in their car, using the dome light to put on the final touches before coming in. One of them was big in the hips, with jeans that pinched at the flesh on the sides of her thighs. She stared at Eugene, a faint smile breaking.

"Hey there," she said. "I brought you a carton of Winstons."

"Winstons?" He said, pulling his chin back. He reached up and took his jacket from a nail on the wall. "I told you Marlboros."

"Winstons are cheaper," she said.

The other girl took off her coat and put it with her purse on the floor against the wall. She was thinner than her friend, with a ruffled blouse that she wore tucked into her pegged jeans. "What's it matter?" she said. "Cigarettes are cigarettes."

"Shows what you know." Eugene stomped past them. "Winstons are shit. If you think they're so good, smoke 'em yourselves." He punched the door with both fists and it slammed open, crashing against the outside wall.

Hank nodded to the girls and led Patrick out. By now there was a swirl of activity near the pelt barn. The window lights showed a big, double-wheeled pickup parked across the way, a flatbed trailer hitched behind. On the trailer bed was a giant metal box the size of a Volkswagen. Patrick could see Tin standing with a few others. One of them was a good foot taller than the rest, noodle-thin, and rocking back and forth on his feet.

Hank stepped in front of Patrick and touched a hand to his shoulder. "Why don't you go wait inside," he said. "Warm up by the heater. We'll give you a holler when we're ready."

Patrick stepped from under Hank's hand and walked to the shed. Eugene was the only one inside, and he stood rubbing his hands over the heater, green flannel untucked and draping to the ass of his jeans. The red bud of his hat poked from his seat pocket. He looked back over his shoulder.

"You're still here."

"Yeah."

Eugene motioned with his head. "Stand over here if you want," he said. "I ain't gonna hit you or nothing."

Patrick came and stood opposite Eugene. He kept his hands in his pockets, and the warmth began seep through his jacket, and it stole the moisture from his eyes and the insides of his nostrils. Eugene was staring at the drum of the heater, his face corrugating in the rising heat.

"So the other night, when you were talking to Marcelle outside Rexall's. What did she say about me?"

"Nothing." He looked down at Eugene's hands. They were pink now, and he worked at them like they were under a faucet.

"Don't bullshit me, Luntz. I wanna know what she said."

"She didn't say anything about you."

"You sure about that? Cause she's been acting real weird lately."

Patrick looked up at Eugene. He continued to stare at the stove and show the yellowed band of his front teeth, and Patrick wondered when the hell they were going to come and tell them it was time to bring the minks to the truck.

"It was about my dad," he said.

"Your dad?" He finally looked up at Patrick. A crescent formed at the edge of his mouth. "About him busting out?"

"Yeah."

Eugene gave a horsey nod and slid his hands into his jeans pockets. The ends of his flannel fell over his wrists like falling water. He dragged his toe along the ground, burrowing a small ditch in the spicy dirt. A low cloud of dust rose and settled on his boot.

"You know, I could have told you," he said. "Anytime. But I didn't. Remember that." He wagged a finger at Patrick. Then he said, "You think he'll come back here?"

Patrick swallowed, and it felt as though the dust had come straight from Eugene's boot and found its way into his throat. The flesh seemed to cling to itself, and he worked his tongue over his teeth and the roof of his mouth, priming whatever moisture he could to quench the desert in his voice.

"I hope so," he croaked.

Eugene's face looked like a sudden fire had flashed in front of him. He drew his head back and repositioned his leg, standing as if he was in mid step.

"Why the fuck would you say that?" he asked.

"Cause he's my dad."

"Your dad's a goddamned murderer, in case you forgot."

Behind them, the door swung open, and Hank came in, followed by two other men.

"Let's move 'em out, boys."

# Patrick Anthony Luntz

And then the people clamored in, six or eight of them, Patrick couldn't be sure. It was a collage of overalls and boots, and canvas jackets, camouflage and denim. They shoved through and hoisted and hauled the cages like they were crates of eggs, groaning from the strain of the lifting and the sudden shift of balance as the minks threw themselves from one side of the cage to the other. And then the squalling came, and it was a needle deep into the brain. But the men just kept marching past Patrick, trailing the smell of cologne and tobacco and the sour odor of musk from the pissed off minks. Someone said, "Kid, don't just stand there with your thumb up your ass, start moving."

In the cage nearest, amid the blur of colors and smells, a fat mink crouched in the far corner of his den, tight against the mesh. He was a pile of blue, and his eyes gouged into Patrick's, black eyes, wide and glassy. And Patrick thought for a moment that with the light over his head the way it was, all white and brilliant, that he could see himself in those marble eyes, his own face looking back at him, his spidery hands reaching out to take hold of the crate. And then he was carrying it down the aisle, past men who swam around him and whooped at each other, and coughed, and knocked hard up against each other's shoulders.

One of the minks in a passing cage jumped up and ran to the other side. Its head swung wildly from one side to the other, maybe following the paths of its fellow mates, perhaps looking for a place where it could escape or targeting when the ride would finally come to an end. In the cage Patrick held, a small female stayed where she was in the far corner, her body curled into a loose knot, head buried into herself as if she was showing that she already knew what she was destined to be.

Outside, the tall man stood with Tin at the back of the trailer, and the door to the big freezer was swung wide open. A half-dozen or more cages lined the floor of the box, and when Patrick approached them, the tall man reached out to take the box from him. His gloved fingers grasped the mesh, and Patrick's held the mesh, and there was a tugging, but to his surprise Patrick could not bring himself to loosen his grip. He felt his heels leave the ground as the cage was pulled from him, and a final tug broke it free. The man slid the crate in the big freezer, and after a couple more found their ways into the space, the door was closed and cinched, the handle dropped like the airlock to a space capsule.

They were gathering closer to the thing now, Tin and the others. Eugene was there among them. The tall man walked to the side of the big box and twisted the spigot atop a large canister, some kind of tank that Patrick had not noticed before. And then they waited, all of them. They waited and even though a couple people tried to make small talk nobody wanted really to answer them, and so they stood quietly, smelling a little of sweat and damp wool, and a couple guys stepped back from the group and lit up cigarettes. Patrick's stomach felt like he had drunk a shot of whiskey—warm and unsure of what would happen next. Finally, the tall man said, "That's it," and he walked over and shut off the valve.

Someone tapped Patrick on the shoulder and said, "Let's go." And then the bodies tripped forward, snatching the cages from the cavernous space. They pushed past Patrick, knocking against him, and the minks lay in dark lumps on the bottoms like old, discarded socks. Eugene's voice broke into Patrick's head, telling him, "Grab a cage, Luntz, don't be a puss."

Something seemed to nudge him then, an unseen hand to the chest, and he felt himself stumbling backward over the crisp, frozen sod. The voices came deep from all sides, and they lobbed over him like softballs, dropping past his ears and rolling around his tangled feet as he danced drunkenly under the haze of a breaking dawn. A camouflaged jacket rushed at him, and Patrick threw up his guard, but the man grabbed him anyway, looping his arms under Patrick's and balancing the boy against his body. It seemed as if they stood like that for hours, this stranger holding him under a bleeding sky, as if they were in a waltz. A cold hand pressed against his forehead and cleared the cotton from his ears, and his legs discovered the ground again.

Eugene stood near the trailer with a toothy grin, his eyes bugging like white stones. The tall man hung back and kept his head low, taking quick, nervous glances at Patrick, but mostly tapping at the canisters and fiddling with things that Patrick suspected were probably fine. Tin sidestepped them all and came over. He put his hand on Patrick's shoulder and leaned in.

"You okay, son?"

Patrick sucked in a chest full of air and nodded.

"What's say we take us a little walk." He turned over his shoulder and yelled, "Goddamn it Eugene, I'm gettin tired of seeing you standing around playing with your pockets. Get the rest of 'em over to the fleshing before I throw you in there with 'em."

The sun was cutting through the trees now, scattering gold over the cobble of rocks skirting the riverbank. Curls of water pressed into the shallow pool, and Doug Fir needle-draped Periwinkles crawled toward the edges, their tiny, spidery legs moving them slowly over the sandy floor. Patrick sat on a tuft of crabgrass, his knees pressed to his chin. Tin stood beside him and drummed his old fingers against his trouser legs.

"Hell," he said. "That wasn't no big deal. I seen a two-hundred pound lumberjack give up his breakfast his first time out."

"I thought I'd be fine," said Patrick. "I thought about it all week. It never bothered me to think about it."

Tin laid his hand on Patrick's head. "You got nothin' to be ashamed of."

They stood there, Patrick listening to the gurgle of the river and the sawing of the jays hiding in the feathery hemlocks on the far side of the water. The frost was melting under Patrick's seat and was soaking into his jeans. Tin bent down and picked up a rock, and pitched it side-armed into the water. It skipped a couple times then disappeared below the surface.

"Does it hurt?" Patrick asked.

He had always wondered how it would be done. In the time since Tin had asked him if he would help, it had been the one question eating away at him. But he couldn't for the life of him figure out how to phrase it, not without sounding either gun shy or bloodthirsty. He'd had formulated all sorts of ideas. Twisting them at the neck, injecting them with poison. Clubbing them. The first time he had gone fishing with his father, he became sick to his stomach when his father took hold of the baton and smashed it against the bass' head. The dull thump, and the splatter of blood against Patrick's naked arm. It had taken three hits to kill it, or at least that was what his father had decided it would take.

"No," Tin said. "I don't reckon it hurts em much. It's a CO2 gas. Puts 'em to sleep."

"But they don't like it," he said. "It still scares them. I can tell that it scares them."

Tin lowered himself to the ground. His knees popped and he groaned some, down in his throat. But he took a seat next to Patrick and removed his hat, and picked at the plastic band with his fingernails. He folded the bill into a C shape, and slapped it against his knee.

"Thing is, Skunk," he said, "there ain't no such thing as a nice way to kill something." He leaned back and looked over at Patrick. In the sun's gouge, his face was like the bark on an old tree. He said, "You can look at it any way you want, but that's the God's honest truth. It don't matter if it's a mink or a mouse or a mosquito. One minute there's a life in front of you, and the next, it's gone. By your hand."

Patrick looked down at Tin's fingers, and the knuckles were like marbles straining against thin tissue. "So you just get used to it?" he said. "And it doesn't bother you?"

Tin fit the cap over his knee. He turned his palms up and held them there, as if he might catch the sunrise in his hands. "I look at it this way," he said. "If it ain't this farm, it's the forest. We cut 'em down, chop 'em up, use 'em to make our houses. Use the pieces to keep us warm. You ever hear a four hundred year-old Doug Fir come down? It's like a old man. It groans and it cries, and it creaks and snaps all over the place. It never feels good to take something that's lived so long and end it, just to make things better for you. But you put some more in the ground, and maybe in a hundred years, some Joe'll come along and do it all over again. And between then and then, all a fella can do is show respect and take care of em the best you can."

"So it doesn't bother you."

He put his hand on Patrick's shoulder and heaved himself to his feet.

"Kid, I learned to live with it," he said. "And someday, it'll be my turn to go. And when it happens, I hope someone makes it as quick and easy as I did for them. I'd say that's about all that any man can hope for."

# Marcelle and Eugene

She went to the kitchen for the third time that morning, this time stopping in the entry, where she slumped against the edge of the wall and pressed her hands over her stomach. It pained her, like broken glass was tumbling around inside there. She was so hungry. She was hungry and sick of everything, of the wallpaper that always screamed around them, and how the tins and bottles cluttered up the counters and the way the scribbled papers and snapshot photos stuck to the refrigerator like confetti. She hadn't even walked out the door yet, and already she wanted to crawl into a closet and just disappear.

Lyla Henry was up to her elbows in suds, pressed against the sink, shoulders working broad circles. "The nurse was clear," she said without turning around. "No food after midnight. Nothing." She ran a plate under the stream of water and slid it into the rack at her elbow. "Go in the living room. Watch T.V. or something. You're driving me crazy with all your pacing."

"What time do we go?"

Lyla tipped her head back and released an exhausted sigh. "I told you. Eleven."

The clock had no numbers, only dots. But it was clear enough to tell there was still well over an hour. She rolled from the wall and retreated to the sofa where she forced her herself to lie down, lifting her feet to the armrest. Eyes closed, she concentrated on the path of her own blood as it traveled down her legs and collected at her chest and her head, making her feel warm in the face and amplifying the beat of her own heart. The sounds of clattering dishes and silverware chimes echoed from the kitchen. She stared up at the ceiling, at the diamond flecks almost hidden within the cottage cheese texturing. *This time tomorrow*, she thought, *it'll be done*. She moved her hand over her stomach again then quickly brought it to the back of her head, touching the dampness still left from her shower. An engine growled outside, heavy and mean, revving two, three times, rattling the old, loose-paned windows before cutting to silent.

"Were you expecting Eugene this morning?" Lyla's voice was strained and tremorous.

Marcelle said nothing but leaned from the sofa to get a better view into the kitchen. Lyla had her wrist to her forehead.

The kitchen door raked open. Marcelle bolted from the couch and stood in the center of the room, her hand cupped over her mouth. Of course it was him. That car, that deep growl that she had once hungered for, that had once meant summer heat blowing through open windows, cruising up the mountain at sixty miles per hour, now sent her scrambling to look busy whenever she heard it. He thumped his hand against the kitchen door as he shoved it open because as usual, the entire house had to be made aware of his arrival.

"Marcelle?" His voice was low and hard, and even though he was out of view, Marcelle could see him there, greasy shirt, hands blackened up to his elbows. There would be a handprint on the door. "Marcelle get out here."

It didn't seem as if anything at all in Marcelle's life could possibly go the way it was supposed to as long as Eugene could find a way to get involved. She slid her fingers into her waistband sat down again on the edge of the sofa. Her stomach began to roll and pinch at her.

Lyla said, "What are you doing here?" She walked past the alcove and glanced into the living room at Marcelle, her hands wringing a dishtowel at her waist. "Aren't you supposed to be at work?"

"I was. Now I'm not." Bootsteps drummed the floor, and just like that, he was standing in the doorway. His arms stretched up, and he gripped the top of the alcove, thumbs smearing black onto the eggshell paint. He was a gorilla, chest puffed out under blotted armpits, legs bowed and rocking himself stupidly from side to side.

"What the hell are you doing?" he asked.

"Nothing."

"Nothing," he repeated. "Get your ass up. You're coming with me."

"I can't," she said. She laid her palms over her knees and the warmth of sweat seeped through her jeans.

Lyla stood behind Eugene, watching Marcelle. She reached up with her hand as if she might touch him on the shoulder or sweep her fingers through his hair. "Eugene, please," she said. "All this fuss."

"What do you care?" His voice sharpened even more, his eyes not leaving Marcelle's for a second. They pinned her to the sofa like nails driven through her legs. "She's my wife, right?" he said, over his shoulder to Lyla. "I always need her."

It had never seemed possible that Eugene might know what she was up to. The only people who knew about what lay ahead were her and Mrs. Luntz and Mrs. Henry. Somebody called the house, maybe. Somebody called and he picked up.

"Come on," he said, moving to the sofa and snatching hold of her wrist.

"Don't!" She pulled back from him and fell hard against the cushion. He reached out to her again, but she lashed out, swatting her arms as if he were a wasp. She knew she couldn't win, not if he was bound and determined to get her out the door. But she wasn't about to make it easy for him.

"I'm sick, Eugene. You want me to throw up in your car?"

He leaned into her and got hold of her again, this time with both hands. "Don't fuck around, Marcelle. I ain't in the mood."

"Eugene!" Lyla came into the living room, her hands clenched at her stomach. "You heard her. She's not feeling good."

"She's fine. We're just going for a ride," he said. He yanked Marcelle from the sofa and shoved her from him, sending her stumbling across the room, through the alcove and past Lyla, all the way into the kitchen.

There was an overlay of words behind Marcelle, Eugene and his mother in useless argument, but she hurried to pull her coat from the hook by the kitchen door anyway. It was a parka, but not the one she had planned to wear to the clinic. This one was the older one, the one with the broken zipper and the cigarette burn on the sleeve. She fought to work her arms into it, and the thing deep inside pushed and pinched at her, just like Eugene. He stomped into the kitchen and began to dig through the cupboard.

"What happened to the donuts?" He moved up and down the wall, opening and slamming doors.

Lyla hurried into the room and stopped in the doorway. She watched Marcelle with eyes that drew down at the sides. Her lips pinched together in a tight frown. "I ate them," she said. "Every last one."

Eugene looked at his mother as if she had just slapped him. His tongue ran over his lower lip, slowly from one side to the other. Lyla held her gaze solid. "The hell you did," he finally said. Then he glared at Marcelle, pushed past her, and swung the kitchen door to the wall. "Let's go."

He stomped down the steps to the car, tumbling his keys from his pocket and popping the trunk. Lyla stood beside Marcelle wearing a limp smile of defeat, lacing her slim fingers over the back of the dinette chair, neatly, as if staged for a portrait. Marcelle opened her mouth to speak. There was still time to stop him, to change his mind. His mother could put her foot down and demand that he leave Marcelle alone. But Lyla waved a hand at her.

"Go," she said. "Just go."

Marcelle crowded against the passenger door as Eugene shot

down the highway, taking in the blur of trees and telephone poles as they clicked past. A set alarm clock beat inside her, or maybe it was a Jack-in-the-box, crouched and winding slowly, inching closer to breaking with every passing minute. Eugene cleared his throat. He sat stony with his hands firmly on the wheel, eyes forward, lids quivering. In small tics, his lips moved as if he was reading directions to someone who lived only inside his head. It was the sort of thing he did when there was something important waiting for him at the other end of the trip. When he had to talk to Benny about the job. Before he and Marcelle went inside to tell Mrs. Henry they were getting married. Anytime he went off to buy a bag of weed from somebody he didn't already know.

They were at the base of the mountain, almost forty-five minutes into the ride before he said a word to her again.

"Take the wheel." He let go before she could get a good hold on it. The car veered toward the shoulder and Marcelle jerked the wheel in an overcorrection, and there was a hard move to the center. Eugene grabbed it back from her and held it, shooting her a look. He thrust his chin at her and she took it again, carefully moving closer to him.

"Jesus Christ," he muttered. He leaned to one side of his ass and reached back, fishing a can of Kodiak from his pocket. He popped the lid, tobacco shavings spilling over his lap, and pinched out a fat, grape-sized clump and stuffed it into his mouth.

"When we get there," he said, "I don't want you doing anything unless I say so. Don't say anything. Don't do anything. Just sit."

"Where we going?"

He reached under his seat and pulled out an empty Coke can. He pressed it to his lip and spit a brown slug into it. "Somewhere," he said. "Business."

"What kind of business?"

"None of yours, that's what." He showed a row of brown-specked teeth. "Just shut up, you're stressing me." He reached into the console and thumbed through a few cassettes, then pulled one and punched it into the player. It was a band Marcelle never really liked but missed listening to, all the nights parked at the AM/PM with the doors wide open, standing behind Eugene with her arms locked at his stomach, waiting for those moments when he would take a break from his friends to turn around and kiss her, in front of everyone.

She slid closer to the door and pulled the parka hood over her head. Now that she wasn't going to the clinic, she wanted food more than ever. Her stomach was fighting her and winning, and the spot where Eugene had grabbed her wrist felt like a sunburn. They were dipping down now, coasting the scoop to the wide river slough separating the rural from the suburban. The white tops of office buildings rose up over a low beltline of bare trees, the endpoint to the long, trestle bridge that stretched over yellowed fields. Here and there, standing mirror patches of water shone on the plain, still left over from the week's rain. Marcelle had ridden over this bridge when the entire thing had flooded into one giant lake. A half-dozen farmhouses littered the land on both sides, filthy and cockeyed, as if they'd each been kicked hard in the side and left to rot through the winter.

Times like this, when Eugene would just toss her aside, Marcelle found herself turning over everything she had ever heard about him, from his own mouth or from the mouths of others. She had decided a long time ago that it was him who had set fire to Mick's Laundromat, that it wasn't Patrick's dad like Eugene had suggested. It was the kind of thing Eugene would do, just because it would set people off. After all, he had done that stupid thing with the soap all over the floor at the school. Anyone with half a brain would have been able to realize what a crazy thing that was to do. How could he not have known that someone could get hurt real bad by doing that, or even killed? Mrs. Henry once told Marcelle that it was like he was stuck at five years old, that he could not ever see more than ten minutes past where he was.

They left the highway finally and emptied onto Pacific Avenue, and for a moment Marcelle wondered again if Eugene did know everything about her situation, if he hadn't known all along. Maybe he was taking her to the clinic himself, to make sure that she did it, so he could watch, to be sure it was done right. He spun the steering wheel, white knuckles, and cut from the arterial into the grid of old bungalows, crisscrossing a few blocks over to Broadway where he turned onto the main drag. They headed north, past the fast food burger joints with their red and yellow painted signs and the taco stands, and used car lots with strings of rainbow teeth flapping in the wind. There were people in long coats and stocking hats pushing grocery carts where there were no grocery stores, and taverns with half-lit neon signs and dented cars crowding the fronts. Just before the street dipped down into a shopping plaza, Eugene hooked the wheel and steered into the parking lot of what looked to Marcelle like a motel.

She leaned over the dash and peered up through the windshield. It was hideous. Marcelle couldn't believe that any decent person would pay a single dime to set foot in there, let alone stay the night. Like the Sleep Inn, there was a separate office hut at the end, with a long stretch of side-by-side rooms that faced the busy street. But that was where the similarities ended. The faded white paint striping barely suggested parking stalls for each unit. Soupy orange paint hung from the clapboard like the place was molting, and a strip of dying grass sprung from the gutters in a long, yellow eyebrow. Mismatched drapes and busted screens scarred the windows. All over the concrete lot a patchwork of oil spots spread from building to fence.

"Why are we here?" she asked. Did he want to have sex with her? They could have done that at home, or off the highway in the car, even. Eugene said nothing, but turned to look out his window at the motel. He pulled his sleeve from over his watch. "Eugene," Marcelle said. "Please talk to me."

He shot her the look and stepped from his seat, hugging

the exterior of the car as he circled to the backend. There was the sound of keys and then Marcelle heard the trunk pop, and a tumble vibrated through to where she sat with her hands tucked under her thighs. The car bounced and shook, and then the trunk slammed shut.

Suddenly he was at her door, thumping knuckles against the glass and waving her out. Draped over his shoulder was a purple sports bag, a bag she had never seen in her life. It sunk heavy at his side, and he scooped his hand under it as if he was cradling a baby, or at least in the halfhearted way Marcelle imagined he might try to. In that moment she could almost picture him as a father, though she had to work hard to imagine what it might look like. Tipping a bottle to his son's mouth, patting it on the back when it cried. Saying, There, there, baby. A bandage of silver tape extended from the bag's bottom. She wound down the window.

Eugene said, "Let's go," then he opened the door and pulled her arm, and she jumped from the seat before he could hurt her again. He walked away, and she followed him to the overhang and down the walkway, coming to a stop in front of number 8.

He stood at the door with his hands to his sides, staring at the number, almost as if he was counting to himself. She wrapped an arm around the post, thinking of just how much all of this was starting to feel like really bad news, the same twist in her stomach as when Patrick had pulled the pills from his pocket. Only this was worse. This was more than a simple unknown, an equal chance of excitement or danger, of putting yourself in the hands of someone who really believed he was giving you something good. There wasn't the slightest bit of good that would come from this place.

Eugene knocked on the door, a drumbeat of dull, clumsy thuds. He jammed his hand into his pocket and stepped back, sidling up to Marcelle as if she was the willing partner in whatever scheme was about to go down. A volley of voices came from the inside, two or three people maybe, and when the door finally opened a man who was both taller and wider than Eugene stood in the doorway, his giant hand wrapped over the door jamb. A dark beard sprayed out from his face, and his head sported a dirty red baseball cap, plain with no writing.

"Jimmy?" His voice was dry and deep, and it croaked when he said the name.

"Yeah," Eugene said. "I'm Jimmy." Marcelle looked at him. He kept his eyes forward, but she knew he must be doing all he could to keep from looking at her. She squeezed the post tighter and looked down at her shoes.

"Who's that?" The man nodded to Marcelle. Behind him, another man sat on the edge of a California king, showing mirrored sunglasses and arms that could have been either sleeves or tattoos. His head was shaved tight at the sides, flat along the top.

"Her? She's my wife." Eugene looked at Marcelle and when he smiled, he might as well have kicked her in the stomach. How many times had she seen that same snake's grin and listened to his voice as he referred to her as his girlfriend, or his fiancé and believed that he really meant it? She had always imagined a bond between them, one that was so much more than what everyone had warned her he was capable of. Now she wanted to pull away from him, to run from this place and leave him alone to soak in whatever might be waiting on the other side of that door.

"Your wife?" The man looked at Marcelle. He moved his lips back and forth and the beard shifted like a sleeping cat. "What are you, twelve?"

Marcelle stepped away from the post and Eugene. "I'm almost eighteen," she said, folding her arms over her chest.

"Yeah," the guy laughed. "Eighteen in about five years." He laughed again and tipped his dirty red cap back on his head. He looked at Eugene. "I don't want no fuckin schoolgirl here."

"She's no schoolgirl," Eugene said.

The man shook his head. "She ain't coming in here."

Eugene moved over so that he was next to Marcelle again. His shoulder pressed hers and Marcelle could feel his tremble. "Come on, man," he said. "It's not a big deal."

"She ain't comin' in." Behind him, the Army guy leaned forward on the edge of the bed. At his feet, an ashtray sat piled with a mound of stubbed filters.

Eugene moved the bag from one shoulder to the other, and the sound of glass against glass came through the fabric. He pulled back and looked at Marcelle. His eyes narrowed at her, as if this complication were all her fault, as if she had been the one to do something wrong. He'd told her to keep quiet, but then she had opened her mouth, told the man how old she was. He gave her a nudge with his shoulder.

"Go wait in the car." He cleared his throat and leaned over and kissed her hard on the cheek. She pulled back and his eyes held onto hers, even as he backed away toward the motel door.

Marcelle held to the post as he disappeared into the room, and then she dug her hands into the pockets of her parka and walked back to the car and climbed inside. The raw smell of Eugene's underarms and his tobacco breath filled the space. He had left his coveralls in a wad on the backseat. She unwound the window and put her elbow on the door, and looked out over the parking lot to the yard past the chain link fence. In the distance a school faced her, lit up windows grinning a long row of yellowed teeth. Kids swarmed everywhere, scrambling over a tight cluster of playground equipment, swatting tetherballs around poles. A smattering of boys knocked a red ball up and down the grassy field. Marcelle's grade school had had a swing set with three swings and a connected slide, and a separate merry-go-round that had been roped off to the kids. She couldn't remember if they had monkey bars or not. She had a vision of drawing a checkerboard hopscotch with a chunk of drywall that she had taken from the bed of her dad's pickup truck, but she couldn't be sure if she had drawn it at school or on her own sidewalk.

The kids ran everywhere, spilling from the slide, darting along the fence, up and down the stairs behind the school, back and forth like ants, always running, running everywhere. It was hard for her to imagine that she ever did that. Run from one place to another, screaming with joy and excitement. But she must have. That's what all kids did. What would happen, she wondered, if you never outgrew it? What would the world be like if grownups sprinted in the mall from one store to another, pushing through the other shoppers, screaming just for fun as they ran from their cars, through the parking lot with the shared goal of getting there before everyone else? She could run far if she had to, if the right thing was waiting at the end for her. Her own apartment. A television and a microwave, where she could watch whatever she wanted and eat as much she desired. Someone who made her laugh, instead of cry. There were things she could still have if she wanted them bad enough.

Her stomach rumbled again and she thought, what the hell, might as well go on across the street to the minimart and get something to eat. Her appointment was definitely dead, and it was not likely that Eugene would be coming out anytime soon. She picked three quarters from the console and opened the glove compartment that was packed full of trash. She dug through the folds of papers and bolts and empty cigarette packs for any other loose coins that might have been tossed in with everything else. A thick yellow envelope pushed itself from the stack, and immediately Marcelle saw a layered band of green bills peeking from the opening. She slid it from the compartment and held it in her fingers, looking out the windshield toward the motel window that remained curtained and still. She took the bills from the envelope and spread them in a tight fan. They were all twenties and she counted twenty of them before she gave up and drew one from the stack and tucked it into her pocket.

"Fucker," she said aloud. He didn't make this kind of money working for Benny. He'd either stolen it from someone or was selling whatever it was he'd stolen from someone. It was dirty money no matter how you looked at it, and the thought of it here in his car, this piece of trash car, was both terrifying and infuriating. How dare he? How dare he have all this money stashed away and yet when she asked to go out for a simple movie or a burger and a Coke, they could never afford it? He might miss it, but she honestly didn't care one bit what he might say. She could pretend not to know a thing about it, not about that twenty or even the whole envelope. Just like she didn't know a damned thing about why she was even there in the first place.

She crossed the lane and paused in the median, bouncing on her toes while a heavy truck downshifted and crawled up the low hill. When it passed, she dashed to the sidewalk and rushed into the store, making a beeline to the chips. She had just taken a bloated bag of cheese puffs from the rack when she heard a woman at the counter say, "Something's going down over there."

They were outside of the motel room now, the two men only, and they stood on either side of Eugene's car, each caught in his own strange moment. The smaller one held the purple bag over his shoulder like it was a huge purse. He was lizardlike, his crewcut head looking from side to side in hard, short ticks. The lumberjack was more casual, the way he just leaned the weight of his body against the car, thick arm propped against the fender like it was a kickstand. It looked to Marcelle as though he were staring right at her, black eyes peering straight through the window into the store. A jacket that he did not have on before draped over him, a long, black thing falling almost to his knees.

Marcelle moved back from the window, retreating to where the sodas packed the refrigerator against the farthest wall. The motor behind the glass hummed and rattled, drowning whatever conversation might be happening at the register. The cashier was a sinewy woman, with yellow hair and dark roots, and she tore strips of lottery tickets like ripping fabric. A geezer in a fisherman's hat stood clutching his wallet, his head shaking slowly. A wad of bills lay on the counter.

The car was still clearly visible from where she stood. Even with the rows of chips and canned food and cookies and magazines between her and the window, she could see the men. They stood like guards, or like hawks waiting on a fence rail for any bit of movement, any reason to pounce. Eugene was nowhere.

He might still be in the room, she thought, but what then? Maybe he was waiting for them to leave or wanted her to come in and get him. For a moment she imagined him dead, sprawled out on the bathroom floor or in the tub, like a clothed Trucker Otis waiting to be discovered. It wasn't the first time she pictured him dead; now and then she found herself bringing certain snapshots to mind: him trapped under his car, or crumpled at the bottom of the basement steps. She hated that about herself. Wives didn't think about their husbands having to die in order to set them free.

For a minute it looked like the bearded one might come to her. He broke from the car and walked a few steps toward the street, quick, with big, lumbering strides. But the skinny guy said something, something that made him stop and turn around. They were talking about something for sure, and then both looked to the office hut, almost in a synchronized motion. And then just like that, they broke loose and ran to the far end of the lot where they climbed into a gray-primered van and squealed out onto the road, disappearing up over the hill.

She waited some time before leaving. There were soda can labels to look at and bags of pepperoni and pretzels, and bean dip to pick up and put back in the same way. She wanted to be sure they weren't playing a trick on her, just driving to the end of the block so they could turn around and come back to surprise her. There was a row of aspirin and vitamins and cough drops in packages smaller than she'd ever seen before.

"Something I can help you with, hon?" The cashier stood against the counter, her pencil fingers tapping the Formica. Lips stretched over marbled teeth, lips chalky and crackled. "Them guys got you scared over there?"

Marcelle pinched her lips together and shook her head.

"You want me to call the cops? I can get the cops here in five if you want."

A small orange Japanese car pulled up to the window and a black woman got out, followed by a little boy in the brightest striped pants that Marcelle had ever seen. The woman took hold of his hand and they walked to the glass doors, the boy not even up to her hips, hips that were so full and round, and the woman walked in hard steps, as if she had a single purpose in life, a purpose to kick the ass of any man who might dare to tell her what to do.

As the doors swung open and the boy followed his mother in, Marcelle darted through them on the backswing. She stood under the awning and stared across the street at the motel, at the door, number 8. No matter what he'd done or why he'd dragged her there, no matter where she might run off to tomorrow or next week or whenever, Eugene was her husband. She owed it to Mrs. Henry at least to get into that room and see what had happened.

She ran at a full sprint across the street, darting between passing cars and through the parking lot, past Eugene's car and straight to the motel door. She blocked her mind to what she might see when she opened the door; she just turned the knob and pushed her way inside.

He lay on the floor, still halfway dressed into his jacket. A sleeve stretched limply from his body, like he had been skinned part way and left to bleed out. All down the front of his t-shirt was an apron of red, and blood ran from his mouth and his nose, shining in the thin blade of light that spilled into the room. She stumbled toward him and he recoiled, creaking out a watery moan. He was alive.

Marcelle screamed, then turned and slammed the door closed behind her, locking it. She went to him, collapsing to her knees and taking his arm in her hands. "Oh god, Eugene. What did you do?"

"Jesus fucking Christ Marcelle," he wailed. "What the fuck is wrong with you?" Blood spattered from his mouth, peppering her face and her hair. He swore at her again and then he mumbled something else, something Marcelle couldn't begin to make out.

"I'll call 911." She jumped up and went to the bedside phone. There were a half dozen peeling stickers framing the grid of buttons, complex directions for dialing out, the codes and the costs. For all the telephones Marcelle had swabbed at the Sleep Inn, she had never imagined she would actually have to use one.

Eugene pushed himself up on one elbow and yelled at her again. His face had begun to swell now, his blue eyes almost completely shut from bloated cheeks. A crescent-shaped slice stretched from his temple to his ear, ending in a dark purple smudge at the base of his jaw. "No cops," he said. "Take me home."

"I can't drive, Eugene." She held the earpiece out from her, as if it was a lifeline she was offering to him. She struggled to even imagine herself behind the wheel of a car, huddled over it like an old woman, hugging the centerline, cars and trucks flashing their lights at her and laying on horns as she careened down the highway out of control.

"Take me the fuck home, Marcelle. I need to get home."

"You need a hospital." She couldn't begin fix him this time. He was probably dying; driving him all the way to Ash Falls would only guarantee it. She set the phone down and walked to him, stood over him as he lay back onto the rug and squinted at the ceiling. His chest was a giant red wave, rising and falling, bubbles popping at the edges of his mouth. He was as helpless as a beat up dog.

"Please," he whispered. "Get me home."

# Marcelle

A thin whisper filled the room. Air seeped from the tank into coils of tubing, curls winding under a fleshy white arm up to his face, where it hissed out of prongs shoved into his nose. Now and then a passing nurse's clipped voice or the elevator bell, or cry from somewhere far off, fell into the room.

Marcelle, Jonas and Lyla Henry sat in chairs far from one another, surrounded by white walls pocked with brass-framed devotionals, and shiny, mottled paintings of beaches with angry waves smashing into the shore. For the most part the women studied their fingernails or gazed out the window, stealing uncomfortable glances at one another now and then. Mr. Henry seemed content to gawk at the football game playing itself out on the television. Each of them looked to Eugene only occasionally. It was as if doing so were an obligation or a curiosity rather than concern, because what if his eyelids suddenly opened, Marcelle wondered, and he caught them paying attention to something other than him? She let her eyes linger on him a bit longer then, but he just lay still and almost completely noiseless, except for a rhythmic, wet clicking sound that was coming from somewhere down in the back of his throat.

Lyla had taken the chair closest to the bed as soon as they entered the room, perching herself on the edge of the seat, her back arched almost inward. For the longest time she stared with her forehead striped with worry, craning her head to the hallway anytime a pair of heels passed by. By now, though, she had settled into a kind of posture that could actually be sustained, slumped low in her seat, her bony hand gripping the bed rail, owlish eyes riveted by something lingering in the dead air, Marcelle didn't know what. Her heavy wool winter coat was buttoned halfway up, obscuring her familiar blue, checked shirt. These were different clothes than Marcelle had remembered from the morning. Lyla had changed out of whatever it was she had been wearing that morning, and the harder Marcelle tried to see the color of the particular shirt, or recall whether she had been wearing pants or a skirt, the more it pressed at her mind. Maybe Lyla had simply given up on seeing Marcelle again that morning, figuring she might as well just go on with the rest of her day. That would make sense. But what if it wasn't like that at all? What if it wasn't until the phone call from the hospital that she had gone to the bedroom and taken the time to lay out a new outfit, even though the nurse must have told her and Jonas to drop everything and get to the emergency room, because they didn't know what might happen with Eugene yet? What did it matter if she wore a buttoned yellow blouse or a sweater to the hospital?

*You made your bed*, her mother had told her. *Now lie in it*. It must be what waited for all mothers, that moment when their son or daughter had gone one step too far, pushing things to the point where they just couldn't do it anymore, not with any real desire anyway. Marcelle's mother had left without so much as a goodbye, just closed the trunk of the car and put her hand out the window as she drove away, not even a real wave. And now even Mrs. Henry seemed to be just going through motions, as if a string had been pulled at her back and was slowly drawing itself back in.

Marcelle found a piece of gum in the bottom of her purse, under the thick envelope of money she had slipped from Eugene's glove compartment, before the police brought her to the hospital. His balloon chest lifted and dropped, his lips barely kissing the clear plastic tubing, the crisp white strips holding it all in, holding his whole face together maybe. The tape traced up and over lips still stained with blood, cheeks big and blue like storm clouds hovering behind stark white, jet airplane tracks. What had only three hours earlier been a limp, bloody rag was now a body that looked pumped full of air, so full that the ears were almost sucked back into his head. Its eyeballs pressed forward from the skull, straining against the thick, crusty eyelids, skin purpling all the way to the temples. This wasn't her husband; this was more of a monster.

And yet his lips curled a little at the edges, as they always did, and she couldn't help seeing him in there, the boy who had held her hand when no one else would, who had told her, "I think you're the one who can fix me, Marcelle." The hissing went on almost silently, and his chest rose, but the plastic tube hardly moved, a tiny bubble perched on the thin surface of blackened lips.

The doctor had directed all that he had to say to Mr. and Mrs. Henry, looking at Marcelle only when Mrs. Henry did so first. There were things Marcelle didn't quite get—white blood cells, protein count—but there was plenty she did understand. Eugene's brain was damaged, and it was getting bigger inside of his not-very-big skull. The guys at the motel had broken some of his ribs. And a lung collapsed. Four of his teeth were gone completely, maybe he swallowed them, the doctor wasn't sure. But he would live. He might not be the same man he was before, but he would at least be alive.

"He'll need attention," the doctor had said to Lyla. Lyla's arms were folded over her chest, and even when Marcelle stepped to the side in order to catcher her attention, she would not look at her. "I can't tell you how much or for how long, yet. Maybe we'll know more tomorrow."

Mr. Henry turned off the television, the gray and pallid outside light giving him a doughy silhouette as he stood from his chair. He ran a hand over what was left of his hair then walked around the foot of the bed, stopping in front of Marcelle.

"I'm going down for some coffee," he said. "You want a

sandwich?" He fished his wallet from his back pocket and opened the fold, leaning into his hands, into the shuffling stack of bills. "I don't even know what they have down there." He flipped the wallet closed and stuffed it into his front pocket.

"I'll pick you up a sandwich."

Marcelle looked past him over to Lyla, who sat with her chin dropped against the clasp of her jacket zipper, her glasses resting halfway down the bridge of her nose.

"Do you want anything, Mrs. Henry?" she asked.

"No." She raised her head and pushed her glasses back up to her eyes.

Mr. Henry said, "We could be here awhile."

"I said no," she snapped. She waved a hand at him. He looked back at Marcelle, sighed, and shuffled from the room with a hundred extra pounds on his shoulders.

The women sat for a good five minutes without speaking. It was strange for Lyla to sit still so long, nothing for her hands to do, no lacework or crossword puzzle or coupon clipping from newspaper inserts. Marcelle found herself wondering more about what was going on in Lyla's mind than what might not be going on in Eugene's. Maybe she regretted not doing more to stop him from leaving that morning. Maybe she was thinking this was just one more burden she had on her lap, once again all thanks to Eugene. She had stopped even pretending to look over at him by now, sometimes glancing over the same ugly, framed paintings whose every brushstroke Marcelle had memorized.

"So," she said, sitting up straight and looking at Marcelle. "What now?" One lens of her glasses was opaque, reflecting the pale sky.

Marcelle started. She hadn't expected to be pulled into this, not as someone who was expected to know what to do next, to say what she thought about anything.

"We need a plan, Marcelle." Lyla ran her eyes over the four walls of the room again, nodding her chin as if she was taking inventory. The IV bag, dangling, dripping as it hung from the gleaming pole. The towering, green-painted oxygen tank with its hissing, coiled tubes. The heavy wood door that opened out into an impossibly waxed hallway. "I don't even know where to start."

"It'll work out, Mrs. Henry." The words dropped from Marcelle's mouth to the floor without a moment's thought. The truth was, she hadn't a clue what was next. One minute she pictured herself away, anyplace that wasn't Ash Falls, alone. No baby to worry about, that was for sure. And then she would look at Eugene swaddled in that blanket, hands curled at his chest and her heart would just sink. If someone as old as Lyla didn't know what to do, how could she ever hope to figure it out?

Lyla closed her eyes. She pounded her fist on the metal bed railing, and Eugene's fleshy face rocked slightly from side to side, the lines from the heart monitor jumping with him.

"Good Lord," she said. "What have I done to earn this?"

Marcelle sat with her hands folded on her lap, the blood moving through her body, warming her arms and legs and working through her middle, through the tiny thing that still grew inside her, that thing that was still part her and part Eugene, not yet taken out but still holding on tight. She could go from that room, right then and there if she wanted to. She wondered if Eugene would even remember he had a wife, and that the two of them slept together in that big bed in the basement, that they had loud fights over things like too much food and not enough sex and dirty socks always left on the floor. She wondered if he would remember hitting her, then waking her the next morning, on his knees, holding a cookie over her face, or a dahlia he'd snatched from the neighbor's garden. And if not—if the memory of all of that was erased—could it be that it never happened? Maybe they could start over again, she being the wise one this time, knowing exactly which things to do differently. And then it could be the way it was supposed to have been all along.

Lyla was snapping through the pages of a magazine now, too fast to really be reading. Mr. Henry came in without saying a word and handed Marcelle a plastic-wrapped tuna sandwich. She took it and unwrapped it, picking at the crusts to be polite.

"For goodness sakes, take her home so she can get some decent food and a bath," Lyla said. "She can't do anything here, anyway."

"You as well," he said. "There isn't anything going to come of you sitting in that chair all night except a sore back. We'll pack you a bag and you can come back tomorrow if you want."

They drove in the same silence that Marcelle had come to expect from the Henrys. Other than a few unintelligible words from Jonas, followed by the cooing response of Lyla, all dialogue flushed from the crackling radio station. Home was sixty miles away, sixty miles of snaking, climbing roadway to remember when Eugene had sworn that his mother would love Marcelle, that they would be close even, smooth words spoken through tobacco breath in the darkness of a canvas tent, lumpy blankets under her body as his scratchy fingertips circled her bare back. Weekend nights lowered carefully from her bedroom window, his buddies sometimes in the car, often not, moonlit roadway reaching deep into the thickness of trees as they drove too fast up the mountainside to the quarry. Sometimes a bonfire would already be lit, and he would hold her by her waist while he tipped the bottle to his lips and swung the empty over his shoulder to send it smashing into the granite wall, yelling and whooping as shards rained on boulders. And she belonged to him then, and his friends saw this, and those girls who would not talk to her in town called her by her name and passed the joint through her hands, and pretended she was one of them.

She had an hour to think about all of this, this plus the first time she'd made him mad enough to hit her, and the tenderness in the apology, the warm, tight grip as he took hold of her in the backseat of the car, and the hot breath on her neck and declarations of just how much he loved her then, right then, and promises that there was so much still waiting for the two of them. She had all the time in the world, staring at the backs of Mr. and Mrs. Henry's heads, to flip the scene over and over in her head, the set teeth and the backhanded swing, the tears and the firm hold on her waist, over and over with only the seasons and the daylight changing in the memories, and the growing coolness of what had once been electric between them. And she had a lifetime to feel the sharpness that seeing those other girls in his car brought her, and the dead, limp stare he gave when she asked him, *What's the matter, Eugene? I'm not good enough for you no more?*

Each township and turnoff along the way brought them closer to Ash Falls. She looked out the window at the passing world, hearing the sound of Eugene's rattling chest and his deep growl through a clenched jaw, and she could see a future with sheets drawn over his pasty chest, his eyes closed or not, the branch of scars that wound up and down his arms and over his face. Her stomach swayed with the bend in the road, and she could feel the sweat on his clammy face, like raw meat, and the dead weight as she struggled to move him to a chair or back into bed, or on the toilet, leaning him into her as she helped clean his seat. Giving him a bath, maybe, if Mrs. Henry did not expect to do it herself.

Everything she remembered or imagined or pieced together as possibility welded another bar to her cage, and for a brief moment Marcelle considered opening the door right then and there and jumping right out onto the highway.

By the time they pulled onto Shale Street, the streetlamps were steady, spreading white pools over the cracked, gray concrete. Marcelle collected her purse to her lap and undid her seatbelt. The second they came to a stop in the driveway she stepped from the car, circling around the trunk to the stripe of lawn that separated them from the neighbors.

"Marcelle?" Lyla stood against the fender of the car, her jacket bunched against her chest. "Marcelle, what are you doing?"

"I think I want to go for a walk. If that's okay."

"Well don't you want to go inside and get cleaned up?"

Marcelle shook her head firmly.

"It's cold," Lyla said. She reached a hand out, as if she might take hold of her from twenty feet away. "It feels like snow, even. You should come inside."

Marcelle tucked her purse under her arm and bit down on her lip. That she felt as if she might start to cry surprised her, that sudden swell in her throat, the molten rush from her stomach up into her chest. It wasn't Lyla or Jonas or even Eugene, but the sense that all she wanted to do was keep walking past that tiny strip of grass, down the sidewalk and on and on, she didn't know where. Someplace where every house was new to her, and nobody recognized who she was. Mrs. Henry had to stop talking and Marcelle had to stop listening to her, just get her feet moving again.

It was so much colder than it had been that morning, the kind of air that slapped at the skin and made ears sting. Soft lights gave away all the living rooms of the block, low, golden squares looking out, drapes still open on some, blinking blue lights of television sets playing to rooms that looked mostly empty. She tucked her purse down into her jacket and quickened her step, weaving through unfenced yards and naked hedges, four streets of forgotten plastic summer clutter, pails and shovels, errant lawn darts and toppled yard furniture. At the end of it all she stopped midway up Maple to sit down on the cold concrete curb, directly across from the Luntz home.

In a dozen breaths, Marcelle took in wood smoke from as many chimneys and the heady odor of moss that crept over the lawn behind her, moss that seemed to find its way into every living thing. She sensed the slice of coming winter, the metallic scent that came down the mountain from the glaciers, and the frigid rivers that wove back and forth under the highway bridges, all the way down to the wide, saltwater bay. All the lights were on at the Luntz house.

She gathered her purse into her arms, set her jaw firm and pushed off from the curb. She marched across the street to the back door, where Mrs. Luntz stood in the kitchen, just on the other side of the paned glass, pulling cans from an open cupboard as if nothing remarkable at all had happened that day.

The moment she swung open the door, Bobbie put her hands to her mouth. Marcelle could feel her scouring every inch of her, as if she were following the quilt of her old parka, over her breasts and the swollen sleeves. She moved her head to one side as she looked over Marcelle's legs, thick and trembling as they must have been, and the bare hands whose nails clung tightly to the cuffs of her sleeves. Reaching out, she took Marcelle by the arm and pulled her from the porch, over the threshold.

"Jesus Christ," she said. "What happened to you?"

That she hadn't realized the extent of it in the hospital made no sense. But under the harsh white globe of the ceiling lamp the rust-colored patchwork came through, blood that had soaked into the pale blue of her jacket and over her jeans, and the drops that had spattered onto the toes of her once white tennis shoes. Bobbie pushed around her and leaned out the door, turning her head right and left before closing the door hard.

"What in the hell's going on? Tell me that's not what it looks like."

Marcelle went to the small table near the living room alcove and sat down. "It's Eugene's," she said, pulling at her stained jacket. "These guys at a motel in Everett beat him up. He's in the hospital."

"What guys?"

"I told the police what I saw. I don't know."

And then Bobbie sat down too. She stared at Marcelle's coat again, her eyes washing over it as if she were hoping to clean her with her mind. At some point she looked up again, brows pulled to the sides, lids welling. It was obvious that she wanted to ask more but she would not do it. She just took hold of Marcelle's hands and squeezed them, holding them together with her own.

"The Henrys drove me home," Marcelle said. "He's going to be there awhile I think. After that, I don't know."

"About him or you?"

"What?"

"After that, you don't know about him, or about you?"

In the room adjacent, the television was on. A man and a woman were fighting over roars of canned laughter. They were outside in a backyard that wasn't real, with fake trees holding up the fat man as he lay back on a hammock with a can of beer perched on his giant belly. The woman paced around him like she was an ostrich, hysterical, slicing at the air with her arms as she ranted.

Then Bobbie said, "You want me to call Patrick in here?"

Marcelle stared down at her thighs again. One of the bloodstains was a handprint.

It was funny how little they said to one another at first, like they were two children meeting for the first time. Patrick's mother held her hand in the small of Marcelle's back, as if she might pull back and run from the house.

"Hey Marcelle," he said. He stared at his socks, stark white with gray toes. His jeans bunched at his ankles, like they always did.

"Hey."

Bobbie said, "You guys can chat in the living room if you want. I was just going to finish up in here and go to bed."

"You want to go outside?" Patrick asked. He looked up at Marcelle then, his gaze moving up the front of her jacket, crisscrossing from one side to the other before settling at last on her eyes.

Tiny flakes swirled in the cone of the streetlight, and in the yellow glow of the porch lamp, the slightest specks of snow had begun to cling to the grass blades. The two of them sat together on the porch steps, close enough for Marcelle to steal some of Patrick's warmth.

"So are you still working at that farm?" she asked. "With those minks, or whatever?"

"Yeah." Patrick leaned forward on his knees. "There was pelting the other day. Killing them and all." He nodded so that his whole body rocked back and forth, and Marcelle could see the forced bravado, the same tone and body language that he used to show when he talked about those weeks he'd been on the run.

"Was it hard?" she asked. "To kill them?"

He shrugged his shoulders and stole a glace at her, lightning-quick. "A little, I guess. But it has to happen. They're not pets."

"Eugene used to always say how nasty they were, how they had it coming."

He sat back on his hands and looked over at her. His eyes widened with a look that shrunk her down into her shoes. "That doesn't mean it's fun to watch them die."

"I never said it was." Marcelle shifted on her rear and tugged the zipper of her jacket down a few inches to let the cold air inside. The snow was falling heavier now, the flakes still tiny yet filling the spaces under the streetlights and beginning to whiten the dark sidewalk that stretched out to the street.

"It was so crazy, in that motel. With Eugene." She rubbed her hands over her knees. "I thought he was dead. By the time the cops came he was shaking so hard they had to put him on a board and tie straps over him. And the whole time he's just staring up at the ceiling, his eyes all big and wide. He looked so scared. And the blood, just running out of him, all over the carpet. They're gonna have to tear it all out and replace it, you know. That much blood won't ever come out."

She looked to Patrick, who leaned forward on his knees with head in his hands. His eyes gave away nothing, not sympathy, not disgust, not even satisfaction at the details Marcelle gave.

"I never seen him look that scared before," she said, "not in all the time we been together. I sure didn't expect that."

Patrick blew into his hands, a plume of steam sifting through his fingers. The light from the porch lamp washed over him, turning the blond streak in his hair a shade of orange. He seemed older than when she last saw him, even two weeks earlier, from Eugene's car at the drugstore. His face looked hard. Stronger, maybe. Maybe it was his father's face that was growing into him.

"So what are you gonna do now?"

"Everything's so different," she said. "I don't even know how I got here." She shook her head, a tear rolling down her cheek, traveling halfway to her chin before she wiped at it with her sleeve. "Sometimes I feel like I want to just get on a bus and go wherever it's headed." She looked at him, but he stared straight ahead. "You know like we used to talk about? Not even look to see where it's going," she said.

"You could do that," he said.

"No I couldn't. That only happens in the movies."

Then it came to her. Before she had a chance to think it through clearly, it was out of her mouth, into there air, impossible to take back.

"Do you think you could talk to that lady? The one you stayed with?"

"Mama T?" Patrick leaned back on the porch step, looking up the street, as if the answer to Marcelle's question would be found somewhere on the next block.

"What's wrong?" she said, as if it was the greatest idea in the world. "I got money. And I can get a job."

For the longest time he said nothing. He wouldn't look at Marcelle, even when she leaned forward and craned her neck to meet his glance. He continued to stare up the street, chewing at his thumbnail and rocking back and forth, all the while snowflakes were caught in the breeze, sweeping up onto the porch where they settled on legs and arms and bare, pink faces.

"You want me to call her now?" he said finally.

She caught her breath. It wasn't something she had planned to do, not then. Not with Eugene in the hospital, with his blood barely dry on her jacket.

"Let me get my coat," he said, standing up.

They stayed to the sidewalks that ran down Maple Street all the way to Main, past dark, stony pillars fronting Harmon Funeral Home and the burned out shell of Mick's Laundromat. Even though everyone in town said it was Eugene, no question about it, it had been Patrick who surprised Marcelle with the idea that it might be one of his dad's sleepwalking things.

"Even he thinks he could have done it," he'd said to Marcelle. "He told my mom the day after it burned down that he woke up behind the library that night."

It was then—as they walked past Mick's—that it occurred to Marcelle she should ask Patrick about his dad. Was there any word from him? Had he been caught? She was curious, but more than that, she knew it was the right thing to do, give him a turn if he wanted. It was how things had been between them before Eugene—they'd talk about parents and school and problems, and all the endless things that tangled the two of them together. His father. But now there never seemed to be a right time to bring it up, a single moment when she thought he wouldn't break apart with just the mention of it, just turn on his heel and head straight back home, to leave her in the same spot she had been before she'd left Mr. and Mrs. Henry in their driveway.

They came to the end of the block and crossed the open street to the grocery store, its massive wall of windows dumping light into the parking lot. Suddenly Patrick dashed into the open and twirled in a circle, arms outstretched, head back, and eyes closed. He turned and turned, fingers reaching toward Marcelle, and it made her laugh to see him behaving so beautifully ridiculous. She swatted at his arm, and he stopped, looked at her and, for the first time that night, smiled.

"What?"

"You know what," she said. "God, you can be so weird sometimes."

"Come on," he said. "It's the first snow. And you're leaving it." His eyes caught the lamplight, glistening and full, and his teeth broke through thin, wet lips. "Goddamn you," he said. "Sometimes you can be such a pain in the ass."

A car pulled into the entrance behind them, its headlamps projecting a moving circle of yellow light over the storefront glass. Giant paper signs advertising weekly specials flashed at them, red and brown numbers blotting the white squares like old bandages.

"Yeah, I know," she said. "I'm hoping to fix that about me." Marcelle felt a momentary lightness and took hold of his sleeve, pulling him with her as she skated gracefully over the snow, all the way to the front doors, the two of them, hands clasped behind backs, their laughter bouncing through the lot as they carved long staccato lines over the jewel-specked plain.

The doors slid open, the warm air rushing over Marcelle as the smell of bread and doughnuts took hold of her, raking the insides of her mouth with an excruciating desire for food. The cashier looked over at her and Patrick, lingering on Marcelle, and once again she considered the condition of her clothing. The woman looked as if she knew Marcelle had done something horrible before coming in, a trail of carnage stretching out somewhere behind her. Through caked blue eye shadow and spidery lashes she studied them both, all the while punching at the register and pretending to pay attention to the pile of groceries that she snatched from the cart. Marcelle worked her hand inside her purse. Her fingers moved through the clutter like they were working a knot, and she kept Patrick in her periphery, knowing he must think her crazy with whatever she was doing inside that purse of hers. She finally drew out a twenty and held it out to him.

"Can you get change? That lady's staring at me like I killed someone."

"Just tell her it's your husband's blood."

"Right, that'll make it all better."

It wasn't late, but the mood in the store felt like near closing. Only a few people waited in line to pay, and there weren't more than three others standing around the produce department, staring at apples and onions and potatoes they held in their hands as if they were things to be hatched rather than cut up and eaten.

In the aisle behind the register, a man and woman stood next to one another. They were an old couple, the man with a full head of hair, brilliant white that he'd combed back in a drift down to the base of his neck. She wore a flowered scarf over her hair, and he had on a heavy knitted sweater that dropped past his waist, maybe something she had made for him. It was that kind of sweater. The man held his wife's arm gently as she stood on tiptoes and pulled cans from the shelf, and set them easily in the cart. It was as if she was on the edge of a cliff reaching for berries and he had to steady her, to be certain she would not slip and fall. She picked up a can, read the label and set it back, and then she turned to him and said something. He nodded, and she reached up and patted him on the cheek three times, said something else, and then walked off in front of him, her arms clasped behind her. He looked around and broke into a big, toothy grin then took hold of the cart, shaking his head as he pushed it down the aisle behind her.

Patrick came to her and dropped a bunch of coins into the slot then pushed at the keys. Turning away, he huddled close to the wood partition of the booth.

"Mama T? It's Spooky." He stood there with his back to Marcelle, fingering the metal cord, talking now in tones too low for her to make out. Finally, after what seemed like three conversations, he handed the phone to her.

Marcelle managed to croak a "Hello."

"Hi baby." The voice was deep and smoky. "My boy Spooky

tells me you in a hard spot. Need somewhere to be for awhile."

"I think so." Marcelle's stomach rose and settled under her coat. "Pretty sure. I got my own money."

"He says you thinkin' of runnin' away from your man. That true?"

"Yes ma'am. I want to leave for a lot of reasons, but he's the biggest one." Marcelle turned and looked down the cereal aisle again. The old couple was long gone. Patrick was looking at her as she talked, glancing down at the mouthpiece in the pauses, as if he could see Mama T responding inside the phone.

"I got money," Marcelle said again.

"I heard you before," Mama T said. "First thing, you make sure this what you want. Things can get real ugly when a man's been left behind. I don't want no drama brought to my stoop. I got plenty of that already."

"Yes ma'am."

There was a heavy sigh on the other end of the line and the sound of something tapping. Marcelle reached over and took Patrick's hand, and he squeezed back. Finally Mama T. spoke again.

"All right then," she said. "You get my number from Spooky. If you make up your mind to do this, you call me. You get yourself to the bus station, and I'll come fetch you."

Marcelle thanked her and promised to call one way or the other, and then she hung up, and her arm felt lighter the second she left the earpiece on the cradle. A pathway opened, a possibility. Something she'd never had before, and it was exhilarating and terrifying at the same time.

They walked the distance from the grocery to Maple Street with barely a word between them but right about halfway, just as they crossed Main, Patrick slipped his arm around Marcelle's elbow. She pushed her hand into her coat pocket and locked him in place. He was warm against her side, and the swell in her throat did nothing to drag down the lightness she felt then, just being with him.

"Someone called the house the other night," he said.

"Really?"

"Yeah." He laughed softly. "It was weird."

"You think it could have been him?"

"I don't know. Maybe. They didn't hang up right away. I could hear breathing."

Marcelle didn't say anything. She'd gotten calls like that before.

"Anyway," he said, "that was it. I don't know what it means. But I hate that I'm back to thinking about him all the time and I don't even know what the story is anymore. It's like my mind is caught in a trap or something. Sometimes I wish he would hurry up and just get caught. Then at least we'd know where he is."

It surprised her, if only a little, to hear him say this. She'd imagined Patrick would want his father to succeed, to keep free of handcuffs and the law. He used to talk about how much his father hated the idea of small spaces, and how great it would be if he broke out, just climbed over the wall and escaped into the world. Now he was wishing for the opposite and Marcelle wondered what Mr. Luntz would do if he found out that his own son had turned against him. That he was hoping the police would find him, descend upon him and stuff him back into his cage.

The house was dark when Marcelle slipped in through the back door into the kitchen. The buttery smell of toast lingered in the air. She opened the breadbox and took a slice of bread from the loaf, walking from the kitchen into the hallway. A spray of light washed over the carpet at the end of the corridor, voices hummed, the blue flickering and dancing from slit at the bottom of the door. She imagined the two of them, on opposite sides of the huge bed, watching their program on the little black and white on the bureau against the wall, Mr. Henry chewing toast from the saucer that sat perched on his stomach. They would have already said all they were going to say about what happened that day, probably throwing in a few things about Marcelle, how they were going to have to take care of both of them now, their son and his wife and, who knows, probably even a little baby on top of everything else.

In the basement, things were just as they had been that morning, when Marcelle had imagined resting in her bed, empty in the very space that still weighed her down like cement. The blankets were tucked neatly under the long, green pillow, the striped afghan carefully draped over the foot as she had left them. Eugene's clothes still overflowed the hamper, waiting to be washed, smothering the few things that Marcelle had tossed in days earlier. She overturned the basket, dumping everything to the floor, kicking greasy jeans and t-shirts and boxer shorts over the floor, the smell of Eugene's pits and feet and crotch rolling up into the air, filling her mouth and her mind with his musk. It was one last time to feel the sensation that his smell could bring her, the rolling surge of electricity in her legs and stomach, and over her breasts, that anticipation of his body heavy on hers, breath hot against her neck, those moments when she felt like she could lie naked for hours, clothes bunched in a heap at her feet, his callused hands scratching over her skin and making her feel like she was worth every second of his time. Beautiful.

A plastic garbage bag, filled enough to still be carried over her shoulder, Marcelle moving so fast but stepping lightly, drawers opened and closed, change scooped into pockets in an almost singularly silent motion. She crept through the room as if she were trespassing or, better yet, escaping from prison, staying low enough to be invisible beneath the sound of the ten o'clock drama that played itself out upstairs. She had plenty of money—almost three thousand dollars—that could last her a long time if she made it stretch. Cars and trucks left the mountain at all hours of the night, too. She wouldn't have to stand for more than twenty minutes in front of The Red Apple or The Flume before someone would stop, open his door, and offer her a ride into the city. She had seen it happen plenty of times. She had twenty seven hundred dollars and some change, and even if she had to spend one night in a motel, there would be plenty left over.

A line of waffle tread trailed far behind as she shuffled over the snow-covered sidewalk, down Shale Street toward Main. But the flakes were big as dandelion seeds now, falling heavily enough to whitewash the bald patches as quickly as she made them. No one in that house would know she had gone, and if Lyla Henry happened to put on her blue bathrobe and step into her white slippers to walk to the living room, pull the drapes back to stare out at the gently falling snow, she would notice nothing out of the ordinary, no shoeprints spotting the driveway out to the sidewalk, down the block into town. There would be nothing to see but naked branches flocked in powder and a growing blanket of white, confirming for her that winter had indeed arrived in Ash Falls. She would realize then that before she called downstairs to wake Marcelle the next morning, she'd be smart to get her brother Hank on the phone. Because, as Eugene had told her the week before, the woodshed along the side of the house was down to its last rows of alder, and the next five months were going to be especially dark and cold.

# Patrick and Tin

Patrick Luntz walked the grid between the mink sheds, splashing the gravy of snowmelt, sawdust, and last year's maple leaves onto the cuffs of his jeans. His toes were numb through his boots from socks too thin, but he was almost done, there being a few hundred less minks to deal with and all. The snow had softened the rooflines and the puffs of huckleberry stands, while the cedar boughs against the hillside reached almost to the ground, sagging under the weight of it all. Along the river edge a field of giant cotton balls lay scattered where rocks had lain only a week earlier.

Christmas was less than a week away. High above the hemlocks, a thin mist screened out all but the craggy peaks of Silver Mountain. The stinging cold that dug into each open button and collar, the persistent, heady smell of chimney smoke—all of it was constant, and it folded the entire mountain into itself. And Patrick's limbs grew heavier each day, as if his blood was slowly coagulating, thickening like the winter sap.

All morning he had watched Tin slosh bowlegged from his travel trailer to the pelt building, into the mink sheds and back out again, over and over. Occasionally he stopped to talk to the Indian guys out front of the Quonset or held up fat Charlie from his rounds with the power feeder, the old man positioned at the front wheels, shoulders hunched over his chicken neck, steadfast just like a traffic cop. Tin carried on with them, throwing steam and hand signals, giving wide sweeps of his arms. And when he finally turned away, one of the Indians smiled and shook his head and the other rolled his eyes and gave a broad masturbatory gesture, then shot a look to the other guy that said, *Christ old man, just go the fuck away.*

It was the end of the day for everyone but Patrick. The younger of the two Indians, the one with the smooth, darker skin and the clipped, cowlick bangs was the last to leave, stripping his coveralls over his yoke shoulders and tossing them in a ball into the passenger side of his pickup. Patrick gave him a wave and he saluted in return, two fingers against his stiff cowlick, then he gunned a rooster tail out of the spongy lot. Patrick returned the hand rake and trowel to the equipment shed where they belonged, then he turned off the lights and secured the door tight. He made his way to Tin's blue and white Shasta, its beveled windows fogged in a sweep that mirrored the snowdrift that had built against the painted siding. He knocked twice before nudging the door open a crack.

"I'm done."

No answer.

"I said I'm done."

"In or out," Tin groused. "This heat ain't free."

The aluminum steps creaked under his weight as he climbed up, closing the door behind him. Inside it was warm, heavy with the dry, sweet smell of a propane flame, and pipe tobacco and rubber boots, and of damp wool drying next to a heater. Tin was seated with his back to the door, at the little dinette booth, a slew of papers in white and pink and blue triplicate spread out in front of him. A chunky calculator held one stack in place, and at the edge of the table sat a mug, half full of milky coffee.

"Sit down," he said, thumbing the opposite side of the table. "And don't mess up my stuff."

Except for a few bundles of newspapers, tied up and pushed against the far wall, the trailer was surprisingly tidy. A percolator sat alone on the stovetop, its glass knob still dotted with condensation, while the adjacent counter space was clustered with a few ceramic mugs, a small jar of powdered creamer, and an opened box of sugar cubes. A pair of matching orange flashlights clung to the door of the tiny refrigerator, each of them pinning a flyer of some kind to the metal. Beside the sink, a bottle of liquid soap slept against the tangs of a dish rack, a terrycloth hand towel draped over like a tiny, blue waterfall. It could have been anyone's vacation trailer, really, sparsely furnished with barely anything to make it appear lived in or even used all that much. There were no discarded clothes hanging wet over the backs of the chairs and dripping onto the floor like he'd imagined there would be, or crusted dishes collecting flies or wastebaskets overflowing with paper towels and beer cans, no cardboard box towers and ma-chine and engine parts, stacks of pelting or fishing magazines, all splayed out over countertops and tables like a corner booth at a community swap meet. Tin was a tidy fellow who obviously liked to know where he stood in the world.

Patrick moved a single, thick phone book along the bench seat before settling in.

"Done already?" Tin asked.

"Yeah."

"You got all of 'em?" He didn't even look up from his papers. The question was as predictable as the rain.

Patrick's teeth ached from the grinding, and the temperature rose along his collar. He sighed, shifting in his seat. "I don't miss cages anymore."

Tin laid his hands on the table and craned his head to look out the window. "What time is it? I guess you got places to be."

"I don't know," he said. "I'm just going home." Patrick looked around for a clock. The walls were a collage of dittoed papers with columns of names and numbers, a single calendar with the scrawl of red and black handwriting filling the squares, and a long row of hooks, gold and silver keys dangling from each.

"I don't know what time it is," he said finally.

"You don't got a watch?"

Patrick showed him his wrists, both sides.

"What kid your age don't wear a watch?"

"You don't wear one."

"I ain't a kid," Tin said. He leaned over and reached across to the cabinet beside the sink, opening the top drawer. He rattled through it, eyes staring at the ceiling, his lower lip pulled over his gums. Finally, he pulled back his hand, a silver banded wristwatch looped over his fingers.

"Here. See if it still keeps time."

Patrick looked down at the face, tiny Roman numerals, black with a bone white background. The pin-like secondhand clicked along.

"Looks like it. Says it's three thirty-five."

"Good. Keep it."

"You don't want it?"

"I wouldn't be giving it to you if I did. Thing's so small I can't see a damn thing on it."

Patrick stretched the band and slid it over his wrist, turning it so the face looked up at him. It was a good enough watch but definitely not the kind that any kid he knew would be caught wearing. It was a nerd watch, old and boxy, something you might see on someone with horn-rimmed glasses, greasy hair, and acne. But it felt good on his wrist. He breathed on the glass and brushed it over his sleeve.

"Thanks. You should still get a clock in here."

"You're just chock full of ideas for me."

Patrick thumbed one of the papers in front of him, and Tin took it from him. "So what'd you ask Santa for this year?" he slid the paper under the stack in front of him. Patrick looked up at his face. Tin gave a half-cocked grin.

"A new stereo."

"What's wrong with the one you got?"

"Nothing really. It's just old."

"Just old." Tin said, then gathered the papers into a single stack and tucked them into a hard manila folder. "You look like you should be asking for a shaving kit." He nodded his chin at Patrick. "With that winter fur you're trying to grow over your lip."

Patrick felt around his mouth. He hardly ever bothered with shaving, the growth always faint and downy against his hand, nothing like the rich coarseness that would cover the face of a real man. He recalled the scratch of his father's cheek against his own as he'd kissed him goodnight. He slid down into his seat.

"I guess," he said.

"Makes you look shifty."

"My dad had a beard." It snapped from him with such a jagged defensiveness it startled even himself. "Has," he said, forcing a softer tone. "Probably he still has it."

"Oh yeah." Tin held his gaze firmly on Patrick, the lids red and moist, turned down slightly at the edges. He picked up his coffee and put it to his lips. "I guess I remember something about that."

Patrick turned the watch until it circled his wrist. "He's out, you know. Out of jail."

"Yeah."

"Yep. Busted out."

"I guess I heard about that, too."

Patrick nodded. This was not privileged information, he realized. They'd known all along—maybe even at the same time— each of them passing by one another each day, dropping small talk about everyone and everything else in Ash Falls, yet never uttering a single word about this. And here they were now, the two of them, sitting across from one another like men laying it all out there so casually as if it was a five year-old story, about someone else's dad or brother, or an old neighbor. The fact that Tin seemed to hold it as normally as the weather, lifted the weight of it all somehow.

"I don't even know where he is," Patrick said. "He could be anywhere."

"I suppose so," the old man said. He looked at Patrick, but his eyes moved over his face, at his mouth, his hair, at the pimples that Patrick knew mapped the skin over his eyebrows. "What do you think about all that?" Tin said.

*What do you think?* The question pushed at his chest with a force that was sudden and firm, and Patrick fell back against the booth. In all this time, he hadn't given himself the notion to consider—really consider—what he thought about it all. There were times when the news excited him, the vision of his father free of his own cage, wandering the countryside like a nomad, making his way, perhaps, back to Ash Falls, crouched in an open boxcar or thumbing for a ride along some lost highway. Even better, somewhere no one would ever find him. Other times, like now, sitting there in the warmth of Tin's trailer with the old man's yellowed eyes holding him so securely, Patrick could only see his father as just another loose mink, slinking along the perimeter of the fence somewhere out there in the snow, searching for an opening or a deep rut where he could slip through and run free. Free, out into the openness of the roadway and a distant light, or directly into the path of an oncoming truck. He didn't know which would be the better fate, and that indecision tore him to shreds.

"Sometimes I think he ought to go back," Patrick heard himself say. "If he's being smart, that's what he'll do."

"You don't want him to escape?"

"I don't know. I used to imagine he could actually make it, like get up into Canada or all the way to Mexico or someplace far away. Except lately I've been feeling really weird about it. Like, this is all some story, and the only way it can end is by him being dead.

Tin swatted the air with his hand. "Try not to worry yourself about it too much, Skunk. Winter has a way of bringing things back inside."

"You think so?"

"I know so."

He got up then from his seat and brought his cup over to the sink. He turned on the faucet and let the water slurp into the mug, then poured it out, setting it back onto the counter. "My old man," he said, "he hit the road when I was about your age. Left us with nothing but a big, weedy piece of land that couldn't even grow a decent head of lettuce. Ate the breakfast my ma cooked for him, kissed my sister on the head, and walked off to town in his suit and hat like it was any other day. Never heard from him again."

"Nothing? No letter or anything?"

"Nope."

"Maybe he died."

"Could be. I thought about that now and then. My sister told me he was gonna come back, like some beat dog with his tail between his legs. And my ma, she'd have taken him back 'cause that's the kind of woman she was." He came back to the table and sat down, across from Patrick. "We made up a little story about him too, my sister and me. That he'd gone off to Mexico, got shot up by some bandits. Some bullshit like that. I guess it helped some. To have an end to the story. But life moves on, even when you think there ain't no way it can."

"And you never wondered about him. You just forgot about him."

"Course I wondered. But time went on. I just figured that he wasn't the kind of man who ought to have anyone wondering about him. I decided that every minute I spent thinking about him was just handing a little bit of myself over. And he sure as shit didn't have that coming to him."

*Time went on.* It didn't take a lot of thinking to add up the years between then and now, and Patrick wondered if he would be as old as Tin by the time he finally stopped wondering.

Tin kept his gaze on his hands. The low winter sun broke through the window just then, coming through the alder stands and laying thick stripes across the table, washing the old man's arms in gold. He turned them over, holding his palms out, steady, as if a forgotten piece of summer were hovering just above them and if he moved in the slightest, it would all vanish.

"All right then," he said finally, leaning to one side and taking his wallet from his back pocket. He cleared his throat and dug out two twenties, tossing them onto the table. "Payday."

"Payday," Patrick echoed. He picked them from the table and slid to the edge of the bench. What little sun had dropped in was now gone, and he became suddenly aware of an itching in his feet. He stood up, pushing them onto the floor, and the itch worked its way over him, up into his legs and over his ass as he tucked the bills into his back pocket.

"Hold up," Tin said, dropping his arm out in front of Patrick like a tollgate. He drew it back and pulled another twenty out of his wallet, handing it over. "Christmas bonus."

Patrick pulled back. He wanted it, but he hadn't earned it. He might screw up something later, leave a cage open, and Tin would cuss him out, bring up this twenty dollars he should have never gotten.

"You don't have to do that," he said. "You already gave me a watch."

"I know I don't have to, numbskull. Besides, I got one less piece of junk in the drawer now. And this," he slapped the bill on the table, "you got coming."

"No."

"Don't argue with me. It's Christmas, goddamn it. Go and buy some more of that yellow for that hair. Or I'm gonna have to start calling you by your real name."

Patrick took the twenty and tucked it into his pocket, and moved from the table to the door. The bones of Tin's shoulders seemed to rise up through his shirt, a landscape of knobs and ridges, his head sunk low, the scallop of vertebrae straining against the neck. He looked as if he might lean all the way forward and go to sleep right there, and it occurred to Patrick then to just go ahead ask the question that had crossed his mind more than a few times that morning as he had watched the old man with fat Charlie and the two Indians, the guys who mocked him so openly as soon as he turned his back on them.

"Hey Tin," he said.

"Yeah?" He opened the folder again and began to spread the papers over the table once more.

"So my mom, she usually does this Christmas Eve dinner," he said. It's nothing, usually just me and her. But I was thinking if you weren't doing anything. You could come by if you wanted to."

Tin picked at the edge of one of the papers, moving the page back and forth as if he was comparing it to the blank table beneath it. "I don't know, kid. You asking me to come and eat at your house, or you asking me for Christmas Eve?"

"Both, I guess." It bothered him that one should matter over the other, and he didn't know which one was preferable. "It'll probably just be roast beef and potatoes and all that," he said. "She likes us to wear Christmas colors and stuff, but you wouldn't have to. It's a stupid thing but it makes her happy. It's not a big deal."

"Roast beef? I'd have to wear my teeth for that. You already ask her?"

"She won't care. She likes you."

"You ask her first," he said. He got up from the bench, taking hold of Patrick's shoulder as a ledge to help him stand. Brushing past him, he made his way to folding door of the phone booth bathroom. "Ask her first and I'll think about it. I don't like putting my teeth in unless I have to."

Patrick pulled up to the library and braked in front of the courtyard, where the giant Ash Falls Christmas tree stood. He looped the chain from his bicycle around the lamppost and locked it in place, checking the time on his watch again, comparing it to the illuminated face over the library doors. A couple minutes off, close enough. He swept the bench clean and sat down, the cold sinking into his rear end almost immediately. The tree towered over him in a brilliant display, and up and down the street were constellations of countless colors, flickering and bathing clapboard and blanketed lawns in a glow that seemed to mimic something close to warmth.

There was a time when all of this shit was exciting, the spackle of lights and frilly tinsel hanging from the store eaves, and the echo of carols coming from any number of tiny box speakers. He used to sit on this same stone bench in the library courtyard, sometimes with Marcelle, once with his mother, after getting a Polaroid with Santa at the firehouse on Virginia Street. He'd stare up at the giant spruce with its silver and blue globes and fake candles flickering on the fingertips of so many branches as he hummed carols, always the carols, and coalesce images of a day far off in the future, himself a father. Sometimes he wore a beard and other times not, and there might be a wife, hazy and nondistinct in the background, no real form or face, nobody he had ever met in his life. Often there would be a man, though, rugged and strong, like the men who sometimes came through town on motorcycles, or with knobby bicycles strapped to the rear ends of their German cars. It had all been so far in the future as he dreamed, sitting in the middle pews of the Episcopal church on Sixth Avenue with his parents, the Christmas Eve service, with the velvet warmth and the richness of incense, when they had all gone that last December 24th in Ash Falls, before Ricky Cordero took away their ability to blend in to it all.

Deep in the branches of the courtyard tree, behind the candles and ornaments, Patrick rediscovered the chill of the prison visiting room and the saltiness of machine-bought chips, and iron echoes of immediate demands bouncing off concrete walls, and the crash of metal doors, three times on the way in, three times on the way out. There was the frigid alleyway behind the old church, the dance club with its deep, muffled breathing against peeling exterior, and the specter of strobe through stained glass, his body huddled against Shadow's, legs warming one another, both of them waiting for the pill to finally kick in. And then later, in the doorway of the big house, the smell of baked bread and the side-eyed stare of Mama T. as she gave them their final warning. "Don't come into my house if you ain't clear-headed." And then there was his mother again, coming down the front steps of their house, almost running to him, legs uncooperative beneath her, a hundred different words coming from a single, longing look. And there was Marcelle and Eugene looming outside of the Henrys' house, fingers entwined like she was a captured bird, and then Shadow, and then Shadow, with his jet black hair and powder blue eyes, so far away, Shadow always hanging up first and never returning calls, Shadow's sweet scent still faint on the shirt kept underneath Patrick's pillow. And Mama T's soft voice saying, "Shadow's just like his name; here one minute, gone the next," and the smell and the noise of the minks, the awful minks, pacing and crazy, and the simple, magic touch of and old man's hand on his shoulder, and the medicine of sitting beside a curling blue-green river.

All of it was so vivid in his mind and yet so distant, none of it repeatable. What lay ahead was as murky as the past was clear, he couldn't begin to even imagine what waited for him. His father. His place in this town. His mother, and the unbelievable love and patience she had for a son who didn't deserve it.

He got up and made his way down the sidewalk, hands dug deep down in his pockets, forging through his own breath as it pushed out in tiny clouds. Awnings yawned under crusted snow, and winking lights cast sheens of red and green into sectioned cement slabs pocked with scatters of salt pellets. Behind the storefront windows, the Fotomat, the attorney and accountants' offices, people moved back and forth in automatic motions, like finger puppets, or as if coasting on wheels. The orange-haired, mustached man who had always managed Hinkle's drifted behind stenciled window snowflakes from shelf to shelf, unfolding and refolding sweaters, glancing up only briefly as Patrick looked over to take in his own reflection. A sharp cackle split the hum of holiday carols, canned music piped out from somewhere, and Patrick turned to see a woman standing under the garland-draped entry to the Louella's Shear Genius Salon, blond hair ratted high so it hovered around her head, backlit like a giant halo.

A kind of force took hold of him then, a gentle tug at his jacket, a calling that at once seemed both sudden and sensible. He felt the wad of cash in his pocket, and he looked back into Hinkle's, at the stacks and rows of useless clothing, and down the block to A&M Electronics, where even the batteries could be counted on to be overpriced. A low station wagon cruised past, the rattle of studded tires rushing over the music. He glanced both ways and cut through the cars parked at the curb, crossing over to P.J.'s Pawn and Loan on the west side of the street, its half-lit sign lurking behind a slush-specked window. The heavy door strained against his weight, and he pushed it harder, the kick of the bell causing the man at the glass wrap counter—not P.J., but someone Patrick didn't recognize at all—to look up from the magazine he had spread open on the glass top.

"How's it going, Sport?" He had graying hair that was almost to his shoulders, and he tossed it back as he tipped his head up.

"Good."

"What can I do you for?"

Patrick walked up to the glass case and stood with his hands behind his back, scanning the perimeter of figurines and coins and jeweled rings and antique locks, and slivers of knife blades splayed out before him. What happened in the lives of these people, he wondered, that they would sell such treasures for so little, maybe hoping to come back and retrieve them when things got better which they would, of course, never do? Family heirlooms, gifts passed from father to son, to grandson, with the intention of forever, never imagining that the gift would one day be a token for someone's next car payment, or a couple cartons of Marlboros, or maybe one more month's trailer space rent before finally packing up to leave town for good.

Patrick pulled at the band around his wrist. It was almost five o'clock. "You have any watches?" he asked.

The man flipped the magazine closed. There was a woman in a bikini on the cover, dark and oiled so she almost looked plastic. "I got watches," he said. He slouched to the back of the store, to an acrylic columned case that sat atop a wide, cherry wood sideboard. The case was lit by a tiny desktop spot lamp with one of those flexible necks, the kind that always reminded Patrick of a robot or a space alien. The wrist and pocket watches in the case looked to span decades, from shiny, digital faces to cloudy, ash-like discs with their elaborate covers tightly clasped shut over the time of day.

"I was needing something with big numbers." He leaned into the case and tapped at the carousel.

"Big numbers? Roman or Arabic?"

"Just regular. Arabic, I guess. That's probably better."

The man took a key ring from his pocket and jimmied the lock on the case, then took out about a half dozen wristwatches, plus a couple pocket watches, snapping open the covers. He laid them out on the sideboard in a clean lineup.

Patrick thumbed a few of them, feeling the smoothness of the glass, the cool plating of the metal bands or the fissured leather, the sweat of some stranger buried deep in the cells of the hide. He held them to his wrist and stretched his hand as far from him as he could, pretending to struggle in order to see the numbers. Maybe he wouldn't want to put something on his wrist at all, whether he could read the thing or not. He picked up the pocket watch with the open cover and turned it over in his hand. The plate was simple, with a relief of what looked like leaves and waves around the circumference. The numbers on the face were big enough, not too fancy to make out. It worked. The tiny sticker on the back said $45.00. He put it back.

"You like that one?"

"Yeah, but it's too much. I won't have hardly anything left."

"Who's it for?"

"My grandpa." It was funny how quickly that lie spilled out, and it gave him a flutter in his stomach when he said it, a pleasant sensation that made him want to laugh, at the mere notion that Tin Dorsay could be anyone's grandfather. It was an absurd image, like something from an old black and white comedy. But it was not an impossible one. He could almost see it.

The man leaned his elbows on the counter and held the watch in one of his hands. He turned it over and looked closely at the face, at the numbers that Patrick could still make out clearly, even from across the counter. He pinched the winding crown and turned it, glancing at Patrick a few times as he did so.

"Tell you what," he said. "Since it's Christmas and all, how about I give it to you for thirty. Can you handle that?"

The movement grew in his stomach, shifting and swelling until it might tip him off his feet. The deal was a good one, he knew, but he didn't want to snatch hold of it just yet. He put his hands into his pockets and felt the crispness of the cash, rocking on his the balls of his feet, looking at the watch, taking it in his hand, studying the engravings on the cover. He was contemplating the offer as a good businessman would. It was past five o'clock, and the shopkeeper no doubt had places to be.

"Okay kid," the man said. He rubbed his hands together then displayed the empty palms. "Twenty-five. Final offer. You'll get a nice watch for your grandpa, and I can close up and get home to my dinner."

# Henry Tomas Kelleher

He noticed it the second he walked into the trailer. Besides the usual fog of cat piss and overripe fruit, the unwashed underarms and aquarium shop moisture hanging in the air, other than the expected image of Susanna shoehorned into her beaten, orange recliner—what really caught his attention was the tree. Where there had always been shoebox towers, sagging lids, and water-stained bottoms, and bundles of yellowed newspaper striations, there now stood a lone Christmas tree. It was one of those fake things, a conglomeration of plastic and twisted wire, and it stood at stark attention in the corner, bound with a string of dim white bulbs and a single, snaking green garland. Spindle branches stuck out like the crossbraces of a telephone pole. A dozen or so tiny balls peeked out like fat, silver birds.

The placement of this tree, in this house, was equally as strange as the absence of one had been in Lyla's. A tree this time of year at the Henry place was one thing Hank could always count on. A big one, pressed into the same dark corner, riddled with the same collection of ornaments, the nutcrackers and glitter-spackled balls, and glass snowflakes, all topped with a writhing, motorized angel she had ordered some years back through a catalog that sold those kinds of things. But not once throughout the past two days—not through the drone of the power drill, the mounting of handrails and cabinet latches and chain door locks, between the countless trips up and down the basement stairs to drag Eugene's boxy furniture to the main floor bedroom—not once did Lyla even utter the word *Christmas*.

Still, he shouldn't have been surprised that the tree was in this trailer. It was, after all, almost Christmas. But he couldn't shake the feeling that nothing about the tree seemed right, not in this place, not with this person. It reeked of the accidental guest, the bride who turns up at the wrong church in the middle of a funeral invocation. Some well-intentioned person had cleaned out that corner and hauled away all the crap that had built up over the years. Then whoever it was dragged the horrible thing in and propped it up, trussed it with some old lights and a garland, threw on a few cheap ornaments and called it a day.

"That's not mine," she said. He looked at her and she quickly cut away, studying the tree as if it were a stray dog that had wandered into her yard. "Tammy my caseworker brung it over in her hatchback. They got a new one this year at the welfare office. She said she thought I might want it."

"Well that was nice of her."

"I didn't ask for it or nothing. She just brung it."

"She sounds like a thoughtful person."

"Yeah, well. All the time she's on my case about how I need to stop getting stuff, that I got no room left in the place. And then here she comes with a Christmas tree in her car." Susanna shrugged her shoulders. The small gesture moved her entire body in the chair.

Slivers of condensation-spotted glass peeked through curtains that were drawn almost to the centers. Hank's bag weighed heavy on his lap, and he thumbed the zipper, feigning interest, still making small talk about the tree and the nice light it gave off in the room, and the kinds of ornaments his mother used to bring home after the holidays, when everything in the Christmas aisle was half price. And when Susanna released a heavy sigh, it was saturated with such disinterest he could no longer pretend he wasn't just rambling. He opened the bag and took out the small plastic pouch.

He knew she was not going to like what he had to say to her, and he tried to be easy with the news, saying the words just as he had rehearsed them in the ride there. He was done, out of the business for good. No, it didn't matter why. Things were just different for him now. "It's simply the way it is, Honey," he said. *Honey*. It wasn't a term of endearment he used often, but he found it could help in circumstances like this.

Nevertheless, her reaction was that of near panic. Her lips came apart with a pop, and she pulled herself into the chair, the strain on springs unnerving. Her eyeballs looked ready to leave their sockets, as if being pushed from behind. He said it again, *Honey*, and she sucked in her lower lip and squeezed her eyelids closed, the thin, feathery lashes trembling against her apple cheeks, her hand pressing into the blotchy flesh above her neckline.

"Now then," he said. He had expected as much from her, this carrying on. The dramatics. It was the reason he hadn't wanted to come at all, why he'd had to force himself, instead of simply calling her on the phone. It was best to do it in person, he told himself, to be sure that in the wake of all the spectacle, she would be okay.

"Oh geez Louise," she said at last. "I'm sorry." She dragged in a rattled breath and opened her eyes again. Fanning her cheeks, she looked down at the tiny plastic bag. "You just caught me off guard. I gotta think this through."

"I'll make some phone calls if you want."

"You mean to get someone new to come over? 'Cause that'd be okay."

Hank took his coat from the chair back. He stood and draped it over his arm, ready to leave, wanting so badly to leave. Susanna sat with her hands folded on her lap, filling the orange chair from arm to arm. The plastic baggie lay on the T.V. tray like a turd, more of an insult than a gift. It wouldn't last her through the week. But that was it; she was going to have to live with it. He wouldn't be bringing any more here on out, not a single gram.

"Maybe I ought to just stop, too," she said. "My brother Nels says I'm turning into a old hippie. Says I'm gonna get myself in trouble if I'm not careful."

Hank didn't have a response. He had always worked to as-suage Susanna's nerves—her fears and the fears of all the oth-ers. It was low risk, he'd told them. "Nobody cares about a little friendly trade between an old guy and a few people needing a little help with their aches and pains." But Nels had a clear point. A person could be careful as hell and still have word get out to the wrong person.

"He's always telling me what to do," Susanna said, picking up the baggie and holding it up in front of her face. "He's been tak-ing stuff from the house. Taking it out to his truck and then going to the dump. He does it when I'm asleep in the bed."

Hank made a move toward the door. "Sneaky guy, too."

"Not so sneaky," she said. "He thinks I don't notice, but I do."

The open door brought in the crispness of winter air, a clean he could feel rushing from the snowy ground on up. Toby's sil-houette popped up in the window, ears perked in a crown on his head, and Hank envied him at that moment, his cozy seat, free-dom from obligation and error, nothing to worry about except food and all the things there were in the world to piss on.

Coming into town, Hank came to a stop at the intersection near The Sleep Inn, its reader board still advertising fall rates over the humming green neon vacancy sign. A housekeeping cart sat parked in front of one of the units, the room door wide open, just letting all the room light out and all the December cold in. The truck heater was cranking now, and Hank twisted to work himself free of his jacket. He was embarrassed that he should feel suddenly anxious, that he would be looking for a particular face to emerge from that open door. A flash of white appeared in the doorway, but the woman who appeared, who took hold of the cart, was a stranger. She was a big gal with thick, bare arms dark as coffee against a stark white short-sleeve. She picked at the cart, hugging bottles and towels to her ample chest, and just as Hank lifted his foot from the brake, she turned and went back inside.

The neighborhood streets that pulled from the downtown core were packed with sand-peppered snow, a contrast to the salted sheen of the main drag. Hank drove on, reaching to his sleeping passenger, running his hand over the soft coat and working his fingers between the ears. Toby's eyes fluttered, and his mouth curled at the edges, and Hank serenaded him from far back in his throat.

*Everybody loves somebody, sometimes.*

*Everybody loves somebody, somehow.*

A half-dozen metallic holly strands straddled the length of Main Street, the final one supporting a banner that screamed "MERRY CHRISTMAS!" in giant Old English script. Hank looked into the rearview, at the long, stretch of roadway that divided the downtown storefronts. They were shops and owners barely clinging to life, facing one another with their freshly painted sandwich boards and paper signs and twinkling lights begging for shoppers, anyone, to come inside. Glancing images of figures dashed from one side to the other, jumping over slush-filled potholes, carrying bags too small to hold anything really significant. He thumped Toby's back before taking the wheel with both hands, stepped on the gas, and cruised under the sign, launching himself into the stretch of road leading up the mountain.

Ahead on the left, a tiny forest of freshly cut Noble and Doug Firs huddled under a necklace of multicolored lights. For as long as he could remember, the Christmas tree lot had been the boy scouts' domain, a good twenty years supplied by Ole Olson's tree farm just down the highway from Hank's place. He had helped out three or four times in the early years, giving the troop a hand with felling the little ribbon-marked trees. He couldn't recall why he'd done it—maybe Ole had called him, or someone from the school had roped him into it. But they were always good kids, the kind of boys he'd have liked to raise if things had been different for him. But then Ole passed on, and the farm and the scouts moved on elsewhere. Hank didn't even know who was supplying trees for them, now, but he did know that the trees they hawked were godawful scrawny and overpriced. A muddy Fifth Wheel trailer stood at the edge near the highway, the blue screen of a portable television flickering through the translucent curtains.

A couple of kids in canvas jackets wrestled with a fat Noble, hoisting it onto the roof of a white Japanese car. Their jackets were open to the waist, khaki shirts and colorful patches and bright red bandanas showing through, and they were all teeth and scrub-faced and freckled, as if they had just jumped out of a Norman Rockwell scene. Hank liked to think that such a thing existed in the world, that level of innocence and unaffected optimism. But nothing he had ever experienced in his life told him it was possible, not with kids in his classroom, certainly not with any kids he'd ever seen raised around him. But the way these kids laughed, as they stretched twine over that hideous tree, working with the care of budding craftsmen, he felt a little hope was there. Hope that there might be a few young men left to keep this town from falling down around itself.

At the base of the Fifth Wheel steps, a woman stood with her back to him, fussing with a bulky leather purse. He recognized the sturdy posture at once, the squared shoulders, the dry, sagebrush hair that brushed at the quilted parka. He slowed to a stop in the middle of the street and wound down the window, tapping the horn.

"That you over there?" he called to her.

She turned around. "Depends on who you think it is."

"You still working at the motel? I just saw some other gal there."

"They got gals besides just me." Roxanne put her hand to her forehead and bent slightly at the knees. "Kelleher?" she shouted. "What the hell are you doing? You're blocking the road."

He looked over his shoulder and cranked the wheel, crunching into the gravel lot. He parked the truck along the edge of the lot and climbed out, meeting her halfway to the tree line.

"That your car under that little fir?" he asked.

"Maybe. What brings you out into the daylight? You ever figure out who busted up your place?"

"I got a pretty good idea," he said. "It's a bigger can of worms than I want to deal with, though."

"Really." She raised her eyebrows in faint surprise, and with a trace of disappointment.

He looked over at the scouts wrestling the twine over the rear bumper of the white compact. "Shouldn't your fella be here doing this for you?"

"My fella walked out of rehab a week ago." Her smile buckled.

Hank pulled back, stung. "Oh hell," he said. "I'm sorry."

"Fucker called me from a payphone, wanted me to Western Union some bus money so he could come home. Shit. I told him he could either march his ass back into rehab or start walking the other direction."

Hank tucked his hands into his jeans pockets. An unexpected coolness crept up his back and over his shoulders. Her smile was there again, a perfect row of white behind rose-pink lips. She wore no makeup as far as he could tell, and her skin was pale and a little dry in the snow-licked wind, but it sure looked as soft as any he'd ever seen. He could reach over and brush his hand against her cheek and it would feel like silk.

"You're one tough little girl," he said.

"Please. It's been a long time since I was a little girl."

A grin stretched tight over his face, and he put a hand to his mouth. "So," he said, smoothing away the smirk. "You gonna tell me whose car that is?"

"Jesus, Kelleher. You're persistent. It's mine, if you gotta know. Melvin's letting me make payments on it."

"It's a shame, them boys getting sap all over it. Next time give me a call, and I'll throw it in the back of my pickup. I'm in the book."

The edge of her mouth drew up again, and she nodded heavy, as if there was no possible way she could agree with him any more than she already did. "I will remember that," she said. "Next time."

"Anytime," he said. "Doesn't have to be a tree, either."

"I figured that's what you meant." She took a pack of gum from her purse and stripped the paper clean before popping it in her mouth, then held the package out to Hank.

"I'm not much of a gum chewer."

"God," she said. "Live a little. *Hank.*"

Then she pushed it at him, and he obliged, drawing one from the pack. He turned it over with his fingers, examined the yellow and black label, taking in the smell of sugar and fruit, a scent that had no existence in natural form, anywhere.

"You already got your tree?" Roxanne asked.

"I got trees all around me."

"Smart ass. You know what I mean."

Hank put the stick of gum in his pocket and looked over her shoulder. The boy scouts had finished with the car and were now rolling twine around a wheel-sized spool, their teenaged voices tumbling over the lot like the notes of a bell choir.

"I don't know," he said. "I'm not really set up for something like that."

"I'm not set up for something like that," she repeated. Her voice was gruff and mocking, but Hank didn't get riled over it. She was teasing him, and he felt a lift in his stomach. "If I didn't do Christmas," she said, "I wouldn't make it through winter without killing myself. I got Christmas decorations like you wouldn't believe. I could set you up good if you wanted."

He never had any kind of desire to put a tree up in his house, needles littering the floor, tinder dry and ready to go up with the slightest spark. He'd had no kids wrap presents for or to let crawl around the trunk and rifle through presents, so what was the use? But she was standing here staring at him like some imploring teenager, her hand on her hip, snapping her gum while she waited for him to give in—he couldn't think of a single way out where he didn't come off like a complete jackass.

A sudden movement, some thirty yards behind her in a grove of white-patched alders, broke the moment. He put a hand on her arm and pointed over her shoulder. "Take a look at that," he said.

A yearling stepped carefully between the naked alder stands, over snow-covered undergrowth. He was a young black-tailed, maybe four points and a promising buck. He dug at the ground with his foreleg, pulling at the groundcover with his teeth and chewing slowly, head low and almost out of sight. Now and then he'd raise his nose and snuff at the air, and look over toward Hank, at the goings on under the lights, maybe. Then he'd stare out and over the open field just beyond the grove and poke his nose back among the salal and sedge cover.

"He's a beauty," Roxanne said.

"Yeah, he is. But he won't last long if he stays this close to town. Between the logging trucks and teenaged drivers."

"Logging trucks and teenagers exist all the way up the mountain," Roxanne said. "If anything, being this far down will keep him clear of the weekend K-Mart hunters."

At that, Hank had to laugh. Many a hunting season began and ended with cameos of idiots wandering onto his property in newly bought flannel jackets and stocking hats, price tags barely plucked free. "Can you point me to the road?" the guy would say, his gleaming rifle held in such a way that the slightest stumble would surely take his own head off.

"Nothing wrong with an eager hunter," he said.

"I never said there was." She circled around him and began walking toward his pickup, and he followed. "I went hunting with my dad all the time," she said. "You ever field dress a deer?"

"Sure," he said. "A couple times."

"Well, I've done it more times than I can count. You wouldn't know it to look at me, but some of my best memories are cold-assed weekends out in the woods with my dad, trying to get a big old buck in the crosshairs." She stopped at the truck and rested her hand on the roof. "Even so, I always thought they were a lot prettier out walking in the woods than hanging upside down from a tree branch, no matter how tight they might fill a freezer."

She opened the driver's side door and sat with one leg still hanging down to the gravel. Toby was up in his seat, already pawing at her jacket.

"He remembers you," Hank said.

"Hell yeah, he does. I'm a pretty unforgettable gal," she said, scratching the dog on his muzzle. "Good or bad."

Hank leaned his arm against the open door. When she had been with him at the house after the break-in, she walked around that place like she belonged there, as if she owned it. Digging the broom from his closet, sweeping up busted glass and loose coins, retrieving scattered knickknacks and setting them where she thought they should go, in all the wrong places. Places where, to this day, they still sat.

He turned and looked back up the highway, where the open sky broke through the trees, at the spread of dirt-colored spec houses had once been a playground thick with sword fern and cedars and hemlocks for Hank and his buddies. "Those houses there," he said. "My buddies and I, we got together one summer and built a tree house right in the middle of that place. It was a dangerous piece of shit, cobbled together with some old pallets and rotten fence boards. But it was something else, for a twelve year-old."

"I remember when it was all just trees," she said. "There are places all over this town that used to be trees. Things change."

"Unfortunately, yes."

She squinted up at him, chewing that gum she still had in her mouth. She shifted in the seat so that she faced him, propping her heels on floor edge. "Why unfortunately?" she said. "You think things ought to stay the same, forever?"

"I don't know," he said. "Some things."

She shook her head. "What's behind us is gone, Kelleher. It's out of our hands. The only thing any of us have control over is maybe the shit that's waiting around the next corner."

She turned slightly, and reached back to find Toby again. She scratched at his ears, and he rolled onto his side to show his stomach, but she didn't notice. Her eyes remained on Hank's, studying him, it seemed, to see where he might be taking this conversation.

"It's just reminiscing is all," he said. "It's what happens when you realize there's more years behind you than there are in front of you."

She swung her leg out and tapped him against the shin. "You ain't as old as you let on. You've got plenty of good years left ahead. Whether you live them up there on the mountain, or down here in Ash Falls, or wherever the hell you want to—just live them. Don't spend your whole life staring at the rearview mirror."

She got up from the seat and brushed off her jeans. "The way I see it, if things never changed, I could be stuck at seventeen, wearing patched-up bellbottoms and working at the Burger Hut, God forbid. And you'd still be trapped in that classroom, trying to teach science to a bunch of kids whose biggest care in life is when the next party is. And then what?"

"And then what?" he repeated.

"Then we wouldn't be standing here," she said. "And I'm kind of liking right now, aren't you?"

She reached up and gave his shoulder a squeeze with a hand that was twice as warm as it should be, a hand so warm it might well have been skin on skin.

"Now quit being a Scrooge and go buy a goddamned tree from those boys. They're dying out here."

"I will," he said. "If the ornament loan offer still stands."

"I'll be there at nine o'clock sharp," she said, giving him one of the best smiles he'd ever seen in his life. "I like my eggs scrambled and my coffee strong."

She walked the whole way without looking back at him, and even when she turned and opened the door to her car and her body was facing him, she kept her head down. It was only when she lowered her purse from her shoulder and tossed it into the passenger seat that she glanced up. It was quick, hardly more than a second or two. But that was plenty.

Hank climbed into his truck and cranked the engine, and turned down the music that seemed to just spill out of the radio. Roxanne rolled past him and gave a wave through the mud-spattered window, and as she pulled up to the edge of the highway, he noted that the left tail light of her car was out. It wasn't good for her to be driving with a dead bulb, he decided. Benny's garage was still open, and he'd have one in stock, probably. The Sleep Inn was on the way to Benny's, too. Mel would tell him just what kind of car it was that he sold her.

# Ernie

It crept low to the ground, hugging the edge of the brush, its eyes peering at him as it slunk back and forth and sniffed at the air. It was a female coyote, a new mother, well fed, with a coat healthy and full, not ragged and patchy as he had seen so many times on the packs that hunted farther up the mountain. He sat on the railroad tie, the medicinal scent of creosote mixing with cigarette smoke, and he watched the coyote as she searched the ground and tore at scraps of discarded paper, and nosed around the garbage cans, her beanbag teats swinging as she moved back and forth. At one point she rose to her hind legs and hooked her paws over the edge of the bin, tipping it to the ground. She yelped and sprang back, and after skulking a good-sized arc around it, she dove in and pulled out a full bag, dragging it backwards into the brush.

Ernie took another pull from his cigarette and tipped the bottle of beer to his lips, a bottle he had walked in and bought himself not ten minutes earlier from the Ash Falls General Store. He didn't know the young gal working behind the counter, but it was the same mom and pop store that had always been there, its phony brick asphalt siding and swaybacked porch roof, an old hillbilly left to rot alone at the edge of town. Anyone could have seen him in there but the girl barely looked at him, keeping most of her attention on the snowy 12-inch black and white propped against the side wall. Nonetheless, his heart drummed in his head. The cigarette was the best one he'd had all week.

Ernie had never really been much of a risk taker, but there were times when the situation called for it, and the high he felt by having trouble so close on his heels was something worth taking hold of. He had planned this night—on this night—with purpose. Come into town, collect what he needed from boxes stored years ago, and get out. It was a night when the streets and sidewalks should be empty, strangers expected. And maybe, if the situation was just right, he'd catch a glimpse of his own family before he lit out for the hills.

He straightened up, still stiff and sore from the long trip out of Everett. He'd ridden the whole way with his back against the cab in the bed of a pickup with no side rails, a bed cluttered with shovels and two kinds of rakes, a few stray pieces of cordwood and a long bar chainsaw that slid from the tailgate to his shins with every change in speed and topography. Cars trailed behind the whole way with headlamps boring into him, sometimes turning one direction or another, but always quickly replaced, the glares passing over his face like searchlights. He pulled the coat collar up to his nose and brought his knees to his chin in a weak effort to hide from them, and to soften the constant exhaust that tumbled up through the patchy corrosion.

He had taken his time to get here, two months and five days to be exact. He could have made the whole journey in a matter of days, but there was never a full day that he was really sure this was where he ought to end up. He was here now, some thirty yards down from the River Road junction with nothing but the clothes on his back and a drawstring nylon bag stuffed with a few t-shirts and three pairs of socks. The winter air was as full of energy as it always was, scoured by billions of fir and hemlock needles and that rolling gray-blue river fed from great glaciers that he had never seen up close, but had admired daily from his house below. Up the road, the Rexall drugstore loitered under a blue vapor light, its bleached shingle siding and hokey wooden bicycle racks dressed to look like weathered hitching posts, all of it standing as a tired welcome to the town. The AM/PM had a new front awning, and the price of fountain sodas was up fifty cents. The gas pumps had rainbows painted on them. For the most part, though, things were just as they had always been. The cloud of blackberry brambles along the back, the rusted tin roof over the pump. All of it left a strange buzz in his head, but why, he asked himself, should it be any different? It wasn't as if he had taken the town with him when he left. Why shouldn't these people just go on post-Ernie as if he'd never even existed?

He stood up, and the coyote lifted her head for a brief moment then went back to tearing up the garbage, her bottlebrush tail swiping lazily at the air. Ernie wondered if her pups might be nearby or hidden some distance away, too far for her to hear their cries should something come upon them while she scavenged.

He circled around the corner of the store then stepped up to a slow jog to cross the highway, to the gravel road that broke alongside the motel. Cutting east, his route took him past the enclave of ranch and split-level homes to the welfare apartments that crowded the north side of the Red Apple market. In the near-empty grocery lot, the post lamps laid a kaleidoscope of blue spots over the snow-patched parking lot.

Ernie's feet were soaked and almost numb by the time he reached the retail strip of Main Street, and he truly was right in the middle of everything then—the shimmering garland and the giant plastic ornaments, and window murals with powder-spray snowflakes, and shops empty and dark, everyone having gone home hours ago. Strings of blinking lights gave off an eerie calm, as if he had sneaked into the bar way past closing time where the low neon signs showed only the closest surfaces. It was as if he were nothing more than a ghost returning to a town that had folded up and forgotten him long ago.

Ernie began to see himself walking into any store on the block, and wouldn't it be something if they greeted him as a brand new face, just some guy who had never even set foot in the place before? They'd smile at him and wish him a happy holiday, and tell him *please come again, sir.* He had covered a great distance already in that town, tonight and certainly years before. The people in Ash Falls, he imagined, had lived through a period in which

Ernie Luntz's name was branded into every waking conversation. Now, it seemed as if he might as well be invisible.

Though it was surely him, the face looking back at him from the shop windows was a stranger. A kid practically, clothes hanging loose from his body, lips thin as noodles and so much skin. It was not the face Ernie was used to, the one that had stared back at him from his cell mirror for the last five years, grizzled and robust, full from inactivity, and so much overcooked potatoes and ham and slop greens. This one was sallow and cadaverous, the product of freeway rest stop coffee and sidewalk panhandling and grocery store discards, and he realized how a few years and a close shave could make a person anonymous. He reached the end of the block, crossed the street, and backtracked all the way up the opposite side.

The only space on this end that appeared to have any life in it was the Mexican restaurant, the Montaña de Plata. It had always been a dive, good for cheap margaritas, greasy nachos, and secondhand smoke. Red and green neon lit the cracked sidewalk, and just as Ernie came upon it, the door opened and a couple stepped out in front of him. The woman turned quickly and nearly walked into him. He put his hands up, and she yelped, jumped back, and took hold of her boyfriend's arm. The two of them stared at Ernie, the woman swaying on unsteady legs, the man red-faced, his lower lip curled to his mustache.

Ernie said, "Didn't mean to spook you."

The man's face dropped, and he broke into a grin. "No problem, man. You just come of out nowhere is all." He looked Ernie up and down. "Hell of a night to be out in summer clothes."

"I'm on a short leash," he said. "Heading home."

The woman kept her brow strained. She stared at Ernie as if he had reached out and torn her shirt from her, or was about to. There was something going on there, something behind those eyes. A journey through years of casual encounters, maybe. Photographs in the newspaper, or on the post office wall.

"Where's that at?" she asked.

"Pardon?"

"Home. You said you were heading home. Where's that at?"

The music coming from the restaurant was a Christmas tune, but a mariachi kind of thing, all waving brass and guitar strumming. Her stony glare, along with the smoky scent of broiled steak and onions, pulled at his stomach and set to work it into a knot.

"I said what?" Ernie took a couple steps back. He looked to the guy, who rolled his eyes.

"Sorry, man," he said. He looked to his girlfriend. "You're drunk, babe."

"I ain't drunk." She looked at Ernie again. "I seen you somewhere," she said. She squinted and wagged a finger in front of him. "You know that girl Phyllis? Phyllis What's-her-name from over at the feed store?" She stepped to one side and put her hand on the doorway.

"No."

"You know her. Phyllis. She gots red hair, and she's real top heavy." She lifted her hands to her boobs and pushed them a couple times. "You go with her?"

Ernie looked around him. The sidewalks were mostly empty; a couple people stood farther down the sidewalk, then cut across the street. "Naw," he said. "I don't know her."

The guy took his girlfriend's arm. "Come on, you," he said, giving Ernie a quick, apologetic glance. He made a wide berth around him, led her down the sidewalk as she wobbled on stalactite heels. She pulled her arm away and turned to give Ernie one more look. There was a rush of adrenaline, a kick as he stood there unmoving, almost challenging her to make the connection once and for all. The boyfriend slid her arm around his waist and pulled her back in line, disappearing into the shadows of the darkened storefronts near the end.

The last of the blinking doorways behind him, Ernie stepped up his pace until he came to Shale, the street where the Henrys lived, that kid who had busted Bobbie's leg, and Patrick's friend, the girl, who Patrick had said married the guy. He looked up the street, to the little cedar-shingled house a few lots up, the fourth one from the corner. There was a single porch light on and a few dull patches of light peeking from behind the hedges. The place looked sleepy with its drapes half open, slim amber slivers seeping out the warmth. Every house on the block, whether lit up ablaze or wrapped tightly in gray looked warmer than where he stood, on the corner of someone's lawn with the snow piled over his ankles.

Before he even reached Maple Street, he could see Bobbie through the kitchen window, above the driveway, over the hood of a pickup truck that he did not recognize. She was at the sink, looking down, rocking back and forth behind the white lace drapes that she always complained about. Yet there they still were, barely shielding her from the street, from anyone who might happen to walk past. As he drew closer, he saw that she was wearing a red blouse and her hair was pulled back with something real nice, a band that shone golden against that beautiful orange hair of hers. He remembered the pomp and circumstance that Christmas Eve always meant for Bobbie. He'd always found it childish and stupid, the sweaters and ribbons and Leave it to Beaver bullshit she seemed to be shooting for. But now, though the blur of the window and so many months alone with nothing but her and Patrick in his head, he'd have given anything to be in there, sitting at the dining table watching the last of the candles melt into the jars. She looked up as he approached and leaned in closer to the window. He sank behind the shed and peered past the holly bush.

Reaching up, she pulled at the neck of her blouse, moving it back and forth, fanning her chest. She brought her fingers to her cheekbones and ran them under her eyes, smoothing at the skin in tiny sweeps. She smiled, and he smiled. More than anything, he hoped that she knew the incredible beauty still living in the face looking back at her.

What would he say if he could talk to her, if he could see her face to face? If she walked out that back door and came up to him and demanded it of him, somewhere in the back of his mind was the speech he had rehearsed, all the things he would put out there and ask, and do, if the possibility presented itself to him and there was no way out of it. The apologies would be there first, all of them, but then there would be that aching wonder of why she had really stopped coming to see him, why she had stopped bringing Patrick. The truth, not the excuses of school and work, and of Patrick acting out and how the last thing he needed was something to add to his stress. Her letters were a cobble of contradictions, the phone calls always cut short with irritated sighs and sudden interruptions. Nothing ever seemed to be the real truth. He'd known there was the chance that Hank Kelleher was back in the picture, and he had tumbled that idea in his head until it had more or less settled itself there. But now there was a distinct twist in his gut seeing that truck parked in the driveway, its windshield and hood dusted with snow, a rectangle of bare concrete underneath. Bobbie moved away from the window, and Ernie slid along the siding, to the shed door.

Their first weekend in the house he had caught a couple of high school boys watching him unload his camping gear into the shed. They sat on their bikes hunched over the handlebars, sometimes talking to one another but never looking away from Ernie or from the shed. He'd told Bobbie to keep an eye on things and left to go to the hardware store, bringing back a heavy-duty steel padlock and clasp and locked that son of a bitch up tight. There was a part of him that hoped Bobbie would have stopped locking it, but seeing it secured as always reminded him that she was too smart to leave it open. If it wasn't the same lock, it was one just like it.

He ran his finger along the undersides of the shingles then tried the concrete pavers at the base of the kitchen steps, firmly sunk in place, not having been budged in years. The garbage cans were empty underneath, and there were no conspicuous rocks lining the shed, or any coffee cans. But the terra cotta pot spilling over with dried grass, and clover was something that had not been there before. He tipped it and saw the gleam of metal just beneath it.

The padlock opened easily. He hooked it over the latch before sliding the door and slipping inside. The overturned wheelbarrow and push mower took up the center, draped with an old canvas tarp like a slouching ghost. There were days that having to lug those things around made him curse ever having taken on the responsibility of the white picket fence that he and Bobbie had wanted so badly. That he had wanted, really. But then there were times when the sun massaged his back as he knelt in the dirt, sinking dahlia bulbs and garlic starts into the loamy soil, that he felt a euphoric rush, as if he finally had everything anyone could possibly want in life.

A clear path circled around the garden tools, with shelving and recycled kitchen cabinetry lining the walls from floor to ceiling. The workbench he'd built of sawhorses and an old pine door, where he and Patrick had carved out that slick gold-painted Pinewood derby car, sat cluttered with canisters and milk crates and loose tools over every inch of surface space.

He slid the door closed and gave himself a minute for his eyes to adjust to the darkness. The outside porch light offered the dimmest of light, spilling through the tiny window that sat over the washer and dryer. It was an old four-pane that Ernie had put in himself, when the thought of a shed with nothing but walls made him lose his breath and break out in a sweat. It wasn't much of one, a little bigger than a shoebox, but it let in some light and, in the summer months, a nice stream of air.

He grabbed a milk crate from the workbench and pushed his way to the back shelf, where the box of camping gear was exactly where he had always kept it. He stepped up and brought the box down carefully and carried it to the dryer where he could see it better. Everything was in there, the propane burner, the utility knives, Patrick's little pocket fisherman, the one Ernie had bought him for his twelfth birthday and he'd hardly used. Somewhere among the shelves in one of the bins would be his old army duffle bag, a tightly rolled sleeping bag and maybe the pup tent. He found a flashlight among the gear and snapped it on, the sleepiest of orange glowing from its tiny bulb.

The window was a cloud of dust and cobwebs, its panes crusted with peeling paint and mildew and overall neglect. There was a sudden movement in the light, and Ernie crouched beside the washing machine. A dull hum of conversation seeped in through the wall. Someone laughed. He moved the crate to the wall and raised himself so he could see out, hanging back from the glass in order to stay securely in the shadows. At the top of the steps Bobbie shared space in the open doorway with someone Ernie didn't recognize, and the unfamiliarity was a momentary respite. It was an old man, a codger half stooped, wrestling to climb into an uncooperative jacket. Bobbie held the collar for him and pulled the sleeve over his arm. She laughed again. The old man shook his head. In the background, lingering under the overhead lamp the slender silhouette of a third person stood.

Patrick. So much taller than Ernie had last seen him, his shoulders were broad and squared at the edges, hands planted resolutely against his hips, sturdy. A young man already. Goddamn.

Bobbie leaned in and hugged the old man, and Patrick in the kitchen lifted a hand to wave and called out a goodbye. And then the door was closed, and the old man hobbled down the steps, gripping the rail, each step as if he were descending a mountain. He traversed the distance from the bottom step to his pickup, his hand sliding over the snow-dusted hood, and he took hold of the side mirror as he reached for the door, opening it and climbing inside to take his seat behind the wheel. He left the door open, and the light above his bald head carved into his face a landscape of shadows, and he was a hundred years old if he was a day. He muscled his arm, and the engine fired up, revving with an angry roar and sending white clouds of exhaust billowing down the driveway to the street below.

The old man leaned back in his seat and began to dig into his jacket, as if he had lost something in the interior pockets. His lower jaw drew a grimace as he searched, and at last he withdrew his hand and held it up, almost touching it to the lamp. The object gleamed under the light like a gold coin, and it was only when the man popped open the cover that Ernie realized it was a pocket watch. He turned it over, one side to the other, rubbing his thumb over the glass. He worked at the crown, winding it some, and then he finally snapped it shut and tucked it back into his jacket. Giving the horn a single tap, he shut the door and the dome light faded as he backed slowly out of the driveway, creaking around the curb and puttering off down the street.

Erine climbed down from the dryer and pulled the last of the boxes from the shelf. He fished out the duffle, musty and coarse, and the flash of every bivouac and jungle march came back to him, the taste of compact chicken and potatoes from a can and the anticipation of tracers lighting up the night. It never failed to intrigue him how the mere touch of that canvas could bring forth such vivid recall, more so than any other trigger. The names of platoon mates, Carter, Diaz, and Bingham, and the lost looks in their eyes as they all waited for mail call and movement orders. He unfurled the duffle and stuffed it with the sleeping bag and the tent and fishing and hunting gear and the propane burner and a clump of dishrags he'd taken from over the washing machine, and all the miscellaneous shit that had littered the bottom of the camping box. Taking hold of the straps he threw the whole thing over his back and cinched it tightly to his chest.

There was a sudden rattle and creak at the door, and the great light that spilled into the space from the porch was a white tsunami, brilliant and devastating. He bolted backward, rushing along the side of the cabinetry, his hands finding everything that had ever been hung from, stacked and leaned against the walls as he stumbled to the far wall at the back of the garage. Just like that, he was caught.

Patrick stood in the rectangle of the doorway like a paper cutout, a plastic garbage bag at his side, his other hand resting precariously on the doorknob. On one side of his head his hair stood up, a cluster of quills, frozen and so perfect. He looked over his shoulder and stepped inside, swinging the bag outside next to the garbage bin.

"It's you, right?" His voice was that of a man's, low and firm from deep within in his chest. There was only the smallest hint of a tremor in his words.

"How'd you know?"

Patrick lifted his arm to the side, the silhouette of the open padlock hooked over his finger, the tiny key jutting from the bottom. He closed the door behind him.

Ernie forced a laugh, desperate, then he stepped forward, leaning against the workbench. His head began to swim. He slipped the duffle from his back and let it drop to the floor, but the weight of it lingered in him, buckling his knees and threatening to drag him down with it. He had imagined so many things he could say to Patrick if he saw him, him and Bobbie, but he hadn't really planned on saying any of it. In the end, it was best for everyone if he just went in, took what he wanted, and got the hell out. What they didn't know would not be able to hurt them.

"Are you okay?" Patrick said. "You're not hurt or anything?"

"I'm fine." He took hold of the duffle again. "I'm not sticking around, son. In case you were thinking I might. I just came to get some things and get out of here."

"So you were just coming to steal a bunch of stuff. Not even say hi or anything." He came closer to Ernie and raised a hand to his own face. "You look really different. You shaved your beard."

"Yeah, well. Circumstances." The backlight from the window darkened the silhouette even more, and Ernie strained to make out a face in the figure moving toward him. He wanted to see him, to take the image with him of this young man who was not a boy anymore. "I'd say I'm sorry, but I guess you already know that."

"Yeah." Now he stopped and leaned against the side cabinetry opposite Ernie.

The window light illuminated Patrick's face now, the hard lines of his cheekbones and the thin-cut lips. His eyelashes reached out like feathers they were so thick. There was a good amount of himself in that face, he could see now, and there was a surge of pride at that, that this boy standing there so handsome might bear some resemblance to his old man.

"Who's the codger?" Ernie said, nodding to the door. "With the truck."

"A friend."

"What do you mean, a friend?"

Patrick stiffened. "Well, technically he's my boss."

"Your boss," Ernie said. The conversation was continuing, and Ernie wanted it to continue, but he knew it couldn't. He couldn't stay here and risk Bobbie coming in, the inevitable hysterics, and then the cops. "You're a working man now."

Patrick nodded, but said nothing.

"That's good." His head felt heavy on his shoulders. Any second that door was going to open again, and she would be there. "Listen," he said. "I don't want to leave you hanging, but I can't stick around."

"You already said that." Patrick bounced against the counter and chewed on his thumbnail. "Probably all kinds of people looking for you, so you gotta go."

He said, "I don't want you to worry about me," and he meant it, though it sounded cold, forced. There was comfort in the idea that his face might pass through Patrick's mind now and then while he was on the run. But what could something like that bring anyone other than pain?

"It was selfish, you know," Patrick snapped. "Taking off like that. Not calling or letting us know anything. You could be dead."

"But I'm not."

"You will be."

A rush of irritation, of frustration flared up in Ernie. This was exactly what he had wanted to avoid, why he'd known he was supposed to just get in and get out and not say a word to anyone. But here he was anyway, barely an arm's distance from his son. And Christ, it was too damned far away.

"I don't want to fight with you. Let's just say our goodbyes and I'll be on my way. And when I get a chance I'll call, okay?" He stopped himself, took a breath, and held it. He let it out slowly. "How about I call, and if you answer I'll tap the phone a few times. And then you'll know it's me and I'm okay. How's that?"

Patrick closed his eyes and clenched his jaw, biting down as he breathed in deeply. Finally, he moved from the cabinet to the dryer and stood with his hands on the surface.

"I'll come see you," he said suddenly. His voice was tightening now, and he was looking at Ernie. "I can take the bus. It's only in Monroe. I can come visit you every month if you want."

"Jesus, just stop." Ernie slapped the wood on the workbench, the loose tools rattling and clanging against one another. His temperature was climbing. He worked his knuckles back and forth and listened to the sound of breathing on the other side of the shed.

Patrick's shoulders slumped and the bones in his legs looked to have turned to jelly. Ernie took a step toward him, but he pulled back, and stepped away from the dryer.

"I love you, kid," Ernie said, "but goddamn it."

Patrick took a breath as if to say one more thing, likely one more attempt to try and turn the tide toward surrender. But he didn't. He just sighed, shrugged his shoulders and turned around, lifting himself on his toes to look over the washing machine, out the window toward the house. "I don't want you to worry about me, either," he said.

"I'll try not to. But you know that's what parents do."

"I got a job, now."

"Yeah, you told me."

"At a mink farm."

"Minks? Well, what do you know?"

Patrick turned to Ernie again, and the light was behind him now so his face disappeared, but Ernie pushed himself to see the young man with the cheekbones and the soft dusting of whiskers needing a shave. There was a time when Ernie could have gone to him and wrapped his arms around him, and Patrick would have folded into him, and they would have sat together on the floor and laughed and told stories, and no matter what Ernie had done or said, it would have been all right. He felt himself being pulled toward him, but something held his feet to the dirt, as if stakes had been driven straight through them into the ground.

Patrick slid the door open, and the light shone for an instant as he squeezed through and closed it behind him. There was the rattle of the garbage can lid lifting and resealing, knocking against the shed wall, and then it was quiet.

He tossed back the duffle flap and went to the back of the shed, retrieving the raingear, the same jacket and pants that he had worn when Patrick had not wanted to go fishing with him but had relented upon the promise of a hamburger, French fries, and chocolate milkshake afterward. He added it to the duffle, tossing in a couple screwdrivers and a hammer, the hammer Patrick had used when he cracked his thumb while building a ramshackle tree house in a friend's old maple. The nail had turned full blue and fell off on its own about a week later when Ernie was not at home. He cinched the pack to his shoulders again. The porch light was suddenly extinguished, and the shed went dark.

Ernie made his way to the door carefully. He waited for a

time, standing against the wall with his hand on the grip, listening to the sound of his own breathing and of the noise under his shoes, the friction of tiny grains of dirt grinding against one another as he shifted his weight from one foot to the other.

He had expected some resistance; the door was heavy after all. He had anticipated the sounds of creaking and of springs straining as the door slid on its track. But what he had not planned on, what gripped his chest and drained the blood from his arms, was the fact that the door slid nicely all of a single inch before it caught, refusing to budge any further. He leaned in close and peered through the sliver, and he could see it clearly.

It was the padlock. That damned padlock gleamed in the moonlight like it was electric, its stainless steel shackle extending at a perfect arch from one end of the lock through the metal loop that pushed through the clasp that he had screwed on so tightly that day, that first Saturday he and Bobbie and Patrick had lived there. He could not see if the shackle was sunk fully into the guts of the lock, holding to them with its teeth until it could be released by the key, or if it had merely been slid through and was hanging open, not locked at all. It didn't matter though, as it was doing its job just as it should, keeping the prisoner inside, no way for him to reach through that slender gap to get hold of that lock and pull it free.

What he felt came in flashes—rage, disbelief—aimed direcly at Patrick. He could see him looping the padlock over the latch and walking away as if it were nothing, and the betrayal was a giant hook, cold and rusted, and it gouged at his chest and pulled him down to his knees. He sat there breathing in the smell of mold and dust, and there quickly came a frantic energy that cut his breath and lit the room on fire. He stood up and pulled on the door again, his jacket constricting his chest and his neck, his arms and wrists crawling as if riddled with spiders. He dropped the duffle and stripped off his coat. His heart racing, he began to pace the perimeter, digging through boxes and pulling out drawers, looking for anything, he didn't know what, since nobody had bothered to keep this shed organized, not in the years he'd been gone, or before. Tools were thrown in crates and left on shelves and some probably in the house, nothing where it should be. He found a crescent wrench loose on the countertop and scrambled to the washing machine. Climbing onto the lid he held tightly with one hand and took a sharp swing with the other, striking the lower right pane, breaking a single square loose in a bell-like ring, where it landed silently on the snow below.

His face was awash with the burst of cold, the glacial air spilling through the window and pushing itself down the open neck of his shirt, freezing the damp skin and bringing the life back into him. And this air was brand new, never having been breathed, and he pulled it into his lungs until his chest could not take any more. He swung his legs around and sat with his shoulder to the wall, and pressed his ear to the frame and stared up into the night. Above the roof and beyond the overreaching dogwood twigs, the sky yawned forever, and it was almost completely black, and stars poked through in tiny pinpricks, white speckles over the entire canvas.

Things went on forever out there, just past this wall that wanted to keep him inside, held by his own son, and Ernie understood what it must have taken for Patrick to do that. He wanted to keep his father, that's all. Scoop the net under him and toss him in the basket where he could take him home, instead of releasing him into the open water where he ought to be.

The breeze slid through the branches and brushed over his ears, and the soft touch of Patrick's breath came to him, his tiny body pressed against Ernie's bare chest, infant fingers that played his beard like a harp. His own voice sounded in his head, the way he used to whisper poems to his son when he was too little to understand them, poems about nature and the valor of soldiers, as his own father had done, the weight of the old man's body pressing down on the handmade quilt as he sat beside him. It came to him, how he once liked to stay up into the early hours of morning looking for Orion's Belt and Gemini, from the upstairs window of his childhood bungalow and later from beneath wide-leafed palms on the night patrols, and the open moon roof of his souped-up Camaro, his sweetest girlfriend resting her head gently on his shoulder.

In the distance, the faint glow of colored lights pulsed against the trees, but it was Christmas after all. Maybe Patrick hadn't said a thing to Bobbie. Maybe she was in the living room watching television and Patrick was back in his bedroom, lying under the covers and staring at the ceiling, contemplating what exactly he ought to do next. Maybe they were standing over the telephone, their hands clasped together, rehearsing what they could possibly say when they finally picked it up and made the call.

The remaining glass, he knew, would fall easily away. There was time to push the duffle out ahead of him and squeeze his body through the opening, first the shoulder and then the head. If he could get that far, the rest would be easy. It would be a short drop to the brush, with a roll onto the crusted snow, and he'd be in the back of a pickup truck or eighteen-wheeler before anyone could show up to stop him. He knew his way up the mountain, to the creek, and there would be no coming back, no sitting in the dim light of the living room of his own house listening to the sounds of his family waking up to another day with Ernie in their lives. Not now, not ever.

He lowered himself from the dryer and took the wrench from the tabletop behind him. Red and blue lights flashed vivid against the fogged windowpanes now, and Ernie leaned back against the counter and considered how it was like the Fourth of July out there, as if fireworks were exploding silently in the night sky. He took up his duffle and held the wrench over his shoulder. He wasn't ready yet. He climbed back onto the dryer and pressed his face against the edge of the window frame, the rough wood grabbing hold of his naked face like claws. He took in the clean, icy air and thought of how beautiful it was, the lights blossoming over that glass like that, the way the radiance pushed its way into the shed and washed everything in a warm, comforting glow. *Patrick should see this*, he said to himself. *It's that goddamned beautiful.*

# Acknowledgements

Many thanks to the faculty of the Rainier Writing Workshop, most especially my mentors, who encouraged me to trust in the vision that was "Ash Falls." To my RWW colleagues and readers: Jessica, Sarah, Jenee and Jeb, thank you for your sharp insight and, when necessary, your blunt recommendations. To my intrepid writing group members, Lynn, Mary, Susan, Caryn and Tina, thank you for encouraging a wider world for those characters whose origins grew from random, "draw from the hat" writing prompts.

Thank you to my incredible husband Shayne for allowing me the time to sequester myself in those moments when inspiration and deadlines just happened to coincide, and our youngest son, Dmitry, for the conversation that helped me form that final chapter. In addition, much thanks goes out to Chris Craggs, for his generous contributions of what would help me shape Patrick and Tin's unique world, and to my mother Nellie, who helped me guide Marcelle through her complicated, often unforgiving journey.

Finally, heartfelt appreciation goes to Kristen Radtke for her brilliant cover art, and to Robert Lasner and Elizabeth Clementson of Ig Publishing, for their partnership in getting these characters I have grown to love so much out into the greater world.